Praise for DEA

'South African crime writer
thriller confirms his place as o stylists.
This is a remarkable achievement from a singular new talent.'
Publishers Weekly

'A breathtaking pace, heart-pounding action set against a psychological backdrop, and a fascinating protagonist makes this book a winner.'
Library Journal

'Nothing is more exciting than a new voice in the thriller arena, especially if that voice also tells us about a largely unknown part of the world . . . A terrific ride on almost every level.'
Chicago Tribune

'Deon Meyer recreates the beauty, wildness, and danger of modern Africa with an immediacy and force no other writer has achieved . . . his work is undeniably "a cause for celebration".'
Sunday Telegraph

If DEAD AT DAYBREAK is anything to go by, we are seeing the rise of a major new, international writing talent. I cannot recommend this book highly enough.'
Big Issue

'A highly entertaining, page-turning transposition of the American private eye genre to an exotic and vibrant setting . . . a terrific new talent.'
Irish Independent

'DEAD AT DAYBREAK is a gripping read with a flawed but human protagonist who invites our compassion . . . This is the second novel by South African Deon Meyer, a fresh voice and a compelling storyteller.'
Manchester Evening News

'Meyer manages to ratchet up the tension so effectively that readers will have a hard time deciding which mystery they wish to pi

Praise for Deon Meyer

'A riveting crime novel . . . a mesmerising read'
The Sunday Times on TRACKERS

'Crime fiction with real texture and intelligence . . . a sprawling, invigorated and socially committed crime novel'
Independent on TRACKERS

'Tells a cracking story and captures the criminal kaleidoscope of a nation'
The Times Literary Supplement on TRACKERS

'One of the most absorbing crime stories you are ever likely to read'
Shots on TRACKERS

'This terrific, action-packed thriller has superbly drawn characters and an enthralling setting'
Mail on Sunday on THIRTEEN HOURS

'Ramps up the suspense to an unbearable degree'
The Financial Times on THIRTEEN HOURS

'Deon Meyer is the undisputed king of South African crime fiction'
The Times

'This guy is really good'
Michael Connelly

DEON MEYER

DEAD AT DAYBREAK

Translated from Afrikaans by Madeleine van Biljon

HODDER

First published in Great Britain in 2000 by Hodder & Stoughton
An Hachette UK company

This paperback edition published in 2012

1

Originally published in Afrikaans in 2000 as *Orion*
by Human & Rousseau

A CIP catalogue record for this title is available from the British Library

ISBN 978 1 444 73072 2

Printed and bound by Clays Ltd, St Ives plc

Hodder & Stoughton policy is to use papers that are natural, renewable and recyclable products and made from wood grown in sustainable forests. The logging and manufacturing processes are expected to conform to the environmental regulations of the country of origin.

Hodder & Stoughton Ltd
338 Euston Road
London NW1 3BH

www.hodder.co.uk

Day 7

Thursday, 6 July

1

He woke abruptly out of an alcohol-sodden sleep, the pain in his ribs his first conscious sensation. Then the swollen eye and upper lip, the antiseptic, musty smell of the cell, the sour odour of his body, the salty taste of blood and old beer in his mouth.

And the relief.

Jigsaw pieces of the previous evening floated into his mind. The provocation, the annoyed faces, the anger – such normal, predictable motherfuckers, such decent, conventional pillars of the community.

He remained motionless, on the side that wasn't painful, the hang-over throbbing like a disease through his body.

Footsteps in the corridor outside, a key turning in the lock of the grey steel door, the grating of metal on metal slicing through his head. Then the uniform stood there.

'Your attorney's here,' the policeman said.

Slowly he turned on the bed. Opened one eye.

'Come.' A voice devoid of respect.

'I don't have an attorney.' His voice sounded far away.

The policeman took a step, hooked a hand into the back of his collar, pulled him upright. 'Come on.'

The pain in his ribs. He stumbled through the cell door, down the paved passage to the charge office.

The uniform walked ahead, used a key to indicate the way to the small parade room. He entered with difficulty, hurting. Kemp sat there, his briefcase next to him, a frown on his face. He sat down in a dark blue chair, his head in his hands. He heard the policeman close the door behind him and walk away.

'You're trash, van Heerden,' said Kemp.

He didn't respond.

'What are you doing with your life?'

'What does it matter?' His swollen lip lisped the 's'.

Kemp's frown deepened. He shook his head. 'They didn't even bother to lay a charge.'

He wanted to indulge in the relief, the lessening of the pressure, but it eluded him. Kemp. Where the fuck did Kemp come from?

'Even dentists know shit when they see it. Jesus, van Heerden, what's with you? You're pissing your life away. Dentists? How drunk do you have to be to take on five dentists?'

'Two were GPs.'

Kemp took in van Heerden's appearance. Then the attorney got up, a big man, clean and neat in a sports jacket and grey slacks, the neutral colours of the tie a perfect match. 'Where's your car?'

He rose to his feet slowly, the world tilting slightly. 'At the bar.'

Kemp opened the door and walked out. 'Come on, then.'

Van Heerden followed him into the charge office. A sergeant pushed his possessions over the counter, a plastic bag containing his slender wallet and his keys. He took it without making eye contact.

'I'm taking him away,' said Kemp.

'He'll be back.'

The day was cold. The wind knifed through his thin jacket and he resisted the impulse to pull it closer around his body.

Kemp climbed into his large four-by-four, leaned across and unlocked the passenger door. Slowly van Heerden walked around the vehicle, climbed in, closed the door and leaned his head against it. Kemp pulled off.

'Which bar?'

'The Sports Pub, opposite Panarotti's.'

'What happened?'

'Why did you fetch me?'

'Because you told the entire Tableview police station that I would sue them and the dentists for everything ranging from assault to brutality.'

He vaguely remembered his charge-office tirade. 'My attorney.' Mockingly.

'I'm not your attorney, van Heerden.'

The ache in the swollen eye killed his laughter. 'Why did you fetch me?'

Aggressively Kemp changed gears. 'Fuck alone knows.'

Van Heerden turned his head and looked at the man behind the steering wheel. 'You want something.'

'You owe me.'

'I owe you nothing.'

Kemp drove, looking for the pub. 'Which car is yours?'

He pointed to the Corolla.

'I'll follow you. I have to get you clean and respectable.'

'What for?'

'Later.'

He got out, walked across the road and got into the Toyota. He found it difficult to unlock the door, his hand shaking. The engine stuttered, wheezed and eventually fired. He drove to Koeberg Road, left past Killarney, onto the N7, wind suddenly sweeping rain across the road. Left to Morning Star and left again to the entrance to the smallholding, Kemp's imported American Ford behind him. He looked at the big house amongst the trees but turned off to the small whitewashed building and stopped.

Kemp stopped next to him, opening his window just a crack against the rain. 'I'll wait for you.'

First of all he showered, without pleasure, letting the hot water sluice over his body, his hands automatically soaping the narrow space between shoulder and chest and belly – just the soap, no washcloth, careful over the injured part of the ribs. Then, methodically, he washed the rest of himself, leaning his head against the wall for balance as he did first one foot, then the other, eventually turning off the taps and pulling the thin, over-laundered white towel from the rail. Sooner or later he would have to buy a new towel. He let the hot tap of the washbasin run, cupped his hands under the slow stream and threw the water over the mirror to wash away the steam. He squeezed a dollop of shaving cream into his left hand, dipped the shaving brush into it, made it foam. He lathered his face.

The eye looked bad, red and puffy. Later it would be a purplish blue. Most of the scab on his lip had been washed off. Only a thin line of dried blood remained.

He pulled the razor from the left ear downwards, all the way across the skin, over the jawline into the neck, then started at the top again, without looking at himself. Pulled the skin of his jaw to tighten it around the mouth, then did the right side, rinsed the razor, cleaned the basin with hot water, dried off again. Brushed his hair. Had to clean the brush: it was clogged with black hair.

Had to buy new underpants. Had to buy new shirts. Had to buy new socks. Trousers and jacket still reasonable. Fuck the tie. The room was dark and cold. Rain against the windows at ten past eleven in the morning.

He walked out. Kemp opened the door of the four-by-four.

There was a long silence that lasted as far as Milnerton.

'Where to?'

'City.'

'You want something.'

'One of our PAs has started her own practice. She needs help.'

'You owe her.'

Kemp merely snorted. 'What happened last night?'

'I was drunk.'

'What happened last night that was different?'

There were pelicans on the lagoon opposite the golf course. They were feeding, undisturbed by the rain.

'They were so full of their fucking four-by-fours.'

'So you assaulted them?'

'The fat one hit me first.'

'Why?'

He turned his head away.

'I don't understand you.'

He made a noise in his throat.

'You can make a living. But you have such a shitty opinion of yourself . . .'

Paarden Island's industries moved past.

'What happened?'

Van Heerden looked at the rain, fine drops scurrying across the windshield. He took a deep breath, a sigh for the uselessness of it all. 'You can tell a man his four-by-four isn't going to make his prick any larger and he pretends to be deaf. But drag in his wife . . .'

'Jesus.'

For a brief moment he felt the hate again, the relief, the moment of release of the previous evening: the five middle-aged men, their faces contorted with rage, the blows, the kicks that rained down on him until the three bartenders managed to separate them.

They didn't speak again until Kemp stopped in front of a building on the Foreshore.

'Third floor. Beneke, Olivier and partners. Tell Beneke I sent you.'

He nodded and opened the door, got out. Kemp looked thoughtfully at him.

Then he closed the door and walked into the building.

He slumped in the chair, lack of respect evident in his posture. She had asked him to sit down. 'Kemp sent me,' was all he had said. She had nodded, glanced at the injured eye and lip and ignored them.

'I believe that you and I can help one another, Mr van Heerden.' She tucked her skirt under her as she sat down.

Mister. And the attempt at common ground. He knew this approach. But he said nothing. He looked at her. Wondered from whom she had inherited the nose and the mouth. The large eyes and the small ears. The genetic dice had fallen in strange places for her, leaving her on the edge of beauty.

She had folded her hands on the desk, the fingers neatly interlaced. 'Mr Kemp told me you have experience of investigative work but are not in permanent employ at the moment. I need the help of a good investigator.' Norman Vincent Peale. She spoke smoothly and easily. He suspected that she was clever. He suspected she would take longer to unnerve than the average female.

She opened a drawer, took out a file.

'Did Kemp tell you I was trash?'

Her hands hesitated briefly. She gave him a stiff smile. 'Mr van Heerden, your personality doesn't interest me. Your personal life doesn't interest me. This is a business proposition. I'm offering you a temporary job opportunity for a professional fee.'

So fucking controlled. As if she knew everything. As if her cell phone and her degree were the only defence she needed.

'How old are you?'

'Thirty,' she said without hesitation.

He looked at her third finger, left hand. It was bare.

'Are you available, Mr van Heerden?'

'It depends on what you want.'

2

My mother was an artist. My father was a miner.

She saw him for the first time on a cold winter's day on Oliën Park's frost-covered rugby field, his striped Vaal Reef's jersey almost torn off his body. He was walking slowly to the touchline to fetch a new shirt, his sweaty litheness, the definition of shoulders and stomach and ribs, gleaming dully in the weak late afternoon sun.

She had told the story accurately, every time: the pale blue of the sky, the bleached grey-white of the stadium's grass, the smallish group of students loudly supporting their team against the miners, the purple of their scarves bright splashes of colour against the dull grey of the wooden benches. Every time I heard the story I added more detail: her slender figure taken from a black-and-white photograph of that time, cigarette in her hand, dark hair, dark eyes, a certain brooding beauty. How she saw him, how all the lines of his face and his body were so irresistibly right, as if, through all that, she could see everything.

'Into his heart,' she said.

She knew two things with absolute certainty at that moment. One was that she wanted to paint him.

After the game she waited for him outside, among the officials and second-team players, until he came out wearing a jacket and tie, his hair wet from the showers. And he saw her in the dusk, felt her intensity and blushed and walked to her as if he knew that she wanted him.

She had the piece of paper in her hand.

'Call me,' she said when he stood in front of her.

His mates surrounded him so she simply gave him the folded paper with her name and telephone number and left, back to the house in Thom Street where she was boarding.

He phoned late at night.

'My name is Emile.'

'I'm an artist,' she said. 'I want to paint you.'

'Oh.' Disappointment in his voice. 'What kind of painting?'

'One of you.'

'Why?'

'Because you're a handsome man.'

He laughed, disbelieving and uncomfortable. (Later he had told her that it was news to him, that he'd always had trouble getting girls. She'd replied that that was because he was stupid with women.)

'I don't know,' he eventually stammered.

'As payment you can take me out for dinner.'

My father only laughed again. And just over a week later, on a cold winter's Sunday morning, he drove in his Morris Minor from the single quarters in Stilfontein to Potchefstroom. She, with easel and painting kit, got into the car and she directed him – out on the Carletonville road, close to Boskop Dam.

'Where are we going?'

'Into the veld.'

'The veld?'

She nodded.

'Doesn't one do it in a . . . an art room?'

'A studio.'

'Yes.'

'Sometimes.'

'Oh?'

They had turned off onto a farm road and stopped at a small ridge. He helped her carry her equipment, watched as she stretched the canvas on the easel, opened the case and tidied the brushes.

'You can undress now.'

'I'm not going to take everything off.'

She merely looked at him in silence.

'I don't even know your surname.'

'Joan Kilian. Undress.'

He took off his shirt, then his shoes.

'That's enough,' he resisted.

She nodded.

'What must I do now?'

'Stand on the rock.'

He climbed onto a large rock.

'Don't stand so stiffly. Relax. Drop your hands. Look over there, towards the dam.'

And then she began painting. He asked her questions but she didn't reply, only warned him a few times to stand still, looked from him to the canvas, mixed and applied paint until he gave up trying to talk. After an hour or more she allowed him to rest. He asked his questions again, discovered that she was the only daughter of an actress and a drama lecturer in Pretoria. He vaguely remembered their names from Afrikaans films of the Forties.

Eventually she lit a cigarette and started packing her painting equipment.

He dressed. 'Can I see what you've drawn?'

'Painted. No.'

'Why not?'

'You can see it when it's finished.'

They drove back to Potchefstroom and drank hot chocolate in a café. He asked about her art, she asked him about his work. And some time during the late afternoon of a Western Transvaal winter he looked at her for a long time and then said: 'I'm going to marry you.' She nodded because that was the second thing she had known with certainty when she saw him for the first time.

3

The female attorney looked down at the folder and slowly drew in her breath. 'Johannes Jacobus Smit was fatally wounded with a large-calibre gun on 30 September last year during a burglary at his home in Moreletta Street, Durbanville. The entire contents of a walk-in safe are missing, including a will in which, it is alleged, he left all his possessions to his friend, Wilhelmina Johanna van As. If the will cannot be found, the late Mr Smit will have died intestate and his assets will eventually go to the state.'

'What's the size of the estate?'

'At this stage it seems to be just under two million.'

He had suspected it. 'Van As is your client.'

'She lived with Mr Smit for eleven years. She supported him in his business interests, prepared his meals, cleaned his house, looked after his clothes and at his insistence had their child aborted.'

'He never offered to marry her?'

'He was no . . . advocate of marriage.'

'Where was she on the evening of the . . .'

'Thirtieth? In Windhoek. He sent her there. On business. She returned on the first of October and found him dead, tied to a kitchen chair.'

He slid further down in his chair. 'You want me to trace the will?'

She nodded. 'I've already explored every possible legal loophole. The final sitting at the Master of the Supreme Court is in a week's time. If we cannot supply a legal document by that time, Wilna van As doesn't get a cent.'

'A week?'

She nodded.

'It's almost . . . ten months. Since the murder.'

The attorney nodded again.

'I take it the police haven't had a breakthrough.'

'They did their best.'

He looked at her, and then at the two certificates on the wall. His ribs were hurting. He made a short, obscene noise, part pain, part disbelief. 'A week?'

'I . . .'

'Didn't Kemp tell you? I don't do miracles any more.'

'Mr van . . .'

'It's ten months since the man's death. It's a waste of your client's money. Not that that would bother an attorney.'

He saw her eyes narrowing and a small rosy fleck in the shape of a crescent moon slowly appeared on one cheek. 'My ethics, Mr van Heerden, are above reproach.'

'Not if you give Mrs van As the impression that there's any hope,' he said and wondered just how much self-control she had.

'*Miss* van As is completely informed about the significance of this step. I advised her of the potential uselessness of the exercise. But she is prepared to pay you because it's her last chance. The only remaining possibility. Unless *you* don't see your way clear, Mr van Heerden. Evidently there are other people with the same talents . . .'

The crescent was bright red but her voice remained measured and controlled.

'Who would be only too pleased to join you in taking *Miss* van As's money,' he said and wondered if the fleck could become any redder. To his surprise she smiled slowly.

'I'm really not interested in how you acquired your wounds.' With her manicured hands she gestured at his face. 'But I'm beginning to understand why.'

He saw the crescent moon slowly disappearing. He thought for a moment, disappointed. 'What else was in the safe?'

'She doesn't know.'

'She doesn't know? She sleeps with him for eleven years and she doesn't know what's cooking in his safe?'

'Do you know what's in your wife's wardrobe, Mr van Heerden?'

'What's your name?'

She hesitated. 'Hope.'

'Hope?'

'My parents were somewhat . . . romantic.'

He rolled the name around in his mouth. Hope. Beneke. He looked at her, wondered how someone, a woman, thirty years old, could live with the name *Hope*. He looked at her short hair. Like a man's. Fleetingly he wondered with which angle of her face the gods of features had fumbled – an old game, vaguely remembered.

'I don't have a wife, Hope.'

'I'm not surprised . . . What's *your* name?'

'I like the "mister".'

'Do you want to accept the challenge, *Mister* van Heerden?'

Wilna van As was somewhere in her indefinable middle years, a woman with no sharp edges, short and rounded, and her voice was quiet as they sat in the living room of the house in Durbanville while she told him and the attorney about Jan Smit.

She had introduced him as 'Mr van Heerden, our investigator.' *Our*. As if they owned him now. He asked for coffee when they were offered something to drink. Strangers to one another, they sat stiffly and formally in the living room.

'I know it's almost impossible to find the will in time,' van As said apologetically and he looked at the female attorney. She met his gaze, her face expressionless.

He nodded. 'You're sure of the existence of the document?'

Hope Beneke drew in her breath as if she wanted to raise an objection.

'Yes. Jan brought it home one evening.' She gestured in the direction of the kitchen. 'We sat at the table and he took me through it step by step. It wasn't a long document.'

'And the tenor of it was that you would inherit everything?'

'Yes.'

'Who drew up the will?'

'He wrote it himself. It was in his handwriting.'

'Did anyone witness it?'

'He had it witnessed at the police station here in Durbanville. Two of the people there signed it.'

'There was only the one copy?'

'Yes,' said Wilna van As, in a resigned voice.

'You didn't find it odd that he didn't have an attorney to draw up the document?'

'Jan was like that.'

'How?

'Private.'

The word hung in the air. Van Heerden said nothing, waiting for her to speak again.

'I don't think he trusted people very much.'

'Oh?'

'He . . . we . . . led a simple life. We worked and came home. He sometimes referred to this house as his hiding place. There weren't any friends, really . . .'

'What did he do?'

'Classical furniture. What other people describe as antiques. He said that in South Africa there weren't really any antiques, the country was too young. We were wholesalers. We found the furniture and provided traders, sometimes sold directly to the collectors.'

'What was your role?'

'I began working for him about twelve years ago. As a kind of . . . secretary. He drove around looking for furniture, in the countryside, on farms. I manned the office. After six months . . .'

'Where's the office?'

'Here,' she indicated. 'In Wellington Street. Behind Pick 'n Pay. It's a little old house . . .'

'There was no safe in the office.'

'No.'

'After six months . . .' he reminded her.

'I quickly learnt the business. He was in the Northern Cape when someone telephoned from Swellendam. It was a *jonkmanskas*, a wardrobe, if I remember correctly, nineteenth-century, a pretty piece with inlays ... In any case, I phoned him. He said I had to have a look at it. I drove there and bought it for next to nothing. He was impressed when he got back. Then I started doing more and more ...'

'Who manned the office?'

'We started off by taking turns. Afterwards he stayed in the office.'

'You didn't mind?'

'I liked it.'

'When did you start living together?'

Van As hesitated.

'Miss van As ...' Hope Beneke leaned forward, briefly searched for words. 'Mr van Heerden must unfortunately ask questions that might possibly be ... uncomfortable. But it's essential that he acquire as much information as possible.'

Van As nodded. 'Of course. It's just that ... I'm not used to discussing the relationship. Jan was always ... He said people didn't have to know. Because they always gossip.'

She realized that he was waiting for an answer. 'It was a year after we began working together.'

'Eleven years.' A statement.

'Yes.'

'In this house.'

'Yes.'

'And you never went into the safe.'

'No.'

He simply stared at her.

Van As gestured. 'That's the way it was.'

'If Jan Smit had died under different circumstances, how would you have got the will out of the safe?'

'I knew the combination.'

He waited.

'Jan changed it. To my birth date. After he had shown me the will.'

'He kept all his important documents in the safe?'

'I don't know what else was in it. Because it's all gone now.'

'May I see it? The safe?'

She nodded and stood up. Wordlessly he followed her down the passage. Hope Beneke followed them. Between the bathroom and the main bedroom, on the right-hand side, was the safe's big steel door, the mechanism of the combination lock set in it. The door was open. Van As touched a switch on the wall and a fluorescent light flickered and then glowed brightly. She walked in and stood in the safe.

'I think he added it. After he bought the house.'

'You *think* so?'

'He never mentioned it.'

'And you never asked?'

She shook her head. He looked at the inside of the safe. It was entirely lined with wooden shelves, all of them empty.

'You have no idea what was inside?'

She shook her head again, small beside him in the narrow confines of the safe.

'You never walked past when he was busy inside?'

'He closed the door.'

'And the secrecy never bothered you?'

She looked at him, almost childishly. 'You didn't know him, Mr van Rensburg.'

'Van Heerden.'

'I'm sorry.' He could see the woman blushing. 'I'm usually good with names.'

He nodded.

'Jan Smit was . . . He was a very private person.'

'Did you clean in here after the . . .'

'Yes. When the police had finished.'

He turned and walked out, past Hope Beneke who was standing in the doorway, back to the living room. The women followed him. They sat down again.

'You were the first to arrive on the scene?'

The attorney lifted her hands. 'Could we have a bit of breathing space?'

Van As nodded. Van Heerden said nothing.

'I would love some tea,' Beneke said. 'If it's not too much trouble.' She gave the other woman a warm, sympathetic smile.

'With pleasure,' said Wilna van As and walked to the kitchen.

'A touch of compassion wouldn't hurt, Mr van Heerden.'

'Just call me van Heerden.'

She looked at him.

He leaned back in the chair. The pain around his eye was surpassing the ache of his ribs. The hangover throbbed dully in his head. 'Seven days doesn't leave me much time for compassion, Hope.' He could see that his use of her name irritated her. It pleased him.

'I don't think it will take either time or trouble.'

He shrugged.

'You make it sound as if she's a suspect.'

He was quiet for a moment. Then he said slowly, tiredly: 'How long have you been an attorney?'

'Almost four years.'

'How many murder cases have you handled during this period?'

'I fail to see what that has to do with you and your lack of basic decency.'

'Why do you think Kemp recommended me? Because I'm such a lovable guy?'

'What?'

He ignored her. 'I know what I'm doing, Beneke. I know what I'm doing.'

4

For years the painting of my father hung on the wall facing their double bed – the lithe miner with his coppery blond hair and muscled torso set against a ridge in the Western Transvaal, bleached by winter. The painting was a symbol of their unique meeting, their unusual romance, the love at first sight that evidently happened more often in those days than it does now.

I don't offer Emile and Joan's meeting as an amusing prologue, but as one of the great factors that shaped my life.

In the shadow of their romance, I would spend most of my life searching for that moment in which I, too, would discover the same immediate and dramatic certainty of love.

It would, eventually, lead to my downfall.

My father was a man of integrity. (How disappointed he would have been had he known his son as an adult.) That – and his body – possibly formed the foundation on which my parents' marriage was built, because they had nothing in common. Even after their marriage, three years later, they lived in separate worlds in the mine house in Stilfontein.

I must admit that I don't recall much of the first four or five years of my life but I did know that my mother, the artist, was always surrounded by her artistic friends: painters, sculptors, actors and musicians, odd people who came on visits from Johannesburg and Pretoria, occasionally filling the third bedroom to overflowing, even bedding down in the living room on some weekends. She guided the conversation, a cigarette in her hand, an open book within reach, music coming from scratchy records, especially Schubert, but Beethoven and Haydn as well. (Mozart, she said, didn't have enough passion.) She didn't like housekeeping or cooking, but there was always a meal for my father, often an exotic dish prepared by one of her friends. And he was a figure on the periphery, the man who came off shift with his hard hat and his tin lunchbox and went to rugby practice. Or went jogging in summer. He was a fitness fanatic years before it became fashionable. He ran the Comrades Ultra-marathon year after year, other forgotten marathons as well. He was a quiet man and his life revolved around his love for her and his love for sport – and, later, his love for me.

Into this household fate shoved me on 27 January, 1960, a boy with his mother's dark features and, evidently, his father's silences.

It was his suggestion that they should name me 'Zatopek'.

He was a great admirer of the Czech athlete Emil Zatopek, and the fact that he shared his first name with him, even if the spelling differed slightly, probably also played a role. For my mother, 'Zatopek' was different, exotic, bohemian. Neither of them, with their ordinary names, could have foreseen what this would do to a boy growing up in a mining town. Not that the children's insensitive teasing left a scar. But neither did they foresee the lifelong irritation of spelling your first name every time a form had to be filled in; the raised eyebrows and the inevitable 'Come again?' every time you introduced yourself.

There were only two events during my first six years that would remain with me forever.

The first was the discovery of the beauty of women.

The applicability of this is multifaceted and you must bear with me, forgive me if I digress from narrative and chronology. But it was a subject that would fascinate me, enchant me and eventually add to the jigsaw of my psyche.

The specifics of the event have been forgotten. I think I was five, probably playing with my toys in the living room of the mine house, among the adults, my mother's wide circle of artistic friends, when I looked up at one of her friends, an actress. And in that moment recognized her beauty, undefined, but with the complete knowledge that she was beautiful, that one was swept away by the sum total of her features. I must admit that I can't recall her face, just the fact that she was small and slender and possibly had brown hair. But it was the first of many such experiences, each one a milestone of growing admiration and meditation on the beauty of women.

The danger, of course, was the possible loss of objectivity. Because all men, after all, admire beautiful women. But I believed that my feeling for beauty, the way in which it impressed me, was above the average. Perhaps, I thought then, when I still had the energy and the hunger for reflection, that it was the only inheritance from my mother's artistic genes – to be enchanted by the shape, the angles, the separate particles that make up the sum total of a woman, as my father's body had enchanted her. The difference was that she wanted to paint it, as she did so many other people's faces and postures. I was always content merely to look and to ponder. To wonder about the unfairness of the gods who conferred beauty in a haphazard fashion; about the devils of old age who could take back the beauty so that only the personality that had been shaped by it remained; about the influence of stunning beauty on a woman's character; about the strangeness of beauty, its many wonderful facets of nose and mouth and chin, cheekbone and eye. And I wondered about the gods' sense of humour, their wickedness and meanness in giving some woman a perfect body and then holding back at the very epicentre of beauty, the face. Or connecting an exquisite face to a hideous body. Or adding a fraction of imperfection to the mix so that it hangs there in no-man's-land.

Oh, and the talent women possess to enhance nature's parsimony, using clothes and colour, lipstick and brush and small movements of hands and fingers to produce an improved, more alluring product.

From that moment, in a living room in Stilfontein, I was a slave to beauty.

The second unforgettable event during my first six years began with an earthquake.

5

'I returned from Windhoek and Jan was supposed to fetch me at the airport. But he wasn't there. I phoned home. There was no reply. So I took a taxi after waiting for about two hours. It was late, probably ten o'clock in the evening. The house was in darkness. I was worried because he always came home early. And the kitchen light was always burning. So I opened the front door and walked in and I saw him, there, in the kitchen. Immediately. It was the first thing I saw. And I knew he was dead. There was so much blood. His head hung low on his chest. They had fastened him to the chair, one of the kitchen chairs. I sold the set, I couldn't keep them. His arms were tied behind him with wire, the police told me. I couldn't go any closer, I simply stood there in the doorway and then I ran to the neighbours. They telephoned the police, I was in shock. They called the doctor as well.'

From the sound of her voice he knew that she had repeated the story more than once: the lack of intonation that repetition and suppressed trauma brings.

'Later the police asked you to look through the house.'

'Yes. They wanted to know lots of things. How the murderer had entered the house, everything that was stolen . . .'

'Could you help them?'

'We don't know how they got in. The police think they were lying in wait for him when he got home. But the neighbours didn't notice anything.'

'What was gone, out of the house?'

'Only the contents of the safe.'

'His wallet? Television set? Hi-fi?'

'Nothing, except the contents of the safe.'

'How long were you in Windhoek?'

'I spent the entire week in Namibia. In the countryside, mostly. I only flew to and from Windhoek.'

'How long had he been dead when you got back?'

'They told me it had happened the previous evening. Before I came back.'

'You didn't telephone here on that day?'

'No. I'd phoned two days before from Gobabis, just to tell him what I'd found.'

'What did he sound like?'

'The same as always. He didn't like telephones. I did most of the talking. I made sure that the prices I'd offered were correct, gave the addresses for the truck.'

'He said nothing strange? Different?'

'No.'

'The truck. Which truck?'

'It's not our truck. Manie Meiring Transport, of Kuilsriver, fetched the stuff once a month. We let them have the addresses and the cheques which had to be given to the sellers. Then he sent someone with a truck.'

'How many people knew you were out of town that week?'

'I don't know . . . Only Jan, really.'

'Do you have a char? Gardener?'

'No. I . . . we did everything.'

'Cleaner at the office?'

'The police also asked me. Perhaps there was someone who knew I was away but we had no other employees. They also wanted to know if I went out of town on a regular basis. But it was never precisely the same time in any given month. Sometimes I was away for only a night or two, sometimes for two weeks.'

'And then Jan Smit did his own laundry and cleaned the house.'

'There wasn't much to clean, and there's a laundry which does ironing as well in Wellington Street.'

'Who knew about the safe?'

'Only Jan and I.'

'No friends? No family?'

'No.'

'Mrs van As, have you any idea of who could possibly have waited for him and murdered him, anyone who could possibly have known about the contents of the safe?'

She shook her head and then, without any warning, the tears ran soundlessly down her cheeks.

'But I know you,' said Mavis Petersen when van Heerden walked into Murder and Robbery's unattractive brick building in Kasselsvlei Road, Bellville.

He hadn't looked forward to his return. He didn't want to count how many years had passed since he'd walked out through these same doors. Virtually nothing had changed. The same musty, wintry smell, the same tiled floors, the same Civil Service furniture. The same Mavis. Older. But as welcoming.

'Hallo, Mavis.'

'But it's the Captain,' said Mavis and clapped her hands.

'Not any more, Mavis.'

'And look at that eye. What did you do? How many years has it been? What is the Captain doing these days?'

'As little as possible,' he said, uncomfortable, unprepared for the reception, unwilling to contaminate this woman with the sourness of his existence. 'Is Tony O'Grady in?'

'I can't believe it, Captain. You've lost weight. Yes, the Inspector is here, he's on the second floor now. Do you want me to buzz him?'

'No, thank you, Mavis, I'll just walk up.'

He walked past her desk into the body of the building, recollections hammering at the door of his memory. He shouldn't have come, he thought. He should have met O'Grady somewhere else. Detectives sat in offices, walked past him, strange faces he had never known. He climbed the stairs to the top floor, passed the tearoom, saw someone there, asked directions. Then he arrived at O'Grady's office.

The fat man behind the desk looked up when he heard the knock against the door frame.

'Hi, Nougat.'

O'Grady's eyes narrowed. 'Jesus.'

'No, but thanks . . .'

He walked to the desk, extended a hand. O'Grady hoisted himself halfway up in his chair, shook hands and sat down again, his mouth still half-open. Van Heerden took a slab of imported nougat out of his jacket pocket. 'You still eat this?'

O'Grady didn't even glance at it. 'I don't believe it.'

He put the nougat on the desk.

'Jesus, van Heerden, it's been years. It's like seeing a ghost.'

He sat down on one of the grey steel chairs.

'But I suppose ghosts don't get black eyes,' O'Grady said and picked up the nougat. 'What's this? A bribe?'

'You could call it that.'

The fat man fiddled with the cellophane cover of the nougat. 'Where have you been? We've even stopped talking about you, you know.'

'I was in Gauteng for a while,' he fabricated.

'In the Force?'

'No.'

'Jesus, wait till I tell the others. So what happened to the eye?'

He gestured. 'Small accident. I need your help, Tony.' He wanted to keep the conversation short.

O'Grady took a bite of the nougat. 'You sure know how to get it.'

'You handled the Smit case. Last September. Johannes Jacobus Smit. Murdered in his home. Walk-in safe . . .'

'So you're a private eye now.'

'Something like that.'

'Jesus, van Heerden, that's not a fucking living. Why don't you come back?'

He breathed deeply. He had to suppress all the fear and the anger.

'Do you remember the case?'

O'Grady stared at him for long time, his jaws moving as he masticated the nougat, eyes narrowed. *He looks exactly the same*, van Heerden thought. *No fatter, no thinner*. The same plump policeman who hid the sharp mind behind the flamboyant personality and the heavy body.

'So what's your interest?'

'His mistress is looking for a will that was in the safe.'

'And you must find it?'

'Yes.'

He shook his head. 'Private dick. Shit. You used to be good.'

Van Heerden took a deep breath. 'The will,' he said.

O'Grady peered at him over the slab of nougat. 'Ah. The will.' He put down the confectionery, pushed it aside. 'You know, that was the one thing that never really figured.' He leaned back, folded his arms over his stomach. 'That fucking will. Because at first I was sure she did him. Or hired somebody. It fitted the whole damn' case. Smit had no friends, no business associates, no other staff. But they got in, tortured him until he gave them the combination, cleaned out the safe and killed him. Took nothing else. It was an inside job. And she was the only one on the inside. Or so she says.'

'Tortured him?'

'Burned him with a fucking blowtorch. Arms, shoulders, chest, balls. It must have been murder, if you'll pardon the expression.'

'Did she know that?'

'We didn't tell her or the press. I played it close to the chest, tried to see if I could trick her.'

'She says she knew the combination, Nougat.'

'The blowtorch could have been for effect. To take suspicion away from her.'

'Murder weapon?'

'Now there's another strange thing. Ballistics said it was an M16. The Yank army model. Not too many of those around, are there?'

Slowly van Heerden shook his head. 'Just one shot?'

'Yep. Execution style, back of the head.'

'Because he'd seen them? Or knew them?'

'Who knows these days? Maybe they shot him just for the fun of it.'

'How many were there, do you think?'

'We don't know. No fingerprints inside, no footprints outside, no neighbourhood witnesses. But Smit was a big man, in reasonable shape. There must have been more than one perp.'

'Forensics?'

O'Grady leant forward, pulled the nougat towards him again. 'Sweet Fanny Adams. No prints, no hair, no fibres. Just a fucking piece of paper. In the safe. Found a piece of paper, about the size of two match boxes. Clever guys in Pretoria say it was part of a wrapping. For wrapping little stacks of money. You know, ten thousand in fifties, that sort of thing . . .'

Van Heerden raised his eyebrows.

'But the funny thing is, according to the type and all that shit, that they're pretty sure it was dollars. US dollars.'

'Fuck,' said van Heerden.

'My sentiments exactly. But the plot thickens. It was the only thing I had to go on, so I put a lot of pressure on Pretoria through the Colonel. Forensics has a money expert. Claassen, or something. He went back to his books and his microscope and came back and said the paper indicated that it was old money. The Americans don't wrap their money like that any more. But they used to. In the seventies and early eighties.'

Van Heerden digested the information for a moment. 'And you asked Wilna van As about that?'

'Yep. And got the usual answer. She doesn't know anything. She never took dollars as payment for that old-fart furniture, never paid with it. Doesn't even know what a fucking dollar bill looks like. I mean, shit, this woman lived with the deceased for a fucking decade or more, but she's like the three little monkeys – hear, see, speak no evil. And that little sexpot lawyer of hers is all over me like a Sumo wrestler every time I want to ask some straight questions.' O'Grady took a frustrated bite of nougat and sank back in his chair again.

'No American clients or friends she knew about.' It was a statement. He already knew the answer.

The fat detective spoke with his mouth full but managed to utter each word clearly. 'Not one. I mean, with the rifle and the dollars, it just makes sense that there is some kind of Yank involvement.'

'Her attorney says she's innocent.'

'Is she your new employer?'

'Temporarily.'

'At least get her into bed. Because that's all you're going to get from this one. It's a dead end. I mean, where's the fucking motive for Wilna van As? Without the will she apparently gets nothing.'

'Unless there was a deal that she would get half of the haul. In a year or two when things had cooled down.'

'Maybe . . .'

'And without her there were no other suspects?'

'Zilch. Nothing.'

Time to eat humble pie: 'I would like to see the dossier very much, Nougat.'

O'Grady stared fixedly at him.

'I know you're a good policeman, Nougat. I have to go through the motions.'

'You can't take it with you. You'll have to read it here.'

6

The earthquake woke me, late at night, the deep, rolling thunder from the depths of the earth that made all the windows shiver and the corrugated roof of the mine house creak. I cried and my father came to comfort me, took me in his arms in the dark and said that it was only the earth moving itself into a more comfortable position.

I had fallen asleep again when the telephone rang, an hour or so later. To call him out.

The rest of the tale was told to me by my mother, patched together from the official announcements, the stories of my father's colleagues and her own imagination.

He led one of the rescue teams which had to bring out the fourteen men trapped a kilometre underground after one of the tunnels had collapsed.

It was hot and confused down there. Other rescue teams were already at work when they got there, taken down the shaft in the rattling, shaking cage, carrying their shovels and their pickaxes, first-aid kits and bottles of water. No one wore the regulation hard hat, it only got in the way. They all, black and white, folded down the top half of their overalls to work in the heat with naked torsos that gleamed in the glaring electric spotlights, shining brightly in one place and casting deep shadows in another. The black men's rhythmical singing provided the universal tempo to which everyone worked – the diggers, the soil removers, side by side, the usually rigid divisions drawn between races and trades suddenly forgotten because four of the trapped men were white and ten were black.

Hour after hour in the eternal dark to move a mountain.

On the surface relatives of the white men had begun to gather, waiting for news with the usual support of the community, friends and colleagues, as well as families of the rescue teams because they, too, weren't safe.

My mother painted during those hours, Schubert's lieder playing tinnily on the radiogram. Calm, she thought my father was invincible, while I knew nothing of the tension of an entire town.

Just before his team was due to return to the surface at the end of their shift they heard muffled cries for help, exhausted moans of pain and fear, and he encouraged them, the thin edge of the wedge which bit by bit moved rock and stone and earth, to excavate a narrow tunnel, the opportunity for rest suddenly forgotten in the adrenalin high of success in sight. Emile van Heerden was in the lead, his lithe body drawing on the fitness of a lifetime to reach the trapped men.

His team had broken through to the small opening that the survivors had dug with bare hands and bleeding fingers.

The news that there were voices down there quickly spread to the surface and the people in the small recreation hall clapped their hands and wept.

And then the earth shook again.

He had pulled out the first three on his own with muscled, sinewy arms and loaded them onto the wood-and-canvas stretchers. The fourth one was trapped up to his chest, a black man with smashed legs who suppressed the pain with superhuman effort, the only signs the sweat pouring off him and the shaking of his upper body. Emile van Heerden dug frantically, the soil around the man's legs moving with the effort of my father's own fingers because a shovel was too big and too clumsy. Then the earth, once again, moved into a more comfortable position.

He was one of twenty-four men they brought out of the shaft three days later wrapped in blankets.

My mother only cried when she pulled the blanket aside in the mortuary and saw what the pressure of a ton of rock had done to the beautiful body of her husband.

7

Van Heerden wasn't the kind of man she had expected.

Kemp had said he was an ex-policeman. 'What can I tell you? A bit . . . different? But he's damn' good with investigations. Just be firm with him.'

Heaven knew, she needed 'good with investigations'.

She hadn't known what to expect. Different? Perhaps an earring and a ponytail? Not the . . . tension. The way he had spoken to Wilna van As. 'Tension' wasn't the right word. He was difficult to handle. Like an explosive.

They had decided on R2,000 per week. In advance. She would have to pay it out of her own pocket at first if van Heerden found nothing. Too much money. Even if Wilna van As paid it in instalments later. Money the firm couldn't afford. She would have to phone Kemp. She reached out for the telephone.

He stood in her doorway.

'I'll have to speak to van As again.' His lean body and his black eye and his fuck-you attitude, a brown envelope in his hand, leaning against her door frame. She realized that she had been startled and that he had seen it, her hand stretched towards the telephone. Her aversion to the man was small, but germinating, like a seed.

'We'll have to discuss that,' she said. 'And perhaps you should consider knocking before you come in.'

'Why do we have to discuss it?' He sat down in the chair opposite her again, this time leaning forward, his body language antagonistic.

She took a deep breath, forced patience into her voice, and firmness. 'Wilna van As, purely as a human being, can justifiably expect our compassion and respect. Added to that she was exposed to more trauma in the past nine months than most of us experience in a lifetime. Despite the little time at our disposal, I found your attitude towards her this morning upsetting and unacceptable.'

He sat in the chair, his eyes on the brown envelope which he tapped rhythmically against his thumbnail.

'I see you're only two women.'

'What?'

'The firm. Female attorneys.' He looked up, gestured vaguely at the offices around them.

'Yes.' She understood neither the drift nor the relevance.

'Why?' he asked.

'I can't see what that has to do with your insensitivity.'

'I'm getting to it, Hope. Are you deliberately a women-only firm?'

'Yes.'

'Why?'

'Because the legal system is a man's world. And out there are thousands of women who have the right to be treated with sympathy and insight when they are prosecuted or want a divorce. Or are looking for wills.'

'You're an idealist,' he said.

'You're not.' A statement.

'And that is the difference between us, Hope. You think your Women's Groups, your all-female practice, and a regular contribution to the Street Children's Fund and the Mission washes your heart as white as snow. You think you and other people are inherently good when you get into your expensive BMWs to go to the Health and Racquet Club and you're so fucking pleased with yourself and your world. Because everyone is basically good. But let me tell you, we're bad. You, me, the whole lot of us.'

He opened the envelope, took out two postcard-size photographs. He shot them across the desk.

'Have you seen these? The late Johannes Jacobus Smit. Tied to his own kitchen chair. Does that fill you with understanding and sympathy and insight? Or whatever other politically correct words you want to dish out. Someone did that to him. Tied him down with wire and burnt him with a blowtorch until he wished they would shoot him. Someone. People. And your untouchable angel, Wilna van As, is in the middle of this mess. Fat Inspector Tony O'Grady of Murder and Robbery thinks she was a part of it because a whole lot of small things don't add up. And when it comes to murder, statistics are on his side. It's usually the husband, the wife, the mistress or the lover. Maybe he's right and maybe he's wrong. But if he's right, what happens to your idealism?'

She looked up from the photos. Pale. 'And you're going to burst my bubble . . .'

'Have you ever met a murderer, Hope?'

'You've made your point.'

'Or a child rapist. We . . .' and then he hesitated for a single heartbeat before he continued, spoke through it, somewhat surprised at himself. 'I . . . I caught a rapist whose victims were children. A gentle, cuddly old man of fifty-nine who looked as if he was a stand-in for Santa Claus. Who lured seventeen little girls between the ages of four and nine into his car with Wilson's toffees and up on Constantiaberg . . .'

'You've made your point,' she said softly.

He sank back in his chair.

'Then let me do my fucking work.'

The north-west wind blew the dark outside against the windows of the house and inside Wilna van As was talking, looking for Jan Smit with words, her hands with the fingers entwined in her lap never wholly still. 'I don't know. I don't know whether I knew him. I don't know whether it was possible to know him. But I didn't mind. I loved him, he was . . . It was as if he had a wound, as if he had a . . . Sometimes I would lie next to him at night and think he was like a dog who had been beaten, too often, too brutally. I thought many things. I thought perhaps there was a wife and children somewhere. Because when I was pregnant, he looked so scared. I thought he had a wife and child who had left him. Or perhaps he was an orphan. Perhaps it was something else but somewhere someone had hurt him so badly that he could never reveal it to anyone else. That much I knew and I never asked him about it. I know nothing about him. I don't know where he grew up and I don't know what happened to his father and his mother and I don't know how he started the business. But I know he loved me in his way, he was kind and good to me and sometimes we laughed together, not often, but now and then, about people, I knew he couldn't bear pretentious people. And those who flaunted their money. I think he probably went though hard times. He looked after his money so neatly, so carefully. I think he was scared of people. Or shy, perhaps . . . There were no friends. It was just us. It was all we needed.'

Only the wind and the rain against the window. She looked up, looked at Hope Beneke. 'There were so many times that I wanted to ask. That I wanted to say he could tell me, that I would always love him, it didn't matter how deep the pain was. There were times that I wanted to ask because I was so dreadfully curious, because I wanted to know him. I think it was because I wanted to place him, because we do that with everybody, place them in a space in our heads so that we know what we can say to them the next time we meet, or what to give them, it makes life a little easier.

'But I didn't ask. Because if I had asked I might have lost him.'

She looked at van Heerden. 'I had nothing. I sometimes wondered whether his father also drank and his mother was also divorced and perhaps he also came from the wrong side of the tracks. Like me. But we had one another and we needed nothing else. That's why I didn't ask. Not even when I fell pregnant and he said that we would have to do something because children didn't deserve the wickedness of this life and that we couldn't protect them. I didn't ask then because I knew he had been beaten. Like a dog. Too often. I simply went and had an abortion. And I went so that they could fix me so I could never get pregnant again.

'Because I knew we only needed one another.'

And then she wiped the drop from the point of her nose and looked down at her hands and he didn't know what to say and knew he couldn't ask his other questions.

The house was a tomb now.

'I think we must go,' the attorney said eventually and stood up. She walked to van As and laid a hand on the woman's shoulder.

They ran across the street together through the rain to their cars. When she pushed the key into her BMW's door, van Heerden stood next to her. 'If we don't find the will, she gets nothing?'

'Nothing,' said Hope Beneke.

He merely nodded. And then walked to the Toyota as the water sifted over him.

While the onions, peppercorns and cloves were boiling, he telephoned.

'I'm cooking,' he said when she replied.

'What time?' she asked and he didn't want to hear the surprise in her voice. He looked at his watch.

'Ten.'

'Fine,' she replied.

He put the phone down. She would be pleased, he knew. She would make assumptions but she wouldn't ask any questions.

He walked back to the gas stove in the kitchen – the only room in the small house that showed no signs of dilapidation and want. He saw that the water had boiled away. He poured a few sticks of cinnamon into the palm of his hand, added them to the ingredients in the silver saucepan. He added olive oil, measuring with his eye, turned the flame down. The onions had to brown slowly. He pulled the chopping board towards him, cut the lamb shanks into smaller pieces, eventually transferred them to the saucepan. He grated the fresh ginger, added it to the stew, along with two cardamom pods. Stirred the mixture, turned the flame even lower. Looked at his watch, put the lid on the pot.

He laid the table with the white tablecloth, the cutlery, salt, black-pepper grinder, the candleholder with white candles. He couldn't remember when last he had lit them.

Back to the work space. He opened two tins of Italian tomatoes.

Had always preferred them to freshly cooked ones. He chopped the tomatoes, took a small green chilli out of the fridge, rinsed it under the tap, sliced it finely, added it to the tomatoes. He peeled the potatoes, put them in a bowl, opened the hot water tap, filled the sink, poured in washing liquid, rinsed the knife and the cutting board. Uncorked the bottle of red wine.

There was something in that safe. Which someone knew about.

In a separate pot, small carrots in a tablespoon of orange juice, small spoonful of brown sugar. A little grated orange peel. Bit of butter later on.

That was all that made sense. Because nothing else was missing from the house: no cupboards ransacked, no beds overturned, no television set taken.

Jan Smit. The lone wolf with the mistress. The man without a history, without friends.

He looked at his watch. The meat had been in for thirty minutes. He lifted the lid, scraped the tomato and chilli pulp into the saucepan, replaced the lid. He switched on the kettle, put basmati rice in another saucepan, waited until the water boiled, added it to the rice, lit the flame, put the saucepan on the stove, checked the time.

He made sure that the front door was unlocked, lit the candles. She would be here soon.

Jan Smit.

Where the fuck did you start?

Orange juice had boiled away. Added a tablespoon of butter.

He walked to the bedroom, took his notebook out of his jacket pocket, sat on the threadbare armchair in the too-small living room, looked at the notes he had made when he had borrowed the dossier from O'Grady that afternoon.

Fuck-all.

Nothing. He stared at the identity number. 561123 5127 001. On 23 November, 1956, Jan Smit's life had begun. Where?

The door opened. She came in on a gust of wind and with a dripping umbrella. She saw him and smiled, collapsed the umbrella and put it down at the door. She had tied a scarf around her hair. She took off her raincoat. He got up, took it from her, threw it over the arm of a chair.

'Nice smell,' she said. 'The chair will be wet.' She moved the raincoat to the small coffee table.

He nodded.

'Tomato stew,' he said, walked to the kitchen and fetched the red wine, poured two glasses, handed her one. She pulled a chair away from the table and sat down.

'You're working again,' she said.

He nodded.

She sipped at the wine, put the glass down, untied the scarf, took it off, shook her hair.

He walked to the kitchen, opened the pot of stew, added the potatoes, some freshly ground black pepper, a teaspoon of sugar, a pinch of salt, tasted, added more sugar. Killed the flame under the carrots. He walked back to the table, sat opposite her.

'It's an impossible task,' he said. 'I'm looking for a will.'

'Sam Spade,' she said and her eyes laughed.

He snorted without anger.

'I'm so pleased,' she said. 'It's been so long . . .'

'Don't,' he said softly.

She looked at him with overwhelming compassion. 'Tell me,' she said and leant back in the chair. 'About the will.' The light of the candles glimmered dark red in the glass of wine when she picked it up.

Hope Beneke lit thirteen candles in her bathroom without counting them. The candles were multi-coloured: green and blue and white and yellow – one was scented, they were all short and stubby. She liked candlelight and it made the small white-tiled bathroom in the townhouse in Milnerton Ridge more bearable

Her temporary house with its two bedrooms and its open-plan kitchen and white melamine cupboards. Her temporary investment. Until the firm started making good money. Until she could buy something that looked out over the sea, a white house with a green roof and a wooden deck and a view over the Atlantic Ocean and its sunsets, a house with a big kitchen – for entertaining friends – and oak cupboards and a bookcase that filled an entire wall of the living room.

She poured in bath oil, swished the water around with her hands as she bent over the bath, her small breasts moving with her shoulder muscles.

Her house by the sea would have a huge bath for soaking in.

She closed the taps and slowly climbed into the warm water, listened for a moment wondering if she could hear the rain outside so that the steam and the warmth and the comfort of bathing could be emphasized. She dried her hands on the white towel, picked up the book lying on the lavatory lid. *London.* Edward Rutherford. Thick and wonderful. She opened it at her Library Week bookmark.

Women's groups. The Health and Racquet Club. He couldn't be much of a detective if he had categorized her so glibly and so incorrectly.

In any case, she wasn't work-out person.

She was a jogger.

If we don't find the will, she gets nothing? As if he hadn't heard it in her office, that first time. As if Wilna van As had eventually penetrated his mind that evening.

We're all bad . . .

Strange man.

She focused on the book.

'That was wonderful,' she said and neatly placed her knife and fork on the plate. He merely nodded. The meat hadn't been tender enough for his taste. He was out of practice.

'Were you in a fight again?' It was the first time she had mentioned his eye.

'Yes.'

'Oh, dear,' she said. 'Why?'

He shrugged, divided the last of the red wine between the two glasses.

'How much was the advance she gave you?'

'Two thousand.'

'You must buy some clothes.'

He nodded, took a gulp of wine.

'New shoes as well.'

He saw the gentleness in her eyes, the caring, the worry. 'Yes,' he said.

'And you must get out more.'

'Where to?'

'With someone. Take someone out. There are so many attractive young . . .'

'No,' he said.

'What's her name?'

'Whose?'

'The attorney.'

'Hope Beneke.'

'Is she pretty?'

'What does *that* matter?'

'I just wondered.' She put her empty glass down and slowly stood up. 'I must get home.'

He pushed his chair back, stretched out an arm for her raincoat, held it for her, picked up her umbrella.

'Thank you, Zet.'

'It was a pleasure.'

'Goodnight.'

He opened the door for her.

''Night, Ma.'

Day 6

Friday, 7 July

8

When I was nine, or eight or ten, somewhere during those forgettable, neither-fish-nor-fowl years, I took part in a rugby game, playing on the rock-hard field of the Stilfontein Primary School. During the typical ruck 'n tumble of little boys, I received a blow that made my nose bleed. The referee, a teacher, I think, came up to me.

'Now, now, my boy, men don't cry,' he said comfortingly.

'No.' My mother's voice was clearly audible next to me. She was angry. 'Cry, my child. Cry as much as you like. Men are allowed to cry. Real men may cry.'

When I think back, it was typical of who she was and how she tried to raise me.

Different. To Stilfontein and its people and their views and way of doing things.

Describing the psyche of a mining town is difficult because one has to generalize. Young Afrikaners with a minimal education and a maximum income made for a heady, combustible mixture. They lived their lives in the fast track – they earned fast and spent fast on fast cars, bikes and women. Their alcohol intake, their tempers, everything matched the speed of potential sudden death in the dark depths of the earth.

And amidst all this was the cultural oasis of Joan van Heerden's home.

The mine gave her, us, a smaller house in Stilfontein. I don't know why she didn't move to Pretoria: her parents and her friends were there. I suspected that it was because she wanted to be near my father, near his grave in the grey cemetery in the wind-blown wasteland on the back road to Klerksdorp.

There was no shortage of money. Life insurance was fashionable among Afrikaners in those days. And my father was provident unto death. But income also came from my mother whose paintings began selling slowly but steadily, the prices rising a little each year, each year an exhibition at a larger, more important gallery.

Perhaps her decision to remain in Stilfontein was partly a desire to stay away from the mainstream of Art – she disliked the pretentiousness of so-called art lovers and critics. And then there were the arty types, peculiar people who believed that exotic clothing and strange hairstyles would guarantee their admission into the inner circle of taste – all they needed to do was to act bohemian and cultured. She couldn't stand them.

So it was just the two of us and Stilfontein. There were a few friends in the town – Dr de Korte, our GP, and his wife, the Van der Walts of the framing shop – people from Johannesburg and Potchefstroom who came on visits over weekends.

Placid and uneventful years of growing up. Until my sixteenth year.

My mother had no other men in her life, except for the husbands of her friends – and the gay men in the art world, like Tony Masarakis, the Greek sculptor in Krugersdorp who sometimes dropped in. When I was nine or ten he mentioned in passing that she had a good-looking son. 'Forget it, Tony,' she had said with finality. He must have taken it to heart because they remained friends for many years.

She was a young widow, in her late twenties. And beautiful. A passionate woman. Would she be celibate for the rest of her life? I never thought about it until I reached my own twenties and then, when I did think about it, it was with a qualm. Because after all, she was my mother and I was Afrikaans.

I don't know if she occasionally sought relief, let alone found it. If so, it was done with the utmost discretion and possibly with the strict injunction to her partner (or partners) of no long relationships, thank you. Perhaps during those weekends when she went to exhibitions in the Cape, or in Durban or Johannesburg and I didn't go with her.

But there was no evidence.

The question, of course, was whether growing up without a father, without a male role model, scarred a boy whose mother had called him 'Zet' from an early age. I would so much have liked to embrace it as an exoneration, make it a part of the greater exoneration, for the compelling wave that eventually spilled me over the edge, dish it up as an easy psychological escape hatch for the fuck-up of my life. But I don't think I can. My mother raised me with ease and patience. Treated me with respect and compassion and discipline, loved me, punished me and cared for me – even if our staple food, when no friends were visiting, was fruit and bread. She played Beethoven, Schubert, Haydn and Bach (J.S. and, to a lesser extent, C.P.E.) without forcing the music down my throat and later, when I wanted to listen to Bachman Turner Overdrive and Black Sabbath, even kept her music in the background. I suspected that she knew which music would stay with me in the long run.

Those were safe years. Until I was sixteen. When I discovered Mozart and books and food and sex and the long arm of the law.

9

He was awake long before the alarm went off at five o'clock. He lay in the dark, staring at the ceiling, and waited for the instrument's electronic beep. He killed it, swung his legs off the bed, checked the pain in his body. The ribs hurt a little less, the eye still throbbed. He knew it would turn purple during the morning. It wasn't his first.

He walked to the kitchen. The crockery was neatly stacked in the drying rack. He put the kettle on. The cold penetrated the worn old police tracksuit. He put instant coffee into a mug, waited for the water to boil, poured it onto the grains, added milk, walked to the combined dining and living area, put the coffee on the small table. Looked for the CD he wanted. Clarinet concerto. Pressed the buttons on the portable stereo, put on earphones, sat down, drank a mouthful of coffee. Adjusted the volume.

He had known since the previous day that he would have to think about Nagel. Since that moment in the attorney's office. *We . . . Nagel and I caught a rapist who preyed on kids*, he had wanted to say.

It was because this reminded him so much of what he used to do. The first time . . . the first time since he had left. The first time since then that he was looking for a murderer again. That was why he would think about Nagel. It was normal. He simply had to be careful. He could think about Nagel, about everything Nagel had taught him.

He just had to stay within those bounds. Then he would be safe. Set the parameters now. Then he could carry on.

Jan Smit.

Play all the angles: Nagel of the deep bass voice, the bobbing Adam's apple, Nagel who couldn't speak English to save his life. *Murder case is like my fuckin' Portapool, van Heerden. Even if everything looks blue and refreshing, even if the sun glitters on the water, somewhere there's a fucking leak. We'll find it if we look everywhere.*

He wrote in the notebook.

1 Neighbours.

He sat back, thought again, wrote.

2 Manie Meiring Transport.
3 What kind of company?
4 Registrar of Companies (referrals) (??)
5 Dept of Home Affairs (??)

He leaned back and swallowed some coffee. Were there other angles?

6 Regular/big clients?
7 Bank?

That was all he had. He chewed the end of his pen, swallowed another mouthful of coffee, put the pen down, leaned back, closed his eyes.

It hadn't been so bad. He could keep Nagel out.

He listened to the music.

He saw the sides of the large trucks, just before the Polkadraai crossing. MMT in huge, exaggerated dark purple letters pierced by an arrow, to suggest speed. He turned off and drove through pools of water and mud to the small building with the sign reading *Office/Reception*. The clouds were dark and low. It would start raining soon. He got out of the car. The wind was even colder today. Snow on the mountains, probably.

A woman sat behind a computer, speaking on the telephone

'The truck should've been there by now, Dennis, they left here on time but you know what it's like at the tunnel, or a damn' traffic cop pulled him . . .'

Blonde and overweight, she smiled at van Heerden, a smear of scarlet lipstick on her front teeth. She listened for a moment, spoke again. 'OK, Dennis, phone me if he isn't there by twelve. OK. Bye.'

She turned to van Heerden. 'Did you walk into a door or did her husband come home early?'

'Is Manie here?'

'If he is, I'd be extremely worried.' She rolled her eyes heavenward.

He waited.

'Manie was my father-in-law, doll. Been in his grave for three years, bless his soul. You're looking for my husband, Danie – or is there something *I* can do to help you?' The underlying suggestion casual, like an old habit.

'I'm investigating Jan Smit's murder. I want to speak to someone who knew him.'

She looked him up and down. 'You look too thin for a policeman.' Then she turned and shouted through the open door to the back. 'Danieeeee . . .' Then back to van Heerden. 'Have you found anything yet?'

'No, I'm not . . .'

'What?' said Danie Meiring when he walked in, annoyed. Then he saw van Heerden.

'Police,' said the woman and pointed at him with a red-painted fingernail. 'It's about Jan Smit.'

Meiring was short and sturdy, with a thick neck trying to escape from the collar of his clean overall. He stuck out his hand. 'Meiring.'

'Van Heerden. I'd like to ask a few questions.'

'Did that fat Mick fuck up?' The small eyes were set close together beneath an aggressive frown.

Van Heerden shook his head, uncomprehending.

'That Irish cop, O'Hagan or something. Couldn't he manage?'

Light dawned. 'O'Grady.'

'That's the one.'

'I'm not from the police. This is a private investigation for Smit's friend, Miss van As.'

'Oh.'

'How well did you know him?'

'Badly.'

'What kind of contact did you have?'

'None, actually. They faxed the orders through to Valerie and every Christmas I delivered a bottle of whisky to his shop. Never got as much as a cup of tea. He wasn't exactly a chatterbox.'

'For how long did you do business?'

'I don't know. Valerie?'

The woman had listened to the conversation attentively. 'Oh, for years. Many years. He was a client of Pa Manie's for a long time.'

'Five years? Ten?'

'Yes, ten, easily. Maybe more.'

'You don't keep records?'

'Not from so long ago.' Apologetically.

'Was there anything odd about his business at any time?'

'The Mick asked that as well,' said Danie Meiring. 'Wanted to know whether Smit didn't perhaps smuggle grass in his old cupboards. Or diamonds. But how would we know? We tucked 'em and trucked 'em. It's our job.'

'Any regular clients or destinations?'

'No, we collected all over. And the off-loading as well, except for the big antique shops in Durban and the Transvaal.'

'How did he pay?'

'What do you mean, "How did he pay?"'

'By cheque? Cash?'

'Monthly account by cheque,' said Valerie Meiring.

'What the hell does that have to do with it?' her husband asked.

He kept his voice neutral. 'There may have been American dollars in the safe.'

'How about that,' said Meiring.

'Were his payments up to date? Regular?'

'Always,' said Valerie. 'If only everyone paid like that.'

Van Heerden sighed. 'Thank you,' he said and walked to the door.

He stood in the enquiry line for a long time at the Home Affairs office in Bellville until his turn came and the coloured woman looked up tiredly to listen to his question. He told her he was from a firm of attorneys, Beneke, Olivier and Partners. He urgently needed a full birth certificate for Johannes Jacobus Smit, identity number . . .

'You must pay R30 at counter C, sir, and fill in the form. It'll take six to eight weeks for Pretoria to process the form.'

'I don't have six weeks. The Master of the Supreme Court meets in six days to decide about Smit's will.'

'Special cases are on the second floor, sir. They must make representations if you want it more quickly. Room 209.'

'But it can be done?'

'If it's a special case.'

'Thank you.'

He completed the form, stood in the queue at counter C for forty-five minutes, paid the R30 and walked up the stairs to the second floor with the form and the receipt. A black man sat behind the desk of room 209. His desk was stacked with folders in neat piles.

'Can I help?' Hoping that the answer would be in the negative.

He told the story.

'Mmm,' said the man.

Van Heerden waited.

'Pretoria is very busy,' the man said.

'This is an emergency,' said van Heerden.

'There are many emergencies,' said the man.

'Is there anything I can do? Someone I can telephone?'

'No. Only me.'

'How long will it take?'

'A week. Ten days.'

'I don't have that long.'

'Generally, sir, it takes six to eight weeks . . .'

'I heard that. Downstairs.'

Then the man gave a deep sigh. 'It would help if you got a court order. Or a judicial enquiry.'

'Then how long would it take?'

'A day. Even less. Pretoria takes court orders very seriously.'

'Oh.'

The man sighed again. 'Give me the details in the meantime. I'll see what I can do.'

Hope Beneke wasn't in her office.

'She's at a business lunch,' the receptionist said.

'Where?' he asked.

'I don't think she'll want to be disturbed, sir.'

He looked at the beautifully groomed middle-aged woman. 'I'm van Heerden.'

No reaction.

'When she comes back, tell her I was here. Tell her I wanted to see her urgently about the Smit case for which we have only six days left but you wouldn't tell me where she was. Tell her I'm having lunch and I don't know when I'll be back but if her employees want to piss away the Smit case, I'll add my little stream gladly.'

The woman slowly drew a diary towards her. 'She's in the Long Street Cafe.'

He walked out. It was raining. He swore softly. There wouldn't be any parking in Long Street. Sooner or later he would have to buy an umbrella.

'Table for one?' the woman asked when he walked in.

'No,' he said and cast his eyes over the crowd looking for Hope Beneke. He saw her sitting at the back, against the wall, and went forward, his wet shoes leaving a trail on the floor. She was with another woman, both leaning forward, heads together, deep in conversation.

'Hope.'

She looked up, disturbed, her eyes widening slightly. 'Van Heerden?'

'We must get a court order.'

'I . . .' she said. 'You . . .' She looked at the woman opposite her. Van Heerden looked at her. She was stunningly beautiful. 'This is Kara-An Rousseau. She's a client.'

'Hallo,' said the woman and extended a slender hand.

'Van Heerden,' he said and shook her hand but turned to Hope Beneke. 'You'll have to come back to the office. I need the information for Home Affairs and it takes six to eight weeks . . .'

She looked at him and he saw the sickle moons rising, slowly turning red.

'Excuse me for a moment, Kara-An,' Hope said and got up. She walked to the door, then out onto the pavement. He followed her, his temper filling him, making him light-headed.

'Who told you I was here?'

'Does it matter?'

'Do you know who Kara-An Rousseau is?'

'I don't care who she is. I have six days left in which to save your client's inheritance.'

'She heads the Corporate Social Involvement Trust of Nasionale Pers. And I won't allow you to speak to me like that.'

'You're probably seeing the rands from NasPers rolling in, Hope. Do you recall someone named Wilna van As?'

'No,' said Hope Beneke, the sickle moons now glowing like stop-lights. 'You have no right to insinuate that I regard the one as more important than the other. Wilna van As isn't my only client.'

'She's *my* only client.'

'No, van Heerden, I'm your only client. And I'm not a very happy one at this moment.'

He couldn't suppress it any longer. 'I don't care.' He turned and walked into Long Street's rain. He stopped in the middle of the street and looked back. 'Find someone else to fuck around.'

And then, as an afterthought. 'And what kind of horseshit name is Kara-An, anyway?' He walked the two blocks to his car oblivious to the rain.

He threw the wet clothes into the corner of the bathroom, walked naked to the bedroom. He opened the cupboard and searched angrily for a pair of jeans, shirt and sweater. He didn't need this, he thought, again. He'd rather go hungry. He wouldn't be fucked around. Not by her, not by Kemp, not by a bunch of fat dentists. He didn't need it. He didn't care.

Who cared if there was money for fuck-all?

Who cared about anything? No one. That's who. He didn't, either. He was free. Free. Free of the ties that bound other people, the incessant striving after nothing, the endless accumulation of status symbols, the empty, meaningless suburban existence. He was above it all, free of the betrayals, small and large, the lying and the deception, the backstabbing, the distrust, the games.

Fuck her.

In a little while he would drive to her office and throw the remainder of her fucking advance onto the neat receptionist's neat fucking desk and tell her to tell Hope Beneke that he didn't need it. Because he was free.

He tied the laces of his trainers and got up. His house was dark, sombre in the early afternoon. Cold. His house was cold in winter. He'd buy a heater one day. Have a fireplace built. He walked through the too-small sitting area, to the door, he would get a drink in Table View. *Fuck her.*

They were all alike. One day Wilna van As was the most important client in the world because there were only seven days left and oh, we have to help the poor woman because she worked her fingers to the bone for a man (as if she had no choice) and the next day it was Caroline Ann of Monaco or who the fuck whatever, head of the National Press Corporate Shit Shop or whatever the fuck it was and all Hope Beneke saw were rands rolling. All of them. Twenty-four hours worth of loyalty.

He closed the door.

But not him. He was free.

The telephone rang behind the closed door.

Fuck that.

Attorneys. Bloodsuckers. Parasites.

The telephone rang.

He hesitated.

Probably Hope Beneke. 'I'm sorry, van Heerden, come back, van Heerden, I'm a stupid cow, van Heerden.'

Fuck her. Fuck them all.

The telephone kept ringing.

He hissed through his teeth, put the key back in the door, opened it, walked to the phone.

'Yes,' he said, ready to take her on.

'Mr van Heerden?'

'Yes.' Unfamiliar voice.

'Ngwema. Home Affairs.'

'Oh.'

'Pretoria says your ID number is incorrect.'

'Pretoria?'

'I spoke nicely to them, said it was an emergency. But your ID is incorrect. Belongs to someone else. A Mrs Ziegler.'

He pulled the notebook towards him, opened it and read the number to Ngwema again.

'That's the one I sent. It's wrong.'

'Fuck.'

'What?'

'Sorry,' said van Heerden, adding, 'It's impossible.'

'That's what the computer says. And it's never wrong.'

'Oh.' Thinking. He'd found the number in O'Grady's file. Now he would have to look for the identity document.

'Not bad, huh,' Ngwema said.

'What?'

'I said it wasn't bad. Two hours and thirty-seven minutes after we received your request. Not bad for black guys working on African time.' And Ngwema laughed, softly.

Hope Beneke heard Kemp's sigh on the telephone. 'Do you want me to speak to him again?'

'No, thank you. I've had it. He's . . . unstable.'

'No, hang on . . . Were you firm with him?'

'Yes, I was firm with him. He obviously has a problem with a woman in a position of authority.'

'He has a problem with *anyone* in a position of authority.'

'Is there anyone else?'

Kemp laughed. 'There's a whole squadron of private detectives in the phone book. And they're all hot when it comes to sneaking pictures for housewives of hubby's hanky-panky with the secretary. But they know nothing about this kind of thing.'

'There must be someone.'

'Van Heerden is the best.'

'Exactly what has he done for you?'

'This and that.'

'"This and that"?'

'He's good, Hope. Doesn't miss much. You need him.'

'No,' she said.

'I'll ask around.'

'I'd appreciate it.'

She said goodbye and put the handset down. The phone rang immediately.

'There's a Mrs Joan van Heerden to see you,' the receptionist said. 'She doesn't have an appointment.'

'The artist?'

'I don't know.'

'Please ask her to come in.'

Her day was like a Dali painting, she thought. Surrealist surprises everywhere.

The door opened. The woman who came in was small and slender, pretty, in her fifties or early sixties, years worn with grace. Hope recognized her and stood up.

'This is indeed an honour, Mrs van Heerden,' she said. 'I'm Hope Beneke.'

'How do you do.'

'Please sit down. Can I offer you something to drink?'

'No, thank you.'

'I'm a great admirer of your work. Of course I can't afford one just yet but one day . . .'

'It's kind of you, Miss Beneke.'

'Please call me Hope.'

'I'm Joan.'

The ritual was suddenly over.

'What can I do for you?'

'I'm here about Zatopek. But please don't tell him that I was here.'

Hope nodded, waiting for more information.

'It's not going to be easy working with him. But I came to ask you to be patient.'

'Do I know him?'

Joan van Heerden frowned. 'He told me last night that he was working for you. He has to look for a will.'

'Van Heerden?'

'Yes.'

'You know him?'

'He's my son,' Joan van Heerden said.

Hope sank back in her chair. 'Van Heerden is your son?'

She merely nodded.

'Good grief,' said Hope. And then saw the likeness in the eyes, the deep, dark-brown intensity. 'Zatopek.'

Joan smiled. 'My late husband and I thought it was a wonderful name thirty years ago.'

'I never realized . . .'

'He doesn't advertise the connection. I think it's a matter of honour. He doesn't want to use it. Misuse it.'

'I never realized.' She was still finding it difficult to connect these two people, mother and son: famous artist, good-looking and dignified and . . . dysfunctional son.

'He's had a hard time, Hope.'

'I . . . he . . . I don't think he's working for me any longer.'

'Oh.' Disappointment.

'This afternoon he . . . he's . . .' She searched for euphemisms, greatly empathetic towards the woman in front of her. 'I find it difficult to communicate with him.'

'I know.'

'He's . . . resigned, I think.'

'I didn't know. I wanted to prepare you.'

Hope made a movement with her hands, a sign of helplessness.

'I haven't come to apologise for him. I thought, if I tried to explain . . .'

'You needn't.'

She leaned forward, her voice soft. 'He's my only child. I must do what I can. He had to grow up without a father. He was a wonderful child. I thought I'd been successful, even as a single parent.'

'Joan, you don't have to . . .'

'I must, Hope.' Her voice was decisive. 'It was my . . . our choice to bring him into the world. I have to shoulder my responsibilities. I have to try to rectify the mistakes I made. I raised him and thought I could be both father and mother if I tried hard enough. I was wrong. I want to tell you what he was like. A good-looking boy, cheerful, who found it easy to laugh, the world a wonderful place, a journey of discovery. He didn't know about the dark side of life. I didn't tell him. I should have. Because when he discovered it, I wasn't there to help him and it changed everything.'

There was no self-pity in her voice, only calm rationality.

'He had a soft centre, still has. They teased him in the police that he was too soft for the work and he liked it, the way we all like to be a little different. And then . . . I was so pleased when he went to university, he was so happy, so enthusiastic and I was proud of him and knew his father would also have been proud of him. But life takes strange byways and he went back to the force and his mentor was shot, right in front of him, and he believes it was his fault and then he changed because I hadn't prepared him for things like death and human fallibility. That's what I think. If he could believe in himself again, if he could be given another chance . . .'

She didn't know what to say, she wanted to reach out. 'Joan . . .'

'That attorney, Kemp, he looks so angry but I think he has a kind heart, he knows my child isn't bad. There were others but they didn't give him much of a chance. And I don't know how many chances he has left. This issue with the will . . . Zet can do it. He needs it so much.'

'I . . .'

'I'm not making excuses for him.'

'I know.'

'He mustn't know that I was here.'

'He won't.'

The telephone rang. Hope frowned.

'Please answer.'

'It must be urgent. They don't usually phone.' She picked up.

'I'm in consultation, Marie.'

'Mr van Heerden is here again, Hope. He's looking for an identity document.'

She closed her eyes. The day couldn't get any worse. 'Tell him to stay where he is and wait. Under no circumstances will you allow him in here.'

'Very well, Hope.'

'I'm on my way.' She put down the receiver very gently.

'Zatopek has just arrived at reception.'

'Damn!' said Joan van Heerden.

'Don't worry, I'll handle it.' She got up, walked to the door, opened it carefully. The passage was empty. She closed the door behind her and walked to the reception area. He stood there, impatient. She saw that he wore dry clothes, jeans, trainers.

He saw her. 'I'm looking for Smit's ID book.'

'Wilna van As has it. Shall I phone her?'

'I'll drive there. I want to see the shop.' He didn't look at her. He stared at a Piet Grobler painting on the wall. It was one of her favourites. *Man with writer's block eating an apricot sandwich.*

'May I ask why you want the ID document?'

'Murder and Robbery have the wrong ID number. I must get the right one for the birth certificate.'

'Will it help us?'

He looked past her. 'I'll know where he was born. Who his parents were. His life before van As.'

'It's a start.'

'I'm leaving now.'

'Fine.' And then, when he'd turned she added quietly and impulsively: 'Zatopek.'

He stopped at the glass doors. 'Fucking Kemp,' she heard and then he was gone. She smiled for the first time since lunch. The day couldn't . . .

The receptionist held out a telephone. 'It's Kara-An Rousseau, Hope.'

She took the call at the reception desk. 'Hallo.'

'Hi, Hope. I'm looking for the phone number of that detective of yours.'

'Van Heerden?'

'Yes, the one in the restaurant today.'

'He's . . . somewhat fully booked at the moment.'

'No, not for a job.'

'Oh?'

'He's very, very sexy, Hope. Hadn't you noticed?'

10

My mother thought it was Nagel's death that had screwed me up. Everyone thought it was Nagel's death.

Why, when people thought about other people's lives, did they only add a few large numbers to make a judgement? But with the arithmetic of their own lives, they were prepared to juggle a thousand figures, to multiply, add, subtract until the books had been cooked, until the sum total suited them.

Had I also been guilty of that? I didn't know. I had tried to leave the unimportant figures out of the equation. And to allow the negatives equal value. But could we ever be trustworthy accountants of our own lives?

I'd keep trying:

I was fifteen years old when she called me to the living room one evening and said she wanted to speak seriously to me. She had a bottle of whisky and two glasses on the coffee table and poured a tot into each.

'I don't drink that stuff, Ma.'

'They're both for me, Zet. I want to talk to you about sex.'

'Ma . . .'

'You're not the only one for whom it's uncomfortable. It's just something we have to do.'

'But Ma . . .'

'I know you know about sex. I too heard all about it from my school friends long before my mother spoke to me.'

'Ma . . .'

'I just want to make sure you hear the right side, the other side as well.'

And then she knocked back the first glass of whisky.

'Humankind is old, Zet. Millions of years. And what we are wasn't created yesterday. We were formed and shaped and moulded when we were still uncivilized, when we still roamed in small groups over the savannahs of Africa and Europe, looking for food, using stone knives and wearing clothes of animal skin. When there was no certainty that we would be the species that would win, we had to survive. And to do that, everyone had to play his or her part. Men and women. The men hunted and fought and protected. And impregnated as many women as possible so that the gene pool wouldn't stagnate, and because tomorrow they might be lion food. And women had to keep their group together and to make sure of that they seduced the strongest, fastest, cleverest men, to survive. We still have these urges, Zet. It's in us and we're not aware of it, because we no longer know ourselves and it's no one's fault, because the problem is that we no longer need it. We've won. We're at the top of the food chain and there are too many of us and if half of us don't procreate, it wouldn't matter.'

She swallowed the second tot of whisky.

'The problem is that the changed situation hasn't really changed our nature. Someone forgot to tell our instincts we've won. And one of these days your hormones will take over and you'll want to share your seed . . .'

'Ma . . .'

'No, Zet, I know you're masturbating but let me me tell you immediately that it's not wrong . . .'

'Ma, I don't want to . . .'

'It's just as uncomfortable for me, Zatopek van Heerden, but you're going to keep quiet and you're going to listen. Your Grandfather van Heerden told your father that masturbation would turn him blind and your father told me that when he was in the school hostel he opened his eyes very slowly every morning because he was so worried. I don't want you to hear such nonsense. Masturbation is normal and healthy and does no harm, it makes no one pregnant and it forces no one. If it helps you, carry on. It's about real sex that I have to speak about this evening, my child, because your instincts don't know we've won. You carry two, three, ten million years of the urge to survival within you and soon it will come knocking at your door and when you open I don't want it to be a stranger confronting you.'

She poured more of the alcohol into her glass.

'Ma, you must watch that stuff.'

She had nodded. 'You know I never drink it, Zet, but tonight is different. I have only one opportunity to do this thing right and if I lose my nerve, I'll have problems. I have to tell you that sex is great. Nature made it great so we can continue procreating, another carrot in front of our noses, just to make sure. It's a joy from the moment we start thinking about it until the moment of orgasm, with the foreplay and the rising passion and everything in between. Lovely and wonderful and intense, it's like a fever of the gods, an incredible enchantment that can overcome us and push any other thought out of our heads. And if you add up age-old nature and the deliciousness and the fever, then sex is stronger than any other urge we have, Zet. You must realize this.'

Another gulp.

'And then Nature has another ace in the hole. She makes us beautiful to each other. From fifteen, sixteen, seventeen she gives us bodies that are irresistible to the opposite sex, that attract like incredible magnets.

'All these facts add up . . .

'The problem with sex, my son, is the product. It's not only the pleasure. It makes babies. And babies cause trouble if you're not ready for them. I want to ask only three things of you tonight, Zet. Before you have sex with a woman, think. Think if you want to have a baby with her. Because to have a baby means you're tied to her for the rest of your life. Think. See in your head the pictures of getting up in the middle of the night with feeding bottles, or lying awake and wondering where the money is going to come from for food and clothes and a decent house. Think whether you want to wake up for the rest of your life with these responsibilities, wake up with the woman when you see her without make-up and without her hair done, and with stale breath, when her body is no longer so slender and so young and so pretty.

'Think, my child, whether you love her.

'Nature doesn't think, when you want to take her for the first time, whether you love her or not. She gives you instant love like a lightning flash but when you've sown your seed, that instant love is gone. Ask yourself whether you *really* love her. Because I can tell you one thing: sex with someone you love is a thousand times better than sex with someone you don't.'

There was a longing in her voice at that moment that I didn't want to hear but would never forget, the first adolescent glimpse that I had of her love for and relationship with my father.

'The second thing I want to ask you is never to force a woman. There are men out there who will tell you that every woman secretly desires a man simply to take her, but let me tell you that's bull. Women aren't like that. It doesn't matter how high your fever burns, that is the one one thing you may never do.

'And the third thing is to leave another man's woman alone.'

For three weeks after the conversation I didn't put a hand on my own body, ashamed because my mother knew. And after that, Nature took its course. And like all young men probably do, I remembered one part of her message more easily than the rest: *I have to tell you sex is great.*

The rest I had to learn the hard way.

There were three women who would play a role in my sexual awakening. Marna Espag was my first girlfriend, Aunt Baby Marnewick was our neighbour. Betta Wandrag was the third. You know who she is.

I was in standard nine, in the winter of 1975, when I fell in love with Marna Espag – my first love – with all the wonderful intensity of puberty. It was as though I saw her for the first time one morning, with her black hair and green eyes and pretty, laughing mouth and she filled my thoughts and my dreams, fired my fantasies of heroic deeds in which I saved her from death time after time.

It took me three months to ask her out, after the usual teenage process of finding out whether she liked me and the covert messages indicating my interest. We went to the movies at the Leba in Klerksdorp. My mother obligingly dropped us there and picked us up again after we'd had milk shakes at the steakhouse adjoining the theatre. My mother liked her. Everybody liked her.

I kissed Marna for the first time during a garage party in Stilfontein, to the close-dance tempo of Gene Rockwell's *Heart* – the kind of standing still, swaying foreplay which my friend Gunther Krause unromantically described as 'knobbly-wobbly'. I remembered her overwhelming perfume and the softness of her mouth and my own lightheadedness when I tasted a woman's tongue in my mouth for the first time, a foretaste of the hidden and divine potential.

We necked with the unbridled enthusiasm and dedication of pioneers – outside her front door, at the garden gate, at parties and sometimes, when the opportunity presented itself, in my mother's or her parents' living room. There was a careful, natural progression that happened over weeks and months. In November I slid my hand experimentally onto the curve of a breast, my heartbeat frantic that she would object. In the reckless time between Christmas and New Year, with the rest of her family away at a barbecue in Potch Dam, I unbuttoned her blouse in their living room, stroking her small breasts for the first time and feeling her nipple growing in my mouth. And in February my finger, untaught and clumsy, reached the holy grail and we both shuddered at the magnitude of the act, the daring and the overpowering pleasure.

Two weeks later I told her my mother was going to Pretoria to watch an opera. And I would be at home alone.

Marna looked at me for a long time. 'Do you think we should do it?'

'Yes,' I said, the fever already spreading.

'So do I.'

In the following few days I set a world record in the masturbation stakes. The anticipation was terrifying in the way it dominated my whole existence. Mentally I played the Great Moment over and over again and in my fantasies it was perfect. I could think about nothing else. All I could do was to count the days and eventually the hours before saying goodbye to my mother at the gate with barely restrained impatience and a huge lie 'that I would be responsible'.

Marna was late and I thought I was going mad. She was a little pale.

'We don't have to do it,' I lied again.

'It's OK. I'm a bit scared.'

'I am, too,' I said, my final lie of the evening.

We drank coffee, discussed school friends and work with little enthusiasm and eventually I embraced her gently and slowly began kissing her. It took an hour, even more, for her to relax, to change from the terrified Marna to the warm, welcoming girl I knew, for her breath to increase in tempo to the wonderful gallop of complete readiness and for her heartbeat to hammer visibly and almost audibly against her small breasts.

Carefully I took off her clothes piece by piece. Until she eventually lay, beautiful and pale and ready, on my mother's enormous living-room couch.

And suddenly the time had come and I had to get rid of my clothes and I got up and undressed feverishly and turned back to her and saw her lying there and the whole time of expectation and fantasies was like an irresistible wave and my entire body was burning and I came, spectacularly, all over my mother's living-room carpet.

11

He walked to the front door of the house. *Durbanville Classic Furniture* was written on a slightly weathered wooden board against the wall. And below it the bell, next to the steel security gate: *Please ring for service.* He pressed and heard the bell inside, a soft, musical sound, almost cheerful, *ding, dong.* He heard footsteps on the wooden floor, then she opened the door.

'Mr van Rensburg,' she said without surprise.

'Van Heerden,' he said.

'Oh,' she said and unlocked the security gate. 'I'm usually so good with names. Come in.'

She walked ahead of him down the passage. To the left and right there were rooms with furniture, all made of wood, all elegant, tables and cupboards and desks. Her office was in the smallest room of the house. Her desk wasn't a classic piece but the wood of the chairs glowed. Everything was painfully neat.

'Please sit down.'

'I only came to ask whether you had Smit . . . *Mr* Smit's identity document.'

'I have,' she said and opened a melamine cupboard behind the door.

He took out his notebook and paged through it to where he had written down the identity number.

She took out a cardboard box and put it on the desk. She lifted the lid and put it down next to the box with neat, economical gestures. She didn't look at him, avoided eye contact. Because he *knew,* he thought. Because she had to share her secrets with him. That was why she couldn't remember his name. A defence mechanism.

She handed him the ID. It was one of the old issues with a blue cover. He opened it. Jan Smit's photograph, younger than the contorted face he had seen in the artistic rendering of the police photograph. He held his finger underneath the identity number, checked it figure by figure. The one he had written down was correct.

He sighed.

'Home Affairs says this number belongs to someone else. A Mrs Ziegler.'

'Mrs Ziegler?' Wilna van As repeated mechanically.

'Yes.'

'What can that possibly mean?'

'Only two things. Either they're making a mistake, which is very probable. Or the ID has been forged.'

'Forged?' There was fear in her voice. 'Surely that's not possible.'

'The other documents in that box. What are they?'

She looked apathetically at the cardboard box as though it had acquired a new dimension. 'The registration of the company and the contracts of the houses.'

'May I see them?'

Reluctantly she pushed the box across the desk. He took out the contents. Durbanville Classic Furniture. Registered as a one-man business. 1983. Registered as a Close Corporation. 1984. A re-registration? Deed of conveyance for this house. 1983. Deed of conveyance for the home. 1983.

'There are no mortgage documents for the houses,' he said.

'Oh,' she said.

'Are they paid off?'

'I think so.'

'Both?'

'I . . . Yes, I think so.'

'The company books. The financial affairs. Who handles them?'

'Jan dealt with them. And the auditor.'

'Did you have any insight into them?'

'Yes, I helped balance the books every month.'

'Are the records available?'

'Yes. It's all here.' Her eyes turned to the white cupboard behind her.

'May I see them?'

She nodded and got up. There was a certain absence in her, he thought.

She opened the cupboard door again, wider this time. 'Here they are,' she said. He looked. Ledgers and hardcover files stood in neat rows covering two shelves, each one clearly marked with a koki pen for each year since 1983.

'May I see the first lot. To '86, perhaps?'

Carefully she took the files out and handed them to him. He opened the first one. Handwritten figures in columns between the narrow blue and red lines. He concentrated, tried to make sense, get a grip on it all. Entries of dates and sums, the figures not large, tens, a couple of hundreds, but obviously chaotic. He gave up.

'Could you explain how it works?'

She nodded. She took a long yellow pencil, using it as a pointer. 'These are the debits and these are the credits. There . . .'

'Hang on,' he said. 'Is this the income, the money he received?'

'Yes.'

'And that's the money he spent?'

'Yes.'

'Where's the bank balance?'

She turned the page, pointed, using the pencil. 'In August 1983 the balance in the books was minus R1 122,35.'

'Is that the amount he had in the bank?'

'I don't know.'

'Why don't you know?'

'This amount shows that the business spent R1 122,35 more than it made. The bank balance could be more or less, depending on the original balance.' Patiently, as to a child.

'Hang on.' he said. He had never been stupid with figures. Only uninterested. 'This isn't the bank balance. Only the difference between income and expenditure.'

'Yes.'

'Where is the bank balance reflected?'

'It's not reflected here. It would be in the bank statements.' She got up, fetched more ledgers from the cupboard.

'Do you have a bookkeeping background?'

'No,' said Wilna van As. 'I had to learn. Jan showed me. And the auditor. It's not difficult, once you understand.' She paged, searching. 'Here. The bank balance for August 1983.'

He looked at where the pencil was pointing. R13 877,65. 'He had money in the bank but the business was losing money?'

She paged back in the bank statements. 'Look at this. The opening balance of the bank account was R15 000. The figures with the minus sign were amounts that he paid out. If you compare it with the figures in the ledger, you'll see that it's the same as the debits. And the other figures are income that is entered in the ledger as credit. The difference between the two is R1 122,35. Subtract that from R15 000 and you get R13 877,65.'

'Aaaah . . .'

He pulled the ledger towards him again, paged to September 1983. The balance was minus R817,44; October: minus R674,87; November: minus R404,65; December: R312,05.

'He began making a profit in December 1983.'

'December is always a good month.'

He drew the following year's ledger and bank statements towards him, studied them with his new-found knowledge. He made notes. The devil was in the detail. His credo. Nagel's scorn. Wilna van As sat opposite him, her hands folded on the table, quiet. He thought briefly about what was going through the woman's head. Later she offered tea. He accepted gratefully. She got up. He paged on. A business that grew conservatively: prices of cupboards and desks, tables and chairs, four-posters and headboards rising steadily, a microeconomic picture of an era. In 1991 the ledger system changed to computer printouts that he had to decipher all over again, with the aid of Wilna van As.

'The houses. Is there no record of the sale of the houses?'

'I don't know.'

'Could you find out?'

'I'll ask at the bank.'

'I'd be most grateful.'

'What does all this tell you?' she asked, indicating the figures scattered in front of him.

'I don't know yet. Something. Maybe nothing. But let me make sure first.'

'Something?' The fear in her voice again, in her eyes.

'Let me make sure first. May I take the ID?'

'Yes,' she said, but hesitantly.

On the way to Mitchell's Plain, he was in the foothills of that curious breakthrough euphoria, the Everest of insight still hidden behind mist and clouds, data stored in his head, in his notes. The columns of the investigation ledger didn't balance yet: a theory, somewhere between the figures and the years and the information of Wilna van As the truth lay hidden. His heart now beating lightly, his head touching on this and that, he felt light as air, fuck, fuck, fuck, it was like the old days, what was happening to him? Was it that easy? Release, liberation, freedom, walking the old roads with the compass of knowledge and procedures and instructions and senses and Nagel's nagging voice in the back of your head?

Not likely . . .

Don't think about it. Like a man climbing, don't look down.

Did he want to climb up? Did he want to get up out of the safe, stinking shit of his existence?

Orlando Arendse's house had been here five, six years ago. Things had changed.

Security wall with razor wire on the top, Fort Mitchell's Plain. He stopped at the gate and got out. Behind the gate a man came walking up, large pistol holstered at his belt.

'What?'

'I'm looking for Orlando.'

'Who're you?'

No respect any more.

'Van Heerden.'

'SAP?' Spelling out the initials.

'Used to be.'

'Wait.'

SAP. They had always had the gift of smelling a cop, even if you were no longer official. Even if you didn't look like a policeman. He looked at the extensive burglarproofing against the windows. Battlefield Mitchell's Plain. Now there were gangs and Pagad – People against Gansters and Drugs – and Chinese Mafia, and Colombian and Nigerian cartels and Russian Mafia and solo flyers and an alphabet soup of splinter groups. No wonder the police couldn't keep up. In his day there were only gangs – jittery teenagers and fucked-up jailbirds . . .

The man came back, opened the gate. 'You'd better bring in the car.'

He drove in. Got out.

'Come,' said pistol-on-the-hip.

'Aren't you going to search me?'

'Orlando says I don't have to because you can't hit a double-door shithouse at two yards.'

'It's always nice to be remembered.'

In at the front door. The living room was furnished like an office. Home industry of organized crime. In the corner sat three more soldiers while Orlando sat at a large table. Older than he remembered, grey at the temples, looking like a headmaster now, still fond of cream-coloured three-piece tailor-made suits.

'Van Heerden,' Orlando said, unsurprised.

'Orlando.'

'You want something from me.' The soldiers in the corner busy with paperwork, ears pricked, ready for action.

He took the identity book out of his pocket, handed it to Orlando.

'Sit,' said Orlando, waving him to a chair. He opened the booklet, put the reading glasses which hung around his neck on a string on his nose, pulled the lamp nearer, switched it on, held the book under the light.

'I don't do IDs any longer.'

'What do you do now, Orlando?'

'You're not official any more, van Heerden.'

He grinned for a moment. *So fucking true.*

Orlando closed the book. 'It's old. And it's not my work.'

'But it's forged.'

Orlando nodded. 'Good job. Could be Nieuwoudt's.'

'Who's Nieuwoudt?'

Orlando put the ID down on the table, flicked it deftly across the surface to him. 'You come in here, van Heerden, unannounced, as if I owe you. You've been out of the Force for five, six years, rumour has it you're a bottom feeder going down, where's your negotiating power?'

'I don't have negotiating power.'

Orlando stared at him, a man with a brown skin and the features of a Xhosa, the unsympathetic genes of his legendary white wine-farmer father and his servant mother. 'You were always honest, van Heerden, I'll give you that. A straight shooter as long as it's not with a firearm.'

'Fuck you, Orlando.'

The hands of the soldiers in the corner grew still.

Orlando folded his hands in front of him, gold rings on each small finger. 'You still touchy about Nagel, van Heerden?'

'You know fuck-all about Nagel, Orlando.' His voice was high, hands shaking. He sat on the edge of the chair.

Orlando rested his chin on his folded hands, his eyes black and glistening. 'Relax,' he said quietly. Soldiers holding their breath.

Steady on, struggling, can't lose control, not now, not here, red tide slowly receding, a deep breath, felt his heart beating, slowly, slowly.

Orlando's voice was gentle. 'You'll have to let go, van Heerden. We all make mistakes.'

Breathe, slowly.

'Who's Nieuwoudt?'

Orlando's eyes and hands were quiet for a long while, measuring, thoughtful. 'Charles Nieuwoudt. Boer. White trash. Been riding the slow train for ten years, even missed Mandela's birthday-bash amnesty.'

'Forger.'

'One of the best. An animal but an artist. But he got sloppy, too much work, too much money, too much weed, too many women. Tried to make a fortune, so he made six millions' worth of twenty-rand notes without the watermark and dumped the printer in the Liesbeek River with a hole in the head to get his hands on his part of the profit as well. So they got him for the murder and the money.'

Soldiers started moving papers around again.

'And this is his work?'

'Looks like it. He was the king of the blue books. The blues were easier to fake. The seventies and early eighties were good years . . .'

'One more question, Orlando.'

'I'm listening.'

'It's 1983. I have dollars. American. Many dollars. I want to buy a house and start a legal business. I need rands. What do I do?'

'Who're you working for, van Heerden?'

'An attorney.'

'Kemp?'

He shook his head.

'So now you're a PI for an attorney?'

'Freelance, Orlando.'

'It's lower than shark shit, van Heerden. Why don't you go back to the Force? We need all the opposition we can get.'

He ignored it. 'Dollars in '83.'

'It's a long time ago.'

'I know.'

'I was small-time in '83. You had to take thirty or fifty cents to the dollar. But if you're looking for names, I can't help you.'

Van Heerden got up. 'Thank you, Orlando.'

'Are there still dollars in this thing?'

'I don't know.'

'Maybe, though.'

'Maybe.'

'Dollars are big money now.'

He only nodded.

'You owe me one, van Heerden.'

12

Aunt Baby Marnewick.

Every time I hear about a new movie in which fearless American heroes save us all from a virus, meteorites or enemy aliens threatening humankind, I wonder why they are so completely unaware of the far more interesting, small, yet life-altering suburban intrigues.

The Marna Espag love affair didn't survive our first clumsy and incomplete sexual effort. There was no sudden dramatic ending, simply a systematic cooling-off, aided by my disappointment in my performance and her shame because she hadn't been able to hide her own frustration.

But at sixteen, seventeen, the soul and the body heal amazingly fast and we remained friends, even when she started dating the head boy, Lourens Campher, during the July of our Matric year. I'll wonder for ever whether she and Lourens managed it successfully and if he gained the trophy of her virginity and restored her faith in men.

On the other hand, I didn't date on a permanent basis again while at school, just some heavy petting here and there. Because Aunt Baby Marnewick would cross the path of my sexual – and later professional – education.

She and her husband lived in the house behind ours. He was a big, strong miner, like ninety per cent of Stilfontein's male inhabitants a shift worker, a rough diamond who dedicated his Saturdays and Sundays to the installation of a three-litre V6 engine into a Ford Anglia. He had to move the whole instrument panel and gearbox back and lengthen the drive shaft and the transmission, which made the basic reason for this task – to give other Anglia drivers a very unpleasant surprise at stop lights – useless. Simply by looking through the window, any idiot would immediately have noticed that Boet Marnewick's car wasn't standard.

Suburban legend had it that he had to win Baby with his fists, way back in Bez Valley, that stewing pot of a suburb in Johannesburg, when he wanted to take her away from from a sturdy Scotsman. She stood on the front veranda of the house and watched the two men snorting and bleeding like two bulls proving their genetic superiority to win her hand.

Because Baby Marnewick was a good-looking woman. Tall and slender with thick, red hair, a full, broad mouth – and formidable breasts. It was her eyes, small and sly, that gave her a touch of sluttishness that, I suspected, men couldn't resist – possibly because it created the impression that she was easy and was also a clue to her real nature.

For years I was barely aware of the neighbours behind us. (Why are neighbours 'behind' us so much more mysterious, lesser neighbours?) The high wooden fence between the two houses probably contributed to it. But for a sexually awakening teenage boy, the sight of Baby Marnewick in her Saturday outfit at the shopping centre was unforgettable. And my awareness of her grew, my interest pricked by vague rumours and the blatancy with which she flaunted her sexuality.

In the early Spring of my last year at school, on a perfect warm afternoon, bored, Marna-less and curious, I peered through a thin crack in the steadily decaying fence, not for the first time, but still a coincidence, an opportunistic moment of wishful thought.

And there in the back yard of the Marnewicks, Aunt Baby lay on an inflatable mattress, naked and glistening with suntan oil, dark glasses covering her sly eyes and a playful hand and calm fingers with painted nails fondling the paradise between her legs.

Oh, the sweet shock.

I stood there, too frightened to move, too frightened to breathe, light-headed, mindless, utterly randy, discoverer of the pleasures of voyeurism, the chosen of the gods, placed there at just the right moment.

I don't know how long it took Aunt Baby Marnewick to achieve orgasm. Twenty minutes? More? For me the time flashed by – I couldn't get enough – until she eventually, with a low, deep groan through her open mouth and heavenly little movements of stomach and legs, gratified herself.

Then she got up slowly and disappeared into the house.

I stood staring at the mattress for a long time, hoping she would return. Later I realized it was not to be my destiny and went to my room to give expression to my own overriding desire. Again and again and again.

And the next afternoon I was at my spyhole in the fence again, ready to resume the wonderful one-sided relationship with Baby Marnewick.

She didn't masturbate in her back yard every afternoon. She didn't lie in the sun, slick and nude, every day. To my great disappointment there was no routine of time or day. It was a game of dice and of yearning, visual theft. I sometimes wondered whether she did it in the morning when I was in school: I even considered being 'ill' for a few days to test the theory. But occasionally, one day a week, sometimes once in two weeks, my avidity was rewarded with the same enchanting scene.

I fantasized about her. Obviously. I would walk round (climbing over the fence was too undignified), stand next to her and say: 'You need never use your hand again, Baby.' Then I would undress and she would welcome me into her with a 'Yes, yes, yes, yes' and after I had taken her to unknown sensual heights on the inflatable we would lie next to one another and discuss how we would run away and be happy for ever and ever.

Fantasy number one.

With variations on the theme.

How different and more interesting than the fantasies would be the reality, the small, life-changing reality.

13

Rush-hour traffic from Mitchell's Plain. He took the N7, in a hurry to get home, still had to phone Wilna van As.

He was amazed at the world in which he lived. Him and Kemp and him and Orlando and who owed whom, the mechanisms of social and professional interaction, the eleventh commandment: be the one who is owed. Kemp: *'You're trash, van Heerden.'* O'Grady: *'Jesus, van Heerden, that's not a fucking living. Why don't you come back?'* Orlando: *'. . . A bottom feeder, going down . . . It's lower than shark shit, van Heerden. Why don't you go back to the Force?'* General consensus about his life, but they didn't know, they didn't understand, they had no insight. They had no understanding of his sentence: he had to serve it, a life sentence, and then, in a moment of investigative euphoria, he had wondered whether he would be released, would receive amnesty. How absurd, fuck, like a man in a cell, dreaming he was outside, only to wake in the morning.

He pulled off at a petrol station for fuel, saw the telephone booth, phoned Wilna van As.

'The bank says they never held mortgages on the properties. I found the deeds of conveyance and the letters of the attorneys but I don't understand all of it.'

'Who were the conveyancers?'

'Please hold on.'

He waited, saw in his mind's eye the woman walking to the melamine cupboard in her office for the documents.

'Merwe de Villiers and Partners.'

He didn't know the firm. 'Could you fax the documents to Hope?'

'Yes,' said Wilna van As.

'Thank you.'

'The identity book. Did you discover anything?'

'I'm not sure.' Because it was Hope Beneke's job to bring the bad news. He was merely the hired help.

'Oh.' Thoughtful, worried.

'Goodbye,' he said, because he didn't want to hear it.

He paged though his notebook, found Hope Beneke's number, put in another coin and dialled.

'She's in consultation,' said the receptionist.

Like a fucking doctor, he thought.

'Please give her a message. Wilna van As is going to fax her the deeds of conveyance for Jan Smit's two houses. I want to know if there were mortgages on the houses. She can phone me at home.'

When he got out of the car and looked up, he saw the sun going down behind the next cold front coming in from the sea, the mass of clouds heavy and black and overwhelming.

He sautéed the garlic and parsley lightly and slowly in the big frying pan, the aroma escaping and rising with the steam, filling the room, and he inhaled it with pleasure and a vague, passing surprise that he could still do it. Verdi on the small speakers. *La Traviata.* Music to cook by.

Jan Smit wasn't Jan Smit.

Well, well, well.

Sometime during or before the year of our Lord 1983 the man formerly known as X acquired American dollars. Illegally. So illegally that he needed a new identity. For a new life. As Johannes Jacobus Smit. A life of classic furniture, life within the law, a private, hidden existence.

Conjecture.

He opened the tin of tuna, poured the brine carefully down the drain of the sink.

You sold a fistful of your dollars on the black market to acquire the house and the business premises, to buy the first pieces of furniture. The business does well. You don't need the rest of your dollars. You build, or have built, a walk-in safe for the rest. How much was left? A great deal. If you needed a walk-in safe. Or did you need to put something else in the safe? America – the wellspring of drug sales, the source of all dollars. Had you wanted to build a safe to hold your little white packets of heroin or cocaine, neatly stacked on the shelves, next to the dollars? Retailer, wholesaler, middle man?

Arms trade. Another reliable source of large amounts of dollars. In '82 or '83 – the flourishing years of South Africa's Armscor and its thousand obscure affiliations and the rest of Africa with its terrorist acronyms and insatiable hunger for weapons.

The walk-in safe wasn't quite big enough. Maybe not arms.

Why? If the business in classic furniture was thriving, why didn't you simply burn the incriminating evidence?

He added the tuna to the garlic and parsley. He chopped the walnuts, added them as well, switched on the kettle.

Fifteen years later Jan Smit, formerly known as X, died. Finis. American assault rifle, one shot, execution style, back of the head.

The return of the original owner of the dollars? A renewed effort to sell the little white parcels – what went wrong?

Put all the little pieces together, van Heerden. Form a picture in your head, create a story, concoct a theory. Adapt it with every new fragment. Speculate.

Nagel.

Boiling water in the pasta pot. Light the gas. Wait until it boiled again. Spaghetti ready. Cut the butter in pieces. Slice a lemon in half. Grate the parmesan. Ready.

Jan Smit alone at home. Knock at the door? Open. 'Hallo, X, long time no see. I've come to have a little chat about my dollars.'

He heard something above the music.

A knock at the door.

His mother didn't knock. She simply came in.

He walked to the door, opened it.

Hope Beneke. 'I thought I'd pop in. I live in Milnerton.' The first, nervous flurry of the cold front blew her short hair in all directions. She had a briefcase in her hand.

'Come in,' he said.

He didn't want her in his home.

'It's going to rain,' she said as he closed the door behind her.

'Yes,' he said, uncomfortably. Nobody came here, except his mother. Quickly he turned down the volume of the music.

'My goodness, something smells delicious,' she said. She put the briefcase down on a chair and opened it.

He didn't say anything.

She took out the documents. She looked at the gas burners. 'I didn't know you could cook.'

'It's only pasta.'

'It doesn't smell like "only pasta".' There was something in her voice . . .

'How did you know where I live?'

'I phoned Kemp. I phoned here first but there was no reply.'

Sympathy in her voice, a patience that hadn't been there before. He recognized it. The reaction of people who *knew*, who knew the public part of van Heerden's history. Kemp. Kemp had told her. Fuck Kemp, who couldn't keep anything to himself. He didn't need her sympathy.

Even if Kemp, and now she, had it all wrong.

She handed him the sheets of paper. 'Marie said you wanted to know if the houses were mortgaged.'

'Yes.' He felt the discomfort of standing while talking, with furniture around them. He didn't want her to sit down. He wanted her to leave.

'It doesn't look like it. That's the usual letter and account that attorneys send out after a property has been transferred to the new owner. To confirm that the registration has been completed at the Deeds Office. If there were mortgages, the accounts would have mentioned them. Generally complete figures about outstanding amounts, or the surplus, if the mortgages were larger than the purchase price.'

He stared at the documents. He didn't quite grasp it all.

'There's nothing about that here.'

'That's why I think there was no mortgage.'

'Oh.'

He looked at the accounts. It established the price of the two houses. R43 000 for the business one, R52 000 for the home.

The water in the pot boiled with an explosive hiss. He turned it down.

'My timing was bad,' she said. 'You're probably expecting guests.'

'No,' he said.

Yes. He should have said. 'Yes'.

'Did you discover anything about the identity document?'

He stood in the no man's land of his kitchen, Hope uncomfortable among his chairs.

Fuck.

'You'll have to sit down,' he said.

She nodded, gave a small smile, tucked her skirt neatly underneath her, sat down in the grey chair with the frayed arms and looked at him expectantly and with empathy.

'Smit isn't Smit,' he said.

She waited.

'The ID is forged.'

He saw her eyes widen slightly.

'Professional forgery. Possibly the work of one Charles Nieuwoudt, possibly done in the late seventies or early eighties.'

He would have to tell her the whole thing now. She sat there, waiting, her attention wholly fixed on him.

'There's more,' he said. 'I have a theory.'

The nod was barely visible. She was waiting, impressed.

Slowly he took a deep breath. He told her about his day, chronologically: Home Affairs. Ngwema's phone call, his visit to van As, the bookkeeping, the dates and amounts, Orlando, gave her an overview. Explained the mental jump based on a piece of paper that, more than fifteen years ago, held dollars together in a neat parcel, linked it to the walk-in safe. The time, all of it in 1983, the cash acquisition of two houses, the R15 000 with which the business was started. Aware that she was looking at him, he was looking past her, staring at the door, putting his theory to her.

'Sheesh,' she said when he'd done. He saw her dragging her fingers through her short hair.

'Someone knew,' he said. 'Everything points to the fact that someone knew. Someone with an M16 and a blowtorch arrived with premeditated intent. It's hardly standard issue when you're robbing a house. At the very least they had had to know that Jan Smit had a fortune in some form or other and that it would take a certain amount of persuasion to get it from him. Someone who knew him in his previous life.'

She nodded.

A wind-driven gust of rain thudded against the window.

'That means Jan Smit knew where to get a forged ID. It means he knew how to get rid of hot dollars. That means he built the safe to hide something, not for security. That means van As never really knew him. Or she's lying, but I don't think so.'

He leant back against a kitchen cupboard, folded his arms in front of him.

'You're very good,' she said.

He tightened his arms. 'It's a theory.'

'It's a good theory,' she said.

He shrugged. 'It's all we've got.'

'And tomorrow?'

He hadn't really thought about tomorrow. 'I don't know. The dollars are the key. I want to find out who controlled the black market in currency in 1983. And who were the major drug dealers. But maybe it's something completely different. He may have stolen the money in America. Or it could've been an arms transaction. Who knows, in this fucking country of ours.'

He wondered whether she would react to his language again. She must leave now, he thought. He wasn't going to offer her coffee.

'I'll dig. There are a few places. A few people . . .'

'Is there anything I can do for you?'

'You'll have to decide what you're going to tell van As.'

She got up, slowly, as if she was tired. 'I don't think we'll tell her anything.'

'It's your choice.'

'There are too many uncertainties. We can speak to her when we have more.'

She picked up her attaché case. 'I have to go.'

He unfolded his arms. 'I'll phone you if I find something.' *Just please don't come to my house again* – but he didn't say it.

'You have my cell phone number?'

'No,' he said.

She opened her case again, took out a card, handed it to him. Then she turned and walked to the door. He noticed that she had a pretty, rounded bottom beneath the skirt.

'I don't have an umbrella.' A statement, almost aggressive.

She stood at the door and smiled at him. 'Is that Domingo?'

'What?'

'The music.'

'No.'

'I thought it was the soundtrack from the movie. You know, Zefirelli's . . .'

'No.'

'Who is it?'

She had to leave. He didn't want to discuss music with her.

'Pavarotti and Sutherland.'

'It's beautiful,' she said.

'It's the best.' Biting his tongue. *It's none of her business.*

She was quiet for a moment. Then she looked at him, frowning. 'You're an odd man, van Heerden.'

'I'm trash,' he said quickly. 'Ask Kemp.' And opened the door for her. 'You have to go now.'

'You did good work,' she said and turned her head sideways against the rain and ran down the stairs. He heard her laugh, one quick sound, and then the BMW's roof light came on when she opened the door and got in, waved to him. The door slammed and the light went off. He closed the front door.

He walked to the CD player and switched off the music. She knew fuck-all about music. *Domingo.* Indeed.

He would have to phone her in the morning. Tell her he would come to her office every day, just before she went home, for a complete report.

She mustn't come here again.

Or he would write a report every evening and take it to her.

The telephone rang.

'Van Heerden.'

'Good evening,' a woman's voice said. 'My name is Kara-An Rousseau. I don't know whether you remember me.'

Hope Beneke drove home slowly on the N7, the windscreen wipers at full speed. This afternoon she had wanted to murder him, this evening she had wanted to hug him. She bit her lip and hunched over the steering-wheel trying to see through the rain. Now she understood. His baggage wasn't anger. It was pain. And guilt.

Now she could distance herself. By understanding.

That's all.

That's it.

Day 5

Saturday, 8 July

14

The house was full of books. And often filled with writers and poets and readers, arguments and animated conversations – late one Saturday night two women almost came to blows over Etienne Leroux's *Seven Days at the Silbersteins*. A reading and a discussion of the work of van Wyk Louw lasted through the night until after lunch on the Sunday.

And into this circle of literary luminaries I brought Louis L'Amour.

I hadn't been an early reader. There were, I thought, far more interesting things to do. As my mother allowed me more freedom, there were the usual school activities and the more informal boys' play (how many gangs we formed!), fishing in the Vaal River (with Uncle Shorty de Jager, live crickets, without a weight), the investigation of the East Shaft's collapsed minedumps, the eternal building and rebuilding of Schalk Wagenaar's tree house.

Then, the discovery of photo-stories. Gunther Krause read Mark Condor. Takuza. Captain Devil. With his parents' permission. (His mother read Barbara Cartland and others of her ilk and his father wasn't home very often.) On Saturday mornings we went to Don's Book Exchange for a new supply for Gunther and his mother and then we went to his house to read them avidly. Until Standard Eight when I almost disinterestedly picked up a L'Amour in Don's, looked at the fiery green eyes of the hero on the cover and lazily, unsuspectingly, read the first two paragraphs and met Logan Sackett.

My mother gave me a few rands for pocket money every month. The book cost forty cents. I bought it. And for the following three years I couldn't get enough.

My mother made no objection. Perhaps she hoped it would lead to the reading of other, more substantial stuff. She didn't know it would lead to my first confrontation with the law.

It wasn't L'Amour's fault.

One holiday morning my mother dropped me and Gunther and another school friend in Klerksdorp early for the movies. The CNA in the main road was on two levels, toys and stationery downstairs, and upstairs, the books. I had been in the CNA before but that day I discovered a new world of Louis L'Amours, new, unread books with white paper – not the faded, faintly yellowed second-hand copies of the Book Exchange. Books that smelt fresh.

I can't remember how much money I had in my pocket. But it wasn't enough. Too little for a movie and a milk shake and a L'Amour. Certainly enough for a book but then I wouldn't be able to accompany Gunther to the movies. Enough for a movie and a milk shake but then I wouldn't be able to make use of this new-found abundance. And in a moment of feverish desire I took my decision: taking a *book* wasn't stealing.

That was the ease with which I crossed the borderline between innocence and guilt, as quickly as that, without thinking. One moment a reader filled with joy at the variety of new choices, the next a prospective thief with an awareness of the potential, casting furtive glances at others around him, looking for an opportunity.

I took two books and pushed them down my shirt. And then walked down the stairs, slowly, nonchalantly, stomach sucked in to hide the bulge, bent forward slightly for further camouflage, a beating heart and sweaty hands, closer and closer to the front door, closer, closer, out, sigh of relief – until she grabbed my arm and used the words with which so many South Africans start a conversation with strangers, that cornerstone of our sense of inferiority: 'Ag, sorry . . .'

She was fat and ugly and the name on the CNA nametag on her

mighty breasts merely read: 'Monica.' She pulled me back, into the shop. 'Take out those books,' she said.

Afterwards I thought of a thousand things I might have done, what I could have said: jerked loose and run away; 'I was only joking'; 'Which books?'; 'Fuck you.' Often, afterwards, when I remembered her face and her attitude, I yearned to be able to say: 'Fuck you.'

I took out the books. My knees were weak.

'Get Mr Minnaar,' she told the girl at the cash register. And to me: 'Today you'll be taught a lesson.'

Ah, the fear and the humiliation, so slow to mature. The implications of my action didn't present themselves as a group but as a long row of individual, unwelcome, purposeful messengers. I knew every one of them long before Mr Minnaar, the bald man with the glasses, had appeared on the scene.

I stood there and heard Monica telling Minnaar how she had seen me on the upper floor, how she had waited until I had gone out of the door.

'Tsk, tsk, tsk,' he said and looked at me with great disapproval. And when she had finished: 'Phone the police.'

While she was busy, he looked nastily at me again and said, 'You'll steal us blind.'

You. With one word I was part of a group. As though I had done it before. As though I was constantly in the company of other criminals.

I think I was too frightened to cry. When the young constable in the blue uniform came in and we went to Minnaar's small office and he took down their statement. When he took me by the arm to the yellow police wagon. When he took me out again at the police station downtown, next to the Indian shopping centre, and took me to the charge office. Too blood-chillingly frightened.

He made me sit down and told the sergeant behind the desk to keep an eye on me. And came back minutes later with a detective.

He was a big man. Big hands, thick eyebrows and a nose that had known adversity.

'What's your name?' the big man asked.

'Zatopek, sir.'

'Come with me, Zatopek.'

I followed him to his office, a grey room filled with Civil Service furniture and piles of files and memorandums arranged in chaotic stacks.

'Sit down,' he said.

He sat on the edge of the desk with the constable's statements in his hand.

'How old are you?'

'Sixteen, sir.'

'Where do you live?'

'Stilfontein, sir.'

'Standard Nine?'

'Yes, sir.'

'Stilfontein High School?'

'Yes, sir.'

'You stole books.'

'Yes, sir.'

'Louis L'Amours.'

'Yes, sir.'

'How often have you stolen books?'

'This was the first time, sir.'

'What have you stolen before?'

'Nothing, sir.'

'Nothing?'

'I . . . once I stole Gunther Krause's ruler in class, sir, but it was more of a joke, sir. I'll give it back to him, sir.'

'Why did you steal the books?'

'It was wrong, sir.'

'I know it was wrong. I want to know why.'

'I . . . I wanted them so badly, sir.'

'Why?'

'Because I like them so much, sir.'

'Have you read *Flint*?'

'Yes, sir.' Somewhat surprised.

'*Kilkenny*?'

'Yes, sir.'

'*Lando*?'

'No, sir.'

'*Catlow*?'

'Not yet, sir.'

'*Cherokee Trail*?'

'Yes, sir.'

'*The Empty Land*?'

'No, sir.'

He sighed and got up, walked round and sat down at his big desk.

'Did any of the good guys in any L'Amour steal, Zatopek?'

'No, sir.'

'What will your father do, how will he feel if I phone him now to tell him his son's a thief?'

Hope, a faint spark. *If I* . . . not 'when I phone him.' 'My father's dead, sir.'

'And your mother?'

'She'll be very unhappy, sir.'

'I have a suspicion you have a gift for euphemism, Zatopek. Your mother will be heartbroken. Do you have brothers and sisters?'

'No, sir.'

'You're the only one she's got?'

'Yes, sir.'

'And you're stealing.'

'It was wrong, sir.'

'Says he now. Now that it's too late. Where's your mother?'

I told him about the movie plans and that my mother would fetch us at five o'clock, after the movie.

He looked at me. For a long time and in silence. Then he got up. 'Wait here, Zatopek. Understand?'

'Yes, sir.'

He walked out and closed the door. I was alone with my fear and my humiliation and my sprig of hope.

He came back after a lifetime and sat on the edge of the desk again.

'There's an empty cell down here, Zatopek. I'm going to lock you into it. It's a dirty place. It stinks. People have vomited and shat and pissed and bled and sweated in it. But it's paradise in comparison with what happens to thieves if they go to jail . . . I'm going to put you in the cell, Zatopek. So that you can think about all these things. I want you to try and picture, while you're sitting there, what it would be like to spend the rest of your life like that. Only much worse. Among other thieves and murderers and confidence men and rapists and all the other scum of the earth. Men who'll cut your throat for fifty cents. Guys who'll think a young man like you is just the thing to . . . to . . . kiss, if you get my drift.'

I didn't really but I nodded enthusiastically.

'I've just spoken to the CNA on the phone. They say they have a great deal of theft taking place there. They want me to make an example of you. They want you to be in court, in front of the magistrate, with your poor mother weeping, so that everyone can see there's no point in stealing from the CNA. They want the people of the *Klerksdorp Record* to write about you so that the non-thieving youth of South Africa will be deterred. Do you understand?'

I couldn't speak, merely allowed my head to indicate agreement.

'I argued with them, Zatopek. I told them I was sure it was the first time, because I'm stupid enough to believe you. I begged them because someone who likes Louis L'Amour can't be all bad. They told me I was wasting my time because someone who steals once will steal again. But I talked them round, Zatopek.'

'Sir?'

'We reached an agreement. I'll lock you up until half-past four because you're a guilty little bugger. And then I'll take you to the cinema and you'll tell your mother it was a nice movie because breaking her heart isn't a good idea. She didn't steal.'

'Yes, sir.'

'And if you ever steal again, Zatopek, I'll fetch you and give you such a hell of a hiding all use you'll ever have for your backside is to hang a pair of pants on and I'll lock you up with guys who'll suck out your eyeballs before cutting off your other balls with a blunt knife simply because they're bored. Have you got that?'

'Yes, sir.'

'Everyone has the right to one chance in life, Zatopek. We don't all get it but we deserve it.'

'Yes, sir.'

'Use yours.'

'Yes, sir.'

He got up. 'Come along.'

'Sir . . .'

'What?'

'Thank you, sir.' And then I cried until my entire body shook and the big man tucked his arm around me and pulled me close to him and held me until I had stopped.

Then he went and locked me up.

15

He shaved at five in the morning, rain in the dark cold outside, and saw himself. It caused a sudden shudder, the unexpectedness of it. He saw his whole body in the mirror: he saw his face, not the yellowing blue of the swollen eye, he saw himself, the heavy eyebrows, the nose with its slight arch, not quite straight; he saw the grey at his temples, saw that his shoulders weren't as broad as they had been; saw the slight roundness of his belly and hips, a softness; saw his legs, the long muscles less defined; saw the toll of the years, saw himself.

He focused on the shaving cream, dipped the razor in water, allowed the rhythm, the ritual to divert him, let the body disappear in the steam of the earlier shower, rinsed the washbasin, dried his face carefully with the towel, put on the tracksuit. He didn't want to listen to music; Hope Beneke who had listened to his music and said, 'You're an odd man, van Heerden.' There was a time when the contradiction of a cop who listened to Mozart had defined him, but no longer. He switched off the living room's light and opened the curtain, looked through the rain at the big house, felt the cold, there would be snow on the mountains. His mother's veranda light was burning. For him. As usual.

His mother. Who had never once said, 'Get your act together.'

She should have said it, a thousand times by now, each day she should've told him but all he got was her love, her eyes that told him she understood, even if she didn't know, even if she knew fuck-all, only two people who knew, only two.

He and . . .

He looked across. His mother's big house over there, his little cottage here, his refuge, his jail.

He jerked the curtain to, switched on the light, sat in the chair, rain against the window, leant back and closed his eyes. He had been awake since two, that feverish, insubstantial, artificial euphoria of insomnia had come visiting again because he had gone to bed sober and today he had to . . .

His heart beat faster.

Lord, not that as well.

He slowly blew out his breath, relaxed his shoulders, released the tension.

Slowly in. Slowly out. His heartbeat steadily decreased.

The first time had been sudden, five years ago now, it was winter, the clouds low, and he was in his car driving somewhere when his heart began beating at a furious rate, terrifyingly out of control, jerking, and beating and galloping in his chest and the clouds pressed down on him, faster and faster and faster, and he knew he was going to kick the bucket, heart attack, no heart could beat that fast, it was just after Nagel, just a month or so after Nagel and he had driven on the N7, and he knew he was dying and he was scared and surprised because he wanted to die but not now and his hands trembled and his whole body shook and he spoke out loud, babbled, no, no, no, slowly, slowly, no, no and forced his breath through his lips, noises, strange noises to slow everything down and then slowly, systematically, it went away.

It happened again, on other days, every time with rain and low clouds, until fear drove him to a consulting room. 'Panic attack. Is there anything in your life you want to discuss?'

'No.'

'I would like to refer you to a psychologist.' Pushing the white paper with the black ink across the table, caringly, that smooth, simulated, practised caring that they could dish up for every patient when the occasion demanded. He had folded the white paper and put it in his pocket and took it out when he was outside, crumpled it and threw it into the north-wester, didn't even see what happened to it, and the panic attacks came and went, the knowledge, naming it made it more controllable. *Is there anything in your life you want to discuss?*

And then it became less with the months that slipped by like embarrassed shadows, less and less until it no longer came, until now, and he knew why.

Theal.

It was going to bring it all back.

How many policemen had Colonel Willie Theal comforted with his endless supply of tact, fuck, how had he, between his mother and Theal and all the other sympathetic eyes, managed to bottle it up? With difficulty, that was how, with difficulty, with so much effort and difficulty but you got used to it, eventually you got used to it. He got up, made coffee. What was the matter with him this morning? It was almost six o' clock, a safe time, it was always such a safe time, it was being awake between two and three that was the dangerous time, the fighting time. It was because he had gone to bed sober the past two nights. Water in the kettle, coffee in the mug, strong, strong coffee, he could taste the full flavour already, perhaps he should put on *Don Giovanni*, there was a fuck-you-all man, even in the descent into hell. He went looking for the CD, put it on, pressed the button, skipped the overture, Don Giovanni filled with bravado, on the way to his first murder, the smell of semen still clinging to him on his way to his first murder, his only murder, Mozart's testosterone notes, his fuck-you-all notes. The water boiled, he poured it into the mug, stood in his kitchen and took tiny sips of the black flavourful liquid and saw the spaghetti, he needn't cook tonight, he could eat leftovers.

He had seen his body this morning.

Kara-An Rousseau had invited him to dinner. This evening.

He had to see Willie Theal today and all the memories would be unlocked in his head.

Why did she want to invite him to dinner?

'I'm having a few people over.'

'No, thank you,' he had said.

'I knew it was short notice,' she had said in her creamy voice, disappointed. 'But if you have something else on, come a bit later.' And gave an address, somewhere near the mountain.

What for?

He sat down in the chair again, put his bare feet on the coffee table, the mug against his chest, closed his eyes, the cold creeping in.

What for?

He listened to the music.

Perhaps he should phone the number.

No.

Hope Beneke woke up and thought about van Heerden, her very first thought was about van Heerden.

It surprised her.

She swung her feet off the bed. The nightdress was warm and soft against her skin, against her body. She walked purposefully to the bathroom. She had a great deal to do. Saturdays . . . They had to be used.

He phoned the number

'The Voice of Love. Good morning.'

'Hallo,' he said.

'Hi, sweetie. What can Monique do for you? What is your pleasure? You want to talk dirty to me?'

'No.'

'You want me to talk dirty to you?'

'No.'

'Can I ask you to do things to me?'

'No.'

'Well, what do you want, sweetie?'

Silence.

'Come on, sweetie, the meter is running.'

'I want you to say something nice.'

'Oh, God, it's you again.'

'Yes.'

'It's been a while.'

'Yes.'

'I don't do "nice", honey. I've told you before.'

'Yes.'

'Are you very lonely?'

'Yes.'

'Poor baby.'

'I have to go.'

'You always, do, sweetie.'

He put down the telephone.

Poor baby.

16

I eventually lost my virginity in the early summer of my Matriculation year.

I don't know how important these pieces are, should you want to piece together the jigsaw of my life. I didn't develop an unquenchable passion for older women. But at least it was the beginning of Mozart and food and poetry and perhaps a general departure from the Louis L'Amour stage of my life. It was a start.

All I knew about poetry in those years was what they taught us in school. And as you can imagine, Betta Wandrag's poetry wasn't prescribed reading by the Education Department. Because so many of my mother's friends were well known, I had no concrete awareness of her fame. In any case, it was only when she published her third volume of verse, *Body Language*, that the Sunday papers created such a furore. But by then I had finished my training at the Police College.

She was, at the time of the Great Event, somewhere in her late thirties, tall, her body no longer young, her hips broad, legs strong, her breasts ample, her hair long and thick and black and her eyes almost eastern, the corners downturned, her skin a dark, immaculate, faultless firmament. But it was only later that I stored these details in my memory bank, because for years she was just another weekend visitor from Johannesburg, another member of the adult circle of friends.

A Friday evening. In Stilfontein. When something was released. The collective sigh of relief of ten thousand miners was almost tangible, giving a certain atmosphere to the town, a sense of expectation, a total discharge of tension, an energy focused, deliberately, on the hard work of enjoying oneself.

My mother was in Cape Town and I was on the dark back veranda considering my dateless Friday evening. I just sat there, the way teenagers sometimes do, sat in a deck chair and stared at the dark, vaguely and disinterestedly aware of noises in the kitchen because Betta Wandrag, the visitor, was one of the people who, over weekends, balanced the scales of my mother's lack of interest in the culinary arts. I can't remember what the time was. It was dark, however. Somewhere, the deep bass boom of Deep Purple's 'Smoke on the Water' sounded on a radiogram, competing with Radio South Africa's Concertina Club from another decibel-loaded direction. Most certainly there were the sounds of cars and insects, the exuberant appeal of young children playing cricket under the street lights further down the road, a rubbish bin their wicket.

I just sat.

Until a new sound, furtive and almost inaudible, reached me, startlingly soft, and slow at first.

Aaa . . . aaa . . . aaa . . . aaa . . . aaa.

The first awareness of it was unidentifiable, a sound I deliberately had to separate from all the other instruments of the early-evening symphony, a musical question mark, a sonic puzzle that teased my ears and stimulated a primitive brain cell somewhere.

It grew gradually louder.

Aaa . . . aaa . . . aaa . . . aaa . . . aaa.

Short, fitful cries, no, exclamations, rhythmic and carnal and deeply pleasurable. Until I caught it, until the sounds became a mental image, until a wonderful insight swept over me. Baby Marnewick. In her backyard. Fucking. Al fresco.

Understanding came slowly and dramatically. With a complexity of perspectives. Someone was doing to the object of my many fantasies what I had yearned to do for so long. There was jealousy, envy, hate. She was cheating on me. But there was also the magical, bewitching rapture of her total bliss and the complete abandonment to what she was doing. The tempo and the pitch of each 'aaa' rose slightly, a bolero of love, a dance of pure, silver lust, on and on in flawless rhythm, a woman totally lost in the intensity of her body.

I don't know for how long Betta Wandrag stood in the kitchen doorway. I was completely unaware of her. My hand was in my shorts, mindlessly, instinctively massaging my body's urgent reaction to the sexual symphony, my ears wide open to the sounds repeated over and over again beyond the wooden fence, *aaa* . . . *aaa* . . . *aaa* . . . and then, rhythmically, a new sound crept into the cries, in the beginning contrapuntal to the end of an *aaa* stanza, later an integral part of Baby Marnewick's love lyric. *Aaa* . . . *aaa* . . . *uh* . . . *aaa* . . . *aaa* . . . *aaa* . . . *uh*, now loudly and unabashed.

Something happened in my head, a new peak of randiness, an unknown summit of desire, so that I, with closed eyes, masturbated quite openly on the back veranda, carried away, lost and focused.

Later Betta Wandrag told me that it was one of the most erotic scenes she had ever experienced. She added that she should beg my forgiveness, she hadn't had the right to invade my privacy, but that she was incapable of stopping herself, the sounds and scene in front of her on the veranda – with a wooden spoon in one hand and wearing an apron, she knelt next to my chair, moved my hand gently away and took me into her mouth.

It would be arrogant to think that mere words can describe the surprise, the shock and the pleasure. It is unnecessary to re-live, in detail, what followed. Let me keep to the salient features of this watershed in my life.

That night (and the whole of Saturday and most of the Sunday) Betta Wandrag initiated me with patience and compassion into the world of hedonism.

First there was sex. Slowly, she transformed my youthful urgency and unquenchable lust to patience and control. She revealed the secrets of a woman's body to me like a gospel, educated me in the minor and major pleasures of women, gently corrected my mistakes, richly rewarded my successes. Somewhere in the middle of the Saturday night, after a long lesson in oral satisfaction, she got up and fetched writing materials, shamelessly sat cross-legged on the bed while I looked at her, and wrote the poem 'For Z' which would later form part of that notorious volume:

cunnilingua franca

Your teeth and your tongue,
Soft sibilants flung,
Fricative.
Your breath and your lips,
Body language slips
Flutter.
Stutter.
Plosive.

In between there was Mozart. On that first night she played the Second Violin Concerto and sometimes, shuddering, with hips straining upwards, would hum the theme in perfect harmony. There was the Bassoon Concerto as well, and one of the Horn Concertos (about which she made a double-edged remark and then gave her deep self-satisfied laugh), the Violin Concerto Number 5 and the Piano Concerto Number 27.

In the hours of recovery between orgasm and the next arousal, she told me about Wolfgang Amadeus, about the small genius with the dirty mouth and the beautiful music, the intrigue behind each concerto, the perfection of each note. During that weekend she connected the music to pleasure and ecstasy in my mind for all time, associated it with the highest level of existence, the human potential to try and achieve perfection, even if it was beyond the reach of most of us.

She also cooked. Wearing only an apron. Naturally we had our *Postman* session on the kitchen table, but she brought other dimensions to the erotica of food. Between it all she spoke about things culinary, about eating, about the sensuality, the art. 'It is the cradle of our civilization. Our culture started around the cooking fires of our prehistoric ancestors. That was where we learnt to socialize and to communicate. And when only the embers of the dying fire remained, the pleasure of a filled belly made them lie down for love in the weak, flickering shadows,' she told me while we consumed her creations by candlelight with a compelling hunger.

Ah, she was clever. The first poem she introduced me to was van Wyk Louw's 'Ballad of the Nightly Hours', with its evocation of a few hours of drunken passion and its erotic yet sad details of such a passion. Until daybreak, when the morning spills the man over the edge of its glass, 'in the hour of the dark thirst'. While I was lying on top of her, empty and sweating after another climax, she whispered it into my ear, so softly that I had to concentrate. And when I heard it, another world opened for me, the words acquired meaning, I probably realized for the first time what art really meant.

She told me that sex would always be like that: post-coital depression was the curse of men. She told me about the French who called orgasm 'the small death' but that sex with the love of your life was the one exception, the cure, the escape hatch. It made a great impression on me. I carried her words with me as another guide in my search for that single great love that my parents' romance and now Betta Wandrag's philosophies forecast and promised, and which I later believed life owed me.

I hadn't realized that the Dark Thirst would become the crystal ball of my life. I didn't know how finally, how dramatically the morning of my life would spill me over the edge like so much flotsam.

But that lay far in the future.

Much closer, far more immediate, was the last great event of my youth that fate so casually created as a detour.

Because barely a week later Baby Marnewick was gruesomely and sensationally murdered.

17

Superintendent Leonard 'Rung' Viljoen was a living legend. He was also a living, walking denial of the medical fact that too many knockout blows in the boxing ring can cause permanent brain damage.

There were four photographs in his office at the South African Narcotics Bureau. The first showed Viljoen in a fighter's pose, taken years ago, a young man with only slight tissue damage around the eyes and a minor defect in the shape of the nose. But what drew the eye was Viljoen's massive muscles, a body trained to the highest point of physical fitness. In the other three photographs the young, muscled Viljoen lay flat on his back. In each one another boxer stood over Viljoen, his arms raised triumphantly above his head. The three joyful boxers were heavyweights Kallie Knoetze, Gerrie Coetzee and Mike Schutte, all our great white hopes, in that sequence, from left to right.

This knockout gallery was known as 'The Three Tenners', Viljoen's clever-for-a-boxer play on words because all three fights were scheduled for ten rounds but in each one he heard the 'Ten!' knockout announcement and was unable to beat the ten-minute margin in any of them.

Below the photos, behind a desk, sat a man whose face looked like a battlefield but whose body, at the age of fifty-four, was in the best possible physical condition. 'To reach the top as a heavyweight, you have to climb the ladder to the top. I was lucky to have been a rung on that ladder for so many successful boxers' were the self-ridiculing words heard in police pubs throughout the country whenever Viljoen's name came up. It was also the origin of his legendary nickname.

'I know you,' said Rung Viljoen when van Heerden knocked on the door frame on Saturday morning.

He walked in and extended his hand.

'No, don't tell me.' He pulled his large hand over his scarred face as if he wanted to wipe off cobwebs.

Van Heerden waited.

'I must just place the face . . .'

He didn't want to be remembered.

'Do you box?'

'No, Superintendent.' Involuntarily his hand went to his eye.

'Call me Rung. I give up. Who are you?'

'Van Heerden.'

'Used to be with Murder and Robbery?'

'Yes, Superintendent.'

'Hang on a second, hang on. Silva, that fucker who shot Joubert's wife. Weren't we on the task team together?'

'That's it.'

'Thought you looked familiar. What can I do for you, colleague?'

'I'm working with a legal firm now.' Manipulating the truth, trying to avoid the PI remarks. 'We're investigating a case for a client that goes back a number of years. Early eighties. Drugs could be involved. Rumour is, if you want to know something about drugs, you ask Rung Viljoen.'

'Ha!' said Viljoen. 'Flattery. Always works. Sit down.'

Van Heerden pulled out the old Civil Service chair and sat down on the worn leather seat. 'We suspect that a big transaction took place in eighty-two or -three in which American dollars were involved, Superintendent.'

'Rung.'

He nodded. 'I'm afraid that's about the extent of our information.'

Viljoen's frown carved deep scar tracks next to his eyes. 'What do you want from me?'

'Speculation. For argument's sake, let's say there was a big drug deal in 1982. Let's say dollars were involved. Who, typically, would have been the players at that time? What would they have smuggled? If I dig around, where do I start digging?'

'Shit,' said Rung Viljoen and dragged the broken-knuckled hand over his face again.

'1982?'

'Somewhere about then.'

'American dollars?'

'Yes.'

'The dollars don't mean a thing. It's the currency of the trade, any place on earth. Tell me, are there Chinese involved? Taiwanese?'

'I don't know.'

'But it's possible?'

'The deceased in the case is a forty-two-year-old white man from Durbanville, an Afrikaner by the name of Johannes Jacobus Smit. It's probably not his real name. The age is more or less correct.'

'The deceased? How did he become deceased?'

'One shot in the back of the head from an American M16 rifle.'

'When?'

'Thirtieth of September last year.'

'Mmmmm.'

Van Heerden waited.

'M16?'

'Yes.'

'Don't know it.'

'Nougat O' Grady says it's an American Army assault rifle.'

'The Chinese prefer smaller stuff. But one never knows.'

'Where do the Chinese come into it?'

'In 1980 there were a few routes. Number one came from Thailand. Heroin, mainly, if we're talking big money in dollars. Through India and Pakistan, Afghanistan occasionally, and then the Middle East, four, five, different agents, to Europe. Number two was

Central America which had just started doing their thing, through the Gulf of Mexico to Texas and Florida. But if you're talking about us, it was probably the other route. Possibly heroin from the Golden Triangle to Taiwan and the Far East. In those years the Taiwanese triads slowly but surely became the big suppliers in South Africa. But we've never been a large market. Too few people with enough money for drugs. If you ask me, it could've been an export transaction. Marijuana, perhaps. Or Mandrax, imported. Makes no difference what it was, the amounts couldn't have been much larger than a million dollars.'

'Why?'

'We're a very small fish in a very big ocean, van Heerden. We're at the arse end of the world, the dope desert. In comparison with the trade in the USA and Europe, we're not even a wart on the ugly face of international drug sales. In the eighties we were even smaller.'

'This guy had a walk-in safe built – too small for missiles and too big for a few hundred thousand dollars in notes. He had to have something he wanted to keep in it . . .'

'In Durbanville?'

'In Durbanville.'

'Fooock.' Rung plaited his fingers behind his head and his biceps swelled impressively. 'What about diamonds?'

'I thought about that. He imported antique furniture from Namibia so it would fit, but stones are too small.'

'But valuable. Lots of dollars.'

'Could be.'

'Durbanville feels more like stones to me. Drugs aren't a Boer thing. But show a white Afrikaner a diamond . . . It's in our genes.'

It was a good argument. He couldn't deny it. But he didn't want to change gears: the lack of sleep lay between him and new thought processes, he wanted to hang onto drugs, the packets of white powder that, in his imagination, lay on the shelves in the safe, neatly stacked, filling Jan Smit's hiding place so tidily.

'Just presume for a moment that it was drugs. Who would've been the local players in those years?'

'Hell, van Heerden . . .' Hand over the face, an odd, unconscious mannerism. 'Sam Ling. The Fu brothers. Silva. It's a long time ago.'

'Where can I find Sam Ling?'

Viljoen laughed, a phlegmy, rattling sound. 'The life expectancy of those guys doesn't exactly have insurance agents rushing for their forms. Ling, they say, was fed to the fish in the harbour. The Fu brothers were shot in a gang war in '87. And you know what happened to Silva. You're looking for shadows. Everything has changed. It's almost twenty years.'

'And if it's stones? Who do I speak to?'

Viljoen smiled slowly. 'You could try the detectives at Gold and Diamonds. But if I were you I'd pay the Horse a visit – if you can get past the gate, of course.'

'The Horse?'

'Don't tell me you've never heard of Ronald van der Merwe?'

'I've been . . . somewhat out of circulation for the past few years.'

'Must have been, because there wasn't a policeman south of the Orange River who didn't gossip about Ronnie. And if you quote me, I'll say you lied like a trooper.'

Van Heerden gave a quick nod.

Viljoen drew his palm over his face, slowly, from forehead to jaw. Van Heerden wondered whether he hoped to heal the damaged tissue. 'Ronnie. Colourful. Big guy. Was at the Diamond branch for years. Calls everyone "Horse". Always greets everyone with a "Hi, old horse". Likes big American sports cars. Drove a Trans Am while he was still a sergeant and everyone wondered how he could afford it and there was always gossip but his arrest record was good. Very good. Captain, later. And about two years ago Ronnie resigned and the news was that he'd bought a house at Sunset Beach, a castle with three garages and a high wall and electronic gates that open by remote control. And now he doesn't know any policeman.'

Van Heerden said nothing.

'They said his ship had come in. All the way from Walvis Bay, if you know what I mean.'

Lonely?

Beautiful
Natasha
wants to
listen
Call her now at
386 555 555

He drove from the city on the N1, then north on the N7, the sun breaking through cloud, the green of the wet Cape glowing in the bright light.

His head was dancing the rhythmless dance of the sleepless, thoughts jumping, unfocused, without depth. It was going to be a long day, a shallow tiredness pervaded his body, why had he phoned the fucking number again? He knew the humiliation would scorch him, like it had before. Why had they pushed the fucking pamphlet under his windscreen wiper? Another great lie, just one more great lie like all the other lies to extend and tighten the world's web of deceit.

That first time. Lord, he had phoned the number with so much expectation, so much consuming loneliness because *Natasha wants to listen* and he had to speak to someone, he wanted to speak to someone, he wanted to tell someone, someone had to embrace him even if it was only with words, had to say 'You're OK, Zet, you're OK, van Heerden', but he wasn't, he was weak, he was trash, he was as big a lie as Natasha and the rest of fuckin' humankind.

He sighed.

And Johannes Jacobus Smit. What the fuck was his lie, his deception?

He knew his leap from one scrap of dollar-wrapping paper in a walk-in safe was very big. Too big. But why do you build such a safe? If you were a normal, law-abiding citizen. You might buy a small gun safe or a jewel safe. Law-abiding citizens didn't bother with false identity documents. Smit-whatever-his-name-might-be was a man who wanted to hide a great deal. Who he was. And whatever the fuck was in the safe.

Not stones.

Stones are small.

Stones are hot. You get them and you sell them fast. You don't amass them in a small room with a steel door.

Not drugs. Drugs weren't a Boer game.

Not weapons. Weapons were too big.

Documents?

Dollars?

Documents.

What fucking kind of documents?

Secret documents.

Secret. God knows this country has enough secrets to fill a warehouse. Documents of death and torture, of chemical weapons and nuclear weapons and ballistic missiles and murder lists and secret operations. Documents of deceit. People deceiving one another on national and international levels. The Great Deceit. Important Documents. Documents that would make people commit murder with an attack rifle and a blowtorch.

Documents . . .

But the dates of Smit's new identity and the hiding of secrets didn't work. If Smit had been Secret Service or BSB or MI or whatever unholy acronym it might have been, the nineties would have been a good time for a new identity.

Not the early eighties.

Documents?

An M16 and a blowtorch?

Not your standard 'Kill a Whitey and Steal the Television Set'.

On the Modderdam interchange to Bothasig. Middle-class. Police suburb.

He remembered the route vaguely, found it easily. Mike de Villiers's house. He stopped in the street, walked to the front door. The garden was simple, neat. Knocked at the front door, waited. Mike's wife opened, didn't recognize him, a wide, waddling body, dish cloth in her hand.

'Is Mike here, Mrs de Villiers?'

Broad smile, a nod. 'Yes, he's busy at the back, come in.' Put out her hand, a woman satisfied in her home.

'Are you well?

'Yes, thank you.'

He followed her – the house was shining and neat and smelt of cleaning materials, laundry on the table – out of the back door.

Mike de Villiers stood in the back yard, screwdriver in his hand, next to the lawnmower, wearing his blue police overall, his bald head reflecting the sunlight. He looked up, saw van Heerden, showed no emotion, as usual, shifted the screwdriver to his left hand, wiped the right hand on the overall, extended it.

'Captain . . .'

'No longer, Mike.'

'Superintendent?'

'I'm out of the Force, Mike.'

De Villiers merely nodded. It had never been his place to ask questions. Least of all of officers.

'Coffee?' Martha asked from the kitchen door.

Mike waited for van Heerden. 'That would be nice,' he said.

'Still at the armoury, Mike?'

'Yes, Captain.' Old habits. The eyelids. Which blinked from the bottom up like a lizard's. 'Let's sit down.' He put the screwdriver in the tool chest and walked to the white plastic furniture under the pepper tree. Square and neat in the sunlight, each chair in its precise place.

'I'm working on a case, Mike.'

Eyelids blinked, waiting, as always, like years ago.

'M16.'

They sat.

'Assault rifle,' said Mike de Villiers. The eyes closed. How many years had it been since he saw it at the armoury for the first time, since Nagel had told him, 'I'm going to show you the biggest secret weapon in the Force' and they had gone to the armoury and looked for Mike de Villiers and fed requests for arms information into the man as if into a computer and stood and watched the wheels turning behind the closed eyes and the information coming out, precise and systematic. Sometimes here, in this house, Nagel who made Martha laugh with his slim body and his deep voice and his charm and then the ritual, *you're our secret weapon, Mike*, drawing on the knowledge and then leaving again, like travelling salesmen who quickly came to use a whore. He was always slightly uncomfortable, wondered what de Villiers thought, if he ever minded.

'The Smit case,' de Villiers said.

'You heard.'

An almost invisible nod.

'Did they speak to you?'

'No.' The bare word, hanging.

'It's an American rifle, Mike.'

'Military. The rifle of their infantry since Vietnam. Good weapon. Up to 950 rounds per minute on fully automatic. Light. From less than three kilograms to just under four. Different models. M16, M161A, M16A2, M-4 carbine, La France M16K sub-machine gun, 5.56 calibre, the whole lot. That's what makes it so odd because it's not popular round here. R1 and AK47 use 7.62, ammunition is freely available.'

'Who would use it, Mike?'

De Villiers looked at him, eyes open now. Nagel had never asked him to speculate.

'How would I know, Captain?'

'Did you wonder?'

The eyes closed again. 'Yes.'

'And what did you think, Mike?'

De Villiers hesitated for a long time, his eyes closed. Then he opened them again.

'It's not a good weapon for housebreaking, Captain. It's big, even if it's light. It's a weapon for the battlefield, for the swamps of the Far East and the deserts of the Middle East, it's a weapon for killing outside, not inside. How do you hide it under your jacket in a suburb? It's not a good weapon for close work, in a house, Captain. A revolver would've been better.'

'What's your opinion, Mike?'

The eyes, the strange, hypnotic eyes closed again. 'There are a few possibilities, Captain. You want to intimidate, people are scared of a large weapon. M16 is in every movie. Or it's your only unregistered weapon and you don't want to leave a trail. Or you're an American. An American soldier. Or . . .'

Eyes open. He shook his head slightly from side to side, as if he wanted to leave it.

'Or?'

'I don't know . . .'

'Tell me, Mike.'

'Mercenary, Captain. M16 is just as available on the black market in Europe as the AK. Mercenaries. Many of them like it. But . . .'

'But?'

'What would a mercenary be doing in Durbanville, Captain?'

Martha de Villiers came out with the coffee and somewhere a Karoo long-tailed tit's clear song sounded in the sunlight.

When he drove away, Mike and Martha de Villiers stood in front of the house, the buxom woman's arm around her husband's waist, a couple in Bothasig in a street with neat gardens and ugly concrete walls and children on bicycles and the low whine of lawnmowers using the sunlit gift of a winter morning and he wondered why his life couldn't have been like that, a woman and children and a small castle with its own little pub built on and a mongrel dog and a career and a home loan. That had been, somewhere in the past, a possibility.

What had driven him to take the wrong turnings to nowhere, to seek the dead ends? The road signs had been so clear, so attractive.

Was that not what he wanted, he suddenly asked himself. Wife and children and a lawnmower?

Yes, he thought.

So fucking badly.

18

Boet Marnewick found his wife's kneeling body in the living room, her hands tied behind her back with masking tape, her feet bound with a silk stocking. Forty-six stab wounds, made with a sharp instrument, in her stomach and her back, her nipples sliced off, her genitals mutilated beyond recognition. Blood everywhere, in the bedroom, in the kitchen, in the living room. A murder that shook the community, caused fear and hatred and was a subject of conversation for years to come. Stilfontein was rough, a town that knew and understood alcoholism and wife-beating and immorality and adultery and assault. Even manslaughter. And, occasionally, murder. But not this kind of murder. The deadly blow in a hot-headed, drunken moment, after an excess of alcohol, that was possible to understand, once in a while.

But this was in cold blood, done by a stranger, an intruder, a thief who, taking his time and with malice aforethought, mutilated and murdered a defenceless woman.

I was in my room, busy with homework, when there was a knock at the door. My mother answered and I couldn't hear the words but the tone of her voice made me walk to the living room and there was my detective, my Louis L'Amour Samaritan, and suddenly my heart beat in my throat because my mother looked shocked.

'Sir . . .' I said and swallowed and then my mother said, 'Baby Marnewick is dead, Zet.'

He pretended not to know me and it was only when he left that he squeezed my shoulder, looked at me and gave me a small smile. But before that he asked his questions. Had we seen anything? Heard anything? What did we know about the Marnewicks?

And I sat there with my fantasies and my intimate knowledge and my voyeurism and merely affirmed my mother's negative replies. We knew nothing.

We got the details later. From neighbours and the *Klerksdorp Gazette* and *Die Vaderland* and *Die Volksblad* and even the *Sunday Times*. A gruesome sex killing had made Stilfontein national news. I read the reports over and over again and listened with the closest attention to each bit of news a new source could supply.

The details upset me. Partly because of my own unclean thoughts about Baby Marnewick. And the fact that they, however slight the connection, linked me to the murderer who had cut and stabbed, driven by lust. Because I had lusted as well – even though our fantasies had been so dramatically different.

And partly because a human being, someone in Stilfontein, one of us, was capable of such a revolting deed.

They never found him. There were no fingerprints. There was semen on Baby Marnewick's body, on her buttocks and on her back but this was in the years before DNA testing and the long arm of the test tube that could reach past your race and sex and blood group to the imprint of your body, that could decipher a microscopic hair or thread from a piece of clothing and dissect you more thoroughly than a scalpel.

There were rumours. Boet Marnewick was a suspect but that was nonsense, he had been a kilometre underground at the time of the murder. There were the rumours of the travelling murderer. Another story was of a man from her past, from Johannesburg, and there was even one about the Scot from whom Boet had taken her.

But they never found the killer.

Day after day I stared at the wooden fence and thought about the strangest things. If Betta Wandrag hadn't interfered, would I have listened at the fence? Perhaps heard something that could have saved Baby Marnewick? Wondered why. How? How did someone do something like that? How do you murder so brutally and without conscience, so bloody and cruel? And who.

Who could have planned something like that? Because rumour would have it that he had brought the masking tape with him, that he had worn gloves. Premeditated, planned murder.

Towards the end of the year my mother put the application forms for Potchefstroom University in front of me, made herself comfortable and said we had speculated about my plans for a long time. Now it was time to go to university and make my choices, because it was better to go to university first and then do the compulsory army training because graduates quickly became officers, even if I only wanted to become a teacher.

'I'm not going to university, Ma.'

'You're what?'

'I'm joining the police.'

19

Profiling.

Johannes Jacobus Smit had been bound, tortured and then murdered because he had to supply the combination to a safe and afterwards he was an unnecessary and unwelcome witness. The motive was known. The *modus operandi* clear. The profile simple. A single-minded thief. Someone who was capable of torture and murder. Psychopath, sociopath, at least some symptoms.

Behaviour established personality. They had taught him that at Quantico. His three American months.

But the magical power of profiling lay in pinpointing the evidently motiveless, the serial killers, the rapists, the sex murderers who were driven by the demons of their pasts: the fucked-up family life, the violent father, the whoring mother. Not in exposing the simplicity of torture and murder committed to get at the contents of a safe. Robbery. Murder. With aggravating circumstances.

Planned robbery. The wire had been brought to the murder scene. The blowtorch was part of the murderer's equipment. 'Here are your sandwiches, love. And don't forget the wire, the pliers and the blowtorch. Is the M16 loaded? Have a nice day.'

He, the murderer/robber, was known to Smit. Maybe. Probably. No sign of forced entry into the house. And the fact that Smit was shot execution-style. Another potential sign. No witnesses left behind.

Perhaps. Possibly. Conceivably.

He parked the Corolla under a tree at the bottom end of Moreletta Street and switched off the engine.

The blowtorch.

There was something about that blowtorch. The murderer knew he would have to torture, which meant that he knew Smit wouldn't talk easily. Which also meant that he knew him. Which meant that he knew Smit possessed something that was worth stealing. Something that was hidden or locked away. But there were many ways to torture that caused pain, inhuman pain. Why use a blowtorch? Why not use the pliers to extract Smit's nails, one by one? Why not beat Smit with the stock of the rifle until his face was unrecognizable and the pain of a broken nose and smashed mouth and cracked skull made him beg to confess, to tell where the documents or diamonds or dollars or drugs were.

Or whatever the fuck was in the safe,

The blowtorch said something about the murderer.

Arson was a primary warning sign of a serial killer in the making. Together with bed-wetting and torturing animals.

They liked fire. Flames.

He took out his notebook.

Crime Research Bureau. Blowtorch-burglaries/crimes

He closed the book, put it into his jacket pocket with the pen.

'You must be able to put yourself in the shoes of the murderer *and* the victim,' they had said at Quantico.

Smit's shoes. The perspective of the victim acquired from the crime scene, the forensic and pathology reports. Smit, alone at home, follows his usual routine: there's a knock at the door – was the door locked, had he always kept it locked, habit of fifteen years, or was the door open and had the murderer simply walked in with his rifle and his blowtorch and his wire and his pliers? Here was something that didn't make sense. There were too many things for one man to carry. 'Hold the door for a moment, Johannes Jacobus, I just want to get the torture equipment.'

Two attackers?

Or one. With a backpack and an M16.

Smit is startled, fear, recognition, after so many years the existence he had crafted with so much care is suddenly threatened. Great fear, adrenalin. But he's unarmed. He steps away from the door. 'What do you want?'

'Oh, you know, Johannes Jacobus, the goodies you stole from me. Where are they, good buddy?'

According to the pathologist there were no wounds to indicate that there had been a fight. Smit had put up no resistance. A lamb led to the slaughter. 'Sit, Smit, and we'll see how long you can hang in there before you tell me where my goodies are.'

Why hadn't Smit put up any resistance? Had he known he would achieve nothing because there were two of them? Or was he simply too scared, terrified?

Force him into the kitchen chair, tie him down.

With an M16? How do you hold a M16 to a man's head with one hand while tying his hands with binding wire and a pair of pliers with your other hand?

There had been more than one 'visitor'.

'Tell us, Smittie, where are the goodies?'

'Fuck you.'

'Ah, so pleasant to have cooperation. Light the blowtorch and strip him.'

Torture him. The blue flame on his scrotum, on his chest, on his belly, on his arms. The pain must've been inhuman.

Why hadn't he simply told them? His business was doing well, he didn't need money, diamonds, drugs, weapons to make more money. Why didn't he just say 'It's in the safe, here's the combination, take the stuff and leave me alone?'

Reason: there was something else in the safe. Of no monetary value. Something else.

Reason: he'd known he was going to die if they found what they had come for.

Van Heerden sighed.

'What the fuck do the shoes of the victim have to do with anything? Except if the murderer's blood is stuck to them,' had been Nagel's reaction. 'The suspect, yes. *His* shoes. That's what counts.'

He stared ahead, didn't see the street, the big trees, the gardens. Didn't see the clouds moving in from the mountain.

Nagel. Who was now thrusting his thin, sinewy arm from the grave. Nagel, he thought, had rested for long enough. Nagel was coming back.

He didn't know how he would handle it.

He got out of the car.

Let the footwork begin.

Like crystal, she thought. The sunshine days between the cold fronts. Clear as glass, windless, a beautiful fragility. Shining jewels in the dark dress of winter.

Hope Beneke was jogging next to the sea at Blouberg beach, somewhat self-conscious about the stares of passing motorists, a small price to pay for the stunning view of the sea and the mountain, the great towering mass of rock with its strange, world-famous shape that guarded the bay, a sentinel of calm, constancy, peace of mind, resignation. Some things always remained the same.

Even if she was changing.

Rhythmically, one running shoe following the other, she took pleasure in the fitness of her body, her breathing deep and even, her legs blissfully warm. She wasn't always fit, she hadn't always been so slender. There had been a time in her last year at university and the clerkship years when she had been ashamed of her legs, when she didn't like her bottom, didn't look good in jeans – the combination of university-residence food and long hours of study and a certain aversion to herself.

Not that Richard minded. He said he liked her Rubenesque curves. At the beginning. When everything was new in their relationship, when he ran his hands over her body for the first time, sighed deeply and said, with a light shining behind his eyes, 'Lord, Hope, but you're sexy.' Richard, with his small bald patch and his laconic accountant's view of life and his passion for news. Richard, who later, when everything was no longer new, would get up after making love to look at the latest news. Or would pick up *Time*, switch on the light and read. *Time!*

Richard, who wanted to get married. No, who wanted to live like a married man long before she had finished with the romance and the eroticism of the game of love.

'You have a red mark on your cheek,' Richard had said without surprise, one summer's night in the middle of the act of love, as if he was reporting the news to an audience without prejudice. After they had had sex for months.

'My whole body is glowing like fire,' she had said, filled with passion and empathy.

'Odd mark,' was his thoughtful reaction.

And when their relationship eventually became as dry as dust and died a quiet death, she had to take stock.

Just to realize that she had been equally to blame. Not that Richard possessed the same unbiased capacity for introspection. Some people dare not run the risk of self-criticism. He was different. He was so satisfied with himself that he never saw the need for it.

But she had to examine her life. And one of the conclusions she came to was that she wasn't comfortable with herself. Not with her body, not with the way she was.

So she did two things. Left Kemp, Smuts and Breedt. And started jogging. And here she was on Blouberg's beach, fit and slender and Richard-less – and a forty-year-old dysfunctional ex-policeman (what was his real age?) was a vague interest, an impossible possibility.

Because he was so different to Richard? Because he was so unpredictable and wounded? Because his mother . . .

She should have her head read.

The sun suddenly disappeared. She looked up. A dark bank of clouds over the bay, over the mountain. Another front. It was a cold winter. Not like last year's. Like life. Always changing, sometimes there wasn't much sunshine, then rare crystal days in between the rain.

* * *

He walked from house to house in Moreletta Street, like a door-to-door salesman, and asked his questions.

No one knew Johannes Jacobus Smit. 'You know what it's like, we all live our own lives.'

The houses on either side of the Smit–van As house: 'We sometimes had a chat across the fence. They were very quiet.'

No one saw or heard anything. 'I thought I heard something like a shot but it might have been something else.'

Everyone at each house, somewhat uncomfortable, their Saturday schedule disturbed, politeness without friendliness, curious. 'Have you found anything?' 'Have you caught anybody?' 'Do you know why he was shot?' Because that was where the threat lay. Someone in their area had been cruelly murdered, too near their personal safety zone, a small breach in the bastion of their white middle-class security. And when he replied in the negative, there was a quick frown of worry, followed by a moment of silence as if they wanted Smit to have earned it in some way or another, because such things simply didn't happen.

Then, before he was ready, he had finished, and he drove to Philippi, to see Willie Theal.

Theal who had phoned him to say, 'Come and work with me.' Theal who had comforted him when his life had burst open like an overripe sick bloody pomegranate and he accepted the comfort because he needed it, but his acceptance was deceit, the big deceit because he had always been trash, from the first time he stole, when he stole with his eyes and his mind through the wooden fence, when he stole from Nagel, the trash in him was always there, just under the surface, like lava, constantly smouldering, bubbling, waiting for a crack in the rock face, ready to break like a volcano through the soft crust of his world.

He braked, suddenly.

Too little time.

He realized it suddenly: five days. *Not enough.*

Say he spoke to Theal, fuck it, he wasn't afraid, it wouldn't make him better or worse, it wasn't because he was afraid of the ghosts that Theal would call up.

It wouldn't make any difference. Because there simply wasn't enough. Too little information, too little time.

And it wasn't going to change. Theal would tell him how and where you could change dollars in the eighties. Or maybe not. And what then? Who would remember Johannes Jacobus X after fifteen years? He could visit Charles Nieuwoudt in Pollsmoor Prison or Victor Verster or whichever jail he might be in and ask whether he falsified the identity document and what would he get?

Nothing. Not in five days.

Because Nieuwoudt's brains had been scrambled by drugs and it had been fifteen years and he wouldn't remember a thing.

That was the problem. The case wasn't ten months old. It was fifteen years old. Someone had known there was something in that safe worth killing for. He didn't know what it was. He might as well admit it. He hadn't the faintest idea what had been in that safe. He could speculate on the basis of a fucking slip of paper until he was blue in the face. He could formulate his clever theories until he died of boredom. It could have been anything. Kruger rands. Gold. Diamonds. Rands or dollars or fucking Monopoly money. It could have been nude photographs of Bill Clinton or the fucking Spice Girls. It could have been a map of pirate's treasure and he would never know because the thing was as dead as a doornail and he couldn't get it breathing with mouth-to-mouth resuscitation or a heart-lung machine.

He knew he was right. More than a thought-through conclusion. Instinct. Everything he had learnt told him that it would take time. Weeks. Months of fine-tooth combing, of talking, of asking questions until something unravelled and gave you a thread you could tug, pull, wiggle.

He pulled off at the Kraaifontein interchange, turned right over the bridge and right again back to the city on the N1. Where had she said she lived? Milnerton.

Curious. He would have placed her near the mountain with her yuppie hair-do and her BMW, the fucking mountain that brooded, he hated that mountain, hated this place that had made him think he could stage a comeback overnight: hi, sweetheart, I'm home, I'm a detective again, isn't it great!

* * *

She was busy digging compost into the oleanders when she heard the cell-phone ringing. She pulled off the gloves as she walked, opened the sliding door and answered the phone.

'Hope Beneke.'

'I want to see you.' His voice dark and abrupt.

'Of course,' she said.

'Now.' He heard the irritating sympathy again, the I-understand-everything-now-and-can-be-patient-with-you tone in her voice.

'Fine.'

'I don't know where you live.'

'Where are you?'

'Milnerton. At Pick 'n Pay.'

She gave him directions.

'Good,' he said and put the phone down.

'Goodbye,' she said, 'Zatopek.' And smiled to herself. He wasn't a ray of sunshine. What did he look like when he laughed?

She walked to the bathroom, pulled a comb through her short hair, applied pale pink lipstick. She wasn't going to change. The tracksuit was fine. She went to the kitchen, put on the kettle, took out the small white tray, put out the mugs, the milk jug, the sugar bowl. She should have bought something at the Home Industry. A tart. It was almost coffee time.

She walked to the mini hi-fi. She didn't really know much about classical music. Was he very knowledgeable? She had *The World's Greatest Arias*. And *The Best Classical Album Ever*. And *Pavarotti and Friends*. The rest was a mixture from Sinatra to Laurika Rauch to Celine Dion to Bryan Adams.

She put on the Dion CD. Universally loved. She turned the volume to low. Heard the kettle switching itself off. Stood at her sliding door and surveyed the small patch of garden, a postage-stamp oasis that she had created with her own hands, even down to planting the grass, the shrubs and the flowers. Now she was preparing for Spring.

She felt raindrops and looked up. The clouds were heavy, the drops fine and light. She had finished just in time. She closed the door, sat down on a living-room chair, checked her watch. He should be here any moment now. Her eyes wandered over the pine bookcase that she had bought second-hand and painted herself, when she was still a clerk.

Did van Heerden read? Richard hadn't. Richard was a news fanatic. Newspapers and television news and *Time* and *The Economist* and radio bulletins, six o'clock in the morning. She had indulged him. A relationship was a question of give and take. For him it was a matter of being given to and taking from.

Eventually he knocked on her door. She got up, peered through the spyhole, recognized him and opened the door. He stood, again slightly damp from the rain, the face reflecting stormy weather. As usual. 'Come in,' she said. He walked in, glanced at the open-plan kitchen, dining area and living room, walked to the breakfast counter, took out his wallet and removed bank notes. He placed them on the counter.

'I've finished,' he said without looking up.

She looked at him. He seemed so defenceless, she thought. How could she have been so intimidated initially? The vague purplish colour around his eye accentuated his vulnerability, though the lip was now nearly healed.

He placed the last note on the little pile. 'We're going nowhere. The thing is dead. It's not ten months old. It started when Smit changed his name and it's too long ago. You can do nothing about it.' He folded his arms and leant against the counter.

'Would you like some coffee?' she asked quietly.

'The advance . . . yes, please.' Somewhat taken aback. She walked around him to the kettle, put it on again, put a teaspoon of instant coffee in each mug.

'I have nothing to serve with the coffee. I'm not good at baking,' she said. 'Do you bake?'

'I . . . no.' Irritated. 'The investigation . . .'

'Won't you sit down? Then we can discuss it.' Voice gentle. She suddenly wanted to laugh: he was so focused, so predictable, his body language an alarm siren, directed at confrontation. He was lost when it didn't come.

'Yes,' he said and sat on the edge of a living-room chair. He was so unbelievably uncomfortable, she thought.

'How do you like your coffee?'

'Black and bitter.' As an afterthought: 'Thank you.'

'I appreciate your honesty about the investigation.'

'You'll simply have to accept that the case is dead.'

'It was worth trying.'

'And there is nothing you can do about it.'

'I know.'

'I just came to tell you.'

'That's fine,' she said.

'What did Kemp tell you?'

'Kemp knows nothing about the investigation.' She poured boiling water into the mugs.

'About me. What did he tell you about me?'

'He said that if there was someone who would be able to find the will, it would be you.' She carried the coffee on her small white tray, put it down on the glass table. 'Help yourself,' she said.

He took a mug, put it back on the tray.

'How could he have said that if he knows nothing about the investigation?'

She bent forward, added milk to her coffee, stirred it. 'Of course he knows I have a client who is looking for a will that was lost in a burglary. He knows it's a sort of criminal investigation. That's why he recommended you. He said you're the best.' For a moment she wanted to add, 'Difficult, but the best,' but she left it at that, raised the mug to her lips.

'What else did he say? About me?'

'That's all. Why do you ask?'

'I just want to tell you, I don't need your sympathy.'

'Why would you need my sympathy? If you say the investigation is dead, then . . .' She wanted to provoke him, she knew she was doing it deliberately.

'Not the investigation,' he said, irritated.

'Do have your coffee.'

He nodded, took the mug off the tray.

'What made you realize finally that the case was dead?' Her tone of voice was accepting, acquiescent.

He blew on the coffee. thought for a while. 'I was at the Drug Squad this morning. And at the neighbours of van As. I don't know. I suddenly realized . . . There is nothing, Hope. And you'll have to accept it. There is nothing you can do.'

She nodded.

'I . . . know van As will be disappointed. But if they hadn't had such an odd relationship . . .'

'I'll talk to her. Don't worry about it.'

'I'm not worried. Because there's nothing . . .'

'That she can do.'

'That's right.'

'Where did you learn to cook?'

He suddenly looked penetratingly at her. 'What's going on here, Hope?'

'What do you mean?'

'I come here to tell you that you and van As can forget it and you talk about food? What's going on?'

She sank back in the chair, put her running shoes on the table, rested the mug on her knees, spoke amiably. 'Do you want me to argue with you about it? You gave me your professional opinion and I accept it. I think you did a good job. I also have tremendous respect for the fact that you've returned the money. Someone with less integrity would have let the case drag on endlessly.'

He snorted. 'I'm trash,' he said.

To which she had no reply.

'I think Kemp told you more.'

'What should he have told me?'

'Nothing.'

He's like a child, she thought, watching him as he stared at nothing in the distance, drinking his coffee. She could see his mother's genes, in and around the eyes. She wondered what his father had looked like.

'There was something in the safe. That's the key.'

'It could have been anything,' she agreed.

'Exactly,' he said. 'It would take a year to examine all the possibilities.'

'If you had more time?'

He tried to read her face for sarcasm. Found nothing. 'I don't know. Weeks. Months, perhaps. Luck. We needed luck. If van As had remembered something. Or had seen something. If the safe had contained something more.'

You make your own luck, Nagel had said.

'Have you anything else you're working on?' she asked.

'No.'

She so badly wanted to ask him about himself, his mother, about who he was, why he was the way he was. Tell him his front was so unnecessary, she knew what hid behind it, she knew he could again become what his mother said he once had been.

'I'm leaving.'

'Perhaps we'll work together again one day.'

'Perhaps.' He got up.

20

I must admit that I remain endlessly fascinated by the small crossroads of life, the forks in the road, seldom indicated, rarely a road sign. Only visible in retrospect.

I joined the police force because I peered through a wooden fence one Saturday afternoon. I joined the police because a detective gave me a second chance with firm warmth – a father figure? Did I join the Force because my father died young? Would I have joined the police if I hadn't lusted after Baby Marnewick? Would I have joined if Baby Marnewick hadn't been murdered?

There was a Gauloise advertisement at the movies in those days. A French artist who made clever charcoal or pencil drawings on paper. At first it seemed as if he was drawing a female nude – the sexy breasts, the hips, the waist. But as he drew on, the female figure became an innocuous Frenchman with a beret, beard and a cigarette.

The crossroads, the road signs, the milestones were only visible when each picture was completed.

I joined the police.

With my mother's blessing. I think she suspected that it had something to do with the Marnewick murder but her perspective was speculative and wrong. I think she had had other dreams for me but she . . . was my mother, she supported me.

What can I tell you about Police College in Pretoria? Bluebottles, young men from every level of society thrown together. We paraded and learnt and carried on like young bulls in the evening, we argued and talked nonsense and laughed and dreamt of more sex and less physical effort. We paraded and perspired in classes without air-conditioning and made beds with perfect edges and learnt to shoot.

Let me be honest. The rest of my intake learnt to shoot. I shut my eyes and eventually, with the minimum number of marks, managed to stay on the course. From the start firearms were my Achilles heel, my Nemesis as a policeman. It was inexplicable. I liked the smell of gun oil, the glimmer of black metal, the cold, effective lines. I picked up the weapons with the same amount of bravado and the same feeling of power as did the other recruits, handled them and fired them. But the projectiles I sent off by pulling the trigger, the physics I initiated, were always less effective than every other bluebottle's. I was teased endlessly about it but it didn't damage my ego, mainly because my achievements in the tests and examinations tipped the scales of mutual respect in another direction. In theoretical work, on paper, with a set of questions, I had no equal.

And then the training was over and I was a constable in a uniform and I asked for Stilfontein or Klerksdorp or Orkney, heaven only knows why, and got Sunnyside in Pretoria and for the next two years locked up drunken students and dealt with disturbing-the-peace complaints and smoothed down marital scraps in thousands of flats and investigated burglaries from cars and served in the charge office and learnt how to fill in SAPS forms, over and over and over again, adding to the tons of paper of the documentation of justice.

And was branded as the classical-music constable, the one who read (but couldn't shoot worth a damn). For the Sunnyside office of the SAP I was what a teddy bear was for the centre-line of a high-school rugby team: a kind of totem, a defence against the darkness of total cultural decline in a city area of grey crime.

Because that was our daily task: not the screaming colours of injustice committed in hatred, but the drab world of minor, white-collar transgressions, of human weakness on the colourless part of the police palette.

I lived in a bachelor pad with a single bed and a table and a chair which my mother gave me and I made a bookcase with bricks and planks and saved for three months for the deposit on a Defy stove and taught myself to cook from magazines and read virtually every book in the library and worked shifts that didn't do much for romance or socializing but did manage, however, among the enormous number of lonely young girls in Sunnyside, to strike it lucky, one or two or three nights per month of wriggling, struggling, despairing sex. They were backscratchers, virtually without exception, as if they wanted to leave a physical mark that would outlast the brief flame of physical passion.

There were times when I could not remember why I was a servant of justice. I first had to think back to Stilfontein, to stand at the wooden fence of shame again, to drink at the fountain of inspiration.

It was temporary, everything, a purposeless existence, a rite of passage, marking time, wasted years, growing years, growing-up years.

21

You make your own luck.

He drove to Table View, the rain sifting onto the shallow lagoon, a discomfort within him, displeased with himself, with Hope Beneke. He knew she knew something, didn't want to say anything, Kemp who probably still let the rumours live, that was what everyone thought, that he had seen Nagel die and it had fucked him up.

Ha.

Discomfort about the whole investigation, there was something he'd missed, he knew it, there was something, somewhere. Something van As had said, something in O'Grady's file.

You make your own luck.

Uncomfortable, he wasn't a loser. With his life, yes, but that was different, you couldn't battle the odds, but this thing was dead, just another murderer who had joined the hordes of the unarrested, just another statistic. It happened, he knew it, sometimes there wasn't enough evidence or enough luck.

He needed a great deal of luck with this case, he needed an explosion, a piece of fucking dynamite that could blow away the cobwebs of fifteen years, blow open the secrets of Johannes Jacobus Smit, blow away the dust so that the facts, the bones and the fossils could be distinguished from the rocks.

How the fuck could he make his own luck with this thing?

How could he gain more *time*?

Gain time.

You must be able to go back in time.

If he could only . . .

Hang on.

No, it wouldn't . . .

Quantico. What had they said?

No.

Yes.

Jesus.

He braked, suddenly and hard, swearing as a car behind him complained with a blast of the hooter, missing him by inches, and he turned, drove over the central ridge in the road, heard the Corolla's undercarriage flattening the shrubs, let the wheels kick up wet sand, turned back to Hope Beneke because he had a fucking idea, he had a bomb, he had a plan to blow away the spiderwebs.

She simply sat, coffee mugs still on the table, unwilling to think about the full implications of his visit, her thoughts random, disappointed.

She had no choice, she had to accept that he had been right, that they wouldn't get any further. The police had achieved nothing either, he had at least achieved a bit more, discovered a false identity. He'd been so positive with his theories last night, she'd been so hopeful, excited that they were going to solve the problem but he wasn't only . . .

She'd been pleased with herself earlier, with her handling of him, her calmness, her avoidance of potential conflict. She'd thought she'd discovered the key to Zatopek van Heerden, the mystery: simply defuse every explosive situation, don't react. She had hidden her disappointment well, she had been so brave when she said that she would tell Wilna van As, but she would find it hard, she knew she would be broken-hearted.

Disappointment. Because van Heerden was out of her life. Better that way. He was, despite the hurt and the defencelessness, trouble. With a capital T.

Was there really nothing else he could do?

No. She had to accept that. He had even returned the advance. She looked at the little pile of notes on the breakfast counter. The testimony of her detective.

She got up, put the mugs on the tray. She had to carry on. Join Valerie and Chris for a barbecue this evening. She needed an evening of laughter and relaxation. It had been a hard week. She walked to the kitchen, put the mugs in the sink. Was struck by a sudden idea.

Joan van Heerden was never going to be her mother-in-law. And she laughed, loudly, above the soft sounds of Celine Dion and shook her head, still laughing, opened the taps, took out the washing-up liquid from the cupboard below, what absurdities the mind could suddenly conjure up, then heard the sound of her front-door bell.

She wasn't expecting anyone, she thought, turned off the tap, walked to the door and peered through the spyhole. Zatopek van Heerden.

Had he forgotten something? She opened the door.

'There is something we can do,' he said and his eyes were bright and his voice urgent and she wondered whether he had heard her laughing.

'Come in,' she said. 'Please,' her voice under control and he walked past her, stood at the counter as she closed the door behind him.

'I . . .' he said. 'It . . .'

'Won't you sit down?'

'We have . . . What we must do is to turn the clock back fifteen years. It's our only chance.'

She stood between nothing and nowhere, decided to sit down. She had never seen him like this, excited, with such urgency in his voice.

'I've just realized I've been speaking to all the wrong people. I've been talking to everyone who didn't know him fifteen years ago. It's time for us to change that. There is a way.'

'How?'

'Publicity.'

She looked at him, not understanding.

'When he was murdered O'Grady didn't know that he had changed his name. Was there a picture of him in the newspapers?'

'No. Wilna van As wouldn't . . . release the identity book's photo to the press. There was no reason . . .'

'One thing has changed since then,' he said. 'We now know he wasn't Jan Smit. No one knew it then. If we can get the photo published now and ask if someone recognizes him, if we say he was someone else, we may be able to find out who he was. And if we know that, we may find out what was in the safe . . .'

'And who wanted it so badly.'

'We can place an advertisement,' he said. 'Small ads, it wouldn't cost much.'

'No,' she said. 'We can do much better than that.'

'How?'

'Kara-An Rousseau,' she said.

He merely looked at her.

'She can get us publicity. Free for all. In every NasPers newspaper in the country.'

'She invited me to dinner this evening,' he said, suddenly sorry he had refused.

Jealousy raised its head. 'Kara-An?'

'Yes,' he said. 'But I refused. I didn't know . . .'

'You must go,' she said. *I didn't know you knew one another so well,* she thought.

'I don't know her.'

'We have so little time. We have to speak to her immediately.'

'Will you go with me?'

She wanted to go, she . . . but . . .

'I haven't been invited.'

'I'll ask if I may bring a partner.'

'No,' she said. 'We don't have to go to the dinner. It's early enough. We can try to see her before dinner.' She got up, found the cell-phone, looked up the number in the memory and dialled. It rang.

'Kara-An.'

'It's Hope. Am I phoning at a bad time?'

'Hi. Of course not. How are you?'

'Crazy at the moment, thank you. Do you remember the case of the will I told you about?'

'Of course. The one Mr Sexy is helping you with.'

'We urgently need your help, Kara-An.'

'*My* help?'

'Yes. I know it's a bad time but we can have a very quick conversation. It would be easy . . .'

'Of course, it sounds fascinating. And you must stay to dinner. I've invited a few people. Come a bit earlier . . .'

'I don't want to disrupt your Saturday evening, Kara-An.'

'Don't be silly. There's enough space and more than enough to eat.'

'Are you sure?'

'Absolutely. I can't wait to become a part of the Great Search.'

They said goodbye. Hope Beneke turned to van Heerden.

'You'll have to take your money,' she said. 'Before I spend it on a new outfit for this evening.'

Eight hours later she would lie in her bed and wonder how an evening that had started so conventionally could end with so much violence and chaos. She would lie there weeping about the disillusionment and the humilation and would contemplate his words again, 'We're all evil', and wonder whether he was perhaps right – and where the badness in her lay.

But when he had come to fetch her and stood at her door in black trousers, white shirt and a black jacket she had felt a warmth towards him, for the effort he had made to conform with the clothes even if the cut wasn't modern and the shoes not really right. His eyes widened slightly when he saw her in the short black dress and he said with undisguised surprise and honesty, 'You look great, Hope' and for a moment she wanted to put out a hand and make physical contact but mercifully he turned and walked to his car before she could act on the impulse.

They drove in comfortable silence in the rain towards the mountain until she guided him through the narrow streets high up on its slope and they stopped in front of a huge house in Oranjezicht, old and Victorian. He whistled through his teeth.

'Old money,' she said. 'Her father was a Member of Parliament.'

The sight of Kara-An in her scarlet dress and bare feet was like a clarion call from his past – the black hair, the blue eyes, the breathtaking, strong line of chin and cheekbone and neck – and he wanted to store it all in his memory bank for later meditation. He had to shake off the feeling almost physically.

There was a lot of activity in the house, young people in white aprons arranging flowers, carrying plates and glasses to the dining room. 'The caterers are still busy, let's go through to the library.'

Caterers? Was that how the rich did it, he wondered and followed the two women, aware of the dark, polished wood of the antique furniture, the expensive paintings, the Eastern carpets, the wealth that glowed in the light of a thousand candles. 'I've invited a few people,' she'd said the previous evening.

Caterers.

Jesus. How could you ask strangers to cook for your friends?

Kara-An closed the door behind them and invited them to sit down. He wondered how many of the books on the dark panelled shelves she'd read, so many leatherbound copies, so many titles stamped in gold. He realized Hope was waiting for him to say something. 'You explain,' he said.

He watched the two women as Hope spoke, careful because he knew there was old, well-known, dangerous terrain here: Kara-An who looked at him every time Hope mentioned his name, Kara-An who listened with great concentration but there was something else in her look, an interest. Then he saw the distance he kept from everything in his life, not for the first time: it sometimes happened when he listened to music, when he looked through a recipe book for a new dish, sometimes it seemed as if life wanted to lure him back, when the pleasures, major and minor, of a normal, happy existence wanted to seduce him into forgetting that he didn't deserve it, couldn't afford it. This time the siren song was stronger – a woman's wonderful beauty, two women in front of him, Hope's eyes that looked pretty tonight, her legs in the black dress, the touchable bottom, he wanted to compare and consider and philosophize and desire, blatantly and obviously desire, and play a light-hearted silly game of love, start a flirtation and talk to someone about it, laugh, Lord, he needed to laugh, he wanted to laugh with someone over a glass of chilled white wine, he missed it, he missed *her* so terribly . . . and then the fear was upon him, overpowering and strong and he retreated from his own thoughts and Hope looked expectantly at him, wanting him to say something.

'What?' he said and he thought his voice sounded scared.

'Was that an accurate version of where we stand?'

'Yes,' he said, withdrawing into his shell in a panic.

'It'll make good copy,' said Kara-An.

'Copy?' said Hope who didn't know the terminology.

'Newspaper article. I won't have much trouble in convincing the news editor . . .'

'There are two important points,' van Heerden said. They looked at him. 'The story must get the angle right. And it must appear in all your dailies. In Gauteng as well.'

'What do you mean by the right angle?'

He took the papers out of his jacket pocket, pages torn from his notebook. Control had returned. 'I tried something but it's not quite right. You'll have to work on it.' He handed it to Kara-An Rousseau. She leant forward, the neckline of the red dress opening for a moment. He looked away. 'It must sound as if we're on the edge of a breakthrough, as if information about Smit is not essential, merely a . . .'

'A bonus,' said Hope.

'Yes. We must make it sound as if we know all about the events of fifteen years ago and just want to tie up loose ends . . .'

'Ah,' said Kara-An. 'You want creative journalism.'

'Lots,' he said.

'I know someone who specializes in it.'

'What are the chances for the front page?' he asked.

'That will depend on other news stories.'

Someone knocked on the door. 'Come in,' said Kara-An.

A young woman in a white apron put her head round the door. 'Some of the other guests have arrived, madam.'

'Thank you,' said Kara-An. She smiled at Zatopek van Heerden, a spectacular sight focused entirely on him. 'We'll talk again when everyone else has left.'

* * *

He sat between the wife of the South African Cultural Attaché, a tall brown woman with very prominent front teeth and thick glasses who spoke very softly, and the Businesswoman of the Year, sharp-faced, thin, hyperactive, hands that were never still, mouth never shut.

'And what do you do?' asked the Businesswoman of the Year before he could seat himself comfortably at the long table. And suddenly his memory threw up the world of senseless socializing of his University of South Africa era, out of nowhere, as if it had been lying in wait, ready to be recalled, the reply to 'What do you do?' establishing your hierarchy in that status-conscious society. In those years he sometimes lied at cocktail parties and lunches and dinners for the sheer hell of it, saying he was an engine driver, or a security guard, then sitting back and watching the person who had asked the question struggle with a reaction. Sometimes he would come to the rescue with an 'Only joking, I'm with the Department of Police Science. Lecturer,' his passport to the select company safe, his visa correctly stamped. Wendy had hated it when he did that, especially when he didn't retract the lie: status was important to Wendy. That and the appearance of happiness and success. Seemingly for Kara-An as well. Earlier on she had introduced them to some of the people. 'This is Hope Beneke, the attorney. And van Heerden, her colleague.' *The* attorney. Not *an* attorney. The status of the article. And the deceit of the selective truth. 'Her colleague.'

'I'm a policeman,' he said to the Businesswoman and watched her eyes but they gave away nothing. She immediately leant over to Mrs Cultural Attaché and introduced herself, then spoke to the man on her right, the Doctor. He looked at the other faces around the table, Hope opposite him, Kara-An at the head, on his right twenty people who still had to conquer the stiffness of new acquaintance without the oil of alcohol. Some he had met during the pre-dinner sherry period, the Writer, the Wine Farmer, the Dress Designer, the dignified ex-Actress, the Millionaire Businessman, the Editor of a Women's Magazine, the Doctor ex-rugby player. And their partners. It was the partners who had looked him up and down. Stared at his clothes.

Fuck them.

And now he simply sat there, a half-hearted auditor of other people's conversations, his mind trailing through memories of the period before Nagel, his Pretoria ascendancy, his relationship with Wendy. Mrs Cultural Attaché didn't say much. They formed an island of silence, she smiled sympathetically at him once or twice. He tasted the caterers' orange butternut soup, perfect, the spiral of cream a nice decorative touch. Garnishing had been the last great challenge to his culinary skill, before his life fell apart and his mother became his only dinner guest.

'. . . Exchange rate is a blessing in disguise. I don't want the rand to recover. But the government will have to do something about the trade agreement with the EU. The excise duties are killing us.'

Mrs Millionaire Businessman's Wife sat opposite him. She was very pretty, without a wrinkle, her cheeks rosy. Her husband sat two chairs further down, pale and tired and old. '. . . Move to the farm, I simply can't cope with the crime any longer. One lives in constant fear but Herman says he can't run the Group from Beaufort West,' she said to someone.

'And the police,' replied the Doctor, his voice deep and self-satisfied, 'steal as happily as everyone else.'

He felt the tension in his belly.

'It must be difficult to be a policeman today,' the coloured woman next to him said, softly and honestly. He looked at her, the eyes large and scared behind the glasses, wondered whether she had heard the Doctor's remark.

'It is,' he said and sipped the red wine, slowly.

'Do you think it will change?'

Good question, he thought. 'No. I don't think so.'

'Oh,' she said.

He drew breath to explain and stopped. Remembered that it wouldn't help.

That it had never helped. Even when he was still on the force and had tried to give some perspective to the figures – too little money, too few hands, too big a gap between the haves and the have-nots, too much politics, too many liberal laws, too much bad publicity, fuck, the publicity had frustrated him so much, the good work and successes on page seven, the mistakes and corruption on page one. Salaries that were a joke, that could never compensate for the working conditions, the long hours, the scorn. He had occasionally tried to explain but people didn't want to hear it. 'It's just the way it is,' he said.

The main dish was Malay mutton curry, steaming and flavourful and meltingly tender, he could taste the cook's pleasure in the making, wished he could meet him or her, ask how do you get the mutton so unbelievably tender. He had read somewhere that you left it to soak overnight in buttermilk, that it worked especially well with curries, made the taste even more subtle.

'It's van Heerden, not so?' the Doctor leant over the Business-woman's plate towards him, mouth still filled with food.

He nodded.

'What's your rank?'

'My what?'

'I heard you saying you were a policeman. What's your rank?'

'I'm no longer in the Force.'

The Doctor looked at him, nodded slowly and turned to the Cultural Attaché. 'Are you still a Western Province supporter, Achmat?'

'Yes, but it isn't the same as in your day, Chris.'

The Doctor forced hearty laughter. 'You make me sound like ancient history, Achmat. Sometimes feel like taking the togs out again, old sport.'

Old sport. Even if he wasn't a doctor, he would still be irritating.

Forget it, he thought. *Leave it be.* He concentrated on the food, placed rice and meat carefully on his fork, tasted the texture and the flavour, then a swallow of red wine, the waiters keeping the glasses filled, the decibels of the conversations around the table rising and rising, people laughing more heartily, more loudly, cheeks coloured rosily by the wine. He watched Hope Beneke, her head at an angle as she listened to and nodded at the Author, a middle-aged, bearded man wearing an earring. He wondered whether she was enjoying the party, it seemed like it, was she another Wendy? An athlete on the social track? She was more serious than Wendy, but so earnest, so focused, so ready to do the right thing, so Norman Vincent Peale, so . . . idealistic. *A practice for women.* As if they were special victims.

Everyone was a fucking victim. Special or otherwise.

Between dessert and coffee, just before the bomb exploded, the Businesswoman asked whether he had children. He said he wasn't married. 'I have two,' she said. 'A son and a daughter. They live in Canada.' He said it must be very cold there and the conversation died an uncomfortable death.

And then the Doctor fucked with Mozart.

The waiters were removing the dessert plates, coffee had already been served to some. A curious moment because the rest of the table was quiet and only the Doctor's strong, rich voice could be heard: he was complaining about a boring holiday in Austria, the unfriendly people, the over-commercialization, the exploitation of tourists, the dull entertainment.

'And what's it with them and Mozart?' he asked rhetorically and van Heerden couldn't help it, he said: 'He was an Austrian,' and he had suddenly had enough of this man and his views and his superiority.

'So was Waldheim and he was a Nazi,' said the Doctor, irritated by the interruption. 'But no matter where you go, it's Mozart. If it isn't the name of a restaurant, they play his music on street corners.'

'His music is very nice, Daddy,' said Mrs Doctor, two chairs away, soothingly.

'So is Abba's until you've heard it for the third time,' said the Doctor.

Van Heerden heard the galloping of the red bull in his ears.

'At the end of the day it all sounds the same. And there is no intellectual depth to his music. Compare *The Barber of Seville* with any of Wagner's works . . .'

'The *Barber* was Rossini,' said van Heerden, his voice a finely honed blade. 'Mozart wrote *The Marriage of Figaro*. A sequel to the *Barber*.'

'Nonsense,' said the Doctor.

'It's true,' said the Actress from the other side.

'It still doesn't give it more intellectual depth. It's still musical candyfloss.'

'Bullshit,' said van Heerden loudly and clearly and angrily and even the waiters came to a halt.

'Your language!' said the Doctor.

'Fuck you,' said van Heerden.

'What does a policeman know about music?' the Doctor, red in the face, eyes widened.

'As much as a doctor about intellectual depth, you cunt.'

'Zatopek!' It was Hope's voice, urgent, pleading but it made no difference.

'You Nazi,' said the Doctor, halfway up, his napkin falling off his lap.

And then van Heerden hit him as he rose, right fist against the head, a glancing blow, not a direct hit. For a moment the Doctor was off-balance but recovered quickly, swung towards van Heerden, but he was ready, hit him again, the Businesswoman of the Year shrieking and holding her head as she cowered between them. He struck the Doctor full on the nose with a right, hit again, against the mouth, felt teeth breaking, more women screaming, Hope's 'No, no, no' shrill and high and despairing. The doctor staggered back against the wall, his foot hooked onto the chair, van Heerden over him, lifting his arm for the last blow, white with anger, then someone held his arm, a calm, coaxing voice behind him. 'Steady on, slowly now,' murmured the Cultural Attaché, 'slowly now, he was only a centre.' He still pulled against the man's firm grip, looked down at the bloody face below him, the glassy eyes, 'Slowly now,' softly repeated, and he relaxed.

Deadly silence. He dropped his arm, moved his foot to regain his balance, looked up.

At the head of the table, almost upright, stood Kara-An Rousseau, an expression of complete sexual arousal on her face.

22

Sergeant Thomas 'Fires' van Vuuren was a caricature, a peripheral figure in my Sunnyside days, a brandy addict who exhibited the evidence of his passion with a map of blue veins on his face and a knob of a nose which he wore gracelessly, a man in his late fifties with a vast belly, unattractive and obtuse.

Of all the people at the station, he would have been the last on the list of my nominees of those who would have a lasting influence on my life. I hardly knew him.

In the police, as in any government organisation, there are a number of them, those rather pathetic people who get stuck at a certain rank because of some deficiency, sometimes blatant laziness or an unforgivable misdemeanour – the cannon fodder of bureaucracy who trundle down the slow track to retirement without haste or expectation. Sarge Fires was always around. I don't think we exchanged more than five words in my first two years.

I sat in the tearoom, swotting, my first set of questions for the promotion examination a month or so away. He came in, made himself coffee, dragged a chair to the table and tinkled the spoon loudly against the cup as he stirred.

'You're wasting your time with the sergeants' exam,' he said.

I looked up, surprised, saw his watery little blue eyes watching me attentively.

'Sarge?'

'You're wasting your time.'

I moved the books and folded my arms. 'Why, Sarge?'

'You're a clever boy, van Heerden. I've been watching you. You're not like most of them.'

He lit a cigarette, without filter, smelly tobacco, and checked the temperature of his coffee with a small sip. 'I saw your service file. Your were the top guy in the college. You read. You look at the shit in the cells and you see people and you think and you wonder.'

I was astonished.

He trickled the cigarette smoke through his nostrils, thrust his hand into his shirt pocket and took out a creased piece of paper, unfolded it and passed it to me across the table. It was a page from the police magazine *Servamus*.

Boost your career now!

Enrol now for for the BA (Police Science) degree at Unisa.

> Since 1972 the SAP and Unisa have offered a degree which is specifically aimed at professionalising your post with an academic background. This is a specialist three-year course with Police Science as a compulsory major subject – and *one* of the following as a second major subject: Criminology, Public Administration, Psychology, Sociology, Political Science and Communication Science.

An address and telephone numbers followed.

I finished reading and looked up at Sergeant Fires van Vuuren, at the red hair that he had allowed to grow long on one side to enable him to comb the strands over the ever-increasing bald patch.

'You must do that,' he said through another mouthful of smoke. 'These other little exams,' waving at my original reading matter, 'are for policemen like Broodryk. And the like.'

Then he stood up, killed the cigarette in the ashtray, took his coffee and walked out. I called 'Thanks, Sarge,' after him but I don't know whether he heard me.

Over the years I would often think about that moment in the Sunnyside station's tearoom. About Thomas van Vuuren and his mysterious interest and encouragement. The 'Broodryk' to whom he had referred was an adjutant in the terminology of the old ranks, a big, brusque, ambitious man who would later acquire notoriety as one of the most merciless operators at the infamous Vlakplaas, who had, in Sunnyside, already shown his willingness to physically abuse those arrested.

Fires van Vuuren never again tried to speak to me. Once or twice I tried to look him up after I had registered as a student at Unisa and started my studies but he had withdrawn behind his rampart of obtuseness, as if our conversation had never happened. What had motivated him to draw my service file (without permission, more likely than not) and to tear out the magazine page carefully and bring it to me, I'll never know.

I can only speculate that the truth lay somewhere in the contrast he had drawn between Broodryk and me. Was van Vuuren's weakness that he saw criminals as human beings? Had his physical unattractiveness hidden a sensitivity that had to be deadened by brandy so that he could get through his daily task?

He died a year or two later of a heart attack, alone in his house. His funeral was small and sad. A son was there, a single member of the family at the graveside, with a set face and a measure of relief, I thought. And the conventional wisdom of his colleagues was 'It was the booze,' said with much shaking of heads,

And the evening after my first graduation ceremony, I quietly drank a toast to him. Because he had given me two gifts: direction. And self-respect. I know it sounds dramatic but one must draw the comparison accurately, rather like those kitsch slimming ads that use the 'Before' and 'After' pictures (often touched up) to convince. After two years in Sunnyside I was firmly on the road to nowhere, frustrated, unstimulated, professionally at sea, unwilling to admit that I had made a mistake in my career choice. The police, more than any other occupation, has a way of blunting one's sensibilities, both by the endless routine and the nature of the work, the constant exposure to the dregs, the scum, the aberrant, the socially and economically deprived and, sometimes, the purely evil.

Thomas van Vuuren had opened a door in this maze.

As I advanced academically, the stimulation and focus would systematically act as the deus ex machina to haul me out of the professional quicksand. I started liking myself.

Oh, the psychology of positive feedback.

'Your essays show singular writing and dialectic skills. It is a pleasure to receive them.'

'Your insight into this subject is impressive and considerably above the level of what is expected from an undergraduate. Congratulations.'

What the lecturers didn't realize and I, on a subconscious level, did, was that the course was a lifeline. I studied at every possible moment, read more than necessary, analysed. I chose Police Science, Criminology and Psychology as my main subjects, unwilling to give up any of the three. I achieved (not without self-satisfaction) distinctions in all three, every year. I was promoted, even though the promotion was due to my passing the sergeants' examination, and transferred to the Pretoria station. The three stripes meant very little to me. I had far higher ideals.

My mother was overjoyed with her son's new-found focus, with the fact that I was acquiring an 'education'.

Day 4

Sunday, 9 July

23

She knocked on his door at seven in the morning and when he opened it, his hair tousled and his eyes sleep-filled, she walked in out of the dark, the red mark on her cheek bright from lack of sleep and the anger in her, the powerlessness because she couldn't understand him.

She stood with her back against the grey wall while he remained at the open front door. 'Shut the door,' she said. 'It's cold.'

He sighed, closed the door, walked to a chair, sat down.

'You're my employer, Hope. You can fire me. It's your right.'

'Why did you hit him, van Heerden?'

'Because I wanted to.'

She dropped her chin onto her chest. Slowly shook her head from side to side, silent.

The silence spread through the room.

'Do you want coffee?' he asked without any tone of hospitality.

Her head was still moving from side to side, she looked at the running shoes on her feet, looking for words. 'No, I don't want coffee. I want answers.'

He said nothing.

'I'm trying to understand, van Heerden. Since you left me there last night with a bleeding man lying next to the table and simply walked out and drove off, I've been trying to understand how your mind works. You were . . .'

'Is that why you're angry? Because I left you there?'

She lifted her eyes to his, silenced him with a look. When she spoke again, her voice was even softer. 'You were a servant of justice, van Heerden. According to all reports a good one. In the past few days I've had enough experience of you to come to the conclusion that you're an intelligent man. Someone who understands causality. Someone who has the capacity to realize that action and consequence cannot be separated, cannot be restricted to those immediately involved. That's what the whole legal system is about, van Heerden. To protect the community against the wider implications. Because there are always wider implications.'

'Have you come to fire me, Hope?'

She didn't hesitate for a moment, would not be driven off course.

'What I can't understand, van Heerden, is that you give yourself the right to hit someone, to wreak your own infantile rage on a defenceless person without giving a thought to the other nineteen people there.'

'Defenceless? He wasn't defenceless. He was a provincial rugby player. And he was a cunt.'

'Do you think it makes you more of a man if you swear, van Heerden? Do you think it makes you strong?'

'Fuck you, Hope. I never asked you to like me. I am what I am. I don't owe anyone anything. You have no right to come into my house, to tell me how bad I am. I hit the cunt because he deserved it. He spent the entire evening looking for it. With his fucking superiority.'

'I don't have the right? Are you the one with all the rights? To go to someone else's house as a guest, as someone who needs Kara-An's help for your work, and then attack one of her friends like a barbarian because you didn't like his attitude? Your fists told him how bad he was. That was your right. But when I do it to you in a reasonably civilized manner, you're suddenly touchy. Where's your sense of fairness, van Heerden?'

He sank back in his chair. 'I told you. I'm bad.'

And then the mark flamed blood-red, a glow that spread over

her entire face. She leant forward, away from the wall, her hands gesticulating as she spoke. 'Ah, the great excuse, the answer to everything: "I'm bad". Extrapolate that, you coward. Just think for a moment about a community in which we all do as we please as long as we admit we're bad. We can murder and rape and deceive and assault, because we're bad. It explains everything, it justifies everything, it excuses everything.'

He rested his chin on his hand, his fingers almost covering his mouth. 'You wouldn't understand.'

'I *don't* understand. That's the whole point. But I'm here because I want to understand. If I have insight into what you are, I can at least try to understand. To comprehend. But you don't want to tell me anything. You live behind the barrier of your senseless excuses, your rationalization based on pathetic arguments. Speak to me, van Heerden. Tell me why you're like this. Then I'll be able to understand. Or at least have some sympathy.'

'Why do you want to know, Hope? What's with you? What does it matter? Next week, when this van As affair is over, you'll be rid of me. Then you can carry on your practice for women, the sad victims of society, and you need never think of me again. So, what does it matter?'

'Last night your behaviour involved me and nineteen other people. You tainted my memory with an experience I didn't ask for. You upset me. You humilated me because the others assumed you were there with me. I was involved by association. I'm now part of your behaviour. That is why, if you don't have the courage to ask yourself questions, I'll do it for you. Because I've been given the right to know, to try and understand.'

He snorted, wrinkled his nose. 'Your reputation as the great female attorney has been dented because you were there with me. And you don't like that.'

'You want to believe that, van Heerden. That everyone is as selfish as you are.'

She walked across to him, her feet soundless in the running shoes, sat on the coffee table in front of him, her face almost touching his, her voice urgent, her words boiling up, tumbling out of her.

'I voted for the National Party, van Heerden. Before ninety-two. In two elections. Because I believed separate development was right. Fair. Believed like my father and my mother. Like my friends. And their parents. Like my teachers and lecturers. Like the whole white population of Bloemfontein. I believed the local Afrikaans newspaper. And Afrikaans radio and TV. I questioned nothing because I saw blacks as we all saw them. As people who believed in witchcraft and the *tokoloshe* and the spirits of their forefathers, who worked in the house and garden and fetched the rubbish and smelled of Lifebuoy soap. I accompanied my father when he took Emily to the location and I looked at the dirty streets and the small, gardenless houses and I knew separate development was right because they were so unlike us. Why didn't they garden? How could people have so little pride? Homelands. If they murdered so easily, let them do it in Thaba' Nchu or Mafikeng or Umtata. I shuddered every time they planted a bomb or shot people in a restaurant. I was angry . . . shake your head as much as you like, van Heerden, but now you're going to listen. I was angry with the rest of the world every time they applied sanctions or criticized us because I thought they didn't know, didn't understand. They didn't know *our* black people. They thought ours were like theirs, Sidney Poitier and Eddie Murphy and Whoopi Goldberg. Ours were different. Destroyers and wreckers, always angry and unfriendly. Ours spoke languages that no one understood. Theirs spoke the same American English as they did. And wore beautiful clothes and played Othello in the movies. And then ninety-two arrived and I was scared, van Heerden, because now they would take everything and make a mess of it so that the entire country looked like dirty townships. My fear made me search for reasons why it shouldn't happen. No logical thought, no open-mindedness, no sense of fairness. Fear. And then I found a book about Mandela, an old biography, written by some Dutch woman or other and I read it and it was like being reborn. Do you know what it feels like to change your opinion of yourself, your views, your people, your parents, your leaders, your background, your history – all within two days? To realize everything you believed, and believed in, was wrong, twisted, without insight, even evil. But I'm proud of one thing, van Heerden. That I had the ability to do it.To open my mind to truth. To see, after being blind for so long. And after I'd assimilated and processed the guilt and the humiliation, after working through my own anger and the anger I felt against all the whites who had assisted in my seduction, I came to a decision. Never again would I make a judgement based on a lack of exposure and knowledge and insight and comprehension. I would search for truth. I wouldn't judge people because of their colour, beliefs or actions before I understood why they were like that. And if you think that I'm going to drop it, that I'll believe your infantile excuses, that I'll be thrown off course by your fencing and flight, you're making a big mistake.'

She sat in front of him, her finger emphasizing each point, centimetres away from his nose and then she laughed at herself, a short derisory sound.

Slowly she released her breath.

'*Talk* to me.' The first word almost pleading.

He looked blankly at the wall.

'Our view of the world differs too much, Hope.'

'How do you know? You don't know me.'

'I know enough, Hope. I know enough of your kind to know. You think life is fair. You think that if you try hard enough, try to live a good life, everything will be fine. You think it's contagious. You think if you try, others will do the same, one after another, a wave of goodness that will cover all the evil in the world. I know you because I was like that once, Hope. No, I was better. I reached my *lucidum intervallum* long before ninety-two. At three in the morning I looked through the bars of of the Pretoria police station cell and among the fifteen or sixteen black people in there, drunks and knife wielders and rapists and burglars, I saw a man sitting on the edge of the steel bench with a book of Breyten Breytenbach poetry open in his hands. A black man. I was the lieutenant, Hope, I was second-in-command. I had him taken out and brought to my office. I closed the door and talked to him. About poetry at first. He was a teacher in the black township, Mamelodi. His Afrikaans was better than mine. He was arrested because he was on foot in a white suburb after midnight, on his way to the railway station, twelve kilometres away. He'd been visiting a professor who taught at the University of South Africa. By invitation. Because he had to discuss the progress of his thesis for his Master's degree on Breyten. They locked him up because what was a black man doing in a posh white suburb at that time of night? That was my moment of truth. It changed me. And suddenly I was the poor man's Afrikaner Gandhi who wanted to bring the message of passive resistance to the tearoom, the bedroom and the living room. In a civilized manner. I made a point of starting conversations with petrol attendants, office cleaners and road-café waiters. Joking and sympathetic, I focused on them as people. I knew we differed culturally but different isn't wrong, different is merely different. Basically we're all human, Hope. I knew that.'

He looked at her. Her eyes were on him, stunned: he was speaking to her, he was speaking like an adult, like an intelligent, live human being.

'And that is the core. I thought that we were all good. Most of us. And let me tell you, that was a giant step, a great achievement for a cop. I made the big mistake of believing we were all good because *I* was good. Inherently, naturally.'

Then he was quiet. He sat in the worn chair in front of her and looked at her, moved his eyes over the contours of her face, familiar by now, saw the intensity with which she listened. He felt she was too near and he got up slowly, careful to keep his body turned away from her, avoiding physical contact. His mouth was dry. He took the few steps to the kitchen corner, switched on the kettle, turned. Her eyes were still fixed on him.

'My mother is an artist. That's her work.' He pointed to the wall. 'She creates beautiful paintings. She looks at the world and she makes it more beautiful on canvas. I think it's her way of distancing herself from the evil that is in all of us. She says one must look at our whole history if we want to understand people. She says we're retrospectively short-sighted, we only look back to the Greeks and the Romans, some even look back as far as Moses but she says we must look back far further. She says that sometimes when she's working in her studio and it's quiet, she hears a sound and she feels all the tiny muscles in her ear contracting to turn the shell in the direction of the sound, like a cat's. She says that's her proof, her reminder that we mustn't forget to look back as far as the animal world. But even my mother won't admit that we're bad. She cannot. Just like you. Because you believe that you're good. And you are. Because you have never had the opportunity to let the evil escape, because life has never given you the choice.'

The water boiled.

He turned away, took out two mugs. *Coffee*, he thought. The planet around which his and Hope Beneke's social contact revolved.

She had courage, he thought. To come here. No one else had ever done it.

'Sugar and milk?'

'Only milk, please.'

He took the carton out of the fridge, poured milk into her mug, carried the two coffees. She moved from the table to a chair opposite his. She wanted to say a thousand things but she didn't want to put this miracle of an eloquent, new, intelligent, other, strange van Heerden at risk with the wrong phrase.

He sat down. 'You see, Hope . . .'

The telephone rang. He looked at his watch, stood up, picked up the phone.

'Van Heerden.'

'Could I speak to Mike Tyson?' It was Kara-An.

'Are you looking for Hope?'

'No, Mike, I'm looking for you. I'm on the Morning Star road and I can't find your house. I'm looking for directions.'

What did she want? 'I don't know where you are.'

'I'm in front of a gate. Next to the gate is a sign with the words *Table Stables*. I presume it refers to the mountain, not a piece of furniture. Otherwise the owner should have his head read.'

'The turn-off is a hundred metres further on.'

'How will I know it when I see it?'

'There are two white pillars. One on each side of the entrance.'

'No cute little name?'

'No.'

'Didn't think so, Mike. I'll be there in a minute.'

'Come to the little house, not the big one.'

'Not the one on the prairie, I trust.'

'What?'

'Never mind, Mike, you're a boxer, not an intellectual.' Then the line went dead. He replaced the phone.

'That was Kara-An.'

'Is she on her way?'

'She's here. Down the road.'

Hope said nothing, merely nodded.

'What does she want?' he asked.

'I haven't the vaguest idea.'

Then they saw headlights approaching the gate.

If she had a penchant for swearing, Hope Beneke thought, she would have employed one of van Heerden's words with a vengeance.

24

The two letters arrived within a week of one another. One was an appointment to Brixton Murder and Robbery, the other offered new, unexpected crossroads.

> Dear Zatopek
>
> I'm not sure whether you read the Careers section in the Sunday newspapers, therefore this letter is to inform you that the Department of Police Science has grown and the increasing number of students necessitates the creation of a post for a lecturer. Applications for the post are being considered.
>
> Best wishes
>
> Cobus Taljaard (Prof.)
>
> PS When are you coming to discuss your Master's?

How does one make such a choice? Not based on salary because there wasn't a huge difference. Not by looking at the potential professional stimulus because both posts offered unique challenges. Working conditions? It depends on what you like.

I believe that I eventually made the decision I did because I could see myself as a lecturer, because it would make me feel even better about myself, the teacher (in contrast to the executive role), the cerebral world. The potential of a title with so much more weight than a rank. Doctor, one day. Still later, Professor.

During my studies in psychology, I developed the theory that most of the decisions we make, if not all, are to feed the ego. The choice of a car, clothes, a suburb, friends, favourite drinks, all are aimed at creating a specific image for the world, to announce 'This is who I am', so that the world's perception can become a mirror to reflect ourselves and, like Narcissus, make us love the reflection. I started working at the University of South Africa's Department of Police Science in February 1989. At the same time I moved to a larger, better flat in Sunnyside. And changed my battered Nissan for an almost new Volkswagen Golf. I was unashamedly and irresistibly on my way to the top.

All I still needed was the Big L.

There were women in my life. The brief interactions of the first years in Pretoria systematically changed to longer relationships. When I look back, I must admit, with a certain degree of shame, that, all in all, they were relationships of convenience. It wasn't conscious exploitation, more a natural way to pass the time until the Damascene experience of Love happened to me, until that intense, wonderful moment when I would look at the face of a woman and know that she was the One.

They all accused me of being afraid of being tied down. ('Commit' was a favourite word, taken I think, from magazines like *Cosmo* and *Femina*, articles with headings like 'Ten Ways to Make Your Relationship Last.') And they were right. I tried to halt deepening relationships with weak excuses ('We don't have to be in such a hurry. Can't we get to know one another better?') and their duration was often directly linked to the levels of patience.

Was I wrong? Given the rules of the game of love, was it unethical of me to use the togetherness, the regular sex, the availability without committing myself?

I'm not always entirely sure. I never lied. I never promised eternal love, evidence of deeper devotion than I was prepared to give. Because not one of them was the One.

But the one thing a woman wants to hear more than 'I love you' are the words that pave the way to marriage.

I'm not sexist. I grant women every possible right they want to appropriate for themselves. To be perfectly honest, I often and easily admit that women do many things much better than men. Especially in the professional field. They have more sympathy, more tact, they're not burdened with the curse of testosterone-driven aggression, they have a natural talent for differentiating between problems in the workplace and the contaminating politics of ambition and (male) ego. But that they're positively *driven* in the identification of a companion for life and the processing of a relationship through all its conventional stages to down-the-aisle-and-up-to-the-altar, I can attest to from first-hand experience.

There was a woman I took to a drive-in on a first date, before I made sergeant, a pretty, decent Afrikaans girl from some small town, Colesberg or Brandfort or Colenso. And halfway through the forgettable film we began necking and tested the physical milestones one after the other – held hands, arm around her shoulder, careful kissing to open-mouthed, tongue-searching kisses, my hand on her breast, blouse unbuttoned, bra off, caressing of hard nipples, hand sliding down. And just there she stopped me with a firm hand and a breathless 'No'. I could hear her ragged breathing, feel her galloping heartbeat – she was, to use the unworthy, chauvinistically popular word, hot.

But the promised land under the elastic of the panties remained out of reach.

'Why not?' I asked yearningly.

'Because we're not going steady.'

Commitment. That would be my passport to Paradise.

I often speculated on the nature of women's sexual morality because I didn't think I'd ever understand it. But the aspects that would fascinate me above all were the conditions they attached to the granting of sex. Love's social contract. I understood that it served as a defence mechanism against the overriding urge of the man, as my mother had put it, to sow his seed. But I'll never forget Miss Colesberg's or wherever's choice of words. Not 'I don't love you'.

'Because we're not going steady.'

Commitment was the currency, the toll to be paid on the road to intimacy. But the most interesting aspect of this conditional morality were the lines drawn. There were women, like the girl from Colesberg, who drew the line those few frustrating centimetres below the navel. Some even declared the breasts a no man's land if there was no possibility of a long-term relationship. Others shifted the border lower and you were allowed to touch the garden of delights but not push your prick into it. You were allowed to kiss and caress and lick and give your fingers free play but if you wanted the portals to open for Mr Delivery, you had to show your passport.

Commitment.

Wendy.

That's where I should be going.

With Wendy I at least thought she might be the One. Briefly.

Cute Wendy.

She came into my office at the University of South Africa while I was still unpacking my boxes, with her cute little body, her blonde bob around her cute little face, a little bundle of bouncing energy and she opened her little red mouth and spoke to me incessantly for four years.

I think Wendy looked at me that day and decided that I was what she wanted.

'We're going to be neighbours, I'm in English Lit across the passage, you must be the new Police Science guy, my Afrikaans is not very good, I come from Maritzburg and I can tell you, Pretoria is a shock, my God, I haven't introduced myself, I'm Wendy Brice.' She extended her small hand, gave mine a firm shake and peeped at me from under her blonde bob like a little girl, a gesture I would get to know very well in the following months and years.

Wendy was an organizer. She constantly reorganized her own life. And she organized other people's lives, often without their knowing it. She knew where she was heading, she was focused. Wendy was a realist. She knew her academic limitations, knew she was a woman in the male world of the university and that the glass ceiling of Senior Lecturer would be her highest step up the ladder. But her aspirations were higher. Different. I won't say it was a conscious and calculated decision of 'If I can't be a professor, I'll marry a man who'll become one' but Wendy had the larger details of her life mapped out. 'I want to get married and have children, Zet. Your children,' ended her hair-peeping plea in an endless series of arguments about my lack of commitment.

The 'Zet' she had heard from my mother and she had leaped on it, like an eagle pouncing on a rabbit.

Wendy was mad about my mother, about her eccentricity, her status as an artist, her encouragement of me in my career. 'I share your sentiments, Mrs V.'

My mother disliked the *Mrs V.* She disliked Wendy too, but as usual was too tactful to say so.

Like most beautiful women, Wendy was also a manipulative operator who couldn't resist the power of her curves. She used them and her pouty little mouth and her fringe-peeping look and her little-girl attitude. Never so flagrantly that it could be pinned down. But subtly, like a pickpocket.

Despite all my retrospective cynicism about Wendy, I was in love for the first few months of our relationship. Because she was so cute and the first woman with whom I could discuss poems and books – from whom I could learn. And Wendy shared her English Lit with more enthusiasm than she shared her body.

Our sex life was peculiar.

At first there was a cerebral relationship, an intellectual discovery, but I must admit that I was attracted to the little body from the start, the hourglass shape of little breasts and waist and hips, the cute little rounded bottom, her legs faultless miniature sculptures – she was small, but a perfect pocket-sized Venus.

Unfortunately, the promise that her body held would remain just that – a promise.

Even now I don't know whether it was manipulation or a real lack of interest in sex. I had to work for every penetration, had to pay dearly for every orgasm. An hour's foreplay sometimes led to nothing and when she made the full sacrifice, she followed it up almost immediately after my climax with a discussion about my career – generally the lack of progress, Wendy yacking away, never a direct attack but a traffic jam of speech that took the longest possible time to get from point A to point B.

But the biggest frustration was her control during the sexual act, her determined clinging to the civilized side of total surrender, her sounds small and cute and premeditated. She never fell into the abyss of passion to lose herself in the primitive, the animal pleasure of it.

I would only understand the full story behind the Brice interest some years after our first meeting. She had heard, before I joined Police Science, of the academic *wunderkind* who was on his way. Professor Cobus Taljaard made no secret of his admiration for my ability and evidently often aired these views to his neighbour in English Lit. Which also made me wonder with how much calculation she had planned that first chatty entry into my life.

The fact of the matter was that my career wasn't on hold. It advanced – quickly, according to me. I found my feet in the preparation of lectures that had to be sent to extramural students, the reading and correcting of papers, the giving of occasional lectures. Carefully and under the watchful eye of the Prof I started to publish and tackled my Master's degree. But Wendy thirsted for titles, (wife of) a doctor, a professor. And a Master's degree was a long way from either.

So she concentrated on two things. Engagement. And Work. All our conversations, all her statements and opinions and little parables eventually came around to one or both of these themes. It was a game, it was the engine room that supplied the energy for our relationship, the dynamo that kept us together for four years – me fencing and delaying and parrying, she accusing and teasing and slowly, systematically closing the pincers, demolishing the excuses one after another.

And yet: it wasn't her putting her foot down or making an ultimatum that ended our relationship. The last straw had nothing to do with her. It was the ghost of Baby Marnewick that came to seduce me.

25

Kara-An Rousseau wore jeans, a white shirt and a blue sweater and looked as though she had had eight hours' sleep.

'The doctor is on the warpath, Mike. He wants to take you to court. He's after your blood. His ego, my friend, was hurt far more than his face.'

'Mike?' Hope Beneke asked.

'Didn't he tell you? Like in Tyson.'

'Forget it, Hope has already tried the crapping-from-on-high bit.'

'He even sounds like Tyson don't you think?' she said to Hope. Then she turned to van Heerden. 'I take it that an apology is out of the question?'

'A woman with insight. A first.'

Hope Beneke saw that he was back in the aggressive shell, the drawbridge raised. She wanted to weep.

'Didn't think you were the type for whom "sorry" was an easy word. That's why I like you so much. But you have two problems, Mike. And I'm the only one who can help you with both.'

He snorted deep in his throat.

'Number one – I believe that I'll be able to convince the good doctor to drop his litigation plans. Not only will I remind him that it will entail very unwelcome publicity for both of us, which we don't need as professional people. But as a last resort I can also remind him of the night he arrived on my doorstep raging drunk and without his wife's knowledge, to tell me how much he wanted me. That should heal the physician, don't you think?

'Your second problem is that of publicity in a certain murder investigation. If you are still able to cast your mind that far back, Mike, you'll remember that I'm the one who was approached for help. Two good reasons for loving Kara-An.'

He looked at her, appraisingly, surprised by the change in her from last night's good hostess to this . . . phenomenon, totally in control. Why, he wondered, this sudden demonstration of power? He made calculations, adding the Kara-An of this morning to the last sight he'd had of her before he left the previous evening, the beautiful woman in the red dress intensely stimulated by a fist fight, a shadow which passed quickly, fleetingly.

Premonitions of evil.

'Fuck you,' he said.

'Ha, predictable to the last. I didn't expect you to fall on your knees, Mike. Your ego is too brittle for that. That's why I've come to sow a little thought. Both the doctor and the media have a price. The story of your life, in writing, when this business of the will is over, in exchange for peace on the medical front. And front-page copy tomorrow morning.' She walked to the door, opened it. 'I don't suppose I have to remind you that time isn't necessarily on your side.' She walked out. 'Bye, Hope,' were the last words they heard before the door closed.

There was silence in the room, only the wind through the trees and the sound of Kara-An's car driving off. Another BMW, he guessed. The younger woman's universal cure for penis envy. The Mercedes would come later, at about fifty-five, when she no longer wanted to look young, just dignified. He looked at Hope Beneke. She had drawn up her legs and was hugging them, her face almost hidden. As if she knew it was all over.

It was.

Because if Kara-An Rousseau thought she could blackmail him, she was out of her mind.

The silence between them expanded. Eventually Hope got up. 'Just do me one favour,' she said quietly.

He looked at her.

'Don't bring the advance back again. Keep it.'

She walked to the door, opened it and walked out without closing it behind her.

He felt his temper rising. Her whole attitude insinuated that the fuck-up was his fault. As if Kara-An's absurd demands were reasonable. The 'curing' of the doctor had nothing to do with the Wilna van As issue. It was Kara-An who wanted to connect the two, who wanted to make the consequences of one dependent on the other. Which was so unreasonable that one didn't need a law degree to work it out. It was like . . .

He felt the cold wind against his back, got up to close the door, saw Hope's BMW moving down the gravel road, his mother riding up, reining in next to the car. Horse-riding in this weather, it was going to rain in a minute, the clouds a blackish grey, the wind sharp. They were too far away, he couldn't even hear their voices, what did they have to say to one another? The rear lights of the BMW went on, Hope turned the car and followed his mother to the big house.

He slammed the door.

She must leave his mother alone. She mustn't interfere.

What did they have to say to one another?

Fuck it. He had laundry to do.

He was hanging up wet clothes in the bathroom when he heard the door open. He knew it was his mother.

'Where are you, Zet?'

'Here.'

She came in, still in her riding clothes, her nose and ears red with cold.

'You musn't ride in this weather, Ma.'

'You can't hang up a shirt like that. Wait, let me do it.' She lifted the shirt off the shower rail. 'Bring me a hanger.'

Obediently he walked to the bedroom to fetch a hanger.

'No wonder your clothes are in such a state. You must learn to look after them.'

'Ma, I'm thirty-eight . . .'

'One wouldn't say so if one had been a doctor last night. Shift that basket nearer. I'm going to put this stuff in the tumble dryer.'

'Ma . . .'

'Zet, you're a man. That's why I overlook many things but sooner or later you'll have to buy decent stuff. You can't do your laundry by hand for the rest of your life.'

He dragged the laundry basket towards her. She took the wet laundry from the bath, put it in the basket.

'But I'm not going to iron it.'

'No, Ma.'

'What did you do last night?'

'It sounds as if you already know.'

She didn't reply, merely filled the basket with laundry.

'Pick up the basket and bring it home. I want to talk to you.' She turned and walked out. He knew that straight-backed walk. He hadn't seen it for a long time.

He didn't want to talk to her about these things.

'Fuck,' he said quietly and picked up the basket.

A fine rain was falling. The wind suddenly dropped as he walked to the big house. The house his mother had built. After she had had the original one demolished because she didn't want to live in such a monstrosity, a Spanish villa, South African style. She watched the bulldozers do their work and later told him it had been one of her most pleasurable experiences in the past decade.

She could have bought a smallholding next to the Berg River somewhere between Paarl and Stellenbosch, she had the money, but she had chosen this one, on the flat stretch behind Blouberg, in the Port Jackson belt between the sea and the N7 'so that I can go to the mountains when I need them', whatever that might mean. And had her house built, simple white lines, large windows, spacious rooms.

And the stables.

He had been surprised by the horses.

'I've always wanted to,' she said.

He lived there in one of the original buildings, perhaps an old tenant farmer's house, that he had half-heartedly restored at her insistence when he didn't go back to work.

He carried the basket into the kitchen where she was waiting impatiently. He saw the tray next to the sink, empty coffee mugs, two of them, and rusks in a bowl. His mother and Hope Beneke.

Intimate.

She opened the door of the tumble dryer, loaded the machine.

'You know I've never said anything, Zatopek.'

'Ma?' The use of his full name wasn't a good sign.

'For five years I've said nothing.' She straightened, stretched, her hands on her hips, pressed the buttons of the machine, pulled a chair away from the large stinkwood table and sat down.

'Sit down, Zatopek.'

He gave a deep sigh and sat down at the table. The tumble dryer increased its speed and sang its monotonous tune in the room.

'I said nothing out of respect for you. As an adult. And because I don't know everything. I don't know what happened that evening with Nagel . . .'

'Ma.'

She held up her hand, eyes closed.

Memories flooded him, his mother in her role as disciplining parent, he knew the mannerisms so well, but it had been so many years. He saw her as she had been in Stilfontein, saw the erosion of age, compassion filled him, she had suddenly grown so old.

'I must do something, Zatopek. I must say something. You're my child. Your age cannot change that. But I don't know what to say. It's been five years. And . . . you can't get over it.'

'I'm over it, Ma.'

'You're not.'

He said nothing.

'My mother believed in emotional blackmail, Zatopek. She would've sat here now and asked "Do you know you're breaking a mother's heart? Don't you care about my feelings?" I'll never do that to you. How everything makes me feel has nothing to do with the issue. And to give you a sermon won't help either because you're an intelligent man. You know that the sense one makes of life, the amount you grow as a human being is in your own hands. You know you have choices.'

'Yes, Ma.'

'And one of the choices is to see a psychologist, Zatopek.'

He looked at his hands.

'As I have it from Hope, there is another choice you have to exercise today.'

'I'm not going to be involved in that stupid blackmail, Ma.'

'Do the right thing, Zet. That's all I ask.'

'The right thing?'

'Yes, my child, the right thing.' She looked at him, her gaze, her eyes, intense. He looked away.

She got up. 'I'm going to have a bath. You have a great deal to think about.'

You can't get over it.

He lay stretched out on his bed, his hands behind his head, briefly aware that this bed, this position, represented forty to fifty per cent of his time in the past few years. His mother's words in his head – she had unleashed the hounds again, she didn't even know what 'it' was. She thought (as his colleagues and friends had thought then, when they still cared) that 'it' meant exaggerated self-blame about the death of Nagel. Because he had missed his target in that life-changing moment and the suspect, the murderer of seventeen prostitutes, the Red Ribbon Executioner had hit Nagel, once, twice. Nagel who dropped without a sound, blood and tissue against the wall, a moment caught in his memory forever. And then he hit the target, from fear, not revenge, from fear of dying and he hit the target, over and over and over and over, suddenly the top marksman for the first time in his life. Saw the Executioner staggering back, drop, fired until his Z88 was empty, crept to Nagel, faceless Nagel, cradled the shattered head in his hands. Nagel who still breathed, each halting breath spraying blood over his white shirt. He saw life leaking out of Nagel and screamed to the heavens, a deep animal sound, because in that moment he knew, with absolute, overwhelming certainty that nothing would ever be the same again, the sound erupting from the centre of his body, from his very essence, as he roared to the sky.

The others found him like that, on his knees with Nagel's shattered head in his hands, Nagel's blood on his clothes and the tears running down his cheeks and they thought he was crying about Nagel and comforted him and loosened his fingers and led him away and comforted him with deep admiration for his loyalty, for his professional love for a comrade, supported him in the days and weeks that followed and when, eventually, he said he wasn't coming back, enfolded him in their understanding: he had been too deeply hurt, too traumatized, it happened, they understood, it happened and it was a good thing, it showed policemen also had feelings, he testified to that.

He had deceived them. Them and his mother.

The truth, the whole truth, lay deeper, far deeper, that moment in the alleyway merely the tip of the iceberg, the bloated body of deceit hidden under the sea of lies.

But he had recovered from 'it'. Worked through 'it'. Found himself on the other side, systematically, two, almost three years later, when the pain of the truth was contained and only self-knowledge remained. His self-knowledge and the extrapolation, that nothing mattered, that no one mattered, that all were animals, manipulative primitive beings who struggled for survival under the thin, artificial layer of civilization.

'It' changed him, that was what his mother didn't understand. And what Hope Beneke didn't understand. Gave him an insight that they didn't have.

Everyone was evil. Most of them didn't know it yet.

And now his mother wanted him to do the right thing.

The right thing was to survive. To make certain that no one fucked with you.

The doctors.

Nagel had still lived in the ambulance, in the hospital.

They worked on him behind closed doors and came out and with a shrug of their shoulders said no, he didn't have a chance, explained his injuries with big words, those fucking big words with which they reduced you from human being to patient, big words to explain the shattered head and the hole in the chest. But they saved the Red Ribbon Executioner, took van Heerden's lead out of him and fastened him to their machines, pumped fluids into him, sewed and closed and let him live and Nagel died in that cold, white-tiled place, the last life going out of his eyes and he had stood outside with the man's blood on his shirt and wanted to scream because he had to drive to . . .

The tip of the iceberg.

And now his mother wanted him to do the right thing.

The right thing was to say to Kara-An Rousseau fuck you and your petty show of power, I won't be manipulated. And to tell Hope Beneke that her good fight was useless, the issue was dead and Wilna van As would survive without a million, life would go on and a hundred years from now no one would even know about the existence of such insignificant souls.

Nothing he did would make a difference.

Except, maybe, putting Kara-An Rousseau in her place.

She wasn't the only one who could play at that game.

But to what purpose?

His mother and Hope Beneke. Probably had a nice chat about him over the coffee and rusks.

Odd that they'd found one another so quickly from here, down the road.

Just a moment or two's conversation at the BMW and suddenly a visit.

Strange.

And now his mother expected.

The one person whom he really owed.

There was only one thing to do.

Deceive.

'Kara-An, this is Hope,' she said on the telephone.

'Hi.'

'I would like to know why you did it.'

A laugh sounded at the other end. 'I didn't think you'd understand, Hope.'

'I'm prepared to try.'

'With due respect, Hope, you're out of your league.'

'My league is Wilna van As. She has nothing to do with the latest developments.'

'It sounds as if you don't think our Mike is going to accept the offer.'

'Please, Kara-An.'

'I'm not the one you should beg, angel.'

She suddenly didn't know what to say.

'I have to go. There's someone at the front door. Strength to your elbow, Hope.' And the line went dead.

'What do you really want?' he asked as she opened the door.

For a moment there was astonishment, then she smiled. 'Come in, Zatopek van Heerden. What a wonderful surprise.' She closed the door behind him, pulled him roughly towards her, put her hands behind his head and kissed him hard on the mouth, her fingers pulling his hair, her body full of little urgent movements pressing him against the door, then he shoved her away and said 'Fuck you' and she stood in front of him, her lipstick smudged and she gasped and she laughed and he said, 'You're sick'.

'I knew you would understand.'

'And bad.'

'Just like you. But stronger. Much stronger.'

'I have a counter-offer.'

'Tell me.'

'Fuck the doctor. He can lay a charge. This is just between the two of us.'

'What's with you and doctors, Zatopek?'

'I'll give you what you want. For the publicity. Purely for the publicity.'

'But only when it's all over?'

'Yes.'

'Can I trust you?'

'No.'

'And if the story of your life isn't all I want?'

'You want me to hurt you, Kara-An.'

'Yes.'

'I saw you last night.'

'I know.'

'You need help.'

She laughed once, a single barking sound which filled the entrance hall. 'And you're going to help me, Zatopek van Heerden?'

'Do you accept my counter-offer?'

'On one condition.'

'What?'

'If you shove me away again . . .'

'Yes?'

'Don't hold back, van Heerden. Let all that rage out.'

26

Sometime during the routine academic years, I took part, late one night, in one of those senseless conversations that people have when they've had just enough to drink to lose their embarrassment at talking utter nonsense. The others taking part have long been forgotten, the proposer of the theory a mere shadow. But the subject was fate – and the possibility of parallel universes.

Just suppose, the argument had started, that reality forked, like a road, every time you took a major decision. Because you generally have two choices, this would cause a split in the universe, an option between broad and narrow roads.

Because difficult decisions were often made on a fragile balance of possibilities, in which the minutest of minute reasons could disturb the knife-edge equilibrium.

And supposing you and your world continued in both realities, together with all the others you had already created with your choices. In each parallel existence, you lived with the results of your decision.

It was an amusing game, a quasi-intellectual exercise, a rich resource for the writer of science fiction, but it haunted me for years.

Especially after Baby Marnewick so suddenly intruded into my conscience again.

It began with two articles in the same issue of *Law Enforcement* about the budding disciplines of the profiling and 'signature' identification of serial killers in the United States. One was by the director of the FBI's Behavioural Science and Investigation Support Unit, the other by a senior detective in the office of the Public Prosecutor in Seattle, Washington. (Both contributors would later become legendary in their own right.)

On a professional level, the contents of the articles were revolutionary and dramatic: a criminological leap that eventually narrowed the gap between applied psychology and practical policing. But for me the experience of reading them was far more personal than academic because the facts, the *modus operandi*, the examples on which both articles based their arguments, were a blueprint of the death of Baby Marnewick. They made our dead neighbour rise up out of her grave, shook loose the memories and paraded them in front of my consciousness with a fanfare.

It made my life's predictable path take an unforeseen direction.

And now I'll have to lecture you because in the subsequent years I learnt that the emotions that serial killers unleash often lead to false perceptions and popular views that are seldom rooted in reality.

The first thing one must understand is the difference between serial killers and mass murderers. The former are the Ted Bundys of this world, tragically damaged people who kill one victim after another in more or less the same way. They are, without exception, men, their targets usually women (unless they are homosexual, like Jeffrey Dahmer) and their most important psychological motivation is a total inability to make an impression socially – although I say this with great hesitation because, by trying to put it in a nutshell, I'm as guilty as the mass media of generalization and one-dimensional explanation of a far more complex phenomenon.

In contrast, mass murderers are those who will climb into the bell tower of a university and start shooting wildly. Or such a killer may be a White Wolf who does the same on a street corner – in contrast to the repeated, planned stalking of single, helpless victims by the serial killer.

Mass murderers are the shooting stars of daylight who, in one moment of flaming evil, swing Death's scythe, are usually quickly caught and finally leave innumerable questions unanswered.

Serial killers are the covert comets of the dark firmament who follow their path of destruction time and time again – prowlers, thieves of the night. Their crime is a show window of power, of the complete domination and humiliation of their victim, pathetic attempts to take revenge for the killers' total lack of normal, healthy social and sexual interaction.

And Baby Marnewick's dossier was a classic example, a perfect fit for the serial killer's psyche.

If the views and theories of the two articles were true, it meant that Baby Marnewick's murderer was identifiable, because the two authors had presented conceptual models of likely perpetrators, their behaviour and lifestyle: often unattractive, usually single men with an inferiority complex, who lived with a domineering or promiscuous female parent and had an appetite for positions of power, such as might be found in the police or the defence force, but who usually lived on the edge of the law-and-order world, as security guards, for example. They were users of pornography with the emphasis on bondage – and variations on the theme.

Predictable, identifiable. Catchable.

It also meant that Baby Marnewick hadn't been the first or the only victim of her murderer. Serial killers are entrepreneurs, according to the authors of the theory, who become more efficient with every murder, more self-confident and for whom each success opens up new vistas of deviant behaviour, of dominance and control and humiliation. The Marnewick case, as I recalled the details – only too well – suggested an efficient, progressive, established operator.

I read the articles over and over again, relived my own shame at the wooden fence, resurrected my unanswered questions with a clarity that surprised me. The new-found knowledge effortlessly blew away the thin layer of memory dust that the years since my youth had laid over the episodes.

I wondered about it. If I could remember everything so easily, so clearly, it meant that Baby Marnewick had been a psycholgical albatross around my neck, a cancerous growth in the psyche which had spread its toxins unseen through my body. Was that the reason for my inability to commit myself, or merely a contributing factor? What other areas of my existence had it soiled? I brooded on all of it.

I was also stimulated professionally. I analysed the implications on the procedures of policing, the influence this would have on all investigative methods, the duty we had as a department to inform the executive arm of law and order of the new insights.

But overriding it all was the urge to act, to reveal the past, to identify and expose the guilty, to bury the ghost.

And the one thing the academic world had taught me was how to plan a task, how to measure each action against the available knowledge, how to take each step on the firm ground of the proven so as not to sink into the quicksand of wild theory.

Step one would be to immerse myself in the subject.

For two weeks I worked on a document that would serve as a proposal for my doctoral thesis and it was only after rewriting it any number of times that I took it to Professor Cobus Taljaard. Academically he was a man of great integrity and equilibrium, and I knew the step I wanted to take onto the new terrain had to be thoroughly motivated. But the potential also existed for us to be co-pioneers, academic discoverers from the backward Third World who might (like Chris Barnard) give this scorned corner of Africa a place in the sun. On our terrain and with humility, we might find acceptance, acknowledgement and a piece of the criminological limelight.

For that reason it didn't take the professor long to approve the proposed doctoral thesis – and, more importantly, the research visit to the United States.

Two months later I packed my bags and began the journey that I believed would lead to the murderer of Baby Marnewick.

27

CAPE TOWN. — A private investigation into the cold-blooded murder of a Tygerberg businessman nine months ago has made a breakthrough which can open a whole network of criminal activities – but also raises new questions about the efficiency of the SAPS.

A large amount of American dollars, forged identity documents and a criminal trail which leads as far back as the eighties are some of the most important revelations made by a former detective of the Murder and Robbery Unit in Cape Town, investigating the death of the late 'Johannes Jacobus Smit' of Moreletta Street in Durbanville.

The names of those involved, which include the murderer, will shortly be handed to the authorities.

Mr Smit (on the right) was tortured in his house last year and 'executed' with a single shot from a M16 attack rifle after which the specially designed built-in safe in the house was ransacked. The contents of the safe weren't known then, but strong suspicion exists today that it contained, in part, foreign currency.

The private investigation was launched by the deceased's business partner, Ms Wilna van As, and her attorney, Ms Hope Beneke. Ms van As and the deceased lived together.

'It has come to light that the deceased lived under a false name for the past fifteen years and was in possession of a professionally forged identity document,' said Ms Beneke.

'We have a strong suspicion about the origin of the dollars and are following up new clues. There is enough reason to believe that Smit's murder can be connected with a crime which occurred some 15 years ago. A final breakthrough is expected within days.'

Anyone who has additional information regarding the murder of Smit or the events which preceded it can call a special toll-free number: 0800 3535 3555. Ms Beneke gave an assurance that all information would be regarded as highly confidential and that anonymity would be strictly preserved.

Mr Z. van Heerden, a former captain in the SAPS, was hesitant to make any comment about the way the police handled the original dossier which yielded nothing.

'We had more time and sources available to us in our attempt to unravel the case. The police work under enormous pressure and one cannot compare the two investigations,' said van Heerden.

He refused to comment on questions such as why a photograph of the deceased hadn't been handed to the media after the murder, why his identity document wasn't subjected to forensic tests or why evidence pertaining to the large amount of American dollars hadn't been pursued.

The SAPS Murder and Robbery Unit wasn't available for comment at the time of going to press.

'I still don't like the political angle,' said van Heerden.

'It gives the story credibility,' said Groenewald, the crime reporter. The night editor, sitting behind his desk, nodded in agreement. 'And your back is covered.'

'You didn't even phone them for comment.'

'They'll issue a statement tomorrow in any case. Which puts flesh on the bare bones of the story – and gets you more publicity.'

'And it'll appear in *Beeld* as well?' Hope asked, her voice soft.

'They don't have space on page one. The Gauteng premier is in hot water again. But it'll be on five or seven. *Volksblad* will let us know but it looks like page one. Fu – ahh . . . very little happens in the Free State.'

'I want to thank you for your help,' Hope said to the night editor. 'It could assist in righting a grave injustice.'

'Don't thank me, thank Kara-An. She was very persuasive.' He smiled across the room at Kara-An who sat on a small couch against the wall, her legs drawn up.

She smiled back. 'I help where I can,' she said. 'Especially when it can improve a woman's lot.'

They went down in the lift in silence, van Heerden and Hope. He was aware of the change in her. After he had been to Kara-An's home, he had telephoned Hope from the newspaper's offices in the NasPers Centre, told her they were waiting for her, he and Kara-An and Groenewald, the story would run on the following day and she said she was coming, without any enthusiasm. He and the crime reporter had worked on the copy, four, five, six versions, before they went to the night editor. Hope had negotiated with Telkom for the toll-free number but she was different, withdrawn, her body language negative and she didn't look at Kara-An.

There was tension in the room.

In the entrance to the tower block they hesitated. It was raining, dark gusts of water sweeping across the street outside.

'What's wrong, Hope?'

She looked uncomprehendingly at him.

'What's with you?'

'I still think we should offer a reward.'

They had spoken about it earlier. He had resisted the idea. A reward drew even more crazies who wanted to accuse their husbands and wives, mothers-in-law and stepfathers,

'Oh,' he said.

He knew she was lying.

She didn't want to go running. She fell down on the couch, listened to the rain against the window, felt the chill in the room.

What's with you?

He had sold his soul to Kara-An.

Did she want his soul?

No. But she was getting into his head, discovering the real person behind all the aggression and the useless fighting and the swearing. And now he was back behind all the barriers and she just couldn't see herself starting again.

She got up. She must run. Things would start happening the next day and she didn't know when there would be another opportunity to exercise.

She didn't feel like it.

In the glass measuring jug, he mixed the balsamic vinegar, the olive oil, the lemon juice, the finely chopped garlic (as always, he loved the aroma) and chillies, cumin, coriander and a bay leaf. He ground black pepper into it.

Pavarotti, as Rigoletto, was singing:

Softly, your tears are useless,
Now you are certain that he lied.
Softly and let it be my task
To take revenge.
Soon. And deadly.
I'll kill him.

He was hungry. And felt like food. He could taste the dish in his mouth, visualize the thick brown gravy, he had bought fresh bread to dip into the sauce when the chicken livers had been eaten.

He rinsed the livers, carefully cut out the membranes.

Hope. And Kara-An.

He put the livers in the marinade, took an onion out of the refrigerator, peeled and chopped it. The tears ran.

In *Good Housekeeping* he had read that if onions were kept in the refrigerator they wouldn't affect the eyes when peeled. It didn't always work.

Hope and Kara-An. The Laurel and Hardy of the female world.

Kara-An, the perverse.

It didn't turn him on.

It was a first for him. A woman who wanted to be hurt.

Her intensity. Her beauty. The gods' sense of humour. Give her everything. A body, Lord, that body, he had felt her, not too soft, not too firm, the breasts against his chest, her hips grinding into him.

Saucepan on the stove, melt butter in it.

A face in which each line was in perfect harmony with the other – a false front, like the buildings in Wild West movies, a beautiful optical illusion because behind the skin and tissue and muscles and the thick head of hair, under the bone of the skull lay the grey matter, the synapses with their faulty wiring.

What had happened? How had Kara-An, the child, changed into a woman for whom physical pain, a scene in which two men knocked one another about, brought her to a high, ecstatic plateau?

Money. Plus beauty and prominent parents. And intelligence. That would do it. Would make life easy, would quickly change the simple pleasures into the boring, would make the appetite for stimulation ever stronger. Eventually wanting the forbidden, the strange, the deviant.

But it didn't turn him on.

Onions in the butter, lower the flame so that they sautéed slowly.

And Hope? Good, faithful Hope, the bearer of the flame of justice.

Rigoletto:

> *Heavenly Father! She was caught*
> *In the execution of my revenge.*
> *Dearest angel! Look at me.*
> *Listen to me!*

The flame no longer burnt so brightly. And it bothered him.

Fuck alone knew why.

He turned off the gas.

The chicken livers had to marinate. Then he would brown them with the onion, add the tomato paste, Worcester sauce, Tabasco and the marinade, eventually the tot of brandy.

And eat.

When last had he been so hungry? Had such an appetite?

He would take his mother a bowlful.

Peace offering.

He walked to an armchair, sat down, closed his eyes.

Let the little livers absorb the flavours.

He listened to the music.

He would eat in a while.

Tomorrow things would start happening.

He gave a deep sigh.

Day 3

Monday, 10 July

28

I spent three months at Quantico, the Federal Bureau of Investigation's luxurious sprawl in Virginia. And two weeks respectively in Seattle and New York.

I won't bore you with descriptions of abundant, bountiful America. I won't comment on the hospitable, superficial, clever, generous people. (I'm becoming a self-conscious author. I'm seduced by the sensuality of the words in front of me begging to be used. I'm overeating at this banquet of self-description, I think it's a natural process: once you start talking about yourself, once you've overcome the initial (typically Afrikaans) unwillingness to egocentrism, it becomes a furious machine, a monster feeding on itself, an irresistible seduction that adds more and more baroque decorations to the storyline, until the meanderings achieve a life of their own.)

So I must practise self-discipline.

At Quantico they taught me to use the media, showed me that television and radio and the newspapers weren't the enemy of the police but an instrument. That you could harness a carthorse to the media's insatiable hunger for sensation and blood (but that you had to hang on to the wagon if the horse took the bit between its teeth).

They taught me profiling, how to establish the psyche of serial killers and even deduce clothing and transport and age with an astonishing measure of accuracy.

I took a green exercise book with me, the nearest I could come to an official dossier, and I reopened the Baby Marnewick case, the private, unofficial version. My first witnesses were the SACs, the Special Agents in Charge, members of the FBI's Unit for Behavioural Science – and every analysed serial killer in America.

And then I came back.

Wendy was at the airport – 'Why didn't you write?' – but she was ecstatic because her unwilling betrothed was eventually on his way to a doctorate. 'Tell me everything,' while my head was in my green exercise book.

A week after my return, I went to Klerksdorp to beg for the official Marnewick dossier, armed with a letter from the Professor and the Commissioner and all the manipulative charm I possessed.

It took another two weeks before I sent out the other letters because it took that long to get all the names and addresses of every officer in charge of every Murder and Robbery Unit in the country.

I rewrote the letter to them five or six times. The balance had to be right: an academic request, a pricking of professional curiosity, just another servant of justice – without insinuating that I was one of them, because I knew the brotherhood, the unique ties that were formed in a daily round of death and violence and scorn.

The letter, apart from the well-considered opening, contained the salient points of Baby Marnewick's death and asked for information on similar murders between the years 1975 and 1985 with all the possible variations on the theme, à la Quantico.

And then I went back to the books and the notes and the theory of my thesis but merely to make the time spent waiting for information pass more easily.

'What's wrong with you, Zet?'

I'm certain that Wendy, at the very least, had an intimation of the threat.

I hadn't told her about my and Baby Marnewick's past history. As far as she was concerned, it was an academic, scientific process that would lead to a doctorate and a step nearer to her dream. Professor and Mrs van Heerden.

What would we call our children? Her father's and mother's names (Gordon and Shirley) and my Afrikaans surname? Not that I worried about it.

I'm losing the thread.

'Is there someone else?'

There was. Behind a wooden fence, six feet under.

But how to explain that?

'No. Don't be silly.'

29

'Hallo, is that the crime number?'

'Yes.'

'Is there a reward?'

'It depends on the kind of information you have, madam.'

'What's the size of the reward?

'There is no official reward, madam.'

'My ex did it. He's an animal, I tell you.'

'Why do you think he did it?'

'He's capable of anything.'

'Is there anything that connects him to this case?'

'I know he did it. He never pays his alimony . . .'

'Does he own an M16 rifle, madam?'

'He has a gun. I don't know what kind.'

'Is it an attack rifle, madam? A machine-gun?'

'He hunts with it.'

That was the first call.

'It was my father.'

'Who?'

'The murderer.'

'Is there anything that connects him to the murder?'

'He's a monster.'

That was the second call.

Hope was waiting for him at the front of the building at a quarter to six in the morning. She unlocked the office and showed him the empty room with the telephone on the bare desk. He asked for writing paper. She brought it. They didn't speak much.

The phone rang at seven minutes past six.

Hope listened to the first twelve calls, got up, went out. He drew three-dimensional squares on the paper in front of him.

'Hallo.'

'Jesus, van Heerden, what the fuck is this?'

O'Grady.

'I didn't write that piece, Nougat.'

'You stabbed me in the back, you bastard. Do you know how this makes me look?'

'I'm sorry . . .'

'That doesn't cut it, arsehole. The Super wants to fire me. He's fucking furious. I trusted you, you . . .'

'Did you read the whole thing, Nougat? Did you see what I said?'

'That doesn't make much difference. You should have come to me with the fucking evidence, van Heerden. You have no loyalty.'

'Come on, Nougat. We've got three days in which to find the will. If I had taken it back to you . . .'

'Bullshit, van Heerden. You made me look like a cunt.'

'I'm sorry, Nougat. That wasn't the intention. I've got a job to do.'

'Fuck you.'

Hope brought more coffee, listened to more conversations. Three jokers. Two useless calls accusing family members. She left again.

He waited patiently. He doodled. He had known there would be primarily useless callers. The sickness out there was widespread.

But perhaps . . .

At 9:27 she opened the door. There was something different in her eyes. Worry?

Two men followed her into the room – dark suits, short hair, broad shoulders. One black, one white. The white one was older, in his late forties, early fifties. The black man was younger, bigger.

'This is van Heerden,' said Hope.

'Can I help you?'

'We've come to terminate the investigation,' said White.

'Who are you?'

'A messenger.'

'From who?'

'Won't you sit down?' asked Hope. Her frown had deepened.

'No.'

Van Heerden got up. The black man was taller. 'This investigation is not terminable,' van Heerden said, his temper flaming.

'It is,' said Black. 'National security.'

'Bullshit,' said van Heerden.

'Easy does it,' said White. 'We come in peace.' There was a calm in him, authority.

The telephone rang. They all stared at the instrument.

'Do you have identification?' Hope asked.

'You mean one of those little plastic cards?' Black asked with a small smile.

The telephone rang.

'Yes,' Hope said.

'That's only for people in the movies, Miss,' said White.

'You have five minutes to leave this room . . .' said van Heerden.

'Before you do what, boy?'

'Before I ask the police to arrest you for trespassing.'

The telephone rang.

'We don't want any trouble.'

'Bring a court order.'

'We came to ask nicely first.'

'You've asked, now get out.'

'He's right,' Hope said uncertainly.

'If you cooperate now you can avoid a great deal of trouble,' said Black.

The telephone was still ringing. Van Heerden looked at his watch. 'Four minutes and thirty seconds. And don't threaten me.'

White sighed. 'You don't know what you're into.'

Black sighed. 'You're out of your depth.'

'You must leave now,' Hope said more decisively.

Van Heerden picked up the phone. 'Hallo.'

Silence.

'Hallo.'

Something at the other end. A sound.

He looked up. Black and White were still standing there. He tapped his watch with a forefinger, pointed at the door.

'Hallo,' he said again.

'It . . .' said a woman's voice at the other end and he identified the sounds. Sobs. A woman crying.

'It . . .'

Van Heerden sat down slowly. 'I'm listening,' he said quietly, his heart hammering.

'It was . . .' Sobs. 'It was . . . my son.'

The door opened. It was Marie, the receptionist. 'There are policemen here, Hope. At reception.'

'So fast,' White said to Black. 'Our five minutes aren't even up.'

'I'm listening,' van Heerden said softly into the receiver.

'The man in the photo . . .' said the woman's voice, faint and faraway.

'Such SAPS efficiency. Makes me feel so safe,' said Black.

'You have to leave now,' Hope said firmly.

Marie: 'The police, Hope . . .'

The red tide rose, overwhelming van Heerden. He got up, put his hand violently over the mouthpiece. 'Fuck off, all of you. Now!'

Marie's eyes huge, her eyes round in a shocked 'Oh', Black and White with small smiles, unintimidated.

'Please,' Hope said and tugged at Black's jacket. Unwillingly, they walked out, Hope ahead, a locomotive pulling reluctant railcars, and eventually the door closed.

'Forgive me,' he said into the receiver, striving to calm his voice. 'I wanted to get silence in the room.'

Sobs at the other end.

'I just . . . want to know what's going on.'

'I understand, madam.'

'Is that the detective?'

'Yes, madam.'

'Van Heerden?'

'Yes, madam.'

'They told me he was dead.'

'He is . . .' He struggled with the words, he would have to play this neatly, 'deceased, madam.'

'No,' she said. 'In seventy-six. They told me he was dead in seventy-six.'

'Who are "they", madam?'

'The Government, The Defence Force. They said he died in Angola. They brought me a medal.'

'Forgive me for asking, madam, but are you sure that photo is of your son?'

He listened to the electronic sounds on the line, the crackle and hum, wondered where she was, where she was phoning from. Another sound, high, heartbreakingly sad. The woman weeping. 'It's him. I still see Rupert's face every day. In my heart. Against my wall. I see it every day. Every day.'

He walked to the reception area of the firm of attorneys. Hope was there, with Black and White, Senior Superintendent Bart de Wit, Superintendent Mat Joubert and Inspector Tony O'Grady, all three from Murder and Robbery.

'I'm sorry, Colonel,' Bart de Wit said to White, 'but you'll simply have to work through the official channels. This is our case.'

'We don't have channels, boy,' said White. Black nodded in agreement.

'Hope, will you please answer the telephone in the meanwhile?' asked van Heerden. She looked at him, looked at the men scrumming in her reception area, nodded, relieved, and walked down the passage.

'Morning, van Heerden,' said Bart de Wit.

'Morning, van Heerden,' said Mat Joubert.

Nougat O' Grady said nothing.

'Reunion,' said Black. 'Charming.'

'Sweet,' said White.

'You possess information that can help us in the investigation of an active case, van Heerden,' said Bart de Wit and rubbed the large mole on the side of his prominent nose.

'We came to get it,' said O'Grady.

Mat Joubert smiled. 'How are you, van Heerden?'

'Rearranging the deckchairs on the *Titanic*,' said White.

'And not a Di Caprio in sight,' said Black.

'Our friends from Military Intelligence were on the point of leaving,' said van Heerden.

'A shot in the dark,' said Black.

'A little knowledge can be dangerous,' said White.

'Seventy-six,' said van Heerden.

White's eyes narrowed almost imperceptibly.

'Seventy-six reasons why you have to leave now.'

There they stood, two large men with short hair and broad shoulders, looking at one another, suddenly silent and without witticisms.

Van Heerden walked to the glass front door, held it open. 'Go and give someone a medal,' he said.

White's mouth opened and shut.

'Goodbye,' said van Heerden.

'We'll be back,' said Black.

'Sooner than you think,' said White. Then they walked out.

'You abused the Inspector's trust, van Heerden,' said Senior Superintendent Bart de Wit, Officer in Command of the Cape Town Murder and Robbery Unit.

'You owe me big time, van Heerden,' said O'Grady.

'Not forgetting the irreparable damage you have done to the good name of the SAPS,' said Bart de Wit.

Mat Joubert smiled.

'Come,' said van Heerden. 'I'll find a place where we can talk.'

The telephone rang and its shrill noise in the quiet room startled Hope.

'Hallo,' she said.

A moment's silence. 'Who's speaking?' A man's voice.

'Hope Beneke.'

'The attorney?'

'Yes, may I help you?'

'The deceased's name was Rupert de Jager.'

Another silence as if he expected a reaction.

'Yes?' she said uncertainly.

'Before he changed his name. Did you already know that?'

'Yes, sir,' she said and sent up a silent prayer that she was telling the right lie, wrote on the paper in front of her: *Rupert de Jager (???)*

'Do you know who the murderer is?'

How did she reply to that question? 'I'm sorry, sir, but I can't give that information over the phone.'

Hesitation on the other end as though possibilities were being weighed. 'Bushy. It was Bushy.'

'Bushy,' she said mechanically.

'Schlebusch. Everyone called him Bushy.'

Her right hand trembled. *Bushy Schlebusch.* 'Yes?' Her voice was trembling, too.

'I was there. I was with them.'

She looked at the door. Where was van Heerden? She was going to paint herself into a corner.

'At the murder?'

'No, no, that was Schlebusch. Just him, I think. I was with them in seventy-six.'

'Oh.' Seventy-six? Should she ask . . . 'How do you know it was him who . . . murdered de Jager?'

'The M16. It's his.'

'Oh.'

'You don't know Bushy. He's going to . . . he's fucking crazy. You'll have to be careful.'

'Why, sir?'

'He's unstoppable.'

'Why do you say that?' Where *was* van Heerden?

'Because they like killing. That's what you have to understand.'

She was speechless for a moment.

'We're . . . ahhh . . . are you prepared to come and talk? Here . . .'

'No.'

'We'll be very discreet, sir.'

'No,' said the male voice. 'Bushy . . . I don't want him to find me.'

'Where do we find Schlebusch, sir?'

'It seems you don't understand. *He*'ll find *you*. And I don't want to be in the way.'

30

Life, people, events are complex, multi-layered, multi-faceted, with innumerable nuances.

In contrast with the poverty of my words. Even more: the propaganda value of every sentence I offer, the misdirection of everything I omit.

My only experience as a writer is in academia and I am struggling to keep that out of these chronicles. The words seem heavy, the style forced, unyielding. But you will have to bear with me. It is the best I can do.

I must try to explain who I was in the year 1991, in the weeks when I waited for replies to my letters to the officers commanding Murder and Robbery Units across the country.

Because eventually the purpose of this story is to measure, to compare, to weigh: who I was, what the potential was of the man who, at thirty-one, obsessively started an academic murder investigation. To guess and to speculate about what might have been.

Because it was a time of possibilities. If I think back on all the aspects of my existence, it is astonishing to know that there were so many tiny details that could have influenced the course of events, that could have made the road fork.

I was on the edge of a conventional future, a hair's breadth away from it. If I hadn't read those two articles, the Marnewick dossier would have held no interest and I might have followed another, more predictable road. Wendy and I might have been married today, Professor and Mrs Z. van Heerden of Waterkloof Ridge, middle-aged and unhappy, the parents of two or three children being systematically poisoned by the frustration of an unfulfilled marriage.

Because, despite all I've said about Wendy Brice up to now, I wasn't wholly unwilling to follow the conventional route.

You see, we were, for all practical purposes, a couple in Pretoria. Our circle of friends was defined – and they defined us. We were Zet and Wendy, we entertained and were entertained, we had our routine, our moments of flickering happiness, our togetherness. We were one another's frame of reference, we fitted into the neat structure of our social milieu.

I'm not about to deviate and philosophize about the ties that bind, but there is substantial pressure in a circle of friends who group you together. Individuality, personal goals are lost in the collective name: Zet-and-Wendy. The circumstances conspire to make you conform, to take your place in the larger destiny of humankind: to procreate, to let the genes live on, to play a conservative role. Even if I knew she wasn't the One.

We were popular. We were in, an item, we could sparkle. I would like to think we could make heads turn, the athletic dark-haired man and the pretty little blonde. It all helped to establish our path, to define our route.

I didn't protest too much. I didn't visualize a clear alternative future without her. I was prepared to give in eventually, like a sacrificial lamb, to marry, have children, to follow my academic career to its logical conclusion, to play golf, cut grass, take my son to watch rugby and possibly own a Mercedes and a swimming pool.

I didn't yearn for it, but I didn't fight it.

I was on the border of the conventional. Close.

Who was I then?

Above all, I believed in myself – and because of that, in others. I don't think I ever sat down to philosophize about the conflict between Good and Evil in me and in others. Because I didn't see myself as evil, the belief coloured the lenses through which I saw everything. Evil was the deviation of a minority which I could study through the safety glass of academe. A phenomenon like a genetic aberration, scattered percentage-wise through the population, according to the natural statistics of evolution. And my task, as criminal psychologist, as criminologist and police scientist, was to read the figures and make deductions, to develop procedures and to institute them, assisting those who had to execute them.

I was on the side of the good. Therefore I was good.

That's who I was.

Despite the obsession with the Marnewick case. Perhaps *because* of my obsession.

31

They sat in Hope Beneke's office and he felt the adrenalin, the blood of the chase coursing through him and for a moment he remembered . . .

'Jeez, van Heerden, I still can't believe you've turned out to be such a complete arsehole. How could you stab an ex-colleague in the back and manage to disgrace the Force at the same time? All you had to do was to give me a call. Just a single call.'

He held up his hands, he was calm, his head jumping from the telephone call to Military Intelligence, to O'Grady and de Wit and Joubert, his body primed for action, but he had to focus here first. 'OK, Nougat, I know where you're coming from and you have my sympathy . . .'

O'Grady's face twisted in disgust and he began to say something but van Heerden went on.

'But just think of the facts for a moment. I had one more clue than you: the false ID. That's all. The rest is pure conjecture and it's pretty flimsy. The thing about the dollars was a huge leap of faith and it's only because I looked at the way the guy set himself up in business with cash, in the early eighties. I have no corroborating evidence. So tell me, do you think think your superior officers,' and he pointed at de Wit and Joubert, 'would have allowed you to go to the newspapers on the strength of that?'

'It's the fucking principle, van Heerden.'

'And the damage you did to the reputation of the SAPS, van Heerden.'

'I'm sorry about that, Col— er . . . Superintendent, but it was the price I had to pay for the publicity.'

'Sold us down the river for a lousy newspaper story.'

'Bullshit, Nougat. You guys get worse publicity every day of the week because the media see you as a political tool to get at the ANC. Are you going to blame me for that as well?'

'You deliberately withheld information that we could use in the investigation of a murder, van Heerden.'

'I'm more than prepared to share, Superintendent. But the time isn't ripe, for obvious reasons.'

'You're full of shit, van Heerden.'

'Seventy-six,' said Mat Joubert.

They all stared at him.

'You stopped the Military Intelligence jokers dead in their tracks with seventy-six, van Heerden. What did it mean?'

He should have known Joubert wouldn't miss a trick.

'First,' he said slowly and in a measured tone, 'we're going to reach an agreement about the sharing of information.'

O'Grady gave a scornful laugh. 'Jesus, just listen to him.'

'I don't think you're in a position to negotiate,' said Bart de Wit, his voice slightly higher, slightly more nasal.

'Let's listen to what he suggests,' said Mat Joubert.

'But we can't trust the motherfucker.'

'Inspector, we've spoken about your language before,' said de Wit.

O'Grady blew out his breath loudly. It obviously wasn't a new topic.

'Superintendent, this is the way I see the situation,' said van Heerden. 'You have the law on your side and you can force me to reveal everything.'

'Indeed,' said Bart de Wit.

'Damn' right,' said Nougat O'Grady.

'But you're also forced to work within the confines of the regulations if you take over the investigation. If Military Intelligence pull strings, you'll have to cooperate. I don't have to. And as long as I share information, you can't stop me carrying on the investigation.'

De Wit said nothing. Finger and mole met again.

'I suggest a partnership. A working relationship.'

'And you call the shots?' Nougat, snorting.

'Nobody calls the shots. We just do what we have to do – and share the information.'

'I don't trust you.'

Van Heerden made a gesture that implied it didn't bother him.

A silence fell.

'Where *were* you?' Hope asked when he eventually opened the door. 'I don't know how to handle the calls. A man phoned to say someone was coming to attack us and the media, the *Argus* and eTV want information and . . .'

'Take it easy,' he said. 'I had to negotiate with Murder and Robbery.'

'A man phoned. He said Smit was de Jager.'

'Rupert de Jager,' said van Heerden.

'You knew?'

'The call that came in when Military Intelligence were here . . .'

'Military Intelligence?'

'The two clowns, black and white.'

'They were from Military Intelligence?'

'Yes. The call was from a Mrs Carolina de Jager of Springfontein in the Free State. Rupert was her son.'

'Good gracious.'

'It seems as if it all goes back to nineteen seventy-six. And the Defence Force.'

'The man who phoned also spoke about seventy-six. He said the murderer was a Schlebusch who was with them.'

'Schlebusch,' he said, rolling the name on his tongue.

'Bushy,' she said. 'That's what he called him. Do you know about him?'

'No. It's new. What else did the man say?'

She looked at the paper in front of her. 'I didn't handle it well, van Heerden. I had to lie because he assumed we already knew a lot of stuff. He said Schlebusch is dangerous. He's going to shoot us. He has an M16.'

He absorbed the information. 'Does he know where Schlebusch is?'

'No, but he said Schlebusch would find us. He's scared.'

'Did he tell you what happened in seventy-six?'

'No.'

'What else did he say?'

'Schlebusch . . . he said Schlebusch likes killing.'

He looked at her. Realized she wasn't up to this kind of thing. She was afraid.

'What else?'

'That was all. And then the *Argus* phoned and eTV.'

'We'll have to hold a news conference.'

The telephone rang again.

'Now you must answer.'

'You must go to Bloemfontein.'

'Bloemfontein?'

'Hope, you're repeating everything I say.'

She looked frowningly at him for a moment and then she laughed self-consciously. Tension breaker.

'You're right.'

'You must fetch Mrs Carolina de Jager.'

He picked up the receiver.

'Van Heerden.'

'I know who the murderer is,' a woman's voice said.

'We would welcome the information.'

'Satanists,' the woman said. 'They're everywhere.'

'Thank you,' he said and replaced the receiver. 'Another crazy,' he said to Hope.

'We've uncovered something nasty,' she said, her face worried.

'We're going to solve it.'

'And the police are going to help us?'

'We're going to share information.'

'Did you tell them everything?'

'Almost. Simply said that we suspect it has to do with the Defence Force and something that happened years ago.'

'Shouldn't we hand the case to them?'

'Are you scared, Hope?'

'Of course I'm scared. This case is getting bigger and bigger. And now we're getting threats from a man who is going to kill us. Because he enjoys it.'

'You'll learn. There are always a thousand stories about something like this. And most of them are pure sh – nonsense.'

'I still think we should hand it to the police.'

'No,' he said.

She looked pleadingly at him.

'Hope, nothing will happen. You'll see.'

He arranged for an answering machine to take messages, upset with himself that he hadn't thought of it before. He tore a piece of paper off the writing pad, made notes of the new information, tried to arrange it in sequence, listened to callers who were acting out their minor delusions, waited for the answering machine to appear.

'I can get a flight to Bloemfontein early tomorrow morning and be back by late afternoon.' Hope came in to report. He gave her Carolina de Jager's phone number, asked her to arrange it all.

The answering machine was delivered, the technician helped him to install it. The number of calls decreased but he knew they would increase when bored children came home from school.

Marie's head appeared again after a soft, scared knock. 'There's an American who wants to talk to you.'

'Send him in.'

An American? He shook his head, drew another square on his notepad. The whole world was in on the deal. Hell, the newspaper article had worked . . .

Marie opened the door. 'Mr Powell,' she said and wanted to close the door behind her.

'Call Hope,' he said quickly and extended his hand. 'Van Heerden.'

'Luke Powell,' said the American in a heavy accent. He was black and middle-aged, slightly overweight, with a soft, round face and eyes that wanted to laugh.

'What can I do for you, Mr Powell?'

'No, sir, it's what I can do for you.'

'Please take a seat,' he said, indicating one of the chairs on the other side of the desk. 'And I must apologize for the fact that I have to answer the telephone.'

'No sweat. Have to do your job.' The wide mouth smiling broadly to reveal flawless white teeth.

Hope opened the door and he introduced her to Powell. She sat down, her arms folded, body language indicating that she didn't want to be there.

'I'm with the US consulate,' said Powell. 'Economic adviser. After we heard about this on the radio, I thought I'd, you know, pop in to offer our cooperation. You know, with dollars being involved and all.'

'That's very kind of you, sir,' said van Heerden.

The broad smile again. 'It's our absolute pleasure.'

Van Heerden smiled back. 'So you have some interesting information for us about the origin of the dollars?'

'Oh no, I was hoping you could tell me. The radio news was pretty brief, you know, just that quite a few dollars could be involved in this thing. But if you guys point us in the right direction, I could pass the information along to . . . I don't know, whoever can help. That's one thing we do have . . . resources.'

'Tell me, Mr Powell, what does an American economic adviser do in South Africa?'

Smile, self-deprecating, hands that showed the work wasn't important. 'Oh, you know, talk to business people mostly, lots of folk want to trade with the US of A . . . Help them with the paperwork, identify opportunities, our government is totally committed to the development of the new South Africa. And then, of course, our own companies back home, they want to enter your market . . .'

'I was referring to your real job,' said van Heerden, his smile genuine, enjoying it.

'I'm not sure I follow you, sir.'

'My problem, Mr Powell, is that I don't know enough about the

American Intelligence community to be able to guess accurately to which arm you belong. But I would say possibly CIA. Or perhaps one of the military groups, you have so many . . .'

Hope's mouth was slightly open in disbelief.

'Lordy,' said Powell, 'is that what you think?' Amused, sincere. *He's good*, van Heerden thought and wondered whether they had sent a black man so that he could be more or less invisible here. With that accent?

'Yes, sir, that would be my best shot.'

'Wait till I tell the wife about that one, Mr van Hieden. Nope, I'm a pretty ordinary minor government official doing a pretty ordinary job. I guess you all shouldn't believe all that stuff on television. Lordy, is that really what you think?'

He saw Hope hanging on the man's words, ready to believe.

'Seeing that you're so honest with us, Mr Powell, I'll level with you, too. The funny thing about this case is that we had almost nothing to go on. And I mean really nothing. Just a tiny piece of paper that Forensics believed was used years ago to wrap dollars. And a huge walk-in safe and a false identity document and a man starting a business years ago with more cash than can be explained. And that was it.'

Powell nodded, listening intently.

'We were at a dead end. There was nowhere to go. So we asked the press for help and built a story that was nothing more than conjecture, fiction if you want, loosely based on one of quite a few possibilities.'

'Is that right?'

'And you know what happened? All hell broke loose. We had calls from all over the country, we've had the most interesting people walking in, and suddenly more pieces of the puzzle than we could've hoped for fell into our laps. If you'll pardon the expression, it was like opening a can of worms.'

'Well, there you go,' said Powell, still the minor government official.

'And, I must add, forty-eight hours ago I thought this case couldn't be solved. Hell, six hours ago I thought it was dead as a doornail. But now, Mr Powell, the case has blown wide open. It seems to me that not only will we solve it but that a great many people will be embarrassed by it.'

'Is that right?'

'Yes, sir, it sure is,' said van Heerden, a slight American accent creeping into his voice. He couldn't help it, he remembered the time in Quantico, the overwhelming, contagious accents. 'And now you have to ask yourself, do you and those who employ you want to be embarrassed as well?'

Powell took a deep breath, the smile intact, calm, unworried. 'Well, sir, I'm grateful to you for sharing that with me, but I'm just . . .'

'A minor government official?'

'Absolutely.' The smile still broad and open.

'But should you care to share what you know, the damage could be minimized, of course. Contained, I believe, would be the right word.'

'Mr van Hieden, sir, let me say that if I'm ever in the position to supply you with any information whatsoever, nothing would give me greater pleasure than to share it with you.' Powell put a hand in his jacket pocket, took out a card. 'Unfortunately, I haven't the slightest idea what you're talking about. But should you change your mind about my employment and need information, be sure to call me.' He put the card down in front of van Heerden and stood up. 'It's been a pleasure, sir, madam.'

And when they had shaken hands and Powell had closed the door behind him, Hope Beneke slowly blew out her breath and said: 'Fuck it!' and amazement spread across her face at the feat of saying the word.

'Is that right?' said van Heerden in a broad American accent and they laughed, deep and relieved, a moment of calm in a stormy sea.

The phone rang.

32

Among the heartbreaking reports of killings from virtually all over the country, I found the trail of the Masking Tape Murderer.

Not immediately but slowly, with orderly hard work, lists and flow charts and notes and graphs and a total, overruling obsession.

The documents arrived one after another, from detectives in cities, from small towns in the country, all with precisely the same theme: a yearning to catch the sick soul, to trap the perpetrator of abhorrent crimes, the same mandate to empower, the same unconditional offer of assistance to solve and close the dormant, dust-gathering files.

In those weeks I discovered the soul of a policeman, the hunting instinct, the personal involvement of a hunter with his prey. Because each file spoke of dedication, of passion, every packet had a letter enclosed in which I was begged to use the new criminological knowledge, to share, so that they could still the pain of an unsolved murder, the gnawing realization that *he* was still out there, carrying out his deadly calling.

It was in those weeks that I discovered my true vocation, experienced my initiation into the brotherhood, alone in an office in the maze of the university's corridors. In those weeks I lost Wendy and found myself, I truly smelt blood for the first time and could not resist the odour.

Of the unbelievable eighty-seven responses that I received from all over the country, only nine were indisputably applicable, with another four or five possibles. The rest were the crimes of other serial killers who had plagued our country for the past twenty years.

Naturally there was the temptation to establish a sort of national register of mass murder (how far ahead of my time I would've been!) but my obsession was too overwhelming, my debt of honour to Baby Marnewick too heavy a yoke.

And when all the information had been processed onto a huge chart that covered one wall of my office, the murder route of Masking Tape had been mapped. It was a chronicle, a casebook study of the rise, apprenticeship and eventual coming of age of a serial killer who had drawn his trail of bloody destruction across the South African landscape.

And he was a miner.

His journey started in 1974 in the Free State gold-mining town of Virginia, with the assault and rape of a fourteen-year-old black schoolgirl who survived the knife wounds in her breasts by sheer will-power after she had been found with her hands tied behind her back with masking tape in an open stretch of veld. His first initiatory deed? Or were there others before that, clumsy, unreported attempts? Or was that the first time he used masking tape? The dossier mentioned that the victim could give no description of the rapist. Didn't want to?

In the same year, a fifteen-year-old white schoolgirl, again from Virginia, was found next to the road, hands bound with masking tape, seventeen knife wounds in her breasts, with one nipple cut off. The police combed the black township and the black mineworkers' compound, interrogated any number of black suspects, the connection between the two victims clear. No arrests were made.

Blyvooruitzicht on the West Rand, 1975: a twenty-two-year-old secretary at a legal firm, slight and pretty, finished her work and went home. No one ever saw her alive again. The following afternoon at 12:22 they kicked in the door of her small flat because they were suspicious. They found her in the only bedroom, hands and feet bound with masking tape, multiple stab wounds in the breasts, both nipples clumsily removed, a teddy bear on her face. (That, said the Quantico model, was a sign that the murderer was ashamed of his deed, that he didn't want to see her eyes.)

16 December 1975: Carletonville. A black farm hand discovered the naked body of a twenty-one-year-old waitress at 06:30 at the side of the tarred road to Rysmierbult. Masking tape, stab wounds in the chest, nipples removed. Where had she been murdered? There were no signs of a struggle where she was found, no trail of blood. No arrests.

March 9, 1976: a thirty-four-year-old prostitute was found in her flat in Welkom. The amount of blood in the room was frightening – one of the knife wounds had sliced through her aorta which spouted a fountain of blood against the walls, over the furniture and the floor, flushing out her life. She had struggled, there was skin under her nails and she had bruises on her face. She was probably dead before he could use the masking tape but it was found where it had rolled under a coffee table. Nipples sliced, knife wounds and, for the first time, horrifying post-mortem mutilation of the vagina.

Rage.

No fingerprints on the roll of masking tape.

Then, in 1979, after three years of silence, the death of Baby Marnewick. For the first time a victim in the kneeling position, semen found for the first time.

Where had he been for three years? After the acceleration between '75 and '76, the increasing aggression, the periods between the murders becoming briefer? Serial killers didn't simply disappear of their own free will. They never stopped, they were moths around the flame of self-destruction, closer and closer, crazier and crazier until they were burnt out, usually in the white flame of justice.

The answer, the FBI said, is very often a jail sentence. Because where there is the smoke of serial murder, there is a fire that sparks off other crimes – even minor acts of white collar theft, arson occasionally, indecent assault and rape or attempted rape. All the studies indicated that a silence of months or years that disturbed a killer's demonic tempo was, in eighty per cent of the cases, due to a jail sentence for another crime.

Three murders in 1980: in March at Sishen, a twenty-three-year-old housewife, kneeling, multiple knife wounds, nipples removed, masking tape around the ankles and wrists.

June, in Durban: A thirty-one-year-old cosmetic sales rep in her hotel room. Exactly the same *modus operandi*.

August in Thabazimbi: A twenty-three-year-old unemployed single woman, possibly a prostitute or a call girl, found in her small home, five days after someone had used the whole terrifying ritual to humiliate and murder her.

And after that, nothing.

The bloody trail ended sharply and suddenly as if Masking Tape had disappeared off the face of the earth. Dead? Jail sentence again? It made no sense.

For a week I stared at the monster on my wall. The flow chart was there, the map, the notes in the margin, the main suspects – not a single duplication. The list of similarities and differences was there, also the gaps.

The trail was there, sharp and clear, but there was no indication of identity. The murderer of Baby Marnewick had a trail now, a history. But, as yet, no name.

For a week I brooded and gazed and reread every one of the nine documents. And the one thing I couldn't find was the murderer of Baby Marnewick. I would have to cast my net wider.

33

In the late afternoon the calls lessened significantly and at 17:00 he connected an answering machine to the telephone. 'This service is closed for the night. Please leave your name and number and we'll return your call in the morning.' He knew that in the small hours of the night, the craziest would emerge from their holes, those who heard voices, those in contact with other planets. Let them talk to the machine.

He walked to Hope's office. The door was closed. He knocked.

'Come in.'

He opened the door.

She smiled at him. 'You knocked!'

He gave her a wry smile in return, sat down in the same chair that he had used when he first saw her.

'We did well today.'

'*You* did well today.'

'You were a great help.'

'No. I was pathetic.'

'Merely a lack of experience.

'It was your idea, van Heerden. Your plan. And it worked.'

He was quiet for a moment, enjoying the praise.

'Do you really think Powell is American Secret Service?'

'Something like it.'

'Why?'

'Regular consular people don't do things like that. They don't walk in and offer to assist with a crime investigation. They are reactive, polite, careful not to interfere in household affairs. And if there was a real need to help, they work through official channels.'

'He looks like someone's uncle.'

'They all do.'

'Except for the two from Military Intelligence.'

He smiled at her. 'That's true.'

'Everything for tomorrow is organized. I'm meeting Mrs de Jager in Bloemfontein and she is flying back with me.'

'You asked her about the things she has to bring?'

'I did. She will.'

'Thank you. There'll be publicity again. I spoke to the *Cape Times* and the *Argus. Die Burger* will also place a follow-up. Just that we've received information which we're processing. And eTV . . .'

'I'll bring Wilna van As up to date. On my way home.'

'Good.'

She nodded. 'Zatopek,' she said softly, almost experimentally.

He grinned. 'Yes?'

'There is something serious I have to discuss with you.'

He put on the Sinfonia Concertante, K 364 for violin, viola and orchestra, turned up the sound, the sweet, triumphant notes filling his dark house and blotting out the howling northwester. He ate leftovers, spaghetti and then the tangy chicken livers, sitting in his battered armchair, notes on the table in front of him.

Hope wanted him to hand over the case to the police.

He had refused. And dished up excuses. They worked on hundreds of cases at once. He had focus. They had procedures and restraints, he was free. If they were so good *they* would have made the breakthrough.

'Please,' she had said again. She was scared, he could see that, scared of the sudden twists, the strange groups involved, scared of the possibility that a psychopath called Bushy was going to get them.

He had refused.

Because he had to.

She couldn't concentrate on the book.

She put it back on the bedside table and leant back against the cushions.

Wilna van As had cried again. Out of gratitude. In anticipation of the meeting with Carolina de Jager the following day. From fear of the skeletons of the past. From longing for her Johannes Jacobus Smit who had become Rupert de Jager, someone whom she didn't know.

'Would you like to spend the night with me?' she had asked, looking at the large, cold house.

'No,' Wilna van As said.

She had stayed as long as she could, until the other woman had realized and said she should go, tomorrow was going to be a long day.

And underlying it all was the knowledge that couldn't be ignored.

Something had changed today. Between her and Zatopek van Heerden. Between them.

They had laughed together, heartily and honestly, even exuberantly when she had sworn, goodness gracious where had that word come from, she hadn't known she had it in her, but he had laughed and looked at her and in that moment he was someone else, all the anger, the unapproachability suddenly gone.

And he had knocked. And spoken to her calmly. When she had shared her fear, when she had said that the police should take over.

Something had changed today . . .

There was a knock at her door and she thought it was him, she smiled, it was becoming a habit, these late-night visits, put on her dressing gown, her teddy-bear slippers, shuffled to the front door, peered responsibly through the spyhole and saw Black and White, two peas in a pod, and said, 'What do you want?'

'We have to talk, Miss Beneke.'

'Go and talk to van Heerden, he's in charge of the case.'

'He works for you, Miss Beneke.' Suddenly 'Miss Beneke', this morning it had been nothing, simply arrogance. She sighed, unlocked the door.

They smiled politely at her, walked into the living room. She followed.

'Sit down,' she said. They sat down to next to one another on the couch, she sat in the chair.

'Pretty place,' said Black with forced appreciation. White nodded his agreement. Hope said nothing.

'Miss Beneke, we were a trifle impetuous this morning,' White said feelingly.

'Thoughtless,' said Black.

'We don't often work with civilians,' said White.

'Out of practice,' said Black.

'We appreciate the work you've done,' said White.

'Unbelievable,' said Black.

'But we would be neglecting our duty if we didn't warn you that there are a number of very dangerous people involved.'

'Psychopathic murderers,' said Black. 'People who kill without compunction. People who could do the South African Government a great deal of harm. And still wish to do so. And we're a young democracy.'

'We can't afford it,' said White.

'We don't want to expose you to the danger,' said Black. 'It's our task to keep you safe.'

'To contain the war to the front.'

'As we understand it, you're looking for a will.'

'A noble crusade.'

'If we promise, on behalf of the State, to find the document when all those involved are under control . . .'

'We want to ask if you at least won't defer the investigation.'

'Until all danger has been removed.'

'Purely for your own safety.'

'And the security of our young democracy.'

'Please.'

She looked at them. They looked at her expectantly, on the edge of the couch, two large, powerful men with impressive jaws and shoulders, fighting hard against natures that usually barked orders, and she suddenly wanted to laugh, with the same exuberance she had shared with van Heerden and in that moment she knew why he hadn't wanted to hand the case to either the police or Military Intelligence, understood the change in him and she said: 'No, thank you, thank you very much, we appreciate it and I'm sure our young democracy appreciates it but there is one problem attached to handing you the case, which makes it impossible.'

'What?' they said in unison.

'If you're so serious about protecting us all, why wasn't Bushy Schlebusch put behind bars a long time ago?'

Rupert de Jager and Bushy Schlebusch and Another. Members of Military Intelligence? The Three Executioners? The Dirty Work Trio? The fingers that had pulled the trigger on behalf of an obscure section deep in the Department of Defence? Richly rewarded for Mission Impossible? Paid in American dollars? 'Go and shoot so-and-so of the ANC or the PAC in Lusaka or London or Paris, boys, and we'll drown you in dollars.'

Go and plant a bomb?

Hell, every Truth and Reconciliation Commission dossier was a clue in this affair.

'Another', who spoke to Hope and said they had been together in '76. Together where? To do what?

And now that the graves had opened and the ghosts were walking, Military Intelligence and the Yanks were scurrying round like trapped rats.

Where in hell did the Americans fit into this puzzle? The M16? The dollars? Was the target of the Deadly Trio an American one? Lend us a small team from your abundant secret army to eliminate Dictator A in South American country B, and we'll help you to bust a few sanctions. The Yanks as guarantors? The great joint struggle against Communism sometimes made for strange bedfellows.

Or were the Americans on the receiving end of elimination?

He stared at the words, the squares, the timetable in front of him.

De Jager, Schlebusch, Another. Together in '76. And in the eighties de Jager came back with a new name. Had Military Intelligence provided him with the new identity? 'Start a new life, take your dollars and keep your mouth shut.'

And then Bushy Schlebusch's dollars were finished and he brought his M16 and his blowtorch to fetch more?

Still too many questions.

But actually none of it really mattered.

Schlebusch mattered, Schlebusch had the will. And the dollars and the M16.

What mattered was how they were going to find Schlebusch.

And he had a plan.

His telephone rang.

'Van Heerden.'

'Military Intelligence were here,' Hope Beneke said.

'At your home?'

'They want us to defer the investigation so that we can protect our young democracy,' she said. 'And ourselves.'

'That's a new approach.'

'They were very polite.'

'It couldn't have been easy for them.'

'It wasn't.'

'And what did you say?'

'I said no.'

He did the dishes and thought about Hope Beneke. Full of surprises. Idealistic, naive, loyal, temperamental, straight, honest, not beautiful but sexy, despite everything, sexy. What would it be like to hold those neat buttocks, to cup his hands around them and to enter her, what would she be like in bed, naive? Or would the same driving force that had brought her to speak to him about beating up the doctor, the same depths which could make the red mark of anger glow . . .

An erection grew against the edge of the sink.

Light falling through his windows made him look up.

At this time of night? A car door slammed, he frowned, dried his hands, walked to the door, it opened and the wind blew in Kara-An, tight black sweater, nipples erect from the cold, black trousers, high heels. She slammed the door behind her, mouth scarlet and wide. 'I came to fetch a progress report,' holding out a bottle of champagne.

'That's not what you came for.'

She looked at him with a small half-smile. 'You know me.'

'Yes.'

They were a step away from one another.

'Take me,' she said, her eyes darkening.

He looked at the nipples, didn't move.

'Take me. If you can.'

34

I found his name among hundreds of others.

I dug, prospected for weeks in the register of every sexual offender between 1976 and 1978 who had served a jail sentence. And found his name in the lists of comparisons that decorated my wall.

Victor Reinhardt Simmel.

It was a fleck of gold in the grey ore of information, it didn't show up immediately and brightly, it was almost invisible. I listed every one questioned in each of the murders. In the investigation into the death of the twenty-one-year-old-waitress in Carletonville, there had been a Victor Reinhardt Simmel. Short notes, a group of regular guests in the restaurant where she worked were questioned. He was there on a few occasions, she served him, among others. He denied any knowledge, expressed his sympathy. There was nothing to lift him out of the mass of other suspects.

And eventually in the sentence register: On 14 July 1976, a Victor Reinhardt Simmel was jailed for three years in the Randfontein Magistrates Court on charges of indecent assault on a twenty-six-year-old librarian and the possession of pornographic material. I traced the investigation and court files. Crime of opportunity: she walked home in the dusk of early evening, put her key into the lock, unlocked the door, Simmel was driving past, stopped at her garden gate, got out of the car, asked for directions in a friendly manner, suddenly grabbed her arm and forced her into the house. She had yelled, he punched her in the face, threatened to kill her.

The neighbour opposite was defying water restrictions during the great drought of '76 by watering her lawn. And she saw what was happening, called her two miner boarders. They burst into the librarian's home. Victor Reinhardt Simmel was tearing off her blouse, his forearm against her throat, her nose broken and bleeding from the punch. They dragged him away, subdued and tied him. In the meantime the neighbour had called the police.

In his car they found pornography – Dutch magazines with explicit photographs of bondage.

Perhaps they also found a roll of masking tape in the car. Maybe they didn't know it was connected to any case.

Victor Reinhardt Simmel.

Not a miner. A technician for Deutsche Maschine, a firm which made and maintained huge industrial water pumps for the mining industry.

There was a picture of him in the dossier of the case. Short and stocky with the innumerable scars of a war lost to acne.

The thread between Simmel and the Masking Tape murders was slender, so terribly slender – a single cameo role in one of the murders but it was all I had, all I needed.

I took his photo and drove to Virginia, looking for Maria Masibuko who would be a thirty-eight-year-old woman by now with scarred breasts and the face of a murderer stored in her memory. I didn't find her there. They told me she had gone to Welkom. Another rumour had it that she was living in Bloemfontein. After another two weeks I traced her to a maternity clinic in Botshabelo, a nursing sister with delicate hands and the memory of pain and hate still showing in the movements of her shoulders.

She looked at the photo, briefly, before her mouth twisted . . .

'It's him,' she said. And walked away to choke back the vomit rising in her throat.

Day 2

Tuesday, 11 July

35

He stood in the doorway, the bathroom light falling across the bed through the steam of the shower, and stared at Kara-An's sleeping shape: the dark hair spread over the pillow, the pale skin of her shoulder and upper arm, the curve of her breast, the beautiful mouth half-open and without lipstick, the narrow white edge of her teeth visible, small, rhythmic sounds of a deep sleep in her throat. So much beauty, even now, so much beauty, the body of an angel, the face of a goddess but the damaged grey matter lay in the skull, God, it had been wild last night, she was like an animal, a leopard trapped in her head, scratching and hissing and biting and crazy, swearing and panting – how much did she hate herself?

He stood naked in the doorway, feeling more pain than the scratch marks and bruises on his body warranted. He had to get dressed, go to work but the contrast between the quiet figure on the bed and the demon of last night held him captive.

He had learnt about himself last night.

He had reached the edge and halted.

'Hurt me,' she had said, begging, reproaching, hitting out at his face. Again and again through grinding teeth, 'Hurt me,' and he could not, in the frenetic moments he had searched for the ability to do so and it wasn't there.

He didn't want to hurt her, he wanted to comfort her. Despite all the aggression in him, despite all the hate and reproaches and pain.

He had tried to draw it from his own rage but there was . . . something else. He wanted to comfort her, give her sympathy. He felt sorry for her, so infinitely sorry. What he felt was not lust but heartbreak.

Eventually he had thrust into her and brought the act to a climax, holding and sweating while she swore at him about his impotence, his cowardice, his betrayal, until he lay on top of her, empty and tired, and the silence between them became as cold and dark as the night outside. And then he had rolled off and lain next to her, staring at the ceiling until he felt her hands soft on his chest and she had shifted her warm body close to his and fallen asleep. He thought about nothing, closing the doors of his mind.

Hope Beneke walked to the airport building in the icy, dry cold of an early Bloemfontein morning and was amazed by the bleached grass and the bright light of the pale sun. When her eyes searched the people in the arrivals hall, she knew the tall, slender, grey-haired woman with the deeply-lined face was Rupert de Jager's mother. She walked up to her, extended her hand and was embraced by the bony arms that hugged her against Carolina de Jager's body.

'I'm so pleased that you've come.'

'We're pleased that we could trace you.'

The woman dropped her arms. 'I won't cry, you don't have to worry.'

'You can cry as much as you like, Mrs de Jager.'

'Call me Carolina. I've finished crying.'

'Is there somewhere here that we can wait? Perhaps have a cup of coffee?'

'Let's go to town, we have lots of time. I'll show you the Waterfront.'

'Bloemfontein has a Waterfront?'

'What do you mean? A beautiful place.'

They walked out of the airport building, back into the cold. Carolina de Jager looked at her again. 'You're so small. For an attorney. I thought you would be a big woman.'

* * *

He played back the answering machine's tape, listened to the messages of the lonely, the disturbed, with the old, familiar astonishment at the damage that people carry with them. Where did Kara-An's damage originate? Perhaps she could point a finger at others, but his was due to the dagger of his own actions, a blade that cut widely, made others bleed.

Focus. He arranged his notes, read the newspaper reports, clever reheating of the investigative leftovers, quotes from Superintendent Bart de Wit: 'Murder and Robbery have always been part of the investigation and we gladly shared our information with the private team. Murder and Robbery will remain part of it and are following up new leads.'

Ha!

The telephone seldom rang now, nothing usable, he had to wait for Hope and Carolina de Jager and the parcel she was bringing, the next big step.

Marie at the door. 'There's a policeman to see you, sir.'

'Send him in.'

Captain Mat Joubert. 'Morning, van Heerden.'

'Mat.'

'You still believe the devil is in the detail.' Joubert looked at the notes, sat down, his voice soft for such a big man.

'How are you, van Heerden?'

'That's not why you're here.'

'No.'

'Bart de Wit changed his point of view?'

'No. The Super doesn't know I'm here. I've come to warn you. The Commissioner phoned this morning. Military Intelligence are taking over the investigation. It comes from on high. Ministerial level. Nougat is preparing the dossier for the handover.'

'And he's mad as a snake.'

Joubert rolled his big shoulders. 'You're their next port of call, van Heerden. They're coming with a court order. Law on Internal Security.'

He had no reaction.

'You opened up something that makes them very nervous.'

'They can't stop it now.'

'They can. You know that.'

'Mat, this thing goes back to '76. Bush War. It's Truth and Reconciliation Commission material. The ANC would welcome it.'

'How many spooks did you see appearing in front of the TRC? I'm not talking about the butchers and semi-spooks like the Vlakplaas men and Basson, I'm talking about the main men. The obscure units inside National Intelligence and MI of which we've only heard rumours. There was nothing on them or about them. There was nothing from Namibia. Do you think it was a coincidence?'

He had never thought about it in that way. 'I didn't follow the TRC with great attention. I was . . . distracted.'

'In the final TRC report they mention masses of records that were destroyed in '93. And there are rumours all over the place. Do you know how much paper was burnt in Iscor's furnaces? Forty-four tons. And Military Intelligence destroyed hundreds of files in Simon's Town in '94. With the knowledge of the ANC. Nothing could stop them then. Nothing is going to stop them now. And with reason.'

'What reason?'

Joubert took a deep breath. 'I don't know. But if I were you I'd make copies of everything. Because they're coming to confiscate everything. And they'll be here shortly.' He got up. 'They mustn't find me here.'

'Why, Mat? Why did you come to warn me?'

'Because we owe you, van Heerden. All of us.'

It was only after he had said goodbye to Mat Joubert in reception and was sitting at the desk again that he realized he had to get hold of Hope. Carolina de Jager and her parcel must not be delivered here. He dialled her cell-phone. 'The number you have dialled is unavailable. Please leave a message after the tone.'

Jesus.

'Hope, don't bring Mrs de Jager to your office. Go . . . I'll phone my mother. Take her there. I'll explain later.'

He looked at his watch. Were they on the return flight already? Probably. Would she listen to messages before she came to the office?

He put out his hand for the telephone again. Had to warn his mother. He dialled her number.

'Hallo,' he heard his mother say.

The door opened.

'Morning, motherfucker,' said White. He held a document in his hand. 'We have a love letter for you.'

Marian Olivier, the other partner of Beneke, Olivier and Partners was an unattractive young woman with a highly arched nose, a small, narrow mouth and a rich, melodious voice like a radio personality's. 'The document is in order,' she said.

'Nice to work with professional people,' said Black.

'Who understand all the big words,' said White.

'Please translate it for Sonny-boy here, in easy-to-grasp concepts. He's not allowed to play with all the dangerous toys any longer.'

'He must go home.'

'Find other toys.'

'Or we'll lock him up.'

'That's correct,' said Marian Olivier.

'Correct,' said White. 'Such a nice, official word.'

'It's also correct that we may search the offices,' said Black.

'Which we would like to do now.'

'We brought some help.'

'Fourteen men.'

'With itchy hands.'

'Who are waiting outside.'

'Out of decency.'

'Politeness.'

'And then we want to visit Sonny-boy at home.'

'To make sure that he's not hiding toys that are dangerous for a child of his age.'

'And unfortunately we'll also have to search Miss Beneke's little place.'

'We apologize in advance for the discomfort.'

'Sometimes our work is hell.'

'That is correct.'

'Everything is in order,' said Marian Olivier.

'In order,' said Black. 'That's another nice one.'

'Correct,' said White and they giggled like teenagers. 'I'll stay here. Major Mzimkhulu will accompany Sonny-boy a little later.'

'Unpack his toy cupboard. As soon as he's shared everything here with us.'

'Like a good boy.'

They ran in the rain to Hope's BMW in the parking area at the Cape Town International Airport. And when they had put the luggage in the boot and closed the doors, Carolina de Jager said, 'Oh, how lovely to see rain again.'

Hope started the car, pulled away.

'We wouldn't mind a bit of sunshine. It's been raining for more than a week.'

'The farmers should be grateful.'

'Too true,' said Hope and pulled her handbag towards her to find money for the parking gate. Saw her cellphone. Better switch it on.

At 16:52 on Tuesday, 11 July, Major Steve Mzimkhulu of Military Intelligence's Special Ops Unit died on the N7, one kilometre north of the Bosmansdam exit.

They drove from the city in silence as if Mzimkhulu's comedy rhythm was disturbed when White wasn't present but the officer's last words were in a more serious vein. 'I must admit, Sonny-boy, you haven't done badly,' he said when they took the N1 exit.

Van Heerden didn't say anything. Later, when he thought back, he realized they had been followed. He had been unaware. He had been thinking about Joubert's words: 'Because we owe you, van Heerden. All of us.' He thought about Hope and Carolina de Jager and the influence of the latest events on his plan and then, beyond the Bosmansdam exit, at about 130, 140 kilometres per hour, the truck in the right lane swung into them. He would only remember the colour, a dirty white, big, bigger than a SUV, with a bull bar, overtaking him, that was all he could remember. It struck the Corolla on the right wing and suddenly he was fighting the steering wheel and then they rolled, right over, the deafening noise of metal and glass breaking and then the car lay on its roof and he hung in the seat belt, the rain on his face and Mzimkhulu's blood against the front window and then there was a gun against the side of his head. 'Are you alive?' He wanted to turn his head but the muzzle prevented him.

'Can you hear me?'

He nodded.

'You have a mother, policeman. Do you hear me? You have a mother. I'll burn her with a fucking blowtorch, do you hear me?'

'Bushy,' he said, his voice faraway.

'You don't know me, you pig, cunt, leave me alone or I'll burn her. We should've burnt the fucking will a long time ago, leave me alone or I'll kill you.' And then the muzzle was no longer against his face, footsteps, he tried to look, saw long hair, long, blond hair, heard the truck leaving, other cars stopping, rain against the Corolla, against his face, *tink-tink* of metal cooling, the smell of blood and petrol and wet earth and he shivered, his whole body shook and he knew it was shock and he wanted to unfasten the seat belt but he didn't know where his hands were.

He was in the Milnerton MediClinic in a six-bed ward and the woman at administration wanted to know who was going to pay because he didn't have a medical fund and he wanted to go home and the doctor didn't want him to leave because he had to stay for 'observation' and until the injection against shock had worked, 'perhaps tomorrow morning' and then White was there and said he was Colonel Brits of the South African National Defence Force and insisted that van Heerden be moved to a private room and that the State would pay if necessary and put two guards in front of the door and the woman from administration said she wanted a letter of some kind, because the State only paid after a fight but they moved him to a private ward and the doctor said Brits had to leave him alone, he wasn't ready to talk, he was going to sleep after the injection and Brits said it was a matter of urgency and then they were alone, he and Bester 'White' Brits, and the man stood next to his bed and said Steven is dead from a head injury and he said he knew, the ambulance men had told him at the scene and Brits wanted to know how it had happened.

His own voice was faraway, his tongue slow and clumsy, his head thick. 'I don't know. There was . . . a truck, we were hit, I . . .'

'A truck? What fucking truck, van Heerden?' And in the wool of his head it registered that he was no longer 'Sonny-boy', that the whole tone had changed. Aggression.

'It happened so fast I couldn't see,' his words slowing down even more. 'Like a Ford F100, the old pick-ups, bigger than an SUV. Left-hand drive,' and then he wondered why he had said it because . . .

'And then?' Huge impatience.

'Overtook us, swung into us, hit the nose of the car. Then we rolled.'

'Fucking Steven. Would never wear a seat belt. And then?'

Don't say anything, don't say anything.

'Come on, van Heerden, what then?'

'Ambulance . . .'

'There are eyewitnesses who said a man or a woman with long blond hair ran away from your car, got into a big cream-coloured truck and drove away when they stopped.'

Don't say anything. He wanted out, to protect his mother, he couldn't keep his eyes open any longer, he heard voices, Brits calling his name, others, he heard his mother's voice, Hope, Nougat O'Grady, forced his attention, his eyes open but could see nothing.

In the middle of the night he woke and he heard her breathing and looked and saw his mother next to his bed in the dark, moonlight through the window.

'Ma,' his voice almost inaudible.

'Yes, my son,' she whispered back.

'Ma, you must stay here.'

She took his hand. 'I will.'

For her own protection, he meant. Not for him.

Her other hand was in his hair, stroking his head. 'Sleep, I'm here.'

His shoulder and neck ached, not excessively painful, the discomfort of stretched muscles. He wanted to ask where Hope and Carolina de Jager were, but he lay still. He'd been eight or nine when he had the high fever, they thought it was meningitis, never really found out what it was and his mother sat next to his bed for five days and held his hand and stroked his head and spoke to him in between the compresses and the medicine and the fever dreams, and he thought, nothing has changed, it was still only the two of them, and everything had changed and then he slept again.

36

I'm dragging my feet over my story, lingering over the murder of Baby Marnewick because it was my professional coming-of-age, my zenith, my fifteen minutes of fame.

But also because it was the final chapter in the history of Zatopek van Heerden the Innocent, the Just, the Good. After this I'll have to begin the prologue to damnation and I hesitate because the mere thought fills me with repugnance – not fear, no longer fear.

So let me close – but without the suspenseful denouement of a second-rate thriller. The truth was far duller.

The trail of Victor Reinhardt Simmel reached a dead end in 1980 and I found the reason eventually at Intercontinental Mining Support (or IMS as it's known). IMS took over Deutsche Maschine in 1987 but had kept none of the lapsed personnel records. It was an ex-colleague of Simmel's, at IMS headquarters in Germiston, who supplied me with the information: the Masking Tape Murderer had emigrated to Australia early in 1981.

'He said it was due to the political situation here.'

I asked the ex-colleague what he could remember about Simmel. 'Not very much. He talked a great deal and he was a liar.'

I knew it wasn't the political situation that had made Simmel flee. It was the heat of the murder inquiries. Somewhere in their investigations of the last two or three murders the police probably came too close. And so I went to Australia, with the permission of the Prof and the University of South Africa picking up the tab. We – Superintendent Charley Edwards of Sydney's Criminal Investigation Bureau and I – went to arrest Victor Reinhardt Simmel in Alice Springs, in the dry, dusty Northern Territory, an unsensational event, an anticlimax. We knocked on the door of his house, asked the short, ugly little man with the powerful shoulders to accompany us and he came along without demur.

In an unbearably hot interrogation room Simmel denied everything. But eventually, after days of fending-off and lying, using the distancing mechanism of most serial killers, he said that 'the other Victor Reinhardt Simmel, the evil one,' had done terrible things – and told us about his murder trail, which ran through South Africa, Australia and even Hong Kong.

I wanted to know about Baby Marnewick and he, the 'evil Victor', could barely remember her. I had to show him the photographs in the yellowing dossier, I had to describe her and remind him how he had followed her from the shopping centre, watched her for two days, humiliated and murdered her.

I looked for absolution in his insanity – and eventually found it. I had to dig for it because ostensibly he was no monster, merely a self-important, unattractive, damaged product of a casual sexual encounter between a slut of a mother who didn't want him and an unknown father and a lifetime of derision about his background, his height, his acne and his social status.

Thirty-seven women. Thirty-seven victims who had to pay the price of his rage. Had to pay the social debt of a community that finds it easier to reject than to accept, that prefers to remain uninvolved.

You, I, every one of us has a share in those thirty-seven murders. Because we're bad by omission.

My absolution had a price.

And a reward. I was a hero in Australia. 'Academic sleuth corners serial killer,' was the front-page headline in the *Sydney Morning Herald*, the first of a storm of newspaper reports, television programmes and radio interviews. And back in South Africa I was the darling of journalists for two long weeks. (But how soon they forget. Only eight years later, with the Wilna van As case, not a single journalist made the connection – not until the end.)

I cannot deny that I enjoyed every moment of the attention. Suddenly I was Someone, I was successful, I was good. Good.

And if all that still doesn't jog your memory: Victor Reinhardt Simmel committed suicide before he could be extradited. In a cell in Sydney, he cut his wrists to ribbons with a sharpened table knife. Not with the neat transverse cuts of fiction and the movies but with the demonic lengthwise slashes of reality.

My life carried on. My life changed. The last great turning point, the prologue to my own downfall, happened two weeks after I had handed in my doctoral thesis. I was in Cape Town to hold a seminar on the profiling of serial killers for Murder and Robbery in those drab headquarters in Bellville South. And Colonel Willie Theal, then the officer in command, came to me after the proceedings.

'Come home,' he said. 'Come and work for me.'

Day 1

Wednesday, 12 July

37

He was awake by five o' clock, his mother still sleeping in the chair next to the bed, and he lay quite still and thought that he hadn't seen it coming, tried to relive the moments on the N7: the truck next to him, just another vehicle passing, he was driving fast, the truck still faster and then it swung into him, against the bumper and the right front wheel of the car. Perhaps there was immediate damage because he had lost control, Lord, the roll was so quick, the disorientated Steve Mzimkhulu hadn't said a word, didn't make a sound, only breaking glass and metal on tarmac, rolling, rolling, rolling and then the Corolla lay on its roof and he hung there and heard the footsteps and the voice of Bushy Schlebusch.

You have a mother, policeman. Do you hear me? You have a mother.

How did he know?

We should've burnt the fucking will a long time ago.

We . . .

It still existed. The document was somewhere but no one had said anything about a will. Not in the *Die Burger* copy, not in the follow-ups the previous day, not to MI, not to the American.

Only he and Hope and Wilna van As and Murder and Robbery.

Wilna van As.

Nougat O'Grady had been suspicious of her.

You have a mother, policeman. Do you hear me? You have a mother.

There was hatred in that voice, pure, intense hatred.

You have a mother, policeman. Do you hear me? You have a mother.

How was he going to protect her? How was he going to do his work and protect her against Schlebusch?

He had followed him in the truck. From the office? For how long had he watched? How had Schlebusch known what he looked like, what kind of car he drove?

Probably not too difficult to find out if you wanted to.

He had to protect his mother. He had to find Schlebusch before Schlebusch found them. He had to fight Military Intelligence's court interdict.

We should've burnt the fucking will a long time ago.

How did Schlebusch know about the will? Because it was among the stolen goods, among the dollars and the documents of Rupert de Jager/Johannes Jacobus Smit and he had reached a conclusion?

Or because Wilna van As had spoken to him?

And if it was gone, why continue with the investigation?

A gun against his head, why hadn't Schlebusch shot him?

Had he seen other vehicles stopping? Or had it never been the aim to eliminate – merely to frighten?

You have a mother, policeman. Do you hear me? You have a mother.

His first responsibility was to protect her.

He looked at her sitting in the chair next to the hospital bed.

Had to protect her first.

And then get Military Intelligence off his back. Which probably wouldn't be too difficult.

And then find Schlebusch.

The man with the long blond hair running away, getting into the truck but there was something . . .

The left-hand drive . . .

Perhaps he had lied about the will. Perhaps it was still somewhere. And if it no longer existed . . .

There were dollars.

We . . .

Chaos.

They were all there: Bester Brits and a new man, Brigadier Walter Redelinghuys, steel-grey crew-cut, square jaw, O'Grady and Joubert, Hope Beneke, his mother, the doctor. He came out of the bathroom dressed in the clothes his mother had brought and they were all there.

'It's a homicide, sir, and therefore it's our case.'

'It's got nothing to do with you, it's our man who's dead.' Staking out territory on the grounds of murder. As he walked in everyone was quiet for a moment. He looked at Hope, hoping for an indication of the whereabouts of Carolina de Jager. She gave a small nod, knew what he wanted. Relief.

'We want a statement, van Heerden,' said O'Grady.

'I forbid you to speak to them,' said Bester Brits and turned to Joubert: 'You got your orders from high up, why are you messing around?'

Mat Joubert stood in the doorway, filling the space with his height. 'The orders changed this morning,' he said calmly. 'Speak to your boss.'

'I'm his boss,' said Square Jaw. 'Walter Redelinghuys,' extending his hand to van Heerden. 'Brigadier.'

'Van Heerden.'

'I know. How do you feel this morning?'

'That's what I'm trying to find out,' said the doctor, a startled young man with a moustache and a small beard and large pebble glasses, a different one from last night's. 'You'll have to wait outside until I've finished the examination,' he said without conviction.

'There's nothing wrong with me,' said van Heerden.

'Then I want to take down a statement,' said fat Inspector Tony O'Grady.

'No, you don't,' said Bester Brits.

'Stop it!' said his mother in a sharp and decisive voice and a silence fell. 'You're like children. You should be ashamed of yourself. A man died yesterday afternoon and you're sqabbling like a lot of school boys. Have you no respect?'

He saw Hope at that moment, her small, secret smile.

'Tell me,' said Joan van Heerden, 'did he have a wife and children?'

'Yes,' said Walter Redelinghuys. 'Three children.'

'Who's with them? Who's looking after them? Who's comforting them? I don't know where you all fit in but that's where you should be now.'

'Mrs van Heerden,' said Redelinghuys, weightily and conciliatory, 'you're right. But there is also a murderer out there and national security is involved and . . .'

'National security? What an absurd concept. What does it mean, General . . .'

'Brigadier,' said Bester Brits.

'Be quiet,' said Joan van Heerden. 'You and your big, empty words.'

'It was Schlebusch,' said van Heerden and they all looked at him.

'Doctor, you'll have to excuse us,' said Bester Brits and, taking the young man's arm, guided him to the door, the eyes behind the pebble glasses huge but he made no objection, allowed himself to be led out and the door closed.

'Who is Schlebusch?' asked Mat Joubert.

'It doesn't matter,' said Brits, 'Privileged information.'

'You can choose,' said van Heerden, the old rage coming back, 'you can stay here and bark like lap dogs and I'm going home or you can shut up and listen. One interruption and I leave. One more reference to national security and I leave.' He pointed at Brits. 'You've got something you want to cover up and I'm telling you I don't want to know what it is. What happened in '76 doesn't matter to me and you can keep your secrets. But I have a job to do and I'm going to do it because I hold all the aces. Forget about your court interdict because you can't stop this thing now. How are you going to keep Carolina de Jager quiet if she goes to the Sunday papers and starts asking questions about why, more than twenty years ago, she was informed of the death of her son and given a medal but he wasn't dead? What are you going to do if Hope Beneke applies for an urgent interdict today to fight your gag and she invites every newspaper in the Cape to the hearing? Can you imagine the headlines?'

Bester Brits was agitated, uncomfortable, and itching to speak.

'I don't want to hear a word, Brits, or I leave.'

He looked up at them, they looked down.

'We know Johannes Jacobus Smit was Rupert de Jager. We know he and Bushy Schlebusch and another man did something for you in 1976 and I can only guess at the unholy shit that was involved. I don't know where the Americans come in but somewhere along the line they have a finger in the pie. We know you paid de Jager in dollars and gave him a new identity. We know Schlebusch murdered de Jager. I suspect he was after the money. But it could be that you asked him to eliminate de Jager. Because he wanted to sing. I don't know and I no longer care. All that matters is that we have one thing in common. We're looking for Schlebusch. You, I assume, want to protect him or keep him quiet. Or stop him from murdering again. Murder and Robbery want to lock him up. This conflict of interests is your problem. All we want is the will.'

'Or his evidence about its existence and its contents,' said Hope Beneke.

'Right,' said van Heerden. 'And let's be honest, you have no idea where to find Schlebusch.'

'Do you?' asked Redelinghuys.

'No,' he said. 'But I'll find him.'

'How?'

'I know where to dig. And you're going to leave me alone until I find him. And then you can argue again about jurisdiction and orders from higher up.'

'You don't know jackshit, van Heerden. About '76. You know nothing.'

'I know enough, Brits. The detail doesn't matter. I know enough. Yesterday afternoon Schlebusch ran us off the road and, while I hung in the wreck, held a weapon against my head and said I had to leave this whole thing alone and now I'm wondering about two things, Brits. Why didn't he shoot me? Because he could have. And why does he want me to stop the investigation? I'll tell you why. He didn't shoot me because he doesn't want to cause more pressure. He didn't know Mzimkhulu was dead and he didn't want the official investigation to escalate due to another murder. Why not? For the same reason that he wants me to drop the case. Because he knows I'm close, Brits. Somewhere I hit a nerve in all the speculation and publicity that made him think I'm close. And he can't run away because if he could, he would have. He has interests keeping him here and he's nervous. He has dollars and a lifestyle and if the affair escalates he loses everything. And I'm going to find him. I'm telling you here and now, I'm going to find him.'

He saw Mat Joubert's smile.

'And one more thing. Yesterday afternoon, with a gun at my head, Schlebusch spoke about the will and I can't stop speculating how he knew about it. Because only we – and Murder and Robbery – know it's the reason for the private investigation. And we didn't talk.'

Leave Wilna van As out of it.

'Oh, no,' said Nougat O'Grady and pointed a fat finger at Bester Brits. 'They knew it, too. They've been talking to me since early Monday morning, very buddy-buddy, we're in this thing together, and now they're trying to take it away, double-crossing bastards.'

'Then, gentlemen, I wonder who informed Schlebusch: Military Intelligence or the SAPS?'

The sunlight was blindingly bright outside, the sky cloudless and blue, the smell of sun on wet earth, the grass suddenly a deep green, the wind icy.

'There was snow on the mountains,' his mother said. He drove home with her on the N7, the river at Vissershok broad and gleaming, she said Carolina de Jager was safe at her house with Hope, they would be waiting for him; she asked if he was really all right, he said yes, only bruises.

'I met Kara-An Rousseau last night,' she said.

'Oh.'

'She came to the hospital.'

'Oh.'

'Is there something I don't know about?'

'No.'

She was silent for a long time until they turned in at the gate. 'I think Hope is wonderful,' she said.

She stopped in front of his house.

'Here are your keys. They brought them to me,' she said, opening her handbag.

'Ma . . .'

'Yes, my son?'

'There is something I must talk to you about.'

'Yes, son?'

'Yesterday afternoon . . . Schlebusch. He threatened me, Ma. He said he'll . . . come and hurt you, if I don't drop the investigation.'

He looked at her, watching for fear in her face. There was none.

'I'm getting help today. I'll get the best there is. I promise you.'

'But you're not going to drop the investigation?'

'I'll . . . get the best, Ma . . .'

She silenced him with a gesture. 'Maybe it's time for me to tell you something, Zet. I went to see Hope. Last Friday. After you'd dropped the job. I went to speak to her. About you. To give you another chance. I'm not going to apologize for it because I'm your mother and I did it for you. I did it because I believed the only thing that could heal you was for you to work like you used to work. I still believe it. I don't want you to drop it. I just want you to be careful. If you want to get someone to look after me, that's fine. But who is going to look after *you*?'

'You went to speak to Hope, Ma?'

'I asked you who is going to look after you, Zet.'

'I . . . No one. I . . .'

'Will you be careful?'

He opened the car door. 'I can't believe you went to speak to Hope.'

She put the car into gear. 'Water under the bridge. And I'm not going to apologize.'

He got out, almost closed the door, suddenly remembered something.

'Ma.'

'Yes, Zet?'

'Thank you. For last night.'

She smiled at him, moved the car forward. He slammed the door and she drove off to her big house.

He stood in the sunlight, his keys in his hand. He saw the daisies, suddenly in flower, a sea of white and orange stretching from his door as far as the gate. He saw the blue sky, the jagged line of the Hottentots-Holland peaks in the east.

His mother had gone to speak to Hope. No wonder they had had such a cosy conversation the day before yesterday.

He shook his head, unlocked the door, drew the curtains in front of the windows, saw white panels of sunshine illuminating his house like spotlights.

He looked through his CDs until he found the right one, turned up the sound to full volume and sat down in a warm patch of sunlight. First the foundation laid by the orchestra, the prologue to the divine, then the voice of the soprano, so sweet, so heavenly sweet, Mozart's 'Agnus Dei' from *Litaniae de venerabilis altaris sacramento*. He sat bathed in the sound, let it flow over him, into him, followed the singer's voice through each note until it released a deep well of emotion in him; listened to more than six minutes of music and knew that it was the closest he would come to expressing his gratitude for being alive.

Then he had a long, hot, pleasurable shower.

'He was a Recce,' said Carolina de Jager. 'And he was immensely proud of it, he and his father, and when we were told of his death, it broke his father. I still claim it was where the cancer originated. His father died in 1981 and I let the farm and moved to town and I don't know what I'm going to do with the land, there is no one to inherit.'

She sat in the sunlight that fell through the windows of his mother's house, a big black writing pad and a cardboard box on her lap and she spoke to Joan van Heerden, not to him and he thought he understood. Wilna van As sat opposite her, next to Hope, a box of tissues next to her, expectantly, four women and him.

'He was at Grey College in Bloemfontein and he wasn't an excessively clever child and he would come to the farm. He was strong because he and his father worked side by side on the farm. He was a good kid, no smoking or drinking. He was an athlete, he ran cross country, he was second in the Free State and then the call-up papers came for 1 Infantry Batallion and he told his father he was going to try out for Reconnaissance Command. They didn't know I was worried, didn't know about the nights I lay awake. His father was so proud of him when he made the grade, his father always said how strict the selection was, everyone had to listen, Sundays at the Springfontein church, "My son Rupert is a Recce, you know how tough the selection is, Rupert is in Angola, I shouldn't really talk about it but they're giving the Cubans what for".'

'Angola?'

'What Rupert did, he wrote letters but he never sent them because of the censors – they put thick black lines through everything, it frustrated his father so much. He waited for the seven days and fourteen days leave and then he and his father would sit on the veranda and read, or on the ridge. His father kept this book, his notes when he reread the letters, when Rupert had left again, with cuttings from the *Volksblad* and *Paratus*, every single bit about the training in South-West and Angola. And then in '76 they arrived on the farm, two officers in a long, black car, the one with a fake bandage on his neck and they said Rupert was dead and they handed us the small wooden chest with the medal and said he'd been brave but that they weren't allowed to say what the circumstances were because it was national security but he had been very brave, he and his buddies, and the country would always be grateful to them and always honour them.

'His father took the medal and walked out without a word. There was a spot on the farm, a ridge where they always sat and looked out over the farm and talked until the sun went down, about farming and life. I found him there with the little chest on his lap and death in his eyes. His eyes were never the same again. And then the cancer came, oh, only a few months later the cancer came.'

It was his mother who wept soundlessly, he saw, not Carolina de Jager or Wilna van As, his mother who sat upright in her chair, clutching the armrest, and the tear which slowly trickled down her cheek, a thin, shining track. Carolina de Jager moved in her chair, physically dragged herself back to the present, looked at Wilna van As. 'And now I want you to tell me about the Rupert you knew, Wilna. Now you must tell me everything.'

'Carolina,' he said softly, addressing her as she had asked him to do, 'I'll have to look at the letters.'

'And the photographs,' she said.

'There are photos?' Hope asked.

'Oh, yes,' she said. 'He took them for his father. At Reconnaissance Command in Natal. And then in South-West and Angola. His father enjoyed them so much.'

He asked Hope and his mother to join him in the kitchen. Leaving the two other women alone, they sat at the kitchen table. 'Schlebusch threatened my mother, Hope, and I'm worried because I can't always be here.'

'What did he say?' Hope asked.

'That he would hurt my mother if I don't drop the investigation. I'm going to fetch help, I'm getting people to stay here until this affair is over.'

'What can he do to an old woman?' his mother asked.

'Ma, we've spoken about it, I'm not going to argue about it.'

'All right,' said his mother.

'He doesn't even know what's happening with the investigation. You should be safe for a day or two. But then . . .'

'Where will you find help?'

'I'll see. But Ma, I want to use the pick-up. Is that OK?'

'Yes, Zet.'

'Hope, is the answering machine still on in your office?'

'I don't know.'

'Would you please check? And I want you to prepare an urgent interdict, just in case.'

She nodded.

'And then you must come back. We have to work our way through the letters.'

She nodded again.

He got up. 'I'll come as soon as I can.'

'You be careful, Zet.'

'Yes, Ma.'

Hope walked with him to the garage where the faded yellow Nissan

1400 stood next to his mother's 'decent car', the Honda Ballade. The pick-up, thirteen years old, was showing patches of rust.

'Where are you going?'

'There's someone. I'm . . . looking for a firearm as well.'

He got in, started the engine.

'Zatopek,' said Hope Beneke, 'get me one while you're at it.'

38

'There's another woman, isn't there?' Wendy Brice had insisted, her mouth stiff, her body language ready to portray the betrayed woman.

And when I think back, in all honesty I can't blame her. Because why should any right-minded man on the edge of a doctorate and a great career in academe, exchange it for Murder and Robbery in Cape Town? Why would anyone give up the status of university lecturer to join the derided ranks of the SAP?

I tried to explain it in the bloody summer heat of a December afternoon in Pretoria, I walked up and down and up and down in the small living room of our flat and talked about the way I'd found myself in the search for the Masking Tape Murderer, how I eventually discovered the hunter in me, my true calling flowering like a vision, explained over and over again my desire to exchange theory for practice until I suddenly realized she didn't want to understand, she didn't want to be it, Wendy Brice didn't want to be Mrs Plod the Policeman's Wife. Her dream, her vision of herself didn't allow it and I had to choose between her and the work that Colonel Willie Theal had dangled in front of me like a challenge.

I made my choice. I was certain it was the right one. I walked to the bedroom, took a suitcase out of the cupboard. She heard the sounds and knew. She sat in the living room and cried while I packed her future with all my clothes. Wendy who had invested so much energy, so many words in her dream.

Let me tell you a secret. Months after the death of Nagel, I wondered about all my choices – and the effects of my decision on her life and on my own life. And wondered what it would have been like and realized again the pain I had caused her. I got into my Corolla and drove to Pretoria to visit her, to give her the satisfaction of knowing that the scales of justice had been evenly balanced, that the way I had acted towards her had been revenged. 'She doesn't work here any longer,' they told me at English Lit and gave me an address in Waterkloof and I drove there and stopped in front of a house and simply sat and watched, and her husband in the Mercedes came home late in the afternoon and two toddlers, a son and a daughter, rushed out, 'Daddy, Daddy,' and then it was Wendy wearing a pinafore and a smile with an embrace for them all, this family which disappeared into the big house with the syringas in the garden, and surely a swimming pool and a patio and a brick barbecue at the back and I sat there in my Corolla, unemployed and broken and fucked-up and I didn't even have it in me to cry for myself.

39

'There are dollars in it after all,' he said to Orlando Arendse in his fort in Mitchell's Plain.

'How much?'

'I don't know yet, Orlando. A million, at least, but I think it's more,' and he knew he might be wrong but would have to press on. 'It's your transaction, if I get it, Orlando.'

'Let me get this straight, van Heerden. You want me to believe that you're going to steal dollars and bring them to me – you, one of the great Untouchables from years gone by?'

'I'm not going to steal them, Orlando, I'm going to get them back for the widow of the deceased.'

'She's no widow, they weren't married.'

'You know a lot.'

Shrug of the shoulders. 'I read the papers.'

'The money belongs to her.'

'And to you?'

'You know me better than that.'

'True.'

'She can't do anything with the dollars. We'll have to convert them into rands.'

Orlando Arendse tapped his reading glasses, which hung on a chain round his neck, with an expensive fountain pen. 'But what's in it for you, van Heerden?'

'I'm being paid.'

'PI fee? It's peanuts. As it should be. I want to know what's in it for you.'

He ignored that. 'I'm looking for soldiers, Orlando. They threatened my mother. I'm looking for someone to protect her.'

'Your mother?'

'Yes.'

'Threatened?'

'Yes. Said he'd burn her with a blowtorch. Kill her.'

'It can't be. She's a national treasure.'

'What do you know about my mother, Orlando?'

Orlando smiled, like a patient parent with a naughty child. 'You think I'm trash, van Heerden. You think I'm a Cape Flats gangsta without style but good enough for a favour here and there. Well, let me tell you, just for the record, there are two of your mother's originals on the walls of my house. My real house. Paid cash, I wish to add, at an exhibition in Constantia. Every time I look at them it touches me, van Heerden, it shows me there's another side to life. I don't know your mother. But I know her soul and it's beautiful.' And then, as though annoyed at himself. 'How many soldiers?'

'How many do I need?'

Orlando thought. 'You want her protected at her house?'

'Yes.'

'Two should do it.'

He nodded. 'That'll be fine.'

'For your ma, only the best. But it doesn't come for free.'

'I can't pay you. That's why I'm offering you the dollar transaction.'

'Suddenly become a player, van Heerden?'

'I no longer have the Force behind me, Orlando.'

'Too true.'

'Will you help?'

Orlando closed his eyes, the clicking of the fountain pen against the reading glasses continuing, opened his eyes. 'I will.'

'And I'm looking for weapons. Firepower.'

Orlando looked at him in disbelief.

'You?'

'Yes. Me.'

'Heaven help us, I'd better throw in an instructor on the deal.' His soldiers laughing at their table, loudly and mockingly.

He sat at his mother's kitchen table, the women in the living room, Hope not there yet. He read the letters in chronological order, the unsensational story of an Afrikaans boy brimful of patriotism who was going to serve his country. Rupert de Jager, called up to 1 Infantry Battalion in Bloemfontein, grateful for the familiar city, the short distance home, surprised by the mix of people in the Army, the city slickers, the farm boys, the graduates, all together now, all equal, all cannon fodder. Taking pleasure in his physical achievements, believing in his chances for the Recces.

Selection at Dukuduku, the hell of testing physical limits, the euphoria of success, naive writing style, conversations with the father he obviously idolized, then, systematically, among long, sometimes boring descriptions of activities and weaponry and ideas for the farm, with the curiosity of a country-bred boy about origins and natures, the names of brothers in oppression.

'Hofstetter is a joker, Pa, he comes from Makwassie . . .'

'. . . And then they allowed us to sleep . . . We were very tired but then Speckle took out his guitar. His real name is Michael Venter. He's very short, Pa, and he has a birthmark on his neck. So they call him Speckle. He comes from Humansdorp. His father is a panel beater. He wrote a song about his town. It's quite sad.'

'. . . Olivier says no one can spell his name, they write it with an "S" but it's spelt Charel, because he's named after a Middle Ages king. He's as mad as a hatter and never stops talking but I think he'll make it, he's as strong as an ox.'

Van Heerden made notes as he read, a column of names that became longer and longer, realized not all would be applicable, some were only mentioned once, others popped up time and time again in the descriptions. He made an extra column with their names, from one base to another, diving course at Langebaan, parachutes in Bloemfontein, explosives at 1 Reconnaissance Command in Durban, nine months of learning, suffering and growth and then, a fully-fledged Recce in South West Africa.

'. . . And everyone here is being redeployed. Only Speckle and I are left of the old group. Our squad sergeant is Bushy Schlebusch and they say he's completely bush crazy because he's been in Angola twice. His eyes are crazy, Pa, but I think he's a good soldier, he swears better than anyone else . . .'

He looked at the date. Early in '76. He read faster, knew he was getting warm, de Jager and Venter and Schlebusch and five others, supply line to Unita in Angola. He made a new column for the squad, his eyes searched the written lines, looking for more Schlebusch, found very little, frustration, because de Jager's letters were sometimes vague and wandering, paragraph after paragraph of descriptions of the landscape and politics and bush-war tactics and propaganda about the efficacy of the Recces. Casual references to 32 Battalion but the squad's main task was to keep supply lines open between Rundu and somewhere in Angola, to ensure supplies – *'I'm not allowed to write much about it, Pa. I'll tell you about it when I get home'* – with occasional skirmishes here and there.

'Last night Sarge Bushy almost drilled Rodney Verster to death because he didn't have his rifle's safety catch on . . .'

'Gerry de Beer's father farms with angora goats near Somerset East. He says we don't know what drought really is but their market prices are far more stable.'

'Clinton Manley can barely speak Afrikaans. He's Catholic, Pa, but he's just like us and a good guy. He's thin and he doesn't know about giving up and he shoots better than any of us, even if he is a city guy from Rondebosch.'

Eight names eventually, on a list with added detail:

1. Sergeant Bushy Schlebusch: Durban? Natal! Surfer.
2. Rodney 'Red' Verster: Randburg. Son of a
   dentist.

3. Gerry de Beer: Somerset-East. Father an angora goat farmer.
4. Clinton Manley: Rondebosch. Western Province Schools rugby.
5. Michael 'Speckle' Venter, Humansdorp. Father owns a panel-beating firm.
6. Cobus Janse van Rensburg. Pretoria. ??????
7. James/Jamie 'Porra' Vergottini. Father owns a fish-and-chip shop in Bellville.
8. Rupert de Jager.

There were three letters left when Hope came back.

'Found anything?' she asked.

'I don't know.' He couldn't keep the frustration out of his voice.

'You upset?'

'He wasn't a good correspondent. He didn't know why we would need the letters one day.'

'My partner will complete the preparation of the interdict. It's virtually ready.'

'Thank you.'

'And Military Intelligence took the answering machine. Marie says the telephone still rings occasionally but she doesn't answer it.'

He nodded. He sketched the background to the letters, explained his plan and notes. He shifted the packet of photographs towards her. 'We're looking for the faces on this list.'

She nodded and picked them up, the faded colour snapshots, bleached to pastel. She saw there were inscriptions on the back, as she put down one face after another, some had dates, some differing handwriting. De Jager senior and junior? She read the inscriptions first, then turned over the pictures. *Boys' faces*, she thought. Too young to be soldiers. Excessive exuberance for the camera. Tired faces sometimes. Sometimes small figures in bush country, savannah, semi-desert.

'Would you like some coffee?'

'Please.'

She went to the kettle, hesitated, walked down the passage. Carolina de Jager, Wilna van As and Joan van Heerden were in the living room. They were speaking quietly, smiled at her as she peeped in. While she waited for the water to boil, she thought about the women who always remained behind, the widows and the mothers and the loved ones.

She took the two mugs back to the table, sat down, looked at van Heerden, reading the letters, a slight frown of concentration, the two of them, working together, a team. She picked up the pile of photos.

Porra, Clinton and De Beer – written on the back of a photo, she turned it over and they stood, arms over one another's shoulders, in full uniform, smiling broadly. They looked so . . . innocent. She put it aside.

Four photos later, *Speckle playing the guitar*. The picture was taken with a flash at night, the lighting bad.

Cobus and me carrying water. She recognized the young Johannes Jacobus Smit/Rupert de Jager. He and a sturdy boy were struggling with a large, evidently heavy, drum through dusty white sand.

Sarge Schlebusch, she saw on the back of one photo. She turned it over. A young white-blond man without a shirt, wearing only Army pants and boots, his torso shining and hairless and muscled, large rifle in one hand, the other shoving a threatening forefinger at the camera, the mouth verbalizing at the moment of the click, the upper lip curled back in derision. There was something . . . a shudder shook her. 'Zatopek,' she said and held out the photograph. He put down a letter, took it, looked at it.

'It's Schlebusch,' she said. He turned the picture over for a moment, read the inscription, turned it back and stared at it, for a long time and intently, as if he wanted to take the man's measure.

Then he looked at her. 'We'll have to be careful,' he said.

'I know,' she said. 'I know.'

The black man was a terrifying size, tall and broad and on his cheek a zigzag scar ran down to his neck. Next to him stood a coloured guy, short and painfully thin, with the finely chiselled features of a male model.

'Orlando sent us. I'm Tiny Mpayipheli. This is Billy September.

The weapons are in the car,' said the black man and gestured with his thumb over his shoulder to a new Mercedes-Benz ML320 at the front door.

'Come in,' said van Heerden. They walked to the living room.

'Lord save us,' said Carolina de Jager when she saw Mpayipheli.

'And protect us,' said the big man and smiled, showing a perfect set of teeth. 'Why don't they write hymns like that any more?'

'You know the old hymn book?' Carolina asked.

'My father was a missionary, ma'am.'

'Oh.'

Van Heerden introduced everyone.

'You'll have to share the spare bedroom,' said Joan van Heerden. 'But I don't know if the bed is going to be long enough for you.'

'I brought my own bedding, thank you,' said Mpayipheli in a voice like a bass cello. 'And we'll sleep in shifts. I just want to know whether there's an M-Net channel here?'

'M-Net?' said van Heerden blankly.

'Tiny is a weird Xhosa,' said Billy September. 'Likes rugby more than soccer. And on Saturday it's the Sharks against Western Province.'

Joan van Heerden laughed. 'I've got M-Net because I don't miss my soaps.'

'We've died and gone to heaven,' said September. 'I'm a *Bold and the Beautiful* fan myself.'

'Do you want to look at the weapons now?'

Van Heerden nodded and they walked to the car outside. September opened the boot.

'Are you the weapons expert?' Hope asked the small guy.

'No, Tiny is.'

'And what's your . . . speciality?' asked van Heerden.

'Unarmed combat.'

'You're not serious.'

'He is,' said Mpayipheli and lifted a blanket from the boot of the Mercedes. 'I didn't bring a large assortment. Orlando says it's window dressing because none of you can shoot.'

'I can,' said Hope.

'You're not serious,' said September, a perfect echo of van Heerden's intonation.

There was a small arsenal under the blanket. 'It'll be better if you take the SW99,' he said to her and took out a pistol. 'Collaborative effort of Smith and Wesson and Walther. Nine-millimetre, ten pounds in the magazine, one in the barrel. It's not loaded, you can take it.'

'It's too big for me.'

'Is there somewhere we can shoot?'

Van Heerden nodded. 'Beyond the trees. It's the furthest from the stables we can get.'

'You'll see, it handles easily,' Mpayipheli said to Hope. 'Polymer frame. And if you can't handle it . . .' He took out another pistol, smaller. 'This is the Colt Pony Pocketlight, .38 calibre. Firepower enough.' He turned to van Heerden. 'This is the Heckler & Koch MP-5, fires from a closed and locked bolt in either automatic or semi-automatic mode. It's the basic weapon of the FBI's Hostage Rescue Team and the SWAT units and it's what you want when you work at close quarters and you're not a good shot. Can you really not shoot?'

'I can shoot.'

'Without hitting anything,' said September, and giggled.

'With that mouth I sincerely hope you're really good at unarmed combat.'

'You want to try me, van Heerden? Do you want first-hand credentials, so to speak?'

'Zatopek,' said Hope Beneke.

'Come on, van Heerden, don't chicken out. Go for it.'

'Billy,' said Mpayipheli.

He measured the small man. 'You don't scare me.'

'Hit me, PI man, show me what you got.' Mocking, tempting, challenging.

And then van Heerden hit at him, open-handed, annoyed, and lost his balance, felt himself falling, and then he lay on the gritty gravel of his mother's drive with Billy September's knee on his chest and his pointed fingers lightly against his throat. And September said: 'Japanese Karate Association, JKA, Fourth Dan. Don't fuck with me,' and then he laughed and put out his hand to help van Heerden up.

40

Nagel.

Captain Willem Nagel, South African Police, Murder and Robbery.

The first sound I heard him make was a fart, an impossibly long, endless, flat sound as I was coming down the passage on my way to his office. It carried on when I walked in and he looked up and went on farting and it was only when the sound had ended that he put out his hand.

He was always and unashamedly flatulent, but that was probably the least of his socially unacceptable traits.

Nagel was shameless. Nagel was a sexist, a racist, a womanizer, constantly on the lookout for a new 'piece', a braggart, a liar, a show-off.

Nagel was a painfully thin man with a hopping, bobbing Adam's apple and a deep voice and a love for that voice and everything it uttered. Nagel dressed tastelessly and lived tastelessly, ate Kentucky Fried Chicken 'because my fucking old lady can't cook to save her life' until his whole office stank of a mixture of farts and the reek of the Colonel's chicken, as did the Ford Sierra we shared as a squad car, and the stench became part of my daily existence.

Nagel was my mentor within the system run by Colonel Willie Theal and I came to love him like a brother.

He listened to Abba and to Cora Marie ('That woman can make me cry, van Heerden') and said: 'Jesus, your classic shit drives me crazy' and all he ever read was 'Advice to the Lovelorn' in a women's magazine he'd discovered in a doctor's consulting room. He spent his evenings in his favourite bars with 'the boys' and told tall tales about the number, variety and type of extra-marital sex acts he had performed and would soon perform again and then, late at night, drunk but upright, he had to go back to the 'chains' of his marriage.

Willem Nagel. Wonderful, eccentric, politically incorrect Nagel. With a legendary detective brain and phenomenal arrest statistics.

I wish I had never met him.

41

Mavis Petersen, the receptionist at Murder and Robbery, said that Mat Joubert was out. 'He's on leave for personal reasons because he's getting married on Saturday,' she said in a confidential tone. 'To Mrs Margaret Wallace, an English lady. Oh, we're so pleased for his sake, we're not made to be alone.'

'Then I'll have to see Nougat, Mavis,' said van Heerden.

'That one will never get a wife,' she laughed. 'The Inspector is in court. He has to give evidence.' She leafed through the book in front of her. 'B court.'

'Thank you, Mavis.'

'And when is the Captain getting married?'

He merely shook his head as he walked away.

'Goodbye, Mavis.'

'We're not made to be alone,' he heard her calling as he went out of the door.

First his mother, and now Mavis.

His mother, arranging things so that he and Hope would share a house this evening.

He drove to the city on the N1, the traffic heavy, even before peak hours. He wondered for how long the Cape roads would be adequate, checked the rear-view mirror for a white truck, realized it was going to be very difficult to establish whether he was being followed, put his hand under the blanket on the passenger seat, felt the Heckler & Koch.

He hadn't shot too badly. Tiny Mpayipheli had said in his almost accentless English: 'It'll do,' enough holes in the paper target, but it was Hope who stole the limelight. She had held the SW99 pistol in both hands, feet planted apart, the curve of earmuffs over the short hair, and pumped ten rounds at ten metres into the target, somewhat spread grouping but all the shots within the outer circle with monotonous regularity, then smiled apologetically at him, van Heerden.

'And where did you learn to shoot?' Billy September asked her in his melodious voice.

'I did a course last year. A woman should be able to protect herself.'

'Amen,' said Billy September.

Mpayipheli took the nine-millimetre from her, reloaded, put up a new target against the Port Jackson and aimed from fifteen metres.

'He wants to show off a bit.'

The pistol was dwarfed in the huge hand. Ten shots. One hole in the centre of the target. Then he turned to them, took off the earmuffs and said, 'Orlando said to make sure you know you're getting the best.'

When they got back to the house, his mother had started the 'Where is everyone going to sleep?' bit.

'Who is going to look after Wilna and Hope?' she'd asked.

'Schlebusch only threatened you, Ma.'

'And if he sees he can't achieve anything here, who do you think will be next on his list?' Joan had looked at Wilna van As and Hope Beneke and said: 'The two of you must sleep here as well. Until this thing is over.'

'My house is safe,' Hope had said with no conviction.

'Nonsense, you're all alone.'

'She's a very good shot,' was Mpayipheli's contribution.

'I won't hear of it. There's room enough here for Carolina and Wilna and the two of you. Hope can sleep at Zet's house. There's room.'

He had opened his mouth to say something, to object – he didn't trust his mother's motives – but she didn't give him a chance. 'There's a madman out there and you can't afford to take chances,' his mother had said in her effective, organizing mode, unstoppable, adamant.

'I must go,' he'd said. 'There's work to do.'

For five years the only women in his life had been a few divorcees, bewildered, broken partners in bed, picked up in Tableview pubs for a night of physical relief – when he was sober enough, when he could scrape together enough energy and courage to complete the ritual. What was his average? Once a year? Perhaps twice when his body screamed at him and the hormones took over in automatic gear. And now there was a different one in his house every night.

Good material for a situation comedy. He and Hope and Kara-An. The Three Stooges.

It wasn't Hope. It was just . . . his house was his sanctuary.

He looked for parking at the magistrate's court. There was none. He had to park on the Parade and walk, through the clothing district. He hadn't been there for a long time, had forgotten the hodgepodge, the colours and smells, the busy pavements.

Hope in his house. Discomfort in his stomach. It wasn't going to work.

O'Grady stood outside the courtroom, in the passage, talking to other detectives, a closed circle, a close brotherhood. He stood on one side and waited, no longer part of it, until Nougat saw him.

'What do you want?' Still unforgiving.

'To share information, Nougat,' but he had to suppress his reaction to the fat man's tone of voice.

O'Grady's little eyes narrowed in suspicion. 'What do you have?'

He took the envelope out of his jacket pocket. 'This is the guy.'

'Schlebusch?'

O'Grady took the photo carefully, by its edge, looked at it.

'Mean mother.'

'Yes.'

Suddenly saw the light. 'You're going to the newspapers again.'

'Yes. And I wanted to warn you.'

O'Grady shook his head. 'Should have done that on Sunday.' He looked at the photo again. 'This dates from 1976?'

'Yes.'

'There is something you can do, van Heerden, that would work nicely. And the newspapers will love it.'

'What?'

Nougat took a cellphone out of the big folds of his jacket. 'Let me make a call,' he said. 'And what I like most about it is that will drive Military Intelligence nuts.'

He dialled a number, put the cellphone against his ear.

'Mat Joubert tried to call you. He had some information, I don't know what it was but there was no answer on that hot line of yours.' Then someone replied on the other end of the cellular network. 'Hi, may I speak to Russell Marshall, please.'

He found the place easily – in Roeland Street, a modern two-storey office complex opposite the State Archives in Drury Lane. He recognized the logo of a brain with a fuse stuck in it which O'Grady had described. He asked for Russell Marshall at reception and a few seconds later the apparition appeared, a tall, thin man, aged eighteen or nineteen, barefoot, hair down to the shoulders, a straggly growth on the chin and more earrings per square centimetre than a collection of kugels.

'Are you the private detective?'

'Van Heerden,' extending his hand.

'Russell. Where's the photo?' Keen, enthusiastic.

He took out the envelope, slid out the photo, handed it over.

'Mmmmm . . .'

'Can you do something?'

'We can do anything. Come through.'

He followed the man to a large area where ten or fifteen people were working on computers, all young, all . . . different.

'This is the studio.'

'What do you do here?'

'Oh, new media, Internet, Web. CD-ROM. You know.'

He didn't know. 'No.'

'Aren't you on the Internet?'

'I don't even have M-Net. But my mother has.'

Marshall smiled. 'Ah,' he said. 'A dinosaur. We don't get many here.' He put the photo on the glass surface of a piece of equipment. 'First we're going to scan the photo. Sit down, shift all that stuff to the floor, so that you can see the screen.'

Marshall sat behind the keyboard of the computer. 'This is the Apple G4 Power Mac with the new Velocity Engine,' he said with a tone of awe and looked at van Heerden for a reaction. There was none.

'You don't even have a computer.'

'No.'

Marshall tossed his hair over his shoulder in despair.

'Do you know anything about cars?'

'A little.'

'If computers were cars this would be a cross between a Ferrari and a Rolls.'

'Oh.'

'Know anything about aircraft?'

'A little.'

'If computers were fighter planes this would be a cross between a Stealth bomber and an F16.'

'I think I understand.'

'State of the art.'

He nodded.

'Cutting edge, my mate, cutting edge, mother of all . . .'

'I know exactly what you mean.'

The photograph appeared on the screen of the Rolls/Ferrari/B1/F16/G4.

'Fine. Just get the levels right, get Adobe Photoshop going with every plug-in ever designed by man . . .'

'Cutting edge,' said van Heerden.

'State of the art,' Marshall smiled. 'You learn fast. The photo is a bit old, repair the colour balance, like this. Nougat said you want to make the guy a little older.'

'More or less forty to forty-five. And long hair. Long and blond, down to his shoulders.'

'Fatter? Thinner?'

'About the same. Not fatter but . . . bigger.'

'Fuller?'

'Fuller. Sturdier.'

'Fine. First the age. Here, around the eyes . . .' He moved a mouse with unbelievable dexterity, chose the applicable area on the screen, clicked here, clicked there. 'We'll give him a couple of wrinkles, just get the right colour mix, he's very pale . . .' Small lines drawn like rays of the sun at the edge of the eyes. 'And here, around the mouth', more movements with mouse and cursor. 'And then the face, a little jowlier around the chin, it could take a little time, the skin colour and the shadows have to be right. No, that's wrong, let's try . . . that's better, just a little, ah, how about that. What do you think, wait, let me zoom in, it's too far, what does he look like now?'

Bushy Schlebusch, older, sturdier, not quite a bull's eye, more of an impression. He looked for a face that would match the voice: *You have a mother, policeman. Do you hear me? You have a mother.*

'I think the face is too fat.'

'OK. Let's try this.'

'Hi,' he heard the voice behind him, turned. Small, slender, brown-haired girl.

A multitude of earrings.

'We're busy, Charmaine,' Marshall said.

She ignored him. 'I'm Charmaine.'

'Van Heerden.'

'Your jacket. It's so . . . so retro. Don't you want to sell it?'

He looked at his jacket. 'Retro?'

'Y-e-e-e-s.' With feeling.

'Charmaine!'

'If you ever want to sell it . . .' She turned away, unwillingly, walked to a desk.

'What does it look like?'

Schlebusch's face filled the whole screen, the lip still curled in derision, the eyes, older, still . . .

'It's better.'

'Who is this dude?'

'A murderer.'

'Oh, cool,' said Marshall. 'Now for the hair. It's going to take a little longer.'

'Jeez,' said the night editor of *Die Burger* when he looked at the photographs. 'You should've told us earlier. The front page is full. So is page three.'

'Can't we move the Chris Barnard story?' the crime reporter asked.

'Lord, no. His new girlfriend is a scoop and the posters are carrying the story.'

'And the Price Line pic?'

'The chief will kill me.'

'If we have a Price Line kicker on the front page and move the photo inside?'

The night editor scratched his beard. 'Hell . . .' He looked at van Heerden. 'Can't we put it on hold for Friday's edition?'

'I . . .' He couldn't afford to lose another day. 'Maybe it's time for me to to tell you about the will.'

'What will?' they asked in an inquisitive chorus.

He only got away after nine. It was cold outside the NasPers building but windless, cloudless, quiet, the city calm on a Tuesday evening and he hesitated before starting the van, not keen on going home, not keen on doing what he had to do.

But he would have to. Switched on the ignition, drove through the city towards the mountain, the traffic lights unsynchronized at that time of night, every red light an avenue of escape until he stopped in front of the large house and saw lights burning. He got out, locked the pick-up, walked up the drive, climbed the steps, heard the rock music. Did she have guests? Pressed the bell, didn't hear it ring. Waited.

He saw a shadow behind the spyhole before the door opened. Young man, tight pants, white shirt unbuttoned to the navel, sweat on the pale torso, pupils too small. 'Hey,' too loudly.

'I'm looking for Kara-An.'

'Come in.' Tight jeans turned, dancing, leaving the door as it was. Van Heerden closed it, followed him, the music louder and louder, and found them in the living room, lines of cocaine on the glass of the coffee table. Kara-An dancing, wearing only a T-shirt, two more young women, Jeans and two more men, all of them dancing. He stood in the doorway, a woman danced past, leather trousers, pretty, a man, overweight, laughed at him, until Kara-An saw him. She didn't stop dancing. 'Help yourself,' she said, waving towards the coffee table.

For a moment he stood there, indecisively, then turned, walked back to the front door, down the steps to his mother's faded van, got in, switched on the ignition, and looked back at the big veranda across the street for a moment. Kara-An stood in the doorway, etched against the light, her hand lifted in farewell. He drove away.

He wanted to tell her that they were not the same.

And perhaps to ask her where her pain came from.

He shook his head at himself.

He heard the Violin Concerto No. 1 before he even opened the front door.

Hope sat in his chair with a mug of coffee, in her dressing gown and slippers, the couch made up as a bed, the light from the kitchen casting a soft glow over her.

'Hi,' she said. 'Forgive me, but I've made myself at home.'

'That's fine. But I'll sleep on the couch.'

'You're too tall for the couch. And I'm intruding.'

'You're not.'

'Of course I'm intruding. Your house, your privacy, your routine . . .'

He put the Heckler & Koch on the kitchen surface, switched on the kettle, saw the flowers. She had picked an enormous bunch of flowers from his mother's garden and put them in a vase on his kitchen counter.

'No problem.'

'I still think it wasn't necessary, but your mother . . .'

'She can be too much.'

While he made coffee, he told her about the photograph, its ageing by Russell Marshall, his struggle with *Die Burger* – until the story about the will became the decisive factor.

'Someone is going to recognize Schlebusch. We're going to find him.'

'If he doesn't find us first.'

'We're ready for him.'

They drank their coffee.

'Hope,' he said, 'if I said your dressing gown is retro, what does it mean?'

She lay on the couch in the dark, warm under the blankets, comfortable. She listened to the sounds of van Heerden in the bathroom, involuntarily wondering what his body looked like under the shower. Her own body was restless, a thief in the night, a response, a tingling that suffused her.

She smiled at herself. Everything was still in working order.

She lay listening to him until the last light went out.

42

It was one thing to leaf through the dossiers of twenty years ago and to stare in aversion at black-and-white photographs of forgotten murders. It was very different being the first on the scene, experiencing death in full colour and with all your senses, the odours of blood, of bodily excretions, of death itself – that strange, loathsome sweetish odour of human flesh beginning to decay.

The visual impact of murder: the gaping, blood-red cave of the slashed throat, the multicoloured mixture of entrails where a shotgun had wrought devastation, the huge rose of the exit wound made by an AK's 7.62mm round; the staring, dull eyes, the impossible angles at which limbs are aligned to the body, the bits of tissue against the wall, the sticky, reddish-brown pool of coagulating blood, the pallor of a decomposing body among autumn leaves and green grass, in contrast with the diners at the feast, the dark insects that show up so dramatically against the pale background.

During the first weeks and months at Murder and Robbery, I often thought about the psychological implications of the work.

My daily task distressed me. It gave me nightmares and kept me awake, or woke me in the small hours of the morning. It made me drink and swear and blunted me on my stumbling path to find ways to cope with it all, become accustomed to it.

It was a permanent state of post-traumatic stress syndrome, a never-ending attack, a constant reminder that we are dust, that we are infinitesimal, that we are nothing at all.

The murder scenes were only part of it.

We worked with the scum of the earth, day in and day out, every day and every night. The trash and the debris, the crazy and the greedy, the hotheaded and the callous, the morally weak, a never-ending exposure to Evil.

We worked long, impossible hours against a constant stream of criticism from the media, the public and the politicians, at a time of great political change in an area where the differences between a white First World population and a deprived black Third World were incessantly fanned by the flames of baser instincts. We were undermanned, underpaid and overworked.

I thought deeply (and still wonder) about the standards set for the police, about the finger-wagging accusations from every corner of the country, about corruption, malpractice, apathy, slow reactions and irregular results.

But I was mostly worried about my own coping mechanisms. I discovered an aggression in myself that I hadn't known existed. I researched the anaesthetic, healing power of alcohol, the result of social withdrawal and a life of limited, superficial thought – and I found a refuge in the safe arms of the Brotherhood of the Police.

I changed, became a new person and justified it all by fighting the good fight, by using every moment to hunt Evil. It was my passion, it was a passion we all shared, the reason for our existence.

And around me I saw the coping mechanisms of others – and the burnt-out human wrecks of some of our colleagues fallen by the wayside.

But I survived to face my fate. Willem Nagel and I.

D-Day

Thursday, 13 July

43

He was jolted awake from chaotic dreams and the radio alarm next to the bed showed an unsympathetic 3:11.

The dreams had been about Schlebusch.

Dreams of escape and confrontation and fear, and he lay in the dark and realized that the accident, the moments on the road and the man with the long blond hair and his threats were stuck in the cells of his subconscious, unprocessed. This was the first time that he had been both hunter and prey. And there was no protection, no SAPS net, not officially.

Rupert de Jager's last three letters had brought no new insights, opened no new vistas, only confirmed the brooding, growing feeling that Bushy Schlebush had taken the road to viciousness some twenty years ago. The signs of psychopathology there, a lack of emotion, an attraction to violence, an explosive personality. He was prepared to bet money, fuck, he didn't have money, that Rupert de Jager/Johannes Jacobus Smit hadn't been the first victim.

The blowtorch. The threat. The curt words when he hung in the wreck of the Corolla.

Are you alive? Schlebusch had asked. With utter, disinterested contempt, the only reason for the question so that he wouldn't have to waste his breath.

You have a mother, policeman. Do you hear me? You have a mother. I'll burn her with a fucking blowtorch, do you hear me? You don't know me, you pig, cunt, leave me alone or I'll burn her.

He wasn't the one under threat, it was his mother. The terrain was known to him, the pathology, the playing field of the serial killer, the woman as helpless victim over whom control must be exercised. And the love of fire. But Schlebusch was different, evidently not driven by a sense of inferiority. For him, killing wasn't a relief mechanism, a levelling of the playing field. For him murder was an instrument, a final solution when the other means of persuasion didn't do the job.

The reaction to the news stories. There was something to learn there. Calculation. He had followed van Heerden, checked up on him, established his route, found out about his family, waited for the right moment and attacked with a ruthless, cool effectiveness. No panic, no running away or hiding. A clinical operation to stay in control.

What did you do when you were hunting such an animal? What did you do if the prey didn't flee or hide? What did you do if the hunted hunted you?

You got a camp *karateka* and a large black sniper and you packed a machine pistol and you shared your house with a woman who sometimes asked questions you didn't want to hear because you were afraid you would answer her. He was prepared to be bad, to accept that he was evil and to live with that, but no one else must know the truth. He didn't want to experience total rejection.

And then the night with Kara-An came and the fucking problem was he'd discovered he wasn't as bad as he'd wanted to believe.

He knew it was her challenge, her implicit invitation. He knew it was her search for someone to share her world, to confirm her own self-disgust, to sink to the dregs with her. And he had been willing to chance the downward spiral with her but then he had balked because he discovered that he didn't have it in him and it made him feel . . . good about himself, Lord, it was a new experience.

And last night Hope's flowers had touched him.

He had been annoyed with himself then, hadn't wanted to feel the small stutter of emotion, the gratitude. No, it was something else. It was the nature of the present, the contrast. Kara-An had blown into his house on a wind of decadence and Hope had brought flowers as if he was worthy of the gift.

He who had made an appalling fool of himself twice yesterday. The first was in the hospital room when he had spelt out his 1976 theory with so much self-confidence. Then he read the letters and they blew his neat theory to kingdom come. Schlebusch, de Jager and Co hadn't worked for Military Intelligence. They weren't the execution squad – simply another Recce unit that had escorted supplies to Angola.

No question of dollars. No sign of American intervention.

Then what the fuck had happened in 1976? What had this valiant group been involved in that the authorities so badly wanted to hide and that had left death and dollars and riddles behind?

Schlebusch was the key. Schlebusch was the piece that wouldn't fit into a puzzle of ordinary eighteen-year-old soldiers thrown together from a host of backgrounds and circumstances.

Damn. The frustration of loose ends. He wanted to know, wanted to yank down the great blanket hiding this thing, wanted to *know*. He and his mother were being hunted by an animal and he was desperate for a head start. The accident had opened a door to fear in his head and he wasn't able to close it and it amazed him, he who had lived the last five years as if looking for a place to die, to be with death, to escape the memories in his head.

And now he was terrified of the black scythe. He had seen the face of death under the long blond hair.

And then he had made an arsehole of himself again by slapping at Billy September and his legs had been swept from under him and there he lay, and Hope and Tiny Mpayipheli and September had simply stood there, all too afraid to laugh, but he knew they'd wanted to. Then he smiled at himself. It must've been pretty funny. He sat up in bed, could no longer lie still, couldn't get up to put on music and make coffee because Hope was sleeping in his living room, but he didn't want to be alone with his thoughts.

Because we owe you, van Heerden. All of us.

Mat Joubert's ironic words.

Why couldn't he have the personal integrity and the righteous pain of the big detective? Joubert, who had lost his first wife some time ago, another casualty in the line of police duty. And through it all Joubert had fought the good fight and bit by bit put his life together again and now he was getting remarried and here sat van Heerden and what were his chances?

The debt Joubert had spoken about was based on a breathtaking misconception that might never be corrected. No one must know how bad he really was.

Joubert, who had a message for him. What message?

He would have to see if he could get hold of the bridegroom today. It was going to be a great day. Schlebusch. The photographs in *Die Burger* were going to arouse anger in that beast. Were two soldiers enough to guard the women against a psychopath with an American attack rifle and a calm, white anger?

He got up in one smooth movement, pulled on jeans, shirt and sweater and sneakers, looked at the figures on the alarm: 3:57. He opened the door very slowly, very softly, stood still, heard Hope's deep, peaceful breathing, put his feet down carefully, closer and closer to her, the woman who had brought him flowers, about whom he had fantasized before Kara-An arrived with her champagne. Hope's face was almost buried in the blanket, she lay on her side, he saw the rapid movements of her eyeballs behind the lids, wondered what she was dreaming of, court edicts and crazy private investigators? He looked at the shape of her nose and her mouth and her cheek. There was something sad in her features, was it because the sum total, the architecture, the final construction formed an incomplete, beauty, forcing the imagination to reconstruct it, rearrange it so that she could be breathtaking? There was something childlike there, something untouched, did that evoke this strange feeling in him? Had that woken the aggression in him during the past week because he didn't want to be reminded of innocence, because it was lost to him forever?

He closed his eyes. He had to get out of here.

He walked softly and carefully to the door. First switch on the outside light, warn Tiny Mpayipheli and Billy September that he was on his way. Pressed the switch, opened the door very, very carefully, closed it behind him, the click of the lock muffled, stood outside, the night quiet and cold, but never as cold as the biting, black-frost nights of Stilfontein. He stood in front of the door, hoping the soldiers had seen him, walked to the big house, looked up at the stars. A satellite winked its orbit to the north.

'Coming to inspect the guard?' Tiny Mpayipheli's deep voice asked.

He hadn't seen him, the black man in the dark coat in a corner of his mother's garden, on the bench under the cypress.

'Couldn't sleep.'

'Only you, or both of you?' Humour in the voice.

'Only me,' and there was far too much disappointment in his voice and Tiny laughed softly.

'Sit down.' Mpayipheli moved over, made room for him.

'Thanks.'

They sat next to one another, staring at the night sky,

'Cold, hm?'

'I've been colder.'

Uncomfortable silence.

'Were you christened Tiny?'

Mpayipheli laughed. 'I was named after the Springbok lock, Tiny Naude, if you must know. I was born Tobela Mpayipheli, which is a joke on its own.'

'Oh?'

'Tobela means "respectful, well-mannered". Mpayipheli is "the one who never stops fighting". My father . . . I think he wanted to work in a counter-irritant.'

'I know the burden of names.'

'The problem with whites is that your names have no meaning.'

'Hope Beneke wouldn't agree with you.'

'Touché.'

'Tiny Naude?'

'It's a long story.'

'It's a long night.'

The soft laugh again. 'Do you play rugby?'

'At school. Socially a few times after that. I never really had the talent.'

'Life leads one into strange ways, van Heerden. I've considered writing the story of my life, you know, about that time when every single soul who was part of the Struggle wrote an autobiography to get a first-class compartment on the gravy train. But I'm afraid only one chapter would be fascinating. The rugby chapter.'

Tiny Mpayipheli was quiet, shifted into a more comfortable position. 'It's colder when one can't move. But the whole point of guard duty is to sit still.'

He turned up the collar of his coat, put his weapon on his lap and took a deep breath. 'My father was a man of peace. Every time the hand of Apartheid slapped him in the face, he turned the other cheek, said he loved the white man even more because that was what the Word told him. And his son, Tobela, was a man of hate. And violence and fighting. Not suddenly, but systematically, with every humiliation I saw my father enduring. You see, I loved him so much. He was a man of dignity, unbelievable, untouchable dignity . . .'

A night bird called somewhere, a faraway truck droned against an upward gradient on the N7.

'I ran away when I was sixteen, looking for the Struggle. I couldn't stay home any longer, I had enough hate to apply 'one settler one bullet' myself and the channels were ready for me, I walked the road to Gabarone and Nairobi and eventually, when I was twenty, big and strong and full of fight, the ANC sent me to the Soviet Union, to a godforsaken place called Saraktash, in the south of Russia, about a hundred kilometres from the Kazakhstan border, a dusty base where their troops prepared for the war in Afghanistan. That was where some of Umkhonto we Sizwe's people were trained, don't ask me why there, but on the other hand, I don't think the struggle at the ass-end of the Dark Continent was high on the USSR's military agenda.

'I was a troublemaker. From the very first day I asked questions about method and content. I didn't want to learn about Lenin and

Marx and Stalin, I wanted to kill. I didn't want to know about battle plans and tank warfare, I wanted to learn to shoot and slit throats. I didn't want to learn Russian and I didn't like the superior attitude of the Soviet troops and the more my comrades told me I had to be patient. because the road to war wound through a diversity of landscapes, the more I rebelled, until the day I and a sergeant in the Red Army, an Uzbek with shoulders like an ox and a neck like a tree trunk, locked horns in the NCO's bar. I didn't understand one word he was saying but his hate was the white man's hate and I couldn't resist.

'They allowed us to fight. Eventually all the troops on the base were there. First we virtually demolished the mess and then we were outside. Fists, feet, elbows, knees, fingers in the eyes, I was twenty and I was big and strong and there were guys who said it was Ali against Liston but it was bad, he hit me until my head stood still, he broke six ribs and I bled in places where I hadn't even known he had hit me.

'The difference, in the final analysis, wasn't the size of the dog in the fight, but the size of the fight in the dog. My hate was bigger than his. And my lungs were clean, he was a smoker and those Russian cigarettes, they told me, were fifty per cent donkey shit. It wasn't a spectacular knockout. For more than forty minutes we had systematically broken one another down until he sank onto one knee, spat blood and couldn't get his breath and shook his head and the small group of South Africans cheered and the Russians turned away angrily and left their man who had brought shame on the world power and it would all have been over if the Uzbek hadn't had a heart attack, later that night, in his bed, dead as a doornail. They found him the following morning and they came to fetch me out of the sickbay, the military police, and I ask you, what chance does a Xhosa have of a fair trial in a country that feels nothing for him – especially when his attitude hardly shows deep remorse?

'The cell was small and hot, even in the Russian late autumn the sun made the corrugated iron crackle and at night it was so cold that my breath made crystals against the metal and the food was inedible and they kept me there for five weeks, alone in a cell as big as an outhouse and in my head I walked the hills of the Transkei and spoke to my father and made love to plump girls with huge breasts and when my ribs had mended I did sit-ups and push-ups and squats until the sweat literally pooled on the floor.

'While I waited for something to happen, other powers were at work to get me out. Odd how life sometimes goes. The officer commanding the base was a rugby fan, only later I realized rugby wasn't unpopular in the Soviet Army, not nearly as popular as soccer but there were enough men who played rugby for Saraktash to be able to send a good team onto the field. They had come second in the previous year's Red Army championships and the league was on its way to playing again when the OC got it into his head that the South Africans, coming from the land of the Springboks, were just the people to give his team a good warm-up before the first league match against the previous year's champions.

'You can imagine, among the one hundred and twenty of us, there were only Coloured guys who knew anything about the game, the rest were Xhosa, Zulu, Tswana and Sotho and Venda and rugby was the sport of the Oppressor and what we knew about it was just about nothing but our Umkhonto leader was Moses Morape and if one of your men is in the cells and you see a gap, you take it. When the Russian OC came to issue the challenge, the guys had an *indaba* and Rudewaan Moosa, one of the Cape Malays, a committed Muslim, who in any case hated the Russians because they were so godless, said he had been a fly-half in the South African Rugby Federation set-up and he would be their trainer because it was an opportunity to put the whiteys in their place.

'Morape went to negotiate. First suggested soccer as an alternative, because we knew we could beat their Soviet arses hollow but the OC wouldn't hear of it. Then Morape said they would play rugby but that Mpayipheli must be freed. And the South African team must get the same equipment as the Russians.

'But Mpayipheli is a murderer,' the OC said, and Morape argued that it had been a fair fight and the OC shook his head and said justice had to take its course and Morape said then there wouldn't be a warm-up match and for two weeks there was coming and going until the OC agreed, but there were two conditions. You have to win.

And Mpayipheli must play, otherwise his troops wouldn't accept the deal and Morape said OK.

'I didn't want to know. I said I'd rather go back to the cells but the chief *indunas* explained the choices: I either play, or they would send me to Zambia where I could be a pencil-pusher in a supply store for the rest of the Struggle – if the Soviet Army's justice system had finished with me. They were sick and tired of me, I had to choose.

'Two days later we had our first practice. Two teams chosen according to size and height and potential talent. It was chaos. Like grade one kids who gather around the ball and yell and run all over the place. The Russians who stood at the side of the practice field laughed so much that we couldn't hear what Moosa was saying and we were so stupid that the writing was on the wall. Three weeks was far too little. We were cannon fodder.

'But Moosa was clever. And patient. The night after the first practice he spent in deep thought. Changed his strategy. Decided to shift the front to the classroom for starters and for four long days we learnt the theory of rugby on a blackboard, the rules, the involved, inexplicable never-ending shower of rules, then analysed every position, memorized every strategy and on the fifth morning, at six o'clock, we were on the field, before the Russians got going. Moosa drilled us: the backline on one side, the forwards on another, line-outs, scrums, loose scrums, rucking, running, walking us through each step painfully slowly, quite literally at first.

'It got better but it was still pathetic, it was as if the guys couldn't get their heads around this whitey game. You should've heard the remarks. All in the line of "It's only the Boers who would be foolish enough to exchange a round ball and two nets for this stupidity." We wanted to dribble and kick, not pick up and pass. It seemed as if our whole nature was against the strange game. Not to mention the offside rule. But Moosa kept his head and Morape gave us courage and on the Saturday, one week before the match, we went out before sunrise for a secret practice in town, the two black teams against one another on an open piece of land next to the river, a kind of test game to choose the A team.

'Pretty it wasn't. Moosa lost his temper for the first time that day, threw his hands into the air and said it was an impossible task, it simply wasn't possible to change a crowd of black idiots from soccer fans to rugby winners. He stormed off the field and went to sit under a large tree, his head in his hands, and we stood there, our bodies steaming in the cold, and we knew he was right. It wasn't as if we hadn't tried. It was simply – the handicap. And our hearts. If you know you're going to be beaten, it's difficult to get your heart in the right positive spirit.

'Morape went to sit next to Moosa and they talked, for an hour or longer. And then they walked back to where we were sitting in a heap and Morape began to speak to us.

'He was a Tswana. A man with a face like an eagle, not tall or big, not very clever but there was something in Morape that made you listen. And that morning, at the arsehole of the world, we listened. Morape spoke softly. Said the match wasn't about keeping Mpayipheli out of jail. Which got me a few dirty looks. He said the match was about the Struggle. The match had come our way in a country that didn't want us there, from people who didn't think we were good enough. Just like at home. And even though we couldn't choose the battleground and the strategy there to suit us, we *could* do it here. Must we look at our country and say, no, the whiteys have more weapons, more money, better comforts, better technology, they hold the high ground, should we surrender? If we surrendered, here in Holy Mother Russia, we could give up the Struggle, because then we would've lost before we started. It was about character. It was about the fighting spirit. It was about daring, about focus, about concentration, the unshakeable belief that you could do anything if you believed in yourself and in the cause.

'Sport, he said, is the poor man's war. With the same principles. Us against them. Standing together against superior forces. Solidarity. Tactics and strategy and the same deep emotion. And just like war, sport eventually teaches us about ourselves. To test ourselves and our capabilities and our individual and collective character . . .

'He wouldn't mind if we lost the battle. It happened in war, it happened in sport, it happened in life. But if we lost because we hadn't done our best, then we weren't the kind of people with whom he wanted to go to war. Then Morape got up and walked away across the green grass and left us there to think.

'That Monday Morape pinned the names of his first team against the noticeboard and my name was there as lock forward and my knees shook. But I wasn't "Tobela" any longer. Moosa had made me "Tiny" Mpayipheli.

'For the rest of the week we practised every day. With Morape on the sideline as a silent reminder of his words, and Moosa, fly-half and coach, who drilled us and then the jerseys came, on Thursday. The OC of the base had had them made in Moscow, green and gold with a Springbok on the chest and Morape said, "Now you're playing for your country" and the whole thing took on a dimension for which we weren't prepared. We wanted to complain about the jersey of the oppressor when Morape asked, "What are the colours of the ANC?"

'That Saturday the soccer stadium in Saraktash was packed with so many Soviet soldiers you couldn't credit it. Each weekend pass had been withdrawn, every military soul had been called up to support their men and when their team came out of the tunnel, it was a sea of red jerseys with a yellow hammer-and-sickle on the chest and the crowd went wild and for most of the game our small group of supporters were too scared to open their mouths.

'It probably wasn't the greatest rugby to watch, especially the first half. To our great surprise the Russians weren't masters of the game. More experienced than we were, but no oiled machine. At half-time they were ahead by 18 to 6 after Moosa had kicked two drop goals and then he said to us, "Guys, these Reds can be beaten, I can feel it, can you feel it?" Perhaps we were no longer intimidated. Maybe we thought it was going to be a superior force that would grind us, bleeding, into the grass and when it didn't happen, we had to admit that he was right. These guys could be beaten . . .

'"They're slow," Moosa had said. "Get the ball to Zuma, doesn't matter how, get the ball to Zuma." Napoleon Zuma was our left wing, he was only nineteen, a Zulu, he was short but he had a pair of thighs each of which you couldn't encircle with two hands and he could run like the wind.

'It took us fifteen minutes to get him away for the first time and then he scored a try, and then it was as if something happened on that field, as if those fifteen South Africans from the townships and the small-town locations and the villages of the Bantustans suddenly had insight into this strange, wonderful game. And we played. And the better we played, the quieter the Red Army crowd became and the louder our small band of supporters shouted on the pavilion steps and Napoleon Zuma scored two more tries and suddenly the score was equal with only ten minutes of play left and then we wanted to win, we knew we were going to win, you should've seen those guys, van Heerden, you should've seen them play, it was wonderful, it was indescribably beautiful.'

And then Tiny Mpayipheli was silent and he looked at the faraway stars in the dark of a Cape winter and he shivered in his big, black coat.

'Is that Orion?' he asked eventually and pointed a finger at the east.

'Yes.' They sat, staring at the morning star, but when the silence became too long, van Heerden couldn't help asking. 'Did you win?'

The black man smiled broadly in the dark. 'The nicest thing was that the referee saw his posting to Afghanistan coming up, but his whistle couldn't save the day though he did his best. On the rugby field that day, South Africa won its only test against the Red Peril, 36–18.'

44

I rented a two-bedroomed house in Brackenfell and neglected the garden and borrowed the lawnmower of my middle-class neighbours, the van Tonders, every second Saturday but I wasn't home very often.

I developed my own unique weekly routine. Every day and most nights I worked with the same blind dedication as my colleagues. Sometimes when the workload permitted, I attended the Thursday-evening symphony concerts in the City Hall, often alone. On Saturday evenings there was a barbecue at someone's house, a closed police gathering with unwritten rules about meat and alcohol contributions where drunkenness was excused as long as it didn't upset the women and children.

On Sundays I cooked.

I went on a culinary journey of all the continents – Thai, Chinese, Vietnamese, Japanese, Spanish, French, Italian, Greek, Middle Eastern. I would plan the dish during the week, shop for the final ingredients on Saturday and would spend Sunday in the kitchen taking time and care, with a glass of red wine and opera on the hi-fi and a woman who was my sole, deeply impressed audience.

I might as well admit it – the more heartless the dossiers on my desk, the greater the yearning for the love of my life, for love in my life, for that mythical soulmate, someone who would welcome and embrace me in a warm bed in the small hours of the night. Someone who on Saturday nights would put down our contribution on the salad table, among other women there, someone to whom I could refer as 'my wife' with the same loving, jealous possessiveness of Breyten Breytenbach's eponymous poem. There was a loneliness in me, an emptiness, an incompleteness that grew over the months. It was as if the nature of my work deepened this lack so that I searched for her with growing determination – the Cape is a Mecca for the unmarried, middle-class man, the ratio of men to women in the Peninsula an attractive statistic, the network for playing find-a-girl-for-a-cop surely the best in the world.

For that reason there was often someone at my side at the barbecue on a Saturday night. And in my bed on a Sunday morning. An admiring assistant in the kitchen where I proved my culinary superiority to my colleagues with the preparation of the seventh day's festive meal for two. And after lunch, sleepy and full of good food, we tried to still that other hunger on the living-room couch or the bed.

Because on Monday it was back to work, back to the dark heart of the world where other basic instincts applied.

With Nagel.

Our relationship was odd. It sometimes reminded me of the way an old married couple spend their lives bickering – a never-ending conflict on the surface but with a deep underlying respect and love that could bear anything.

It was a relationship forged in the furnace of policing, the pressure cooker of violence and blood and murder. For two years we stood side by side in the firing line and investigated every possible crime committed by people against people and hunted the guilty with total dedication.

Nagel was an ill-educated man with no respect for book learning. He proclaimed that you couldn't get on top of police work using a textbook or lecture notes. He had no patience with pretence, even less with the butterfly dance of humankind's social interaction – the small white lies, the fake politeness, the striving for superficial status symbols.

'Shit, man,' was his general, head-shaking reaction to anything that sounded to him like a senseless statement and he used it often, that and the general applicable possibilities and unlimited declensions of the word 'fuck'. It was Nagel who taught me to swear – not deliberately, but the man's handiness with it was a revelation, and contagious, like a deadly virus.

Nagel was the only detective at Murder and Robbery who was untouched by the heartlessness of our work.

He accepted the criminality of our species as a given – and his role was simply to let justice be done, to hunt and corner the murderer and the rapist and the thief, without thinking about it, without introspection, without tormenting himself over what the sometimes horrifying crimes said about him as a member of the same species.

It wasn't as if all this was merely the petrified crust over a soft centre. Nagel was one-dimensional and because of that he was probably the best professional of the long arm of the law that I knew.

Bickering. About the nature and motive of the murder, about the psyche of the murderer, about the ghostly traces at the murder scene that indicated an investigative direction, about the course and priority of the investigation itself. He was aware of my impressive academic career but he wasn't intimidated by it. Perhaps Colonel Willie Theal had known Nagel would be the only mentor for whom my background posed no threat. He was certain of his views, his methods.

In the solution of crimes he was sometimes right with his astonishing instinct and feeling – and sometimes my pages and pages of annotations, my precise notes, my endless study of detail, my methodology in psychology, which the Americans now so pretentiously refer to as forensic criminology, provided conclusive proof. Only to hear Nagel saying that 'Lady Luck shat on your fucking front porch again.'

Within months we were the investigative team everyone talked about – the first team, the main men who were called in when others failed, but Nagel was the undisputed leader, the spokesman, I the assistant, the student once more, Tonto to his Lone Ranger, Sancho Panza to his Don Quixote. And it suited me because Nagel was my admission ticket to acceptance by Murder and Robbery. His frequently repeated alternative views soon made my doctorate seem just an incidental piece of paper to his colleagues, his constant teasing about my notes gave it an acceptable, eccentric colour.

I was respected by my colleagues as I had been at the Academy.

And what a narcotic the drug of positive feedback can be. It was more than enough to make me accept and enjoy my new lifestyle and what I had become.

I can't say I was consciously happy but I wasn't unhappy and in this life that's quite something.

But I still had the one desire, even if my status as bachelor caused so much envy among my colleagues – the desire to meet the One, to fall in love, totally and irrevocably.

I yearned. And wished.

You must be so careful what you wish for.

45

Just after six in the morning, he and Hope drove to her office and he kept looking back, but only saw the lights of other vehicles, unidentifiable in the dark.

'What do you think he's going to do when he sees the *Burger* story?'

'Schlebusch?'

'Yes.'

He thought for a while. 'It wasn't clever of him to show himself on the N7. He's not patient. He's a doer, not a thinker. The right thing would've been to sit back, lie low, go away, even out of the country, until this whole thing is over. Why didn't he? Because he couldn't suppress the urge to hit back? Because he's been conditioned to solve all his problems with violence?'

'Ahh,' she said, 'the poor man's Zatopek van Heerden?'

There was gentle teasing in her voice but for a moment the comparison unnerved him. 'If he's hopelessly stupid, he'll shoot. If he wants to survive, he'll negotiate.'

'Will you ever go back to the Police Force, Zatopek?'

'I don't know.'

She chewed on it. 'And the Academy?'

'I don't know.'

Then she was quiet and when they passed Ratanga Junction on the N1, he said: 'One day, perhaps, I'll have to find something else to do. Maybe I can't go back to either of the two.' And then he turned and looked back again.

At the office building he held the Heckler & Koch under his windbreaker until Hope had unlocked the doors. While Hope went to make coffee, he walked straight to the small room with the phone, arranged his notepad and his pen, sat down.

Notepaper and guns. He had always preferred the former.

Hope came back with two mugs. 'Are there going to be a lot of useless calls again?'

'There always are.'

'Why do you think people do it?'

'There's so much damage in the world, Hope. We do things to one another . . .'

She sat opposite him, her face gentle and looked at him, eyes searching his face. Then she asked him, softly, 'How much do we do to ourselves?'

The telephone rang, the first call of the morning.

'Hallo.'

'Is that the helpline of that Schlebusch guy?'

'That's right.'

'I want to remain anonymous.'

'Certainly, sir.'

'I think I'm one of his neighbours.'

'Oh?'

'He lives on a smallholding. Here, in Hout Bay.'

'Do you know what kind of car he drives?'

'A large white truck. I think it's an old Chevrolet.'

'Yes,' he said, his heartbeat increasing. He bent forward, his pen quiet on the paper. Hope heard it in his voice, put her coffee down, tense. 'Could you explain where the smallholding is?'

'Do you know Huggies Animal Farm?'

'No.'

'It's a farm zoo for children. You know, city kids can stroke a lamb and milk cows and ride a pony.'

'Oh.'

'And that Schlebusch guy lives next door, the place is pretty neglected, plot forty-seven, it's on the Constantia Neck road, the turn-off is just beyond the local authority's nursery.'

'Are you sure about the truck?'

'Oh, yes. It's in front of the house now.'

'Now?'

'Yes, I can see it.'

'Are you sure you want to remain anonymous?'

But then there was a click and the line was dead and he sat with the receiver in his hand and the adrenalin pumping and said, 'Hope, I want to borrow your car and your cellphone,' and he got up, taking the machine pistol.

'A smallholding,' she said.

'At Hout Bay.' He looked at his watch. 'We can still catch him in bed. Unless he's an early riser.'

'You can't go alone.'

'That's why I want the cellphone. I want to phone Tiny. As soon as I've established that it's not a false alarm.'

'Come,' she said and walked ahead of him down the passage to her office, found the keys and phone in her handbag.

'You must answer the phone while I'm away.'

'I . . .' she said reluctantly.

'It could be a false alarm. Someone must stay here.'

She nodded. 'Be careful,' she said.

Already the traffic to the city was a frustrating sluggish stream but he drove in a different direction, worked the gears and the clutch and the accelerator and rode the BMW hard, wondered if Hope ever used the power of the engineering to its full capacity. De Waal Drive, it was dark, fucking winter, past the University and the Botanical Gardens, right at Constantia Neck, down to Hout Bay. He vaguely remembered where the nursery was, drove past it, had to turn. He was slightly anxious, had to breathe deeply, found the large board that read 'Huggies Farm' with paintings of children and farm animals cartoon-style, realized it was getting light, cloudy morning, and then he stopped, Heckler & Koch under the jacket, cellphone in his pocket, looked at the faded wooden sign with 'Forty-seven' in words on it, the gravel path turning off, many trees, little light. He walked down the path, his trainers crunching on the surface, put the machine pistol's strap over his shoulder, took off the safety, his breathing shallow, his heart beating, fucking coward. Hope saying *How much do we do to ourselves*, funny time to think about that. He saw a light down there, he could see the house, then, suddenly, the truck when he jogged around the corner, just the outline in the grey dawn. He crouched behind a tree, breathing hard, everything quiet down there, only a light above the front door, the overwhelming sound of birds in the early morning. He narrowed his eyes, it was the truck, it was his truck, took the cellphone out of his pocket, punched in the number, waited.

'Joan van Heerden.'

'Ma, I have to speak to Tiny Mpayipheli,' tension in his whispered voice.

'What's the matter, Zet?' Worry.

'Ma, just get Tiny, please.'

'He's sleeping, I'll get Billy,' and then she was gone and he swore, he didn't want to speak to September, he needed the big sniper.

'Yo?'

'Billy, wake Tiny and tell him to come to Hout Bay. We've got Schlebusch. He's still sleeping but I don't know for how long. Get a pen because I want to explain the route.'

A moment's silence and then September said, 'Ready.'

He kneeled behind the tree, calmer now, Schlebusch must be sleeping late this morning. How would you hunt a prey who hunted you? You crept up to the place where he slept, fucker. He wished he had binoculars, how long did it take from Morning Star to Hout Bay, forty minutes if you drove like hell but the N1 and the N5 were nightmarish at this time of morning, an hour perhaps. He looked at his watch: 07:42, Mpayipheli should be here by 08:00, perhaps by quarter past. It was getting light fast, the truck's faded cream clearly visible, where would the house of the neighbour who had telephoned be, Schlebusch's place lay low down in the valley, what was wrong with the vehicle as he remembered it, the problem was he couldn't simply rush in and shoot, he needed him alive. Quarter past was going to be too late, Schlebusch wouldn't sleep that late, why was it so quiet down there, lights should be going on, coffee time for a hunted man, no, he should have been awake long before now.

He heard vehicles behind him, a deep droning, looked, but the road ran behind the rise. Probably a smallholding truck. Footsteps, exclamations, he looked round, something was wrong, many feet, they came running over the crest of the hill, soldiers, steel helmets and rucksacks and R5 rifles held in front of them. They saw him, fell flat, 'Throw down your weapon,' not anxious voices, certainly not, authoritarian, he slowly stood up, the Heckler & Koch in front of him, put it down on the ground. Where the fuck had they come from, two jumped up, R5s aimed at him, bulletproof vests, reaction team, grabbed his machine pistol. 'Lie down. Now!' He moved slowly, heart beating, lay face down, heard the others coming nearer, many boots, felt hands on him, taking the cellphone. 'He's clean,' and he smelt the dew-sodden grass, the earth, heard more footsteps. 'Only the cellphone.'

'Get up, van Heerden.' Bester Brits.

Rage engulfed him when he recognized the voice, the insight too late. He jumped up in one movement. 'You cunt,' he screamed, grabbing the Military Intelligence officer's throat, soldiers dragging him away, forcing him onto his knees.

'You bugged my telephone, you cunt.'

Brits laughed. 'You think you're so clever, van Heerden.'

'He's mine, Brits.'

'The two of you stay here with him. If he doesn't behave, kneecap him.' He lifted a two-way radio to his mouth. 'Alpha, are you ready?'

'Alpha ready.'

'Bravo ready?'

'Bravo ready.'

'Let's go in.'

'I hope you have armoured-car back-up and air support, Brits.'

'If he's going to lie here talking shit, put a bullet through his knee,'

Bester said and then they were gone, down the steep gravel road, the sharp sound of assault rifles being cocked. Van Heerden looked up at the two soldiers staring down at him, sharp, watchful faces. He waited for the rifle shots from the house, angry, he should've thought, but what could he do, it wouldn't have helped to change the number, Jesus, what a first-class cunt. Why was it so quiet at the house, Schlebusch still sleeping? Minutes ticked past, he sat up, the soldiers kept their weapons trained on him.

'Since when have you been on alert?'

They ignored him.

'Could I have my cellphone back?'

No reply.

He got up, looked down the road, shifted a few steps to see better.

'Stand still.'

He stood still. He could see the truck, the garden area. Soldiers kneeling at the front door, at the truck, all at the ready, the door open. Why didn't they shoot, why didn't Schlebusch shoot? Someone came out, a soldier came up the road, comfortable jog, no hurry, something wasn't right, the soldier came up to them.

'Van Heerden?'

'Yes.'

'The Colonel wants you down there.'

He started walking, only the one soldier accompanying him. 'You let Schlebusch get away.'

Silence. Crunch-crunch on the unpaved road, the soldiers' boots loud, his trainers soft. The smallholding opened out ahead of him, neglected, the white paint on an outside building peeling off, long grass, climbing plants growing wildly against a stone wall, weeds in the orchard. As he walked past the truck, he looked, something wasn't right with the fucking truck, what was it? The soldier walked to the veranda, nodded at the front door.

'First door to the right.'

He walked in. Bester Brits stood there, arms folded. On the carpet lay Bushy Schlebusch, half on his face, or what was left of it, the blood a reddish-brown irregular pool on the parquet floor, eye and nose lost in the exit wound, hole in the back of the head, hands tied behind the back.

He looked, flabbergasted, made the connections, one shot, execution-style, in the back of the head and then he knew what was wrong with the truck as he remembered it on the N7. Schlebusch had climbed out on the left-hand side. He had assumed it was a left-hand drive, like Kemp's imported Ford, but Schlebusch wasn't the driver, there was another one, or more than one. He swore, he should've thought, it wasn't the neighbour who phoned, how the fuck could a neighbour remain anonymous, it was . . .

'You killed him, van Heerden.'

'What?'

'The photo in the newspaper this morning. They couldn't afford to let him live.'

He stuttered, a thousand thoughts in his head, nothing made sense. Schlebusch was one, the leader, that was how he'd seen it. Schlebusch was his prey. He struggled with the new information. 'They. Who are "they", Bester?'

'Do you think I would be standing here if I knew?'

He took a step forward, drew a finger through the blood, it was thick and sticky but it wasn't dry. Lord, it must've happened a few hours ago and then he saw the events in his own head: they must've waited for the newspaper, somewhere, waiting to see, every morning since the first copy, made plans. They must've shot Schlebusch this morning and then phoned, the voice on the phone, so calm, so innocent. They knew he would come and then the fear came like a paralysis, his mother, his mother, his mother and he screamed, 'Jesus!' and he ran, out of the door, back to the soldiers who had his cellphone, swearing furiously at his own lack of insight.

'Van Heerden,' Bester called after him.

'My mother, Bester,' he screamed, hearing this morning's call in his ears, that calm, assured voice. Not the voice of a hate-filled psychopath, but of a calm strategist which was worse, much worse.

Billy September saw them coming and he grabbed the AK47 and realized he had to protect the women in the house first: Carolina de Jager in the bathroom, Wilna van As in the kitchen, Joan van Heerden outside somewhere, at the stables. Four men coming from the front, from the road, weapons in their hands, openly moving between trees and shrubs, full of self-confidence, blatant, secure in the knowledge that Joan van Heerden was alone. He screamed at Wilna van As, 'They're coming, get to the bedroom, lie flat', hammered at the bathroom door, 'Trouble, now, come on out.' Wilna van As's eyes white, he pointed at her, 'Look there, please stay in the bedroom.' He ran to the kitchen, looked out towards the stables, didn't see Joan van Heerden, ran to the living room, looked through the big window. They were closer. The bathroom door opened, Carolina de Jager in a pink dressing gown. 'What's the matter?'

'They're here, madam, four with guns, go to the bedroom, lock the door, lie flat.'

'No,' said Carolina de Jager. 'Get me a gun.'

He ran up the sloping road, Bester Brits pounding behind him. 'Van Heerden!' He ran on, Tiny Mpayipheli was on his way here, only September and the women, and they, whoever they were, knew that. He reached the soldiers. 'The cellphone,' he grabbed it out of the man's hand, kept running, heard the soldier behind him, heard Bester: 'Leave him, let him go,' pressed the buttons, held the instrument against his ear, ran. He realized he needed his weapon, turned, tried to take the Heckler & Koch, but the soldier jerked it away. The telephone ringing, ringing, ringing, ringing.

He grabbed at the weapon again, 'Give me the fucking thing,' they surrounded him threateningly and heard Bester's voice, just as breathless as his. 'Give it to him.'

He grabbed, the phone rang, rang, rang, Lord let them answer. He saw the BMW between the Army troop carriers, the fuckers had parked him in. Three soldiers with a big black man, Tiny, the Mercedes-Benz ML 320. Tiny saw him coming.

'We've got to move,' he yelled. 'Schlebusch is dead. This morning.' Mpayipheli just nodded, he couldn't catch the words, only the urgency. He ran to the car, as the telephone rang and rang and rang.

* * *

She jumped, startled when the telephone rang. She was working, had fetched her files to work next to the telephone. The phone was quiet this morning and she had thought about van Heerden's replies to her questions and then it suddenly rang.

'Hallo.'

'Is that Hope Beneke again?'

She recognized the voice, the same male voice. 'Yes.'

'How did you get that photograph of Bushy?'

'We . . . why do you want to know?'

'Have you got photos of all of us?'

'Yes.'

'Are you going to publish them?'

'If it's necessary.'

'Necessary for what?'

'To get the will.'

'But I have nothing to do with the will.'

'Then you have nothing to fear.'

'It's not that simple.'

Billy September heard the telephone ringing, ran to the bedroom where he had slept and grabbed his carry bag from under the bed, hauled out the Remington 870 shotgun by its stock, chambered one shell, gripped the gun in his hand, ran back, gave the weapon to Carolina de Jager. 'There are four shots in the magazine, one in the breech, wait until he's close.' She took the gun, obviously not a first for her. He looked out of the window, the telephone kept ringing, who would phone now? The four armed men were just twenty metres away, he would have to shoot now, where the fuck was Joan van Heerden? He ran to the back door, looked out towards the stables, saw nothing – wait, there she was, carrying a pail, wearing green gumboots, on her way back to the house, he couldn't shout, they were too close. He ran to the living-room window, telephone ringing, aimed the AK over the burglar-proofing, lined up the one with the beret, drew a bead on his lower body, pumped out three shots, saw him fall, the others scattering. Suddenly not so calm any more, suddenly frenetic. He laughed, high and tense, as the window in front of him exploded in a thousand pieces, holes in the plaster, Wilna van

As screaming in the bedroom. He fell flat, blood dripping, the glass had cut him. He saw Carolina de Jager behind the couch with a small smile on her lips and the Remington in front of her, putting out her hand to the telephone. He pushed the AK's barrel through the window, pulled the trigger a few times, crept to the front door, hearing the automatic fire outside. He knew he'd got one, Jesus, Billy September, you're an expert in unarmed combat, look at you shooting the whiteys now.

Bester Brits ran into the door of the Mercedes and banged on the closed window with his hands. 'Van Heerden! Wait!'

He wound down the window, telephone against his ear, still ringing. Tiny Mpayipheli started the engine. 'What is it?'

'Where are you going?'

'My mother. They're going to attack my mother.'

'How do you know?'

'I know, Bester. It was . . . a trap.'

'I have a helicopter, van Heerden.'

'Where?'

'In the air. Behind Karbonkelberg.' Bester waved his hand towards the west.

'Carolina?' he screamed into the cellphone, hearing gunshots in the background, knowing he was right.

'There are four of them,' she shouted. 'Four of them,' and then the phone went dead and he threw it against the front window of the Mercedes with all his might and roared something indecipherable and jumped out and grabbed Bester by the chest. 'Are there soldiers in the chopper, Brits? Tell me!'

'Yes,' said Bester, softly and calmly, and pulled van Heerden's hands away from his jacket. 'There's a radio in the Unimog.'

Hope Beneke tried to remember the names on van Heerden's list because the man at the other end was one of them and she wrote: Red. Manley. Porra. She couldn't remember more than that.

'Have you got all the new names?' he asked.

'Sir, I'm not authorized to share the information with anyone over the telephone.'

'Please, I understand that. I just want . . . I have nothing to do with the will. How can I prove it?'

'By coming to talk to us, sir.'

'They'll kill me.'

'Who?'

'Schlebusch.'

'You said *they*.'

'You know who. You know.'

'We can meet somewhere.'

'Is this line safe?'

'Of course.'

'Will you keep the photos out of the newspapers until we've talked?'

She had an inspiration: 'I can only keep them back for today, sir, tomorrow *Die Burger* will be placing everyone from 1976.'

'No,' he said, his voice filled with fear. 'Please. I'll phone again in an hour. I'll meet you somewhere.'

The line was suddenly quiet. She smiled. This was better. Much better. Then pressed the button on the phone. She had to tell van Heerden about this.

They. He had said they.

Her stomach contracted.

'The subscriber you have dialled is not available . . .'

On his uniform the pilot wore the badge of 22 Squadron with the inscription *Ut Mare Liberum Sit*. He turned the helicopter's nose in the direction of Robben Island. 'Eleven, twelve minutes,' he said.

'It's too slow,' Bester's voice crackled over the radio.

'It's an old Oryx, Colonel, with a top speed of about 300. It's the best I can do.'

'Bester out.'

The pilot pressed the intercom button. 'Hot insertion, ten minutes,' he said and heard the sudden activity at the back, fourteen men of the Anti-Terrorist Unit who were clicking clasps, cocking weapons. *Hell,* he thought, *at last.* Something more exciting than a fishing trawler on the rocks.

46

Her name was Nonnie and when she opened the door the wait of a lifetime was over – because I knew she was the One.

How can I describe that moment?

I've played it in my head, over and over during the past years, that first, magical moment, that overwhelming awareness, that euphoric, immediate knowledge when I looked at her. My eyes drank her in with the thirst of thirty-four years, this gentle, gentle woman, her laughter. She stood there in a one-piece bathing suit because she had been lying next to the small cheap plastic pool and when she opened the door her eyes and her beautiful mouth had laughed (the one front tooth was just a millimetre skew) and her voice was sweeter than Mozart. 'You must be van Heerden,' and I looked into her eyes, deep and green and large and shining. There was so much life there, humour and sympathy and heartbreak and joy. I looked at her body, those curves, she was tall, feminine, fertile, forgive me but it seemed as if nature shouted out of her body, her divine hips, the handfuls of breasts, the small curve of her stomach, her legs strong, her feet small. She was a siren, irresistibly seductive, her short brown hair, her neck, her shoulders, her eyes, her mouth, I wanted to drink her, to taste, to swallow, to slake that unbelievable thirst.

'Come through, then we'll have something to drink at the pool.' She had walked ahead of me down the passage, my eyes on her, past the bookcases, my eyes consuming her, the guilt scurrying through my head like a nocturnal animal, out to the back yard where a book lay. A poetry book. Betta Wandrag: *Morning Star*.

I knew. She knew, in those first moments.

But I couldn't understand it.

Why?

Why should the One's name be Nonnie Nagel?

The wife of my friend and colleague.

47

There was a tall, narrow window next to the front door and when he raised himself off the floor to pull away the blind with the barrel of the AK, they shot Billy September. He felt the bullet breaking through his collarbone, the violence of it slammed him back against the entrance-hall wall, more glass in his face, his arm paralysed. Again he reached forward, looked down, blood pouring out of his chest, out of his stomach. He groaned, his body, they were messing with his body, pockmarks in the wall, deafening noise, his blood on the floor. He was going to die, suddenly he knew it, this was where he was going to die, pressing his hand against the wound in his neck. So much blood, hell, he looked at the sun that shone through the holes in the door, then a man burst in, stood in front of him, a big white man with a stubble beard and a grin, just for a moment, then moved away, to the living room. Billy September heard the thunder of the Remington, one shot. He turned, slowly, his arm was dead, his body a long way away, pain in his stomach, turned slowly, saw Stubble Beard on the living-room floor, on his back, his face blasted away. Billy September smiled, you don't fuck with a *Boervrou*, silence now, deathly silence, there were two more outside, and he had to stop the blood.

The Oryx flew low, 200 metres above the ground, over the coastline at Bloubergstrand, the big engines droning powerfully, fully open, the whole framework vibrating.

'Five minutes to insertion,' the pilot said over the intercom and looked at the ground-speed meter, 309 kms per hour. 'Not bad for an old lady,' he said, then remembered the intercom was still on. He smiled, embarrassed.

'I don't know,' said van Heerden. Tiny Mpayipheli was driving like a maniac, almost losing control at the Constantia Neck circle, fighting the steering wheel, the gears and the clutch.

'I don't know, Jesus, I was stupid, they played me from the start.' He picked up the phone, but the screen was dead. He pressed the 'on' button again, the screen lit up, it was still working. 'Enter pin code.' He swore, threw it down again.

'Here,' Tiny fished a mobile phone out of his pocket, turned left for the Botanic Gardens, swerved for a jogging middle-aged woman with cellulite legs, swore in Xhosa.

Van Heerden took the cellphone, punched in his mother's number, got an engaged signal, tried again, the same frustrating sound. He pressed the phone-in number where Hope Beneke waited – engaged – his mother's number again – engaged – and then he broke through the fear and rage and frustration to a calm sea, took a deep breath, there was nothing he could do. He leant back in the seat, closed his eyes. Thought.

Joan van Heerden saw two men with guns coming round the corner of her house on their way to the back door, no shots now after the terrifying noise. Her heart beating in her throat, she slid back behind the corner of the stables to get out of their field of vision, her eyes looking for a weapon. She saw a spade leaning against the wall, took it in both hands, peered cautiously round the corner. They were at the back door. She put the spade down, pulled off her boots, took the spade again, looked again, they had disappeared into the kitchen. She ran, from shrub to shrub, her footfall light on the sandy soil.

Wilna van As heard the silence and lifted her head from where she was lying on the floor next to the bed, her hands, her whole body shaking, what was going on, was it over now? She got up slowly, as if her legs had no strength, heard a groan. It was Billy September, they needed her help inside. She opened the bedroom door, the passage ahead of her was empty. 'Billy,' she called softly. No reply. She moved down the passage, slowly. 'Billy,' slightly louder, the end of the passage, a hand over her mouth, someone grabbing her roughly from behind, 'Billy is dead, bitch.' She smelt the man's sweat and terror paralysed her.

Hope Beneke grabbed the telephone before it could complete a single ring. 'Hallo.'

'Hallo, Hope.' Intimate, at ease.

'Hallo.'

'You don't know me but I know you.'

'Who's that?'

'You're not getting very far with Rutherford's *London*, Hope, only sixteen pages in the past three days.'

'Who are you?'

'And what was last night like with Zatopek van Heerden, Hope?'

'I'm not having this conversation.'

'Yes, you are, Hope, because I have a very important message for you.'

'What message?'

'I'm getting to it.' So calm. 'First want to share something else with you, Hope. About Kara-An Rousseau. Who kept your place warm in his house on Monday night.'

No words in her head.

'Thought that would leave you speechless but I reckoned it was time for you to know. The real reason why I phoned, Hope, is about Joan. By this time she should be in great pain.'

Carolina de Jager lay behind the couch, the Remington on the floor in front of her. She heard the voice, looked up, saw two of them with Wilna van As.

'You're not Joan van Heerden,' the dark one said and looked at her, his firearm aimed at her.

'Where is she?' the other one in the camouflage pants asked and shoved Wilna van As away from him, so that she fell on her knees on the living room carpet.

'I don't know,' said Carolina de Jager and slowly raised the Remington behind the couch.

'You're lying,' said the dark one, coming closer.

Clattering noise outside, getting louder and louder, aircraft? The two men looked at one another.

'Here I am,' said Joan van Heerden, hitting Camouflage Pants with the spade, the noise outside even louder, the dark one spinning round, taking aim at Joan, Carolina swinging up the Remington, firing without aiming, a thunderclap. He fell, and the noise was suddenly identifiable, helicopter, deafening over the roof of the house.

The helicopter wasn't there when van Heerden and Mpayipheli turned in at the gate in the Mercedes, soldiers in front of the house, army brown body bag in the garden. He saw the damage, the broken windows, the front door hanging on one hinge, the pockmarks against the wall, ran in, 'Ma!' Two more body bags on the floor, cold filled him, 'Ma!' The damage was bad, a great pool of blood in the entrance hall, blood spattered against the walls.

She came out of the kitchen, her eyes swollen and red and he embraced her and she said, 'They shot Billy September, Zet,' and cried.

He held her tightly, overwhelmed with relief. 'I'm sorry, Ma.'

'It wasn't your fault.'

He wasn't so sure but he left it at that.

'Come, they need us,' said his mother.

The other two women were in the kitchen, Wilna van As at the kitchen table, Carolina de Jager at the counter busy with mugs and sugar and tea and milk, their faces pale and set.

'Who . . .' he asked and pointed to the living room.

'Them,' his mother said. 'Billy has gone to hospital in the helicopter but . . .' she shook her head.

'Is he still alive, Ma?'

'He was alive when they put him in the helicopter.'

He counted the body bags. 'There were four?'

'Your mother hit one with a spade. He's also in the helicopter.' Carolina de Jager didn't look up from her busy hands, her voice a monotone.

'Carolina shot two,' said Joan van Heerden.

'Lord,' he said.

'The Lord was on our side today,' said Carolina de Jager.

'Amen,' said Tiny Mpayipheli behind him and then Carolina cried, for the first time.

In the calm before the storm, before Hope came in her partner's car, before Bester and his troops arrived, before the police, with Mat Joubert in command, turned up, before the media and their squadrons streamed in at the gate, before the glaziers could start their repairs, before Orlando Arendse and his retinue, before Kara-An, he walked to one of the two body bags outside and pulled down the zip.

'What are you doing?' asked the soldier with the pack radio, sergeant's stripes on his sleeve.

'Identification,' he said.

'The Colonel said hands off.'

'Fuck the Colonel.' The face in the body bag was that of a stranger, no similarity to Rupert de Jager's photographs of twenty years ago. He slid his hand quickly over the jacket, looking for a wallet.

'That's enough,' said the radio man.

He got up, walked to the other body bag, unzipped it, the soldier watching him. He tried to turn his back on the man, the pale face in the bag unknown, quick hands in the jacket, nothing. He got up, walked to the one in the living room, not wanting the sergeant to follow him, bent over the body, opened fast, found a bulge in the clothing, pushed in his hand, wallet, took it out. He heard footsteps, looked at the face but didn't recognize it, zipped the bag, stood with his back to the door. When he looked round, the sergeant was there, suspicious.

'I don't know them.'

'Samson, Moroka, come and fetch this one, put him with the others.'

Van Heerden went to the kitchen, transferred the wallet to his own pocket.

He borrowed Mpayipheli's cellphone and phoned Murder and Robbery, looking for O'Grady because he wanted them here. Then he phoned the newspapers one by one and the radio stations and the television. He didn't trust Bester Brits, wanted non-military involvement, everything open and above board, transparent.

Hope arrived first, fear in her eyes, wanting to know what had happened, the mark on her cheek bright. She pulled him aside, told him about the second call, but didn't tell him everything.

'He watched us, van Heerden, every move we made. They were in my house, they know what book I'm reading and how fast I read.'

He merely nodded.

'He had a message for us. Your mother . . . the attack . . . he said they'd warned you, Schlebusch had warned you.'

'Schlebusch is dead.'

'Dead?'

'They shot him. This morning. Bester said it's because I put the photo in the paper, because Schlebusch became a high risk. I think it's only part of the story.'

'He said he found the will in the safe.'

'Who?'

'The man who phoned this morning. He said he would've given it to us but then we went to the newspapers. So he burnt it yesterday. He said there was nothing left, we can drop the whole thing now.'

'He's lying.'

'Do you think it still exists?'

'It's leverage, Hope. He would be stupid to destroy it.'

'Why would he say so?'

'I don't know.' He looked at her. At the way she controlled her emotion. *She's strong*, he thought. Stronger than he was. 'Shall we drop it, Hope?'

'I want to get him, van Heerden, with everything I've got but I'm scared. Billy . . . your mother . . .'

'We don't need a will. Those dollars belong to Wilna van As.'

'There was another caller as well, one of the '76 ones. He was scared that we would use his photo as well. He wants to meet us. He said he'd phone back. I told Marie . . .'

'Bester and company tap our phone, Hope.'

'How?'

He laughed without humour. 'Any way they like.'

'Did they hear everything? This morning?'

'They were in Hout Bay a few minutes after me.'

'What do we do now?'

'If he phones again, tell him . . . Jesus, it's difficult . . . they're probably tuned into your cellphone as well.' He thought. 'Tiny's phone. If he phones again, tell him the line isn't secure. Tell him to phone Tiny's cellphone. I'll get the number in a minute.'

'And if he's already phoned? Spoken to Marie?'

'What will Marie tell him?'

'There was a crisis, I'm not available, he must phone at two o'clock this afternoon.'

'He'll phone again. He's frightened.'

She nodded. She said she was going back, perhaps the other call would come in, and he went to fetch her cellphone and Tiny's number and walked with her to her partner's white BMW and then they saw Bester Brits and his convoy of troops arriving and he felt the rage growing in him again, but suppressed it.

Brits jumped off the truck, barked orders left and right, walked to the sergeant, ignored van Heerden.

Then they heard the sirens, saw the blue lights.

The SAPS, he thought. *The cavalry. Too late*. But it pleased him. He would thwart Brits. In every possible way. Just wait until the media arrived.

At first there were five juniors from Murder and Robbery and then, fifteen minutes later, O'Grady, Superintendent Leon Petersen and Mat Joubert arrived in a white Opel Astra. 'You're going to spoil my wedding, van Heerden.'

'You'll thank me one day.'

Joubert looked at the damage, whistled through his teeth. 'What happened?'

'Four of them attacked the house this morning.'

'Them?' asked Petersen.

'I only see three body bags,' said O'Grady.

'Who was in the house?' Joubert asked.

'My mother, two female guests and a . . . a . . . security guy. He's critical, in the Milnerton MediClinic. One of the attackers was still alive. The SANDF took him away as well.'

'And the women?'

'They're safe. And very shocked.'

'One security man handled four armed attackers?'

'He shot one. A farmer's wife from the Free State got two with a shotgun and my mother hit the other one with a spade.'

They looked at him, waiting for him to say he was pulling their leg.

'I'm serious.'

'Jesus,' said O'Grady.

'That's the general feeling,' said van Heerden.

'And what are Brits and the SANDF doing here?'

'It's a long story. Let's talk in there.' He gestured to his house, away from it all and undamaged. They walked towards it.

'You were looking for me yesterday?' van Heerden asked. 'A message?'

Joubert had to think for a moment. 'Oh, yes, I think I know how they found out about the will. I asked around. Someone phoned Murder and Robbery, said he was from the Brixton branch in Gauteng, made all the right noises, could they possibly help, and asked a lot of questions. Snyman who took the call is young. He swallowed the story and gave the information.'

'But it wasn't Brixton.'

'No.'

They were at van Heerden's house but Mat Joubert halted. 'Wait.' He walked over to Bester Brits, alone with his men, a clique in camouflage.

'Brits, I don't need you here. It's a crime scene and your men are ruining all the forensics.'

Van Heerden hung back, filled with satisfaction.

'The hell they are, Joubert, it's my jurisdiction.'

Joubert laughed. 'You don't have any.' He turned to Petersen. 'Leon, get the uniforms from the Table View branch. And you might as well get Philadelphia and Melkbos and Milnerton's people as well, tell them we need crowd-and-riot control. Live ammunition.'

Petersen turned, walked to the Opel Astra. Van Heerden watched Brits. Extremely uncomfortable. He couldn't afford to lose face in front of his troops. 'Unless you want to talk, Brits. Share information,' he called.

Brits tore himself away from the clique, walked up to them, stood too close to Joubert.

'You can't do it, rozzer.'

'"Rozzer"?'

'Jeez, that's old-fashioned,' said Nougat O'Grady. 'Even "pig" would be more up-to-date.'

'What about "flatfoot"?' van Heerden offered.

'Go shit yourself.'

Mat Joubert laughed in his face.

'Uniforms on their way, Mat,' Petersen shouted from the Astra, very loudly. 'In their serried ranks.'

Joubert and Brits stood virtually head to head like two elephant bulls, Joubert slightly shorter, the shoulders somewhat broader.

'Come and talk to us, Brits,' said van Heerden. He wanted to add *please*, but stopped himself. He wanted information. Badly.

O'Grady: 'Our cocks are longer than yours, Brits. Face it.'

'I have nothing to say to you.'

'How many photos must I still publish, Brits?'

'I'll gag the press.'

They laughed as one – van Heerden, Joubert, O'Grady and Petersen.

'Look there, Brits,' van Heerden pointed over Brits's shoulder.

The panel van of eTV turned in at the gate.

'Those men are hungry,' said Petersen.

'You're surrounded,' said O'Grady.

'Custer's last stand,' said Petersen.

'At Little Little Horn.'

Then the two detectives chuckled and van Heerden recalled Brits and Steven Mzimkhulu's mocking. What goes round comes round.

The inner turmoil in Brits ended. 'Ten minutes,' he said. 'That's all you're getting.'

'Thank God you're not a lawyer. It would've cost us a fortune.'

'We have eight members of 1 Reconnaissance Command who ran a supply route from South-West to Angola, Brits.' He closed his eyes, trying to recall the names, his notebook was at Hope's. 'Schlebusch, Verster, de Beer, Manley, Venter, Janse van Rensburg, Vergottini and Rupert de Jager.' He opened his eyes. Brits was pale, trying to hide the shock of the names but his face betrayed him. 'And then two officers appeared on de Jager's parents' farm and told them he had died in the service of his country but more than twenty years later he lived again as Johannes Jacobus Smit with a false identity document and a safe full of American dollars dating from the previous decade. And he was shot with an M16 and I'm reasonably certain it was Schlebusch, the non-commissioned officer who led the group in '76.'

He looked up. Brits evaded his eyes.

'You're doing everything in your power to manipulate the investigation, to get it stopped. Which means that you know what happened in '76 and you want to suppress it at all costs. Which means it was bad, wet work or chemical warfare or some unholy operation.'

Brits snorted contemptuously.

'You can snort all you like, Brits, but your secret is going to come out. Now Schlebusch is also dead, after his picture appeared in the paper. But I have all the photographs, Brits, and I'm giving them to the newspapers and television and I'll sit back and watch all hell breaking loose. And I'll tell them about your efforts to undermine the investigation and see how you handle that.'

They sat in van Heerden's house in the dark living room, his couch and his dining room chairs filled to capacity, Petersen, O'Grady, Mat Joubert, Brits and Tiny Mpayipheli whom he had merely introduced as a colleague.

Brits stood up slowly, his face contorted as if he were in severe pain. He walked down the passage and back again, the others watching him, down the passage and back again, then looked at van Heerden.

'I can't,' he said.

He walked back and forth again, the others quiet, aware of his inner struggle. 'I can't. I've lived with this thing for twenty-three years but I can't talk about it, it's bigger than . . .' His hands embraced the group in the living room. '. . . Than this.'

He walked, thought again, sat down, gestured with his hands, looked for words, breathed out with a sharp exhalation, then slumped back in the chair. 'I can't.'

A silence fell, there was nothing to say. Bester Brits leant his head back, as if the weight of the past was too much for him. And then his voice, almost inaudible. 'So many dead,' he said. And whispered: 'Manley.'

Breathed out. In.

'Verster.'

Out. In.

'De Beer.'

Again the breath, as though he could hear a shot with every name.

'Van Rensburg.'

Van Heerden's heart beating, hammering in his chest, too scared to breathe, too scared that he wouldn't be able to hear, but the officer's voice had stopped. He waited for the last two names but they didn't come.

Then, whispering as well: 'What about Venter and Vergottini?'

Brits closed his eyes as if he was tired to the bone. 'I don't know, van Heerden, I don't know.'

'How did they die?' Almost inaudible but the moment had passed. Bester Brits sat up again.

'It doesn't matter. It was . . .' He bit off the words sharply.

'It matters, Brits.'

Brits started to rise. 'It doesn't matter to *you*, van Heerden, it has absolutely nothing to do with you. Take my word for it. They're dead.'

'Who shot Schlebusch, Brits?'

'I don't know.'

'Vergottini? Verster?'

'I fucking well don't know. I don't know, are you deaf?'

Mat Joubert said softly: 'It must be hard, Brits, to live with this for twenty-three years.' He wanted him in memory mode again, van Heerden thought.

'It is.'

'And to pray it'll never come again.'

Brits dropped his head into his hands. 'Yes.'

'Unload it, Brits, the whole burden. Lay it down.'

He sat like that for a long time, the big hands moving slowly over his eyes and his nose and his forehead, rubbing, rubbing as if comforting himself. Then he got up with difficulty and his body shivered. 'Do you know how much I'd like to? All these years. Do you know how close I sometimes came? Do you know how close I came just now?' Brits walked to the front door, opened it and looked out. He looked back once at the men who remained seated, then shook his head as if saying 'No' to himself and walked out. They listened to his footsteps on the paving and then there was only silence.

48

Perception. And reality.

The perception of Nagel's 'chains': a large battleship with curlers in her hair and a permanent frown, a complaining, nagging millstone, a sloppy television addict, a caricature of a wife in a suburban comic strip.

The reality: this dream woman, this beautiful, gentle, laughing miracle who walked ahead of me through a painfully neat house filled with books, to the small garden at the back, an enchanted spot created with her own hands.

Why had he hidden her? Why, over so many months, had he created the false impression? So that we – I – should have sympathy with his chronic extramarital wanderings, his drinking with the boys?

He had telephoned from De Aar, where he'd gone to investigate a serial rapist case, to say that he had left his service pistol at home. 'I know my fucking wife, she'll let the thing go off and someone will get hurt and then it's a disciplinary hearing and I don't know what other shit, so can you fetch the fucker and keep it with you until I get back?'

I phoned his house first and her voice hadn't prepared me, there was politeness but the technology hadn't carried the music, the beauty, there was no forewarning. That day we talked and couldn't stop.

We sat next to the little swimming pool and later went inside and I prepared supper in her kitchen and we talked, I can't remember what about, it wasn't important, it was what was implied between the words and the sentences, it was the thirst for one another. We ate and talked and looked and laughed and I couldn't believe it, the search of a lifetime and here she was, here I was.

I didn't touch her that evening.

But I was there again the following day after I had phoned Nagel and heard that he was making slow progress and I was glad, my first act of treason, that call, my first betrayal of my friend and colleague, 'Hallo, Nagel, how's it going?'

'Did you get the pistol?' and I went ice-cold because I had forgotten about the weapon, it was still lying around in her house.

'Yes.' And then I realized it was an excuse to go back and I stopped talking, heard he was still going to be busy for days, there were a few suspects but 'the country members of the Force are hopeless, let me tell you,' and then I drove back to Nonnie Nagel.

The story of their marriage unfolded gradually during our conversations, the true story, not the imaginary tales Nagel would dish up to anyone who would listen.

It had been a whirlwind courtship. He was a smooth-talking lover who promised her the world, who painted a dream future for them, told her he was on his way up in the South African Police and she was enchanted by the charm, the humour, the self-assurance. She, a junior school teacher who had reported a burglary in her Bellville flat and found Nagel, Detective Constable Willem Nagel, the man who had the culprit behind bars within days and then used his considerable ingenuity to put her in a prison as well.

It went well for the first year or two. She worked, he worked, they went visiting, had barbecues and sometimes went to the movies and then when he couldn't get her pregnant, he sent her to a doctor, time after time. Every time the message came back – she was normal, there was nothing wrong – and every time he swore and said there had to be and gradually he lost interest in her, in sex and, on top of it, he was promoted to Murder and Robbery as sergeant, his talents recognized, his prophecy of promotion fulfilled, his hours longer and longer, endlessly longer and the green monster of jealousy began raising its ugly head.

She said she believed he had realized that the problem of conception lay with him. Perhaps he had had tests done without her knowledge, discovered that he was infertile or had too low a sperm count, she could only guess, but something triggered the jealousy, only insinuations at first, then hints, later direct accusations as if he was afraid that someone else would make her pregnant. That was all she could imagine, there was no other reason, until one evening, when she was at a school concert, he came to fetch her, out of the hall, dragged her to the car and told her she was going to be a housewife from now on, she was going to resign, he didn't want to come home and find no food, his work, the tension, the hours, the stress, he needed her at home. She had cried that evening, through the night and he had said: 'Cry, it's no use, your place is at home.'

And then he would phone. At any hour of the day or night and if she wasn't home, there was trouble. No, he had never hit her, only verbal abuse.

Mornings between eight and ten were safe. He never phoned before ten and it became her library time and when he gave her money, it was her bookshop time, the second-hand bookshops of Voortrekker Street, her Book Exchange Circuit she called it, and she cooked with distaste, gardened with enthusiasm and wrote stories by hand, the manuscripts stacked high in her wardrobe. I asked her why she didn't send them to someone and she merely shook her head and said it was fantasy, not literature and I asked her if there was a difference and she laughed.

That second night we succumbed to our urges, on that second night I – we – completed the betrayal, not like illicit, guilt-stricken lovers but like released prisoners, with joy and humour and an unbearable lightness of being.

That second night and every night after that until Nagel returned.

49

'You know I have great respect for you, van Heerden,' said Mat Joubert.

He didn't reply, knowing what was coming.

'As far as I'm concerned you're one of us. One of the best.' He sat on the edge of a living-room chair in van Heerden's house, spoke seriously. 'But this morning things changed. Now there are civilians in the firing line.'

Van Heerden nodded.

'We'll have to take control, van Heerden.'

He simply nodded. 'Control' was a relative concept.

'We don't want to exclude you. It's Nougat's case. You'll work with him. Share all your information.'

'You already know everything.'

'Are you sure?' O'Grady's voice was suspicious.

'Yes.' Except the call that was coming at two o'clock and the wallet in his pocket.

'This woman, Carolina de Jager. She was the mother?'

'Yes.'

'I'd like to talk to her.'

'I'll take you to her.'

'And I'll need those photographs.'

'Yes.'

O'Grady looked sharply at him as if gauging his sincerity.

'I'm sorry, van Heerden,' said Joubert, as if perceiving his disappointment.

'I understand,' he said.

'How do we play the media?'

Van Heerden thought for a moment. Minutes ago he had wanted to use the newspapers and television to break Brits, to use the natural aggression of the media as his battering ram to gain information about the whole cover-up. But now, after seeing the man's struggle, he was no longer so certain.

'Say we're cooperating. Everyone, the Defence Force as well. Say the investigation is at a sensitive stage and we must keep back certain information. But a breakthrough is imminent. Keep them hungry.'

Joubert gave a little smile. 'You should come back, van Heerden.' He rose. 'Let's go and feed the monster.'

They walked out, stood outside. The Murder and Robbery detectives led the way to the media lines, the press suddenly moving in anticipation. Then, behind it all, van Heerden saw a new row of cars moving along the driveway. Right in front, in a white Mercedes-Benz, was Orlando Arendse.

'I wanted to warn you,' said Tiny Mpayipheli behind him. 'The boss phoned to say he's on his way.'

There was something surreal about the scene. While he was briefing the repairmen, he looked out over the smallholding. In front of his mother's house stood Orlando Arendse's 'soldiers', all their weapons concealed under their clothing, self-conscious and uncomfortable about the proximity of the squadron of blue police uniforms that had formed a line close to his house – and on the other side stood the cream of the SANDF, the pick of the Urban Anti-Terrorist Unit. The fourth group, the soldiers of the media, was now depleted – only the patient crime reporters who had made the connection between art and Joan van Heerden remained.

Opposite, in his house, Nougat O'Grady was questioning Carolina de Jager. Behind him, in his mother's living room, one of the main bosses of organized crime in the Western Cape was talking to Joan van Heerden about the merits of postmodern art in South Africa while in another room a doctor was treating Wilna van As for shock.

He shook his head.

This thing.

He needed silence now, thinking time. He wanted to read the letters again, comb them for information about Venter and Vergottini, he wanted everyone to go on their way. But he would have to wait.

Orlando had come back from the hospital, said Billy was in Intensive Care, it didn't look good.

Tiny Mpayipheli shaking his head and saying it was just like the Anglo-Boer War: the people of colour who had nothing to do with the fight were in the middle. They were the ones who died.

'Billy is a fighter. He'll make it,' said Orlando.

He had phoned Hope before Joubert and the others had commandeered his living room. Told her the SAPS had officially taken over the case. But they didn't know about the 14:00 call. She must take it. And contact him on Tiny's cellphone.

'Good,' she'd said. Their conspiracy.

He had told her the one who phoned might be Venter or Vergottini.

The others were dead.

Six out of eight.

She was quiet at the other end of the line. And then she said she would phone.

What had happened, two decades ago, to make Death so frequent a visitor now?

Brigadier Walter Redelinghuys arrived, went over to Bester Brits. They talked for a long time, then walked towards him. He went to meet them, heard someone behind him. It was Orlando Arendse.

'I have a stake in this, don't look at me like that.'

He shrugged his shoulders.

Joubert, O'Grady and Petersen came out of his house, saw the new grouping, also came over. The detectives' eyes widened when they saw the crime baron.

'Orlando,' said Mat Joubert without warmth.

'Bull,' Orlando said in acknowledgement, using the nickname Joubert had earned on the Cape Flats.

'What is he doing here?' Joubert asked.

'It's my man who's in hospital.'

'Who are you?' Walter Redelinghuys wanted to know.

'Your worst nightmare,' said Orlando.

Mat Joubert, frowned deeply. 'What are you doing, van Heerden?'

'I'm doing what I have to do.'

'I want to know how we're going to cooperate,' said Walter Redelinghuys.

'I won't work with him,' said Joubert, nodding in Arendse's direction.

'Just as well, I have a reputation to uphold.'

'Orlando and his men made a valuable contribution to the investigation,' van Heerden said uncomfortably.

'You're one of us, van Heerden. If you needed cover fire, we would've helped.'

'Without asking questions?'

And they all stood there.

'We've just taken over the case with van Heerden's support, Brigadier.'

'Nonsense,' said Redelinghuys.

Joubert ignored him. 'I'll leave ten uniforms here,' he said to van Heerden. 'You don't need Orlando.'

He did. Because of the dollars. But he couldn't say that.

'I want Tiny Mpayipheli.'

'He also Orlando's?'

Van Heerden nodded.

Walter Redelinghuys: 'Bester is also in.'

'No,' said van Heerden.

'Why not?' Heavily.

'He creeps around this thing like a thief in the night. He tried to get me off the investigation, he lied like a trooper, he withholds information, putting people's lives in danger. He contributes nothing and he bugs my phone calls. Bester is out. We've kept you out of the media but more than that I bloody well won't do. He can carry on creeping if he wants to but up to now all he's done is cause trouble.'

'I contributed what I could.'

'Have you told Murder and Robbery about the body in Hout Bay, Brits?'

'Which body, Brits?'

'Schlebusch.'

'Jesus.' Joubert turned. 'Tony, Leon, we've got to go.'

'There's nothing left for you,' said Brits.

'Did you interfere with a murder scene?'

'I solved a military problem.'

For a moment van Heerden thought Mat Joubert was going to hit the Defence Force officer, but then Joubert gave a deep sigh. 'I'm getting married on Saturday and on Sunday I'm going on a honeymoon to the Seychelles. It gives me two days in which I'll use every possible channel to get you of out this thing, Brits . . .'

'I object,' said the Brigadier.

'Fat lot of difference that's going to make,' said Orlando Arendse. 'You don't know the Bull.'

Redelinghuys opened his mouth but was forestalled by a woman's high, distraught voice.

'It's you!'

Carolina de Jager came walking up, her finger pointing at one of them.

'It's you,' she said, her voice breaking. She walked past them to Bester Brits, hit him on the shoulder.

'It's you. You're the one who took away my son. What did you do, what did you do to Rupert?' She hit the man on the chest and he simply stood there, didn't stop her. She hammered at him, weeping, until van Heerden reached her.

'Easy,' he said in a soft voice.

'It's him.'

'I know.'

'He brought the news of his death.'

He took her hands away from Brits, held her against him. 'I know.'

'Twenty years. And I'll never forget his face,'

He held her.

'He was the one who took Rupert away.' She cried uncontrollably, the sorrow of a lifetime. He could do no more, heard Bester walking away without a word.

There was nothing he could say to comfort her.

Shortly before one, he closed and locked the door of his house behind him, arranged a few loose papers on the table in front of him, put down a pen and tugged the wallet out of his pocket.

Worn leather that fastened with a stud. Two hundred and fifty rands and loose change. Bank cards. Absa Mastercard in the name of W.A. Potgieter. Absa cash card with the same name. Receipts. All in the past week. Van Hunks Tavern, Mowbray, R65.85. The Mexican Chilli, Observatory, R102.66. Hollywood Video Rental, Main Road, Observatory. Pick 'n Pay, Mowbray, R142.55 for groceries, a credit card slip from the Girls to Go Agency, 12th Avenue, Observatory, R600.

That was it.

He gave the little pile a disappointed look. It wasn't much help. It needed work. He fetched his telephone guide, looked up the number of the Absa Card Division, dialled. 'Art World Frames and Studio, Table View, here. I have a client at the counter,' he said in a whisper, 'of whom I want to make quite sure.'

'Yes, sir.'

'He wants to buy a painting for nearly a thousand rand. His card number is 5417 9113 8919 1030 in the name of W.A. Potgieter and the expiry date is 06/00.'

'Just a moment.'

He waited. 'The card hasn't been reported as missing, sir.'

'What is his registered address? I want to make doubly sure.'

'It's . . . er . . . 177 Wildebeest Drive, Bryanston, sir.'

'Johannesburg?'

'Yes, sir.'

'Thank you very much,' he whispered and put the phone down.

That didn't help much.

But what was W.A. doing so far from home? Why was he hanging around the Cape's southern suburbs?

He leant back in the chair, tried to make sense of the day's events, tried to slot the new information into what he had.

So many dead. And now only Venter and Vergottini remained.

Bester Brits had been the messenger of death then. Involved from the start. But not involved enough to know everything. Like who the protagonist behind it all was.

One of them would telephone at 14:00, one of them wanted to come in and talk, one of them said he wasn't part of the thing.

And the other one had sent four men to shoot his mother.

What kind of man . . . What was so big, so important, so wicked that he needed to send four armed henchmen? Was it the money, the huge stack of American dollars? Or was it because he wanted to cover up the evil of twenty-three years ago at all costs?

Schlebusch. Why shoot your eastwhile team leader if he was on your side?

And if Schlebusch wasn't the evil behind the whole thing, who the hell was?

The timing.

Brits had said it was because Schlebusch's picture had been in the newspaper that he was shot. But the timing was too tight. Between five, six o'clock when *Die Burger* appeared and the phone call, there was too little time to commit a murder, develop a strategy to lure him, van Heerden, to Hout Bay and send troops to Morning Star.

It hadn't worked that way.

Shit, he didn't know how this thing worked but he had one thin string he could pull on to see what unravelled. The contents of the wallet.

He looked at his watch. 13:12. Still time to drive to Observatory before the 14:00 call came. He would have to call Tiny. He replaced the contents of the wallet, snapped it shut, put in back in his pocket.

Walked to the door. The Heckler & Koch stood against the wall next to the door. He looked at it. The thing was too big. Too unwieldy. Too obvious.

He paused.

Perhaps it was time?

No.

What had Mat Joubert told Bester Brits? *Unload the burden.*

A moment's doubt, the old, familiar tug in his stomach when he thought about the Z88, and then he walked to the bedroom, opened the cupboard door, shifted the sweaters in front of the small safe, turned the combination lock and clicked it open. He took out the old police service pistol and magazine, banged the magazine into the grip – don't think, he didn't want to think – pushed the gun into his belt at the back, pulled his sweater over it, walked to the front door, picked up the Heckler & Koch – he must give it back to Tiny – opened the door.

'Hallo, Zatopek,' said Kara-An Rousseau, her hand in the air, about to knock. She looked at the machine pistol. 'Still love me?'

50

We stood next to the body of the Red Ribbon Executioner's first victim when Nagel said: 'If anyone ever messes with my wife, I'll shoot him. Like a dog.'

Unprovoked. He had bent over the middle-aged prostitute and studied the red ribbon with which she had been strangled and suddenly straightened and looked me in the eye and his Adam's apple had bobbed with each word. And then he looked away again and studied the crime scene.

And my heart skipped a beat and my palms sweated and, terrified, I wondered how he knew, he couldn't know, we were so incredibly careful. After the second time I didn't even park my Toyota near the Nagel house, I left it two blocks away in a café's parking lot and walked, stooping, like a suspect, like a criminal.

I who, despite my minor sins of self-satisfaction and selfishness, had taken the conscious decision to strive for integrity, to live with honesty and self-control. I, for whom each crime scene brought a new determination to range myself on the side of the good, to fight and to tame the evil and the bad, the monster which crouched in others.

Then, and in the years thereafter, I turned that moment over and over like a piece of evidence in my hands and examined it from all sides for clues to Nagel's words.

Had my attitude towards him changed when he came back from De Aar? I thought I'd hidden it so well, we still bickered, joked, argued as we'd always done but perhaps the thin light-headedness of guilt when I met his eyes was visible, tangible.

Or was it Nonnie's subtly altered behaviour when he came home? Had he perhaps found her in the kitchen, softly singing, had she said, or not said, something?

Or was it the famous Nagel instinct, the extra sense that, despite all his shallowness, he was blessed with?

Was it Jung who said that there was no coincidence? Had Nagel sent me purposely or subconsciously-consciously to Nonnie that first day? I even considered that possibility but the psychological byways formed a maze of speculation in which I quickly became trapped.

To my deep shame I must admit that his words, his throwing down of the gauntlet as it were, gave an extra element of excitement and adrenalin to our secret relationship. It was a factor that bound us more closely in our deceit, tightened the bonds of our love. In our stolen moments, in her house, in Nagel's bed, when we lay in one another's arms, we would speculate conspiratorially about his suspicions, we would discuss our behaviour, looking for moments in which we might possibly have betrayed ourselves – and each time came to the conclusion that he had no reason to suspect.

The time we could spend together was so heartbreakingly limited: sometimes an hour or two in a day, when the slow-moving judicial system held him captive as a witness in a court case; when he made himself comfortable on a bar stool for an evening's 'serious drinking' and the oh, so rare sweet days and nights when he had to leave the Cape to stretch the long arm of the law into the countryside.

In those months Nonnie Nagel became my whole life. I thought about her from the moment I opened my eyes in the morning until, with painful longing, I eventually went to sleep at night. My love for her was all-encompassing, all-prevailing, a virus, a fever, a refuge.

My love for her was right, just, good. Nagel had rejected her, I had discovered her, embraced and cherished her, made her my own. My love for her was pure, beautiful, gentle. Therefore it was right, despite the terrible daily deceit. I rationalized it for myself, every hour of every day, told her he had had choices, had made his decisions. Together we elevated our relationship to a crusade of love and justice.

Why didn't she just leave him?

I asked her that once and she simply looked at me with those beautiful, gentle eyes and made a gesture of infinite helplessness and I came to my own conclusions. I suspected she was, like many abused women, the victim of a destructive relationship in which one word of praise was the dependency-inducing lifeline in a stormy sea of criticism. I suspected that she didn't think she could stand on her own any longer, she didn't believe she was capable of a life without him.

I didn't ask again, knew I would have to take the lead.

But perhaps it was also the very nature of our relationship that allowed so little time for discussion of the future, perhaps it was because we wanted to be sure, perhaps we didn't want to dilute the excitement of the forbidden so soon. We never really spoke about the way in which she should leave her marriage.

And one afternoon (he was in court again), when we had let the sweat of lovemaking dry on our bodies, I uttered the words that would change so much.

What I should have said was, 'Nonnie, I love you. Marry me.'

What I did say had the same tenor, was the product of my feeling of guilt, my fear, my focus.

'How do we get rid of Nagel?' I asked, without thinking too deeply, without measuring the meaning of my words.

51

Bart de Wit and Mat Joubert had Tony O'Grady on the carpet.

'Van Heerden made something of this case with nothing – no forensics, no team of detectives, no squad of uniforms, nothing. Now's the time for you, Anthony O'Grady, to move your arse because the SANDF is laughing at us and the media are laughing at us and the District Commissioner screams over the telephone and the Provincial Minister of Justice phoned to say you've got to move it, it can't carry on like this. You're in charge now. Tell us what you need. Make things happen.'

And now he was standing in front of an impressive matron of the Milnerton MediClinic and his meaty face blushed a dark red and his lumpish body shook with rage and his mouth was struggling to choke back words that shouldn't be used in front of a woman.

'He's *gone*?' he managed eventually.

'Yes, sir, he's gone, the military people took him away against the wishes of the entire medical team.' Her voice was calm and soothing; she saw O'Grady's red face and shaking torso and wondered whether he was going to have a heart attack in her office.

'Fffff . . .' he said and controlled himself with superhuman effort.

'Just about ten minutes ago. Not even in an ambulance.'

'Did they say where they were taking him?'

'Into custody. When I objected they said they had medical treatment available for him.'

The curses were poised on his tongue but he bit them back.

'What was his condition?'

'He was stable but we were about to run tests on him. A blow like that to the head, there could be major brain damage.'

'Was he conscious?'

'Delirious, I would say.'

'Coherent?'

'I don't know.'

'Who took him?'

'A Colonel Brits.'

The frustration, the impotent rage washed through O'Grady's big body. 'The bastard,' he said, and then he could no longer hold the obscenities back. 'The motherfucking, absolute, total, complete cunt of a bastard,' he said and deflated like a big balloon.

'Feeling better now?' asked the matron. But O'Grady didn't hear her. He was on his way down the passage, cell-phone in his hand. He was going to speak to that dolly-bird attorney but first he would phone Mat Joubert. Joubert must phone Bart de Wit. Bart de Wit must phone the Commissioner and the Commissioner could phone whoever he wanted but Bester Brits was going to get fucked before the day was out.

He was wrong.

The man whose skull had been cracked by a spade was sitting on a wooden Defence Force chair, in a prefab building in a forgotten area in a Port Jackson thicket on the far edge of the Ysterplaat Air Force base. He wasn't tied down or shackled. Bester Brits, standing in front of him, was in complete control: there was no need for restraints.

Outside there were four soldiers with R5 rifles and, in any case, Spadehead wasn't in great shape. His head was lolling, the eyes rolling up every few seconds, his breathing fast and uneven.

'Does it hurt?' Bester Brits asked and slapped Spadehead on the purplish-red head wound.

The sound that came through the swollen lips was just decipherable as 'Yes.'

'What's your name?'

No reply. Brits lifted his hand again, poised threateningly.

A sound.

'What?'

'Ghaarie.'

'Gary?'

Nod, head rolling.

'Who sent you, Gary, to the house to attack the women?'

Sound.

'What?'

'Please.' Hands lifted to protect the wound.

Brits swept the hands aside, slapped again. 'Please? Please what?'

'My head.'

'I know it's your fucking head, you moron, and I'll keep on hitting it until you talk, do you understand? The faster you talk, the faster . . .'

Sound.

'What?'

'Oh-ri-un.'

'Orion?'

'Yes.'

Brits hit him again with the frustration of more than twenty years, all the hatred, the rancour in him that opened like an old, stinking sore. 'I know it was Operation Orion, motherfuck,' the words unlocking memories.

Gary moaning, 'No, no, no.'

'What do you mean, "no"?'

'O-ri-unShh . . .' The word slurred in the saliva that ran from a corner of his mouth.

'What?'

No reply. Gary's eyes were closed, the head flopping.

'Don't pretend to be unconscious, Gary.'

There was still no reply.

'I can't talk to you now,' van Heerden said to Kara-An Rousseau.

'I heard it on the radio. About the shooting.'

'I've got to go.' He stood in the doorway of his house, machine pistol in his hand.

'Why were you at my house last night?'

'I wanted to . . . tell you something.'

'Tell me now.'

'I've got to go.'

'You want to know why I am like I am.'

He shifted past her. 'This isn't a good time,' he said and walked towards his mother's house. He had to get Tiny.

'Because you're afraid you're like that, too.' Not a question.

He halted, turned. 'No,' he said.

She laughed at him. 'Zatopek, it's in you too. And you know it.'

He looked at her beauty, her smile, the perfect teeth. Then he walked away, faster and faster, to get away from the sound of her laughter.

At four minutes past two Nougat O'Grady walked into Hope Beneke's office and said, 'We have taken over the case. Completely.'

'I know,' said Hope Beneke and wondered how she could get rid of him in the next few minutes.

'I believe van Heerden has not been absolutely frank with us,' he said and wondered why this female attorney always wore clothes that hid her talents. He suspected there was a nifty body underneath it all. He sat down on a chair opposite her. 'A lot of people have died, Miss Beneke. And unless you share everything with us, the killing won't stop. Now, do you want that on your conscience?'

'No,' she said.

'Then please . . .'

The phone rang. She started.

'Been expecting a call?' he asked and knew instinctively that something was cooking here. 'Please go ahead. We're a team now, so to speak.'

* * *

The owner of the Girls to Go Agency in 12th Avenue, Observatory, looked like a retired film star – long, elegant nose, square jaw, black hair flecked with grey, bushy Tom Selleck moustache – but when he opened his mouth to speak he showed a set of teeth that were terrifying in their decay: stained yellow, crooked, half of them missing.

'It'th confidenthial informathion,' he said to Zatopek van Heerden and Tony Mpayipheli, lisping slightly.

'A prostitute's destination is not confidential information,' said van Heerden.

'Thyow me your badge.' The lisp was more marked.

'I'm a private investigator, I don't have a badge,' he said slowly and patiently. But he didn't know how much more of the man's attitude he would be able to take.

'Here's *my* badge,' said Tiny Mpayipheli, the impatience strong in his voice as he opened his jacket to show the Rossi model 462 in its shoulder holster.

'I'm not thcared of gunth,' the film star said.

The Xhosa took out the .357 Magnum revolver and put a hole in the 'O' of 'Go' in the sign behind the man, the noise of the gunshot ear-splitting in the small room. Behind a door a few women shrieked.

'The next one goes through your knee,' said Mpayipheli.

The door opened. A young woman with green hair and big eyes asked: 'What's going on, Vincent?'

'Nothing I can't handle.' Calm, unintimidated.

'The address, Vincent,' said van Heerden.

Vincent looked at them with eyes that had seen everything, looked at the Rossi aimed at his leg, slowly shook his head back and forth as if he didn't understand the universe and patiently pulled a large black book towards him, took the credit card slip which van Heerden had put on the counter and lazily started leafing through the book.

Tiny put the weapon back under his jacket. They waited. Vincent licked a finger, leafed on.

'Here it ith,' he said.

'This telephone is tapped by Military Intelligence,' Hope said to the man on the phone. 'I must ask you to phone another number, a cellphone number. My colleague is waiting for your call.'

A moment's silence. 'No,' he said. 'Go to the Coffee King at the Protea Hotel next to your building. I'll phone there in five minutes.'

'Fffff—' said Hope Beneke and bit back the word. 'I've got to go,' she said and stood up swiftly behind the desk.

'I'm coming with you,' said Nougat. 'Where are we going?' They ran down the passage, out through the door, down the stairs and out of the building, a fit Hope ahead, a puffing O'Grady a few yards behind her.

'Wait up,' he shouted. 'They'll think I'm trying to assault you.' But she kept on running, jerked open the door of the Coffee King and stopped at the counter.

'I'm expecting a telephone call.' she said to the Taiwanese woman.

O'Grady steamed in, breathing hard.

'This is not a telephone booth,' said the Taiwanese woman.

'It's police business, madam,' said O'Grady.

'Show me your identification.'

'Jeez, everybody watches television these days,' he said, still trying to catch his breath as he put his hand in his pocket.

The telephone next to her began ringing.

'This man urgently needs hospitalization,' said the captain with the insignia of the SA Medical Services on his uniform.

'Not necessarily,' said Bester Brits.

'He's dying.'

'He has to talk before he turns up his toes.'

The captain looked disbelievingly at the officer from Military Intelligence. 'I . . . I thought the Truth and Reconciliation Commission had eradicated your kind.'

'I wasn't always like this.'

'Colonel, if I don't get him stabilized in Intensive Care, he's never going to speak again. We have half an hour, maybe less.'

'Take him, then,' said Bester Brits and walked out. He walked to a Port Jackson, leant against the trunk. Hell, he wished he still smoked.

Oh-ri-un.

Orion.

'No, no, no,' Gary had said. Not *Operation* Orion?

What, then?

Oh-ri-unSh . . .

Tiny Mpayipheli held the Rossi in both hands and stood next to the door while van Heerden knocked, on the sixth floor of a block of flats in Observatory with a view over the mountain and Groote Schuur Hospital.

'Yes?' A male voice on the other side of the door.

'Parcel for W.A. Potgieter,' said van Heerden, imitating the bored voice of a delivery man.

Silence.

'Get away from the door,' said Tiny.

Van Heerden stood aside, pushed his hand down inside his jacket, felt the butt of the Z88, knocking again with his other hand. 'Halooo.'

The bullet holes splintered out in that nanosecond before they heard the automatic gunfire, the cheap door exploding in a rain of wooden chips. They dropped to their knees, he held Z88 in his hand now, the other hand protectively over his eyes, then sudden silence.

'Shit,' said Tiny Mpayipheli.

They waited.

'You should have kept the Heckler & Koch.'

'Maybe.'

'And that?' Tiny nodded at the Z88.

'It's a long story.'

'We've got time,' said Tiny and grinned.

'Is this the only door? The fire escape is in front, next to the lifts.'

'He can only get out through here.' Tiny pointed the Rossi's barrel at the remains of the door.

'And they have the heavy artillery in there.'

'Yes, but you have your Z88.' Sarcasm.

'Anything in your Russian training for this situation?'

'Yes. I take my anti-tank missile out of my backpack and blow them to smithereens.'

'We need them alive.'

'OK, scrap the missile. You're ex-SAP. You ought to know what to do.'

'Gunfights were never my strong point.'

'I've heard.'

Voice from inside. 'What do you want?'

'His ammunition is finished,' said van Heerden.

'Is that a wish or a fact?'

'Do you want to bet?'

'One of your mother's pictures that's hanging on your wall.'

'What do I get if I'm right?'

'The Heckler & Koch.'

'Forget it.'

From inside: 'What are you looking for?'

'I see you're also hopeless with women. Your mother's painting against a guaranteed formula for getting the attorney into bed.'

'That Russian training was thorough.'

'Come in with your hands up. Or we'll blast you,' the voice yelled from inside the flat. From somewhere in the streets outside came the sound of the first sirens.

'He's bluffing about the "us",' said Tiny.

'You want to bet?'

'No.'

'There's something else I have to tell you,' said van Heerden.

Tiny sighed. 'Fire away.'

'I was a policeman for a long time but I never had the opportunity to do the kick-open-the-door-and-rush-in-shooting bit. And to do it for the first time scares me more than you can ever imagine.'

Voice inside: 'We're counting to ten.'

'All I need. A cowardly whitey.'

'We going in?'

'Yes,' said Tiny. 'You first.'

'Fucking cowardly Xhosa,' said Zatopek van Heerden and then he moved, rose from the crouch, shoulder first, and burst through the door.

52

He first used a red ribbon because it was there, in the prostitute's hair: he picked her up in his Volkswagen Kombi in Sea Point and drove up to Signal Hill where he strangled her after oral sex. He dumped her body, spread-eagled her arms and legs, put her in the middle of the road, his 'signature', his statement that she meant nothing to him, that he despised her and her kind. And when the media focused on the red ribbon, he bought a roll of it at Hymie Sachs in Goodwood and either strangled or decorated the next sixteen of his victims with a metre of red ribbon. He broke the ribbon strangulation habit with the thirteenth and used his hands but the red strip was still tied around the necks of his spread-eagled victims. His mocking message to Nagel and me. His mark of superiority. His relishing of the media spotlight.

He sent a letter to the *Cape Times*, after the third murder when they had described him as the Red Ribbon Murderer. 'I AM NOT A MURDERER. I AM AN EXECUTIONUR,' he had written, bad spelling and all, in block letters. And then he became the Executioner, the criminal whom I hated more than anyone else in my whole career because he kept Nagel in the Cape and me away from Nonnie.

The hunt placed enormous tension on my partnership with Nagel. The pressure, because of media interest, was unbearable towards the end, when he so unexpectedly uttered his warning about his wife.

In all the previous cases that we had investigated, the competition between us had been amiable, always on the safe side of the border drawn by mutual respect. But it seemed as if Nagel used Red Ribbon as a measure of who deserved Nonnie. Like those head-butting rams that have to prove their genetic superiority in order to mate with the ewe, he tackled me on my one area of speciality, the serial killer, and questioned and refuted my every profile, every possible statement, every conceivable judgement, forecast and trapping method.

With the first victim I had already forecast that he would kill again: all the signs were there.

'Bullshit,' said Nagel.

But with the second it was he who shared his 'theory' with the media: 'We have a serial killer here, ever since the first murder I have had no doubt about it.'

As the death toll grew, as the media hysteria increased, as the pressure from the commanding officer and top structure became stronger, the friendship and professional partnership between Nagel and me crumbled. His criticism of me and his passing remarks became personal, disparaging, cutting. The one big difference between us, the fact that I could never get used to the heartlessness and the violence of murder scenes, the fact that I was constantly shocked and upset, evoked no sympathy, merely scorn during the months when I vomited again or, with a pale face and shaking hands, tried not to. He deliberately emphasized his own icy approach, the detachment he had built up over the years. But now the gloves were off. 'You don't have the heart of a policeman,' he said, with so much disapproval that it cut me like a knife. It was only my conscience, my guilty, guilty conscience, and the quiet knowledge that Nonnie was mine, not his, that prevented an all-or-nothing confrontation, that allowed me to give way, even when I knew with absolute certainty that he was wrong about the methods needed to stop Red Ribbon.

I'll always believe that we could have caught the murderer sooner if it hadn't been for the dispute between us. The opportunities slid past one by one while Nagel fought for dominance.

And eventually he solved the case with forensic evidence from tyre tracks and the fibre of the Camper's carpets. 'Not your psychological shit,' he'd said, on that last evening when we were on our way to make the arrest.

Lord, and that last evening had started so well.

53

'Meet me at Café Paradiso on Kloof Street in ten minutes,' the man on the telephone said to Hope.

'How will I know you?'

'I'm wearing a brown leather jacket,' and then the line went dead. She replaced the receiver. 'Thank you so much,' she said to the Taiwanese woman and ran out of the door.

Nougat O'Grady swore softly and ran after her.

'Have you heard of fat guys who are incredibly nimble on their feet?'

'Yes,' she said.

'Well, I'm not one of them.'

'Who sent you?' Bester Brits had asked Gary and the answer was Oh-ri-un and he didn't want to hear it because his head was filled with the past and then he began to think, think, think and here he was, with the telephone book, his finger moving down the list: Orion Motors, Orion Printers, Orion Telecom Corporation, Orion Solutions, Orion Wool & Crafts, all printed in heavy black letters except for Orion Printers and Orion Solutions.

Oh-ri-unSh . . .

All obvious business enterprises except Orion Solutions.

Oh-ri-unSh . . .

Just the name of the firm and the number, 462–555, no address, no fax number, nothing. They had kept the name, were they that arrogant, that challenging?

Bester Brits dialled the number of Orion Solutions.

'Leave your name and number. We'll call back.'

Not exactly client-friendly.

He dialled another number.

'Sergeant Pienaar.'

'Pine, it's Bester Brits.'

'Colonel!'

'I'm looking for an address for a telephone number. I don't want to go through the channels.'

'Give me five minutes, Colonel.'

He leant back. Rank had its advantages.

He was wrong about the ammunition: the R4 stuttered out as he rolled into the flat. He kept on rolling, the bullets stitching a row behind him and he shot wildly, one, two, three shots with the Z88, hopelessly wide of the mark, fear injecting adrenalin, chunks of plaster and wood, dust and splinters, ear-splitting noise. Tiny Mpayipheli's Rossi 357 Magnum thundered once and then everything was quiet and he rolled to a halt behind the cheap sitting-room chair, his heart beating, blood hammering through his body, his hands shaking.

'He lied about the "us",' said Tiny.

Van Heerden got up, shook the dust from his clothes, saw the man, the top of his head shot away by the heavy-calibre pistol. The sirens were close now, loud and clear. 'We don't have time,' he said. 'We must be out of here before the police arrive.'

He shoved his hands into the dead man's pockets – the fifth corpse today, he thought – revulsion against the bits of brain and bone and blood rising in his throat. He found nothing, looked round at the spartan flat, empty pizza boxes on the melamine kitchen counter, empty beer bottles on the coffee table, empty coffee mugs in the sink, two small boxes of ammunition on the floor, one open.

'I'll choose my painting later, thank you.'

Mpayipheli walked to the bedroom while van Heerden jerked open drawers and cupboards in the kitchen.

Nothing.

'Have a look at this,' Tiny called from a bedroom. He went through: R1 and R5 attack rifles leaning in a bunch in a corner, clothes strewn on the bed, two-way radios on the floor. Tiny stood in front of a cupboard, staring at an A4 sheet taped to the door, a printout from a dot matrix printer.

Shift schedule:

00.00–06.00:	*Degenaar and Steenkamp*
06.00–12.00:	*Schlebusch and Player*
12.00–18.00:	*Weber and Potgieter*
18.00–00:	*Goldman and Nixon*

Sirens in front of the block. He knew the police procedure, they would come up the fire escape, two would cover the lift on the ground floor. He didn't know how many uniforms there were by now, didn't want to speak to the police now, this was no time to be caught up in the machine. He jerked the paper off the cupboard door. 'Come on, got to go,' he said and walked, Tiny following him, taking one last look at the body and the damage, out of the door. He pressed the call button for the lift and the door opened immediately. They walked in, pressed 'P' for the parking garage. As the door closed and the lift moved, he held his breath, it mustn't stop on the ground floor.

'Your pistol,' Tiny said softly.

'What?'

'You can put it away now.'

He gave an embarrassed grin and looked at the lights above the door, *ground floor* which flashed once, the lift moving, *parking garage*. His gaze fell on the handwritten note against a side panel of the lift.

Two-bedroom flat for rent in this building.

Call Marla at Southern Estate Agents,

283 Main Road.

When the door opened he took the note down. They walked out. He looked at his watch: 14:17. Why didn't Hope's contact telephone? Why didn't Hope phone?

Sergeant Pienaar's call was was two minutes longer than the promised five. 'The number is registered in the name of Orion Solutions, sir. The address is 78 Solan Street, in Gardens.'

'Solan?'

'I don't pick 'em, Colonel, I just dig 'em out.'

'Thanks, Pine, you're a star.'

'Pleasure, Colonel.'

Bester Brits put the pen down and rubbed his hands over his face with slow, rhythmic movements, softly, soothingly, comfortingly. *Tired*, he thought, *so tired, so many years of searching.*

Another dead end?

He would have a look.

Alone.

He walked out of the office. It was suddenly cold outside, the north-wester tugging at his clothes, the fine rain, preceding the cold front, sifting down. He was hardly aware of it.

They wouldn't be so arrogant.

Orion Solutions.

The hatred was all-encompassing.

As usual there was no parking in Kloof Street, so she parked the BMW in a side street. She wanted to get Zatopek van Heerden on the cellphone, but decided against it, first she must check to see whether the caller was here. She took her umbrella from behind the seat, handed it to O'Grady.

'Be a gentleman,' she said.

'No running?' He took the umbrella from her and got out.

'No running,' she said.

They walked from the corner to Café Paradiso, she and the fat detective under the umbrella, the rain gusting.

'He's not expecting someone else with me,' she said.

'Tough shit,' said O'Grady. 'It's my case.'

'He might run when he sees you.'

'Then you'll have to catch him. You're the fast one in this little team.'

They walked up the stairs, the wooden tables outside empty, the light inside shining through the windows. He opened the door for her, shook out the umbrella. Her eyes searched the room, saw the man sitting alone at a table, cigarette in his hand, brown leather jacket, late thirties, gold-rimmed glasses, dark hair, black moustache. He looked up, saw her, his face tense and he half-rose, nervously stubbing out the cigarette as she walked up to the table.

'I'm Hope Beneke,' extending her hand.

'Miller,' he said and shook her hand. She felt the dampness of the sweat on his palm, saw the wedding ring on his finger. 'Sit down.'

'This is Inspector O'Grady of Murder and Robbery,' she said.

He looked at Nougat, confused. 'What's he doing here?'

'It's my case now. As a matter of fact, it's always been my case.'

They sat down at the table. A waiter approached with menus.

'We don't want anything,' said Miller, 'we're not staying long.'

'I'll have one,' said O'Grady and took a menu. 'You can bring me a Diet Coke in the meanwhile. A big one.'

'Is Miller your real name?' Hope asked when the waiter had gone.

'No,' he said.

'Are you Venter? Or Vergottini?'

'I have a wife and children.'

'It says here they have a Mediterranean buffet,' said O'Grady from behind the menu.

'As you going to publish my photo as well?'

'Not if you cooperate.'

He was visibly relieved. 'I'll tell you all I can but then you'll leave me alone?' A begging question, hopeful.

'That depends on your innocence, sir.'

'No one is innocent in this thing.'

'Why don't you tell us about it?'

He looked at them, looked at the door, across the room, eyes never still. She saw the sweat glistening in the light of the restaurant, small, silver drops on his forehead.

'Hold your horses,' said Nougat O'Grady. 'I want to have a look at the buffet before you start spilling the beans.' He hauled himself upright.

The sniper's bullet that was meant for Miller punched through the window of the restaurant and ploughed through the fat policeman's body between the fourth and fifth ribs, nicked a corner of the right lung, went through the upper right ventricle of the heart, exited through the breastbone and buried itself in a wooden beam above the bar in the centre of the restaurant. There was no sound of a shot, only the window shattering and O'Grady being thrown across the table by the impact of the bullet, his considerable weight smashing the table under him. He fell to the floor in a welter of broken wood and blood but he was unaware of it all.

Miller was the first to react. He was up and running when the first screams erupted, not towards the front door but in the opposite direction, the kitchen. Hope sat transfixed, paralysed. The breaking table had injured her knee, O'Grady had fallen half across her. She looked at the policeman's face, the staring eyes.

'God,' she said softly, looking confusedly at him, at Miller's retreating back, at the window, hearing screaming tyres outside. She half-rose, saw a white panel van driving down Kloof Street, her legs shook. She reached for her handbag, she had to stop Miller, the restaurant staff were hypnotized, bug-eyed and Miller had disappeared. She ran after him, shoved her hand into her handbag looking for the SW99, stumbled, her legs shaking, ran on.

'We want to know who rents 612 Rhodes House,' van Heerden said to Maria Nzululuwazi of Southern Estate Agents.

'You're from the police,' she said, knowledgeably.

'It's a murder case,' said Tiny Mpayipheli.

'Hoo,' said Maria, looking Tiny up and down and shuddering. 'Wouldn't mind being chased by you.'

'I can always arrest you.'

'What for?'

'You're way over the beauty limit.'

'Rhodes House,' said van Heerden.

'612,' said Tiny.

'A sweet talker,' said Maria and tapped on the keyboard of her computer. '612 isn't to let.'

'We want to know who rents it now.'

'It's not let, it's owned.'

'Who owns it?'

Typed again, looked at the screen. 'Orion Solutions.'

'Do you have an address?'

'I do, I do, I do,' she said and looked at Tiny.

'Can we get it today?' asked van Heerden.

'He's real good with the ladies,' said Tiny.

'I've noticed. It's Solan Street in Gardens. 78 Solan. Do you want the telephone number as well?'

'I do, I do, I do.'

Miller ran down the side street, Hope Beneke saw him through the gusts of rain. 'Miller,' she screamed, hysteria in her voice, as he ran on.

'I'm going to publish the picture, Miller.' Despairing, angry, upset, O'Grady's staring eyes filled her head. She saw Miller halting, looking round, waiting for her. Her hair was soaked, she kept her hand on the weapon in her handbag and when she reached him she took out the SW99.

'You're not going anywhere, do you hear me?'

'They're going to kill us.'

'Who the fuck are they?' she said, distraught.

'Orion,' he said. 'Orion Solutions.'

'And who are you?'

'Jamie Vergottini.'

They drove to town, to Gardens, 78 Solan Street, in the Mercedes. Tiny's cellphone rang. 'Mpayipheli,' he answered. 'It's for you,' passing the phone to van Heerden.

'Hallo.'

'I've got Vergottini,' said Hope.

'Where are you?'

'In the rain in Kloof Street, on the corner, at Café Paradiso and I know who's behind it all.'

'Venter?'

'Orion Solutions.'

'I know.'

'You know?'

'We tracked the clues.'

'O'Grady is dead, van Heerden.'

'Nougat?'

'They shot him. In the restaurant. I, we . . . it's a long story.'

'Who shot him?'

'They shot from outside, I didn't see. Vergottini says the shot was meant for him. O'Grady got up to fetch food . . .'

'Jesus.'

'What do I do now?'

'Wait for us, we're on De Waal Drive, we'll be there in five minutes. Give me the street's name.'

'O'Grady is dead,' he said to Tiny Mpayipheli when he'd finished talking, the cellphone shaking in his hand.

'The fat policeman?'

'Yes.'

'Now the shit is going to hit the fan.'

'He was a good man.'

Rain on the window, wind blowing from the harbour, the Mercedes swerving as they drove across the spur of the mountain on De Waal Drive.

'A good policeman,' said van Heerden.

'I saw you in the flat, searching that body' said Mpayipheli. 'Your heart is soft.'

'It's all getting too much.'

'Why did you become a policeman?'

He shook his head.

'You're a good person, van Heerden.'

He said nothing. He would have to phone Mat Joubert. But first, the dollars.

It was all getting too much.

54

Nonnie Nagel had phoned, just after five that afternoon. 'He's going to a meeting about the Red Ribbon affair, he told me he wouldn't be home until after twelve. Fetch me. At eight o'clock. We're going out.'

We never went out. We were either at the Nagel house or at mine but we never went out because we were too frightened that someone would see us. Our love, our togetherness was between four private, clandestine walls, but we hadn't seen one another for more than three weeks and there was excitement in her voice, a playfulness, a recklessness. I wanted to refuse, we shouldn't chance it, but the longing was too great, the possibility that she might announce, tonight, that she was ready to leave him.

'Where to?' I asked when she got into the car two blocks away from their home.

'I'll explain.'

I wanted to ask her why, why this evening, why were we going out, what about when we went back, what if he was at home by then but I said nothing, just drove, with her hand on my thigh and that secret smile on her face.

It was a dance hall in Bellville, just off Durban Road, not a night club, a place for ballroom, packed, the music loud, the light subdued.

There was festivity in the air, she looked beautiful in a simple white dress, sleeveless, and white sandals and when we walked in she took my arm and we moved over the floor and she threw her head back and laughed, deeply, with joy and abandonment and the bass of the loudspeakers throbbed through our bodies.

I have never been a good dancer. My mother taught me in the living room in Stilfontein but she was no expert. I could get along well enough not to make a fool of myself.

That evening, with her, the music moved me. We stayed on the floor for the first hour, one tune after another, pop from the seventies, sixties, eighties, Afrikaans rock. We kept dancing, dripping with perspiration. My shirt, her dress clung to our bodies, her eyes glowed, her laughter, her joy shone, there for everybody to see.

And then she wanted a beer and we dodged through the crowd to a bar counter and swallowed our ice-cold beers and ordered two more, looked for seating and drank the second beer more slowly, our eyes on the other dancers. A thin little guy in black pants and a white shirt and a black waistcoat asked her to dance and she looked questioningly at me and I nodded. She rose and went to dance with him and I watched her with a lightness in me, light-headed with love and tenderness, watching her as she glided expertly over the floor with him, remember at that moment van Wyk Louw's poem *The hour of the dark thirst*. I heard Betta Wandrag's voice again, reciting those sadly beautiful words: *At eleven o'clock your body was / A hunger and thirst in me . . .*

And then she came to fetch me again and we danced and at ten o'clock she looked at her watch and said 'Come' and pulled me to the car, to my house and we threw off our clothes from the front door to the double bed in our feverish haste to reach skin and flesh and love and Betta Wandrag was right, because love with the One was different, so divinely different.

At one o'clock your hair,
caught my hand in an evil web,
your body like black, still water,
your breath a little sob.

Sometime after eleven we lay in one another's arms, whispering as we always did, whispering to safeguard the secret of our togetherness, a laughing, pointless conversation when he hammered at my door, a deep *dhom, dhom, dhom* of his fist on my door and we lay there, petrified. I pulled on shorts. 'Don't open,' she'd said, whispering, urgent, despairing, begging. I walked out. 'Please,' I heard her say, as I walked down the dark passage. *Dhom, dhom, dhom* against my front door, I opened it and Nagel stood there, fire in his eyes.

'Get dressed. We know who Red Ribbon is.'

Facing one another, on the threshold of my house, we knew he knew she was inside and there was hatred between us, deep, black hatred until he turned away.

'I'll wait in the car.'

55

Speckle Venter, he thought, the only one left. '. . . *And then they allowed us to go to sleep. We were very tired but then Speckle took out his guitar. His real name is Michael Venter. He's very short, Pa, and he has a birthmark in his neck so we call him Speckle. He comes from Humansdorp. His father is a panel beater. He wrote a song about Humansdorp. It's quite sad.*'

A guitar-playing country boy. Behind all this?

He punched a number into the cellphone.

'Murder and Robbery, Mavis Petersen speaking.'

'Mavis, it's Zatopek van Heerden. Tony O'Grady has just been shot in Café Paradiso, in Kloof Street. You must get hold of Joubert. And tell de Wit as well.'

'Good Lord,' she said.

'Mavis . . .'

'I hear, Captain, I'll tell him.'

'Thank you, Mavis.' He cut the call. All hell was going to break loose. But before that happened . . . 'We'll have to get a map of Cape Town,' he said to Tiny Mpayipheli.

'There's one in the glove compartment.'

He opened it, took out the map book, looked for Solan Street in the index, found the reference, turned to the map.

'It's just below us.'

'But are we fetching the attorney first?'

'And James Vergottini.'

Then this whole affair would be sliced open, this Pandora's box, this can of worms.

At last, a live witness.

Mpayipheli let the Mercedes ML 320's tyres scream around the corner of Kloof Street and the corner Hope had mentioned. An ambulance stood in front of Café Paradiso, a white Opel with blue police lights. They saw Hope's BMW further up the street, drove nearer, stopped next to the car.

There was no one near the car.

'Fuck,' said van Heerden.

'You should become a writer,' said Mpayipheli. 'Such a gift for language.'

Van Heerden said nothing. He felt exhausted. Too little sleep. Too much adrenalin. Too much struggling.

Tiny's cellphone rang again. He answered, listened. Eventually, slowly, he put the phone down.

'That was Orlando. Billy September is dead.'

'Too many,' said van Heerden. 'Too many.'

'Someone will pay,' said Mpayipheli. 'Now someone will fucking pay.'

They drove up Solan Street. Warehouses, engineering works, panel beaters, a clothing factory, a Vespa scooter-repair shop.

Number 78 was on the corner, an old, run-down, greyish-blue single storey, long and low, without signboards, its small, high windows protected with excessive burglar-proofing. They turned, drove past again. The front door was in Solan Street, a single door on the pavement, in the side street a big double door allowing entry for vehicles, a small brass plate next to the front door with a barely legible *Orion Solutions* on it.

'Video cameras,' said Tiny and pointed but van Heerden saw nothing.

'Where?'

'Under the overhang of the roof.'

His eyes searched, saw a closed-circuit camera in the shadows, barely visible, then another one.

'Lot of security,' he said.

'What do they do?'

'Rob and murder.'

'For a living?'

'I don't know.'

'They know we're here. Those cameras have seen us.'

'I know.'

'You have a plan?'

'Yes.'

'Like the one at the flat?'

'Yes.'

Tiny Mpayipheli shook his head but said nothing. He parked the Mercedes a block away.

'You can't call the police because you're looking for the dollars.'

'Yes.'

'Let me call Orlando. Back-up.'

'I'm not going to wait for back-up.'

'Jesus, you're a stupid whitey.'

Van Heerden put his hand into his jacket pocket. 'Here's a list of their shift schedule,' he said, unfolding the piece of paper that had been stuck to the door of the cupboard in the flat. 'There are eight names. Schlebusch is dead and I presume the four who were at my mother's house are on it because Potgieter led us to the escort agency and the flat. That's five, plus the one in the flat. Six dead or out of action. And Venter. Do you think we can handle three guys?'

'You want to go in at the front door, where they can see us coming a mile away. Where's the strategic advantage?'

'Tiny, if Orlando sends a busload of soldiers, it'll attract attention so fast that the police will be here within minutes.'

'True.'

'Phone Orlando but tell him to give us half an hour. No. An hour.'

Mpayipheli nodded and dialled, spoke. 'Orlando's giving us sixty minutes.' He took out the Rossi, reloaded it with bullets from his jacket pocket. 'Never thought I'd go into battle with a white ex-cop,' he said and opened the car door.

They walked down the road side by side, through the sifting rain, the wind lifting their jackets. Van Heerden looked up at the bulk of the mountain above them, the well-known flat summit covered in low, dark cloud. Just as well. Wouldn't have been a good sign if it had been clear.

Those weeks after Nagel's death.

All he had done was stare at the mountain. A huge, unavoidable, permanent reminder of his guilt. Of his badness.

They stood in front of the door. The brass plate bearing the name of the firm was dirty. He put his hand on the latch, turned it. The door swung open. He looked at Tiny who shrugged his shoulders. They walked in. A large area, dim inside, an empty warehouse, the grey paint faded, the floor a rough cement surface, dusty, dirty. In the gloom he could see a table in a corner. A man sat there, a dark shadow, unrecognizable, a heavy mass. They walked nearer, Tiny's hand on the Rossi in the shoulder holster.

The figure at the table started clapping its hands, slowly, the sound of palm upon palm sharp and echoing in the great, empty space, keeping pace with their footfalls on the cement floor. They walked up to the table, the shadows forming themselves into something human: broad, thick neck, shoulders and chest bulging under the camouflage overall, squat, powerful, the face familiar, like a vaguely remembered friend and then van Heerden saw the dark mark on the neck, a splash as big as a man's hand and the rhythmical clapping stopped and it was suddenly quiet, only the rain pattering softly on the corrugated iron roof.

'Speckle,' he said.

The face sunburnt, the eyes bright and intelligent, the smile sincere, wide, and winning.

'You're good, van Heerden, I have to hand it to you. You achieved in . . . what, six, seven days, something that took the entire SADF twenty-three years.'

It was the voice from the telephone that morning. Quiet. Reasonable. 'And now it's over,' said van Heerden.

The smile widened, white teeth gleaming. 'You're good, van Heerden. But you're not that good.' he said again.

'But he's not alone,' said Tiny Mpayipheli.

'Shut up, kaffir, the white bosses are speaking now.'

Van Heerden felt Mpayipheli stiffen as if an invisible knife had sliced into him.

'It's over, Speckle.'

'No-one calls me Speckle now.' The smile vanished.

'Where's the will, Speckle?'

He hit the metal table with the flat of his hands, a thunderclap in the room. 'Basson!' The exclamation an explosion, he was halfway up, but Tiny's Rossi was in his hands, big black hands gripped around the stock, the barrel gleaming, a deathly hush in the air.

Slowly Venter sat down again. 'They call me Basson,' he said softly, his eyes on van Heerden as if Mpayipheli didn't exist. His whisper filled the echoing space.

'Where's the will?'

'Didn't you get my message?'

'I didn't believe your message.'

The smile back again. 'Dr Zatopek van Heerden. Criminal Psychology, if I'm not mistaken.'

Van Heerden said nothing.

'The will is at the back.' The hand indicating a door behind him was large and weather-beaten, the fingers and wrist thick.

'Let's fetch it.'

'You fetch it. The kaffir and I want to discuss white domination. If he's not scared of putting down his little gun.'

Mpayipheli turned the Rossi in his hands, holding out the butt to Van Heerden.

'Take it.'

'Tiny.'

'Come on, Speckle.' The Xhosa's voice was a deep growl, like an animal's. He tore off his jacket, threw it aside.

'Tiny!'

'Fetch the will, van Heerden,' said Mpayipheli, his eyes on Venter. He thrust his hand into his collar, ripped the shirt off his body, buttons flying, material tearing.

'Open that door, Doctor.' Venter stood up behind the table, short, impossibly broad, unzipping the military overall, massive muscles rippling, a network of tattoos covering the impressive torso. They stood facing one another, the tall, athletic black man, the short white man, a freak of thick bundles of tissue and bulging blue veins.

'Open that door.' Venter had eyes only for Tiny, his voice a bark, an order.

For a moment he was undecided.

'Go,' said Tiny,

He took two, three steps to the door, opened it.

He froze.

Hope Beneke, Bester Brits and another man, all on their knees, arms manacled behind their backs. The barrel of a gun in each of their mouths, three men standing there. They didn't look at him, kept their eyes on their targets, fingers on the triggers. Behind them stood a Uni-Mog truck, the back covered with a tarpaulin, and a white panel van.

'You see, Doctor, it's not over. It's not over by a long chalk.'

He looked back at Venter, saw the two men facing one another in the murky light, both crouching, ready, swung back to the other room, saw Hope's shivering body, her lips around the barrel of the M16, the tears rolling down her cheeks, her eyes turning towards van Heerden. He lifted the Rossi, saw his hands shaking, aimed at the soldier in front of Hope.

'Take the gun out of her mouth.'

'I planned it differently, Doctor.' Speckle Venter's voice came from behind him. 'I assumed you would come on your own, the way you handled the investigation. Alone. And then we would've negotiated. Hope Beneke and the will for you, Bester Brits and Vergottini and the dollars for me. The will is there, do you see it?'

The document, rolled up and pushed down Hope's neckline.

'The dollars are on the truck, a few gemstones, and my little arsenal.

And we would ride heroically into the West, against the setting sun and everyone would've been happy . . .'

And then he spat out. 'But then you brought the kaffir. And now things have changed.'

Van Heerden didn't look round, his eyes and the Rossi still on the soldier in front of Hope. He could see they were young, rough, tough, like the bodies in front of his mother's house.

'Take the gun out of her mouth.' His heart jumping, Lord, he'd got her into this.

A shuffling of feet in the room behind him, the two big men circling one another.

'Now you're going to close that door, Doctor. And if the Xhosa opens it, you must take your chances in there. And if it's me we can negotiate again.'

'No,' he said.

'But first, to show you how serious I am, Simon is going to shoot Bester Brits. And it's ironic, Doctor, because twenty-three years ago I shoved a Star pistol into Bester's mouth and he survived, can you believe it. I should've blown his brains out and I simply shot out his teeth. But now we have more time.'

'No.'

'Simon is going to shoot Bester and if you don't close the door Sarge will shoot Vergottini. And then the attorney, but I don't know how you'll feel about that because it seems to me you can't choose between her and Kara-An.'

The Rossi shook in his hands, with powerlessness, rage, fear.

'Shoot Brits,' Speckle barked from the warehouse behind them.

He shouted and at the same time the shot rang out. Bester Brits was thrown back, fell. He aimed the Rossi at Brits's murderer, fired, the big weapon jerking in his hands, and missed. Simon pointed the M16 at van Heerden.

'I've heard about your problem with firearms,' said Venter. 'Put that thing down now and shut the door. Otherwise Beneke is next.'

He stood, paralysed.

'Sarge, I'm counting to three. If he doesn't do as he's told, shoot the woman.'

Van Heerden bent slowly, put the Rossi on the floor, turned and started to close the door.

'I'll be there in a minute,' said Tiny Mpayipheli.

Venter laughed and then the door was closed and he stood looking at Bester's body lying on the floor and Simon and the M16 aimed at him and Hope's whole body shaking and Vergottini with his eyes closed as if he was praying and he wondered how he would get his Z88 out from above his tailbone, how he could keep down the overpowering nausea that was rising in his throat, how he was going to control his fear. And then he heard the sounds on the other side of the door, brutish cries, flesh smacking against flesh, someone hitting the wall between the two spaces with a dull thud and the building shaking, then silence. He looked down at Bester Brits's still form, lying on his back, one arm thrust out, the blood oozing from the wound at the back of his head, the red pool slowly growing. He looked at Simon, the M16 that hadn't moved, the black eye of death staring at him, then more sounds from the other side, the battle starting all over again, Hope Beneke crying jerkily, her tears dripping onto the document against her neck.

'She's a woman,' he begged the man standing in front of her. Neither the man nor his gun moved. 'Don't you have a conscience?'

He put his hand under his jacket, felt the stock of the Z88, curled his fingers around it. He didn't stand a chance, he wouldn't even have it out before they shot him down like a dog. Someone bellowed in the other room, someone screamed, hate and pain combined, dull blows, wood breaking, the table. How could Mpayipheli win against that brute mass?

'Please, let her go,' he said. 'I'll kneel, I'll put my mouth around your fucking gun,' and he moved closer, the Z88 out of his belt, still behind his back, still under the jacket.

'Stand still,' said the one in front of Hope, the one Venter had called 'Sarge'.

He stopped. 'Are you in charge?' he asked Sarge.

'Just stand still. Then she'll be safe. You too.' The man didn't even look at him, simply stared at Hope's face down the barrel of his firearm.

'She's a woman,' he said.

Heaving, grunting, the sick sound of heavy blows to a body, an unidentifiable voice that went *hu, hu, hu, hu.* He didn't know how much longer he could stand like this, the adrenalin crying out for action, reaction, movement, the total aversion to the scene in front of him, Brits, Hope, his hand clamped on the Z88, sweating. Lord, he couldn't shoot, Lord, he mustn't miss, the one in front of Hope first, then they must shoot him.

The awareness sank over the whole group – the three soldiers, Hope, Vergottini, van Heerden – that it was quiet in the warehouse, the scraping of feet on the floor, the blows, the cries suddenly silenced.

He stared at them. Simon stared at him, Sarge and the other one only had eyes for their targets.

Rain on the roof.

Silence.

Safety catch of the Z88 off, slowly, slowly, slowly, mustn't make a sound, his fingers wet with sweat. He was going to die here today, die today, but he'd been here before, he wasn't scared any more, he'd already been here at the gates of death. He would dive, to the right first, pistol extended, shoot, shoot Sarge away from Hope, that was all he would be able to do, he must not miss. The silence stretched and stretched and stretched.

'What are we going to do if no one comes in?' His words hoarse, his throat dry, no saliva left.

Sarge's eyes darted towards him, the eyes off the target for the first time, then they flashed back. He saw a drop of sweat on the man's forehead and something happened in his head, the panic receded, they were only human after all, they hadn't bargained on this, they were waiting for Venter, Basson, whatever they called him.

'What do we do?' Louder, more urgently.

'Shut your fucking mouth.' Sarge's voice echoed in the large space, uncertainly and when he realized it, he repeated it, quietly, more in control. 'Shut your mouth. Basson will come.'

'The police as well,' he lied. 'You shot a detective this afternoon.'

'It was an accident. We wanted Vergottini.'

'Tell that to the judge, Sarge.'

He knew he had to keep on talking, he knew he had inserted the thin edge of the wedge, caused uncertainty.

'If we could find you, so can the police, Sarge . . .'

'Shut up, if you speak again, if you say one fucking word I'll blow away the bitch's face.'

Sweat on everyone's faces now despite the cold outside, the chill in the room.

What now? he wondered. What did he do now?

Rain on the roof.

Seconds ticking away. Minutes.

'Simon,' said Sarge. 'You must have a look.'

Silence.

'Simon!'

'It could be a trap.'

'For fuck's sake, Simon, after that fight?'

'Basson told us to stay here.'

'Come and take my gun.'

Indecision, van Heerden's eyes moved from one to the other, looking for a moment of distraction, just a moment and then he heard something.

Not in the warehouse. Outside. In the street.

Sarge looked up, he had heard it as well and then all hell broke loose.

The Mercedes burst through the wall, steel on steel and concrete and bricks and then he had the Z88 out and he stood with his feet wide apart and he saw that their eyes were on the wall, all the eyes, and he shot Sarge, the one in front of Hope Beneke, saw him fall, turned the weapon, missed Simon, Jesus, not now, fired again, the barrel of the M16 angling towards him, fired again, hit him in the neck, swung the Z88 and then the lead tore through him, hot as hell, lifted him off his feet, threw him against the wall, another bullet. Where was his pistol? Fuck, it hurt, he was so tired, he looked at his chest, such small holes, why were the holes so small, so many shots in the room, so much noise, someone screamed, high and scared, Hope, it was Hope, why was it so terribly dark?

56

'I'll tell you how one catches a fucking serial killer, van Heerden, I'll tell you, not with fucking theories and forecasts and personality profiles and psychological analyses, van Heerden.' Nagel was driving, a brooding, tense spring at first, a thin man behind the steering wheel, and when we turned up on the N1 beyond the Pick 'n Pay Hypermarket in Brackenfell, he let it all out in that deep voice of his but there was a new, sharper edge to him, a deep rage and he talked, spit flecking the windscreen, Adam's apple bobbing wildly. 'I'll tell you, you do it with fucking hard police work, that's how, elimination, van Heerden.' He reached his arm out and half-turned and the car swerved on the freeway, I didn't know whether I should duck, and he picked up the dossier from the back seat and threw it in my lap.

'There it is, there's your fucking textbook, study it. I don't have a fucking degree, van Heerden, I grew up too poor even to imagine something like that. I had to work for everything, I didn't have time to fuck around on a campus and leaf through little books, I had to work, shitface. I couldn't sit and meditate and philosophize and dream up theories and that's how one catches a fucking serial murderer – look in there, van Heerden, open the fucking file and look at the forensics, look at the lists of carpet fibres and car models, look at the photos of the tyre treads, look at the list of retreads, look at the list of motor registrations for fucking Volkswagen Kombi Campers, look how I drew a line through them, one by one, van Heerden, while you . . .'

And then he was quiet for a moment, his knuckles white on the steering wheel. We drove at 160 kilometres per hour on the N1, weaving through the traffic while he carried on his tirade and I thought he wanted to write us both off but when he was suddenly silent, when he hesitated on the dreadful brink of a direct accusation, I had a momentary insight into the pain I was responsible for.

Willem Nagel knew it was his own fault that he had lost Nonnie. He knew that it was what he had done that had driven her away, made her vulnerable. That was what stopped him from shooting me or hitting me or confronting me. His own culpability.

But he didn't want to give her to me.

Perhaps he had hated me from the start. Perhaps what I had accepted as friendly teasing had been a far more serious game for him. Perhaps the yoke of inferiority about his background, his growing years in Parow, his infertility, all of it was too heavy a burden for him to realize that I was no threat. Perhaps.

He had hidden the evidence of the carpet fibres and tyre treads and registration details from me like a jealous, selfish child who didn't want to share his toys. This was the first I had heard of it and it made me realize how much all of it must have meant to him. To prove his superiority.

If he couldn't keep Nonnie . . .

I said nothing. I didn't open the dossier. I simply stared ahead.

It was only when we had passed the Green Point Stadium that he spoke again, in the same tone of voice, as though there had been no interruption. 'Tonight we'll see what kind of a policeman you are. Tonight it's only you and me and George Charles Hamlyn, the owner of a Volkswagen Kombi Camper and a fucking long piece of red ribbon. We'll see, we'll see. . .'

In Sea Point he parked near the ocean, took out his Z88 and let the magazine drop into his hand, then shoved it back and took off the safety catch and walked in the direction of Main Road with me following, sheepishly checking my weapon as well. Suddenly he walked into the foyer of a block of flats, pressed the button for the lift, not looking at me. The door opened and we walked in and we rose in silence and the only thought I had was that this wasn't the way policemen went to fetch a suspect. He got out on a floor somewhere, high up, you could see the mountain, Signal Hill and the lights against Table Mountain and he went ahead and stopped at a door and said: 'Knock, van Heerden, then you fetch him, show me you're a fucking policeman,' and I knocked loudly and urgently, my pistol in my right hand, my left hand against the door.

I knocked again.

No reaction.

We didn't hear the lift doors opening or closing. We merely sensed the movement and looked back and saw him in the long passage and his eyes widened and he spun round and ran, with Nagel after him and me behind Nagel, down the fire escape, five, six stairs at a time.

I fell, somewhere on the way down, lost my footing and fell, banging my head. My pistol went off, a single shot, and Nagel laughed without looking round, a scornful laugh as he descended the stairs faster and faster. I got up, there was no time to think about the pain, down, down, down, ground level at last. He was up the street, we followed him, three men in a life-or-death race and he ran up an alleyway and Nagel rushed round the corner and came to a sudden halt and then I stopped too, almost bumping into Nagel and when I looked up George Charles Hamlyn stood there with a gun in his hand, aiming at us and Nagel squeezed the trigger of his Z88 and there was nothing, only silence. He squeezed again, swore, a nanosecond that stretched into eternity. I aimed my pistol at Hamlyn and saw him aiming at Nagel and my head said *Let him shoot, let him shoot Nagel, wait, just wait one small second, just wait*. My head, dear God, it came out of my head and then he fired and Nagel fell, two shots as fast as light and then the barrel of Hamlyn's gun swung towards me and I shot and I couldn't stop shooting but it was too late, it was so fucking completely too late.

57

He was aware that he was alive long before he regained consciousness, floating between dream and hallucination. His father, lunchbox in his hand, walking with him through Stilfontein, long conversations, his father's voice low and sympathetic, his father's smile indescribably happy. Hand in hand with his father until he drifted away again to a blackness without awareness, and out on the other side only to experience the blood and the death of Nagel and Brits and Steven Mzimkhulu and Tiny Mpayipheli and Hope Beneke, the shock and the horror, every time he hurled himself into the hail of bullets, every time it passed through him, every time he screamed uselessly, his cries disappearing into the mists. And then Wendy was there, Wendy and her two children and her husband, 'Oh, Zet, you're missing so much,' and his mother, he knew his mother was there, around him, with him. He heard her voice, heard her singing, it was like being in the womb again and then he was awake and the sun shone and it was late afternoon and his mother was with him. She held his hand and the tears ran down his cheeks.

'Ma,' he said but he could barely hear his own voice.

'I knew you were there somewhere,' she said.

And then he was gone again, to dark, peaceful depths. His mother was there, his mother was there and then he came back slowly, up, up, up, a nurse bending over him, shifting the hanging drip. He smelt her faint perfume, saw the roundness of her breasts under the white uniform and then he was there, awake, his chest hurting, his body heavy.

'Hallo,' said the nurse.

He made a noise that didn't quite work.

'Welcome back. Your mother went to have breakfast. She'll be back in a moment.'

He just looked at her, at the pretty lines of her hands, the fine blonde hairs on her supple arms. He was alive, looking at the sunlight through the window.

'We were worried about you,' the nurse said. 'But now you're going to be OK.'

Be OK.

'Do you have any pain?'

He nodded slightly, his head heavy.

'I'll get you something for it,' she said and he closed his eyes and opened them and his mother was there again.

'My child,' she said and he saw tears in her eyes. 'Rest, everything is fine, all you have to do is rest,' and then he slept again.

Wilna van As stood next to his mother. 'I just want to say thank you. The doctor said I'm only allowed a few minutes, I only want to say thank you very much.' He could see she was uncomfortable, self-conscious. He tried to smile at her, hoped his face was cooperating, and then she repeated 'Thank you,' turned, took a step, turned back, came to the bed and kissed him on the cheek and walked out quickly and there were uncontrollable tears in his eyes.

'I bought this for you,' his mother said softly. She had a portable CD player in her hands. 'I know you'll need it.'

'Thanks, Ma.'

He had to stop crying, hell, what was it with all the crying?

'Never mind,' his mother said, 'never mind.'

He wanted to raise his hand to wipe away the tears but it was anchored somewhere under drip needles and blankets.

'And the CDs.' She had a handful. 'I just grabbed some from your cupboard, I didn't know what you'd want to listen to.'

'Agnus Dei,' he said.

She looked through the CDs, found the right one, slid it in, put the small earphones in his ears and pressed the 'play' button. The music filled his ears, his head, his soul. He looked at his mother. 'Thank you,' he mouthed, saw her reply, 'It's a pleasure,' and then she kissed his forehead and sat down and stared out of the window and he closed his eyes and drank in the music, every note, every single blessed note.

In the late afternoon he woke again.

'There's someone to see you,' his mother said.

He nodded. She walked to the door, spoke to someone there, then came in followed by Tiny Mpayipheli. A bandage round his head covered one entire ear and he walked somewhat stiffly in his dressing gown and hospital pyjamas. Relief flowed through him that the big man was alive but the bandage around his head that looked like a turban set awry, as if he was doing an Arab parody, made him want to laugh. There was something about Tiny – an awareness that he looked absurd, a self-consciousness that deepened the humour – and the laughter welled up. He shook, the pain of his wounds sharp and urgent but he couldn't stop himself or the sounds emerging from his mouth. Mpayipheli stood there grinning in a sheepish way and then he laughed as well, holding his ribs where they hurt. They looked at one another, wounded and pathetic and Joan van Heerden, standing at the door, was laughing too.

'You don't look so great yourself,' Tiny said.

The laughter stopped. 'I dreamt you were dead.'

The black man sat down on a chair next to the bed, slowly, like an old man. 'It was pretty close.'

'What happened yesterday?'

'Yesterday?'

'Yes.'

'Yesterday you slept as you did on each of the previous six days. And I lay and felt sorry for myself and moaned at the nurses about the fact that this hospital's affirmative action is so far behind schedule that there are only thin white nurses on duty with unpinchably flat bottoms.'

'Six days?'

'Today's Thursday. You've been here a week.'

Amazement.

'What happened?'

'Bester Brits is alive, can you believe it? They say it's a miracle, the bullet missed his brain stem and exited from the back of the neck, almost exactly like the bullet of twenty years ago. What do you think the chances are of that happening? And he's going to make it. Only just, like you – evidently you whiteys are too soft.'

'And Hope?'

His mother replied: 'She comes every day, twice, three times. She'll probably come again a bit later.'

'She's not . . .'

'She was very shocked. She spent a night here for observation.'

He digested the information.

'Vergottini?'

'In custody,' Tiny said. 'And when Speckle Venter's fractured skull and various other bits of bone have healed, he'll be behind bars too.'

He looked at Tiny, at the eyebrow ridges that were still swollen, at the lopsided bandage, at the unnaturally thick bundle under his arm. 'And you?'

'Ear almost torn off, seven broken ribs, concussion,' Tiny said.

Van Heerden could only stare.

'He's strong, that one. Strongest I've ever fought against. It was hell, I've got to hand it to him. Merciless, an animal, he has more hate than I have, he's got murder in him. I was scared, I tell you. He had my head in a vice and he banged it against the wall and when I felt his strength and saw those crazy eyes I thought, "This is how I'm going to die", but he's slow, too many muscles, too many steroids, too little wind but fuck, he's strong,' and he touched the bandage round his head and looked round guiltily. 'Sorry, ma'am.'

'You two talk,' she said smiling. 'I'm going outside.' She closed the door softly behind her.

Mpayipheli looked at the door.

'And then?'

Tiny turned back, shifted something under the dressing gown, his mouth pursing with pain. 'Strong. Held my head with one hand and with the other took hold of my ear and tore. God, van Heerden, what kind of a human are you to want to tear off another's ear? I kicked, because of the terrible fucking pain, I kicked him with my knee, with everything I had and got loose somehow and knew that the only way to walk away alive was to stay clear of him. At some stage we went over the table and I grabbed one of the legs and I hit him against the head, hard enough to break the wood and he bled like a pig and shook his whole body like a wet dog and he came at me for more I tell you, I was frightened because no one can keep standing after such a blow, but he wanted more, his hatred is so enormous and then I had to dodge and hit and dodge and hit. I've never been so tired, van Heerden, I tell you, he kept coming, his whole face a bloody mess. I hit him with everything I had and he would spit, teeth and red gob and he would come . . .'

Mpayipheli got up slowly. 'Need some of your water first.' He shuffled to the jug and the glass on the table, poured the liquid into the glass, ice cubes falling, water splashing on the table.

'Ah,' he said. 'Fortunately they'll think you're the messy one.' He emptied the glass in one gulp, refilled it and walked back to the chair.

'Want some?'

Van Heerden nodded. Tiny held the glass for him, helped him drink.

'I hope you're allowed to drink. Might leak out of a hole somewhere.'

He swallowed the ice-cold water. It tasted sweet, fresh, delicious.

'He hit me a few more times, swinging blows which you could see coming a mile off but I was too tired to duck. I know now what a tree feels like when you hit it with an axe, it goes right through you, you feel it here.' He put a fingertip on his forehead.

'He fell eventually, forwards, like a blind man who doesn't know where the floor is. I can't tell you how pleased I was because I was finished, completely finished. I collapsed, on my knees. I wanted to come and help you but nothing wanted to work, it was like swimming in treacle, head not thinking, so I rested.'

He took a sip of water.

'I didn't know what to do. I couldn't just walk through that door and say "OK, boys, the boss is over and out and we're taking charge." And then I thought it can't be that door, what about the other one, outside, the big one and I went out to the car, slowly. Odd, my ear wasn't so bad then, it was the ribs that were screaming, big black spots in front of my eyes. I don't know how long it took me to the Benz and then I knew there was no time and I took another firearm out of the back and I drove and I looked for the door and I couldn't find it because everything was so confusing. So I made my own.'

Mpayipheli swallowed the last of the ice water, got up to fetch some more, and sat down again.

'And then you shot the lot. There was only one left for me and it was just as well because the first shots went completely wide.'

The door opened and the blonde nurse came in.

'He must rest,' she said.

'And I must do all the talking,' said Tiny. 'Nothing will ever change in this country.'

Late afternoon. He was alone in the room. A thick brown envelope with his name on it lay next to the bed. Slowly he wriggled his left hand out from under the blankets. He saw that his forearm was red and swollen just below the puncture where the drip entered. He moved his right hand over slowly, touching the wounds in the chest and shoulder, a burning, sharp as fire, but he managed to reach the envelope. He lay back, let the pain subside slightly, and tore the envelope open with difficulty.

A note on top. 'You owe me a honeymoon. And a huge favour for the document. Pleased that you're recovering. Destroy when read. Please.'

Signed by Mat Joubert.

He looked at the document, typewritten A4 pages, stapled together in the top left-hand corner.

Transcription of interrogation of Michael Venter also known as Gerhardus Basson.
Sunday 16 July, 11:45, Groote Schuur Hospital.
Present: Superintendent Mat Joubert, Superintendent Leon Petersen.

He turned over the first page.

Superintendents Mat Joubert and Leon Petersen in interrogation of suspect Michael Venter, also known as Gerhardus Basson, in the investigation of the murders of Rupert de Jager aka Johannes Jacobus Smit and John Arthur Schlebusch aka Bushy Schlebusch, aka . . . er . . . Jonathan Archer, and attempted murder of Colonel Bester Brits of the South African Defence Force. The interrogation is being taped and the suspect has been so informed. Official permission from Doctor Laetitia Schultz has been obtained. The doctor has already certified that the suspect is not under the influence of any medicine or drug that could affect his comprehension or consciousness.

Q: Could you please give your full name and surname for the record?

A: Fuck you.

Q: Are you Michael Venter who is also in possession of a forged South African identity document in the name of Gerhardus Basson?

A: Fuck you.

Q: The charges against you have already been read to you. Do you understand them?

A: Fuck you. I'm not saying another word.

Q: Your rights as a suspect in this investigation have already been read to you. Do you understand them?

A: (No reply.)

Q: Let the record show that the suspect did not respond to the question. You have the right to have a legal representative present during this interrogation.

A: (No reply.)

Q: Let the record show that the suspect did not respond to the question. You are aware of the fact that this interrogation is being taped and that anything you might say during it, may be used as evidence in a court of law.

A: (No reply.)

Q: Let the record show that the suspect did not respond to the question. Mr Venter, can you recall where you were on the night of 30 September last year?

A: (No reply.)

Q: Let the record show that the suspect did not respond to the question. Were you in, or near, the home of one Rupert de Jager also known as Johannes Jacobus Smit, in Moreletta Street, Durbanville?

A: (No reply.)

Q: Let the record show that the suspect did not respond to the question. Were you . . .

Q: We're wasting our time, Mat.

Q: I know.

A: Fucking right, you're wasting your time. Fucking cunts.

Q: Will you answer further questions?

A: (No reply.)

The transcript of the first interrogation ended.

Transcription of interrogation of James Vergottini also known as Peter Miller.
Sunday 16 July, 14:30, Interrogation Room, Murder and Robbery, Bellville South.
Present: Superintendent Mat Joubert, Superintendent Leon Petersen.

Q: Superintendents Mat Joubert and Leon Petersen in interrogation of suspect James Vergottini also known as Peter Miller, in the investigation of the murder of Rupert de Jager aka Johannes Jacobus Smit, and John Arthur Schlebusch aka Bushy Schlebusch, aka Jonathan Archer and attempted murder of Colonel Bester Brits of the South African Defence Force. The interrogation is being taped and the suspect has already been advised of this as well as of his rights.

Q: Could you please state your full name and surname for the record.

A: James Vergottini.

Q: You are also in possession of a forged South African identity document in the name of Peter Miller?

A: Yes.

Q: The charges against you have already been read to you. Do you understand them?

A: Yes, but I had nothing to do . . .

Q: We'll get to that in a moment, Mr Vergottini. Your rights as a suspect in this investigation have already been read to you. Do you understand them?

A: Yes.

Q: You have the right to have a legal representative present during this interrogation but you have already waived that right.

A: Yes.

Q: You are aware that the interrogation is being taped and that anything you may say during it may be used as evidence in a court of law.

A: Yes.

Q: Mr Vergottini, where were you on the evening of the evening of September 30, last year?

A: At home.

Q: And where is that?

A: 112 Mimi Coertse Drive, Centurion.

Q: Near Pretoria.

A: Yes.

Q: Can someone confirm that?

A: Listen, can't I take this whole thing from the beginning?

Q: Mr Vergottini, can anyone confirm that you were at home that evening?

A: My wife.

Q: You're married?

A: Yes.

Q: Under which name?

A: Miller. Please, I'll tell you everything I know. I had nothing to do with Rupert's death. It's a long story but I swear it was Speckle and Bushy.

Q: Venter and Schlebusch?

A: Yes, but I hadn't seen them in years. It was only when the picture appeared in *Beeld* . . .

Q: When last did you see them?

A: Last year.

Q: But you said you were with them in '76?

A: That's what I'm trying to tell you. You must understand the whole thing. The whole story.

Q: Tell us, Mr Vergottini.

A: I don't know what you know. Where shall I start?

Q: Assume that we know nothing.

A: It was in 1976. That's where it all started . . .

58

'There were eight of us in the squad and Bushy was squad sergeant . . .'

'A total of nine?'

'No, eight, with Bushy. We had a . . .'

'What year are you talking about?'

'Seventy-six.'

'You were all Recces?'

'Yes. Bushy had already completed a year and then he signed for another two. He wanted to turn PF but he said he'd have to see first because they took a stripe away in '75 because he was in a fight in a bar . . .'

'PF?' Petersen asked.

'Permanent Force.'

'And the rest of you?'

'We were only troops, doing our military service. We were the first intake to do two years. Clinton Manley complained about it, he wanted to go to university, he already had a rugby bursary to the University of Stellenbosch. We had . . .'

'Who were the other members of the squad?'

'Bushy, Manley, Rupert, Speckle, Red, Gerry de . . .'

'Red?'

'Verster, he came from Johannesburg . . .'

'Did he have another name?'

'Yes . . . um . . . um . . . I can't remember, he was just Red.'

'Carry on.'

'Gerry de Beer, have I mentioned him? Koos van Rensburg, wait, let me count, Bushy, Speckle, Rupert, Clinton, Red, Koos, Gerry. And me. Eight.'

'Good.'

'We had a supply route, in the north, between Mavinga and wherever the Unita bases were – ammunition, food, sometimes a few documents in an attaché case. Every six weeks or so we were back in Katima Mulilo. It was hot and dry and we walked or rode at night. It was rough, in the dark, you couldn't see a thing and when the moon shone everything was grey and then suddenly shots rang out or you saw something coming and you lay in ambush and then it was LPs or goats . . .'

'LPs?'

'Local populace . . . or even Portuguese from the mines in the north who were still trying to get through, sometimes it was Swapos and contact and then you wondered if you were going to die when the bullets hit the ground next to you or sang over your head and you lay behind a shrub. But the Swapos avoided us, they were on their way to South West, they lay low, it was only when we met virtually face to face . . .

'Our nerves were shot, I didn't realize it then, only later, after weeks in the bush. The whole time you knew anything could happen in that darkness, later landmines as well, and you slept badly during the day and you ate badly, and sometimes the waterholes were dry and it was only tension all day, all night, even if Bushy and Speckle pretended they liked it. They never stopped saying they wanted to shoot more ters, they were looking for more contact, but the tension got to them as well in the end. It was tension that caused the whole mess with the Parabats.'

'The Parabats?'

'We were two weeks away from fourteen days leave when we came back from a drop in Angola at night, on foot, and Bushy indicated that we should fall flat. We saw them coming through a dry river bed, only the shadows and the rifle barrels, you couldn't see much more than that – twelve of them, spread out, the way Swapos did – and Bushy told us to form an ambush. We took up our positions, we had practised it over and over again, each one knew what to do, where to lie. We knew we had to wait for Bushy to shoot first. They came up, not even knowing about us. Then Bushy shot and we all fired and they fell and screamed and I knew this was what Bushy had been waiting for, a dozen kaffirs. You must forgive me but that's all they spoke about, they were the biggest racists I've ever known, Bushy and Speckle. We all were, at that time. They taught us . . .'

'Carry on,' said Leon Petersen.

'We mowed them down, they didn't stand a chance and when everything was quiet we heard one of them calling, in Afrikaans, "Help me, Ma, help me," and then I heard Clinton Manley saying, "Oh, my God," and we knew something was wrong. Bushy got up and signed to us and we crept closer and when we came to the first one we saw the dog tags and he was a Parabat from Bloemfontein. No one had told us they would be there. Ten were dead, fucked-up dead, shot to pieces. One was dying, he was the one who shouted, and one was still alive, shot through both legs, but he would've made it.'

'*Would've* made it?'

'Speckle shot him. But it wasn't that simple. You can imagine. We stood next to the Parabat and he knew we were Recces and he asked, over and over again, "Why did you shoot us?" And then he moaned with pain and we were shit-scared because it was a major fuck-up, jeeze, we had killed our own people, do you know what it feels like? We were all panicky, I think it was Red who asked what we were going to do now but no one answered him, we were in such deep trouble, and the guy on the ground was hysterical, "Why did you shoot us?" And he moaned, on and on, jeeze, all I wanted to do was run. I wanted to get away and Bushy simply stood there, as white as a sheet, he didn't know what to do either and then Speckle came up and he shot the guy in the head and Gerry de Beer said "What the fuck are you doing?" and Speckle said "What the fuck do you want us to do?" He wasn't calm, Speckle, he was just as scared as the rest of us, you could hear it, you could see it, Christ, it was bad but then it was quiet, dead quiet and Red threw up and so did Clinton Manley and the rest of us stood there among ten dead Parabats and we all knew no one would ever talk about it. We all knew before I said it, I mean it was an accident, it was genuinely a helluva accident, what could we do and then I said we'd never talk about it.'

Silence.

'Mr Vergottini?'

'I'm OK.'

'Take your time, Mr Vergottini.'

'I'd rather you called me Peter. It's the name I'm used to.'

'Take your time.'

'I'm OK. We buried them. The ground was hard and we didn't want to bury them in the river bed because in the rainy season . . . We worked until two o'clock the following afternoon, covering their heads first. I don't think we could handle the eyes and the faces. They were our guys. Our people. We picked up every cartridge case, covered every spot of blood, buried everyone. And then we went on. Without speaking. Speckle in the lead. I'll never forget it, suddenly Speckle was in the lead, Bushy behind him. Speckle was the new leader without a word being said. For two days we walked, night and day, without a word being said, everyone's head busy with only one thing and when we reached the camp, Lieutenant Brits was waiting and he wanted to see us . . .'

'Bester Brits?'

'Yes.'

'Go on.'

'He wanted to see us and we thought someone knew something because we knew he was Intelligence and we were scared and Speckle said he would talk, we must just keep our traps shut, but then it was another story altogether, a completely new story.

'Every day for the past twenty-three years I've thought about it. Coincidence. If Brits had asked for another squad. If the Parabats had followed another route. If we could've distinguished a R1 from an AK in the dark . . . Coincidence. The Parabats. And then Orion.'

'Orion?'

'Operation Orion, Brits's operation. He said he knew we were tired but it was just one night's work and then we would get fourteen days, immediately, get onto a Hercules and go home but we were the only experienced squad that was available and the operation was the following night. All we had to do was to ride shotgun on a Dak . . . that's a Dakota, a DC 10, an aircraft . . . all we had to do was see that two parcels were exchanged and he was going along, he wanted us for peace of mind, that was his phrase, peace of mind. And then he organized a helluva meal for us from the officers' mess and said we weren't sleeping in tents, he had organized a prefab for us and we could sleep as late as we liked, he would make sure no one bothered us. We had to be fresh the following afternoon, one night's work and then we'd be going home.

'We ate and showered and went to the bungalow but no one could sleep. Red Verster said we would have to tell someone, suddenly, as if he'd decided. Speckle said no. Clinton said we must talk to someone, Rupert de Jager said what good would it do, they were dead, it wouldn't bring them back and Koos van Rensburg said no, we wouldn't be able to live with it and the guys began yelling at one another, Rupert and me at Clinton and Gerry and Red and Koos until Speckle beat on a tin trunk and we all looked at him and he said we were tired, we were all tired and shocked and it would only cause trouble if we fought about it now. We must wait. Until we came back from Orion. Then we would vote. And then we would do what the majority wanted.

'Bushy Schlebusch just lay there staring at the ceiling. And Speckle Venter was in control. And then we all lay down and I think we slept a little towards morning and then Bester arrived at 11:00 and said there was breakfast and were we OK and he was all over us, trying to be one of the boys and we all ignored him because of the Parabats and because all Intelligence officers were like that, shit-scared men who sat at the base and then tried to sound like old hands who had seen contact. But he was too much, kept saying "Orion is big, guys, Orion is really big, you must be on your toes, one day you can tell your children you did a great thing."

'And that evening he handed out live ammunition and hand grenades and we drove in a Bedford to the airfield and there the Dak stood and we got in and before take-off Brits said he wanted to brief us. He said it was top secret but we would see what was going on in any case, we weren't idiots and he knew he could trust us. We were going to a mine in Cuango to fetch stones, diamonds, and then we were crossing a border or two, flying over without permission and we would exchange the diamonds for something Unita wanted very badly because they were struggling against the rest of Angola and the Cubans, but as far as we were concerned we had seen nothing. And then we would leave on our fourteen-day pass with a little extra in the pay packet, a little extra to make the fourteen days rich and enjoyable, and he tried to make his voice sound like some fancy radio announcer selling coffee creamer. He was a real joker, he so badly wanted to be one of the boys.

'Generally we slept on anything that flew but not that night. We sat there with our hands on our rifles and our eyes on one another and I think we all wondered who would be the first to crack, the first to talk. Rupert de Jager and Speckle Venter and I who thought we should keep quiet, Red and Clinton and Gerry and Koos who wanted us to talk, and Bushy Schlebusch with nothing in his eyes. I didn't know where he stood. Tension, hell, there was so much tension between us you could have cut it with a panga, but Brits had no clue, he was too busy with his maps and papers and his little flashlight and every few minutes he would check whether we were staring at him.

'We landed at a godforsaken stretch somewhere in northern Angola, they'd lit fires to mark the runway. We climbed out and positioned ourselves on one knee, rifles facing outward as Brits had briefed us, while he spoke to two guys. And then first they brought petrol for the Dak in a tank on a small van and then a whole lorryload of Unitas arrived and Bester told us to relax, it was part of the plan, as if he was our squad leader. They brought a wooden box which it took four men to carry and loaded it into the plane and Brits said we must get in and we took off and I tried to keep my bearings but in the air at night it's impossible. I thought we were flying south or east and we sat there again with our red eyes and memories of the Parabats in our heads and Speckle got up and went to sit next to Bushy and spoke to him for a long time, right in his ear, and then he sat in his own seat again.

'After two hours in the air we descended again and Brits said now we had to be alert, this was the sensitive part of Operation Orion and we went in and landed, somewhere, it was an endless stretch of bushveld and grass and stones. This time there were flares next to the landing strip and Brits was the first to get out and we followed again in V-formation and then two men came driving up in a Land Rover. They got out and Brits went over to them and chit-chatted. Then he looked in the back of the Landy and came back and told Bushy we must take out the wooden box and bring it. Bushy pointed to Speckle and me and we climbed back in and brought it, it was heavy, and put it down. The two strangers came across and Brits opened it and there were uncut diamonds everywhere, wrapped in plastic bags. One guy whistled and said, "Will ya look at that" in a thick American accent.

'"Shall we make the exchange?" Brits asked and the other Yank said, "You betcha" and Brits closed the box and told us to put it in the back of the Landy and load the stuff in the Landy onto the plane. Speckle and I took the box and carried it to the back of the Landy, the Americans and Brits with us. In the back of the Land Rover there were cartons, a whole load of them, with the names of tinned food on them, closed with masking tape, and I thought it was odd, diamonds for tinned food until I picked one up and it wasn't tinned food. I didn't know what it was, we each carried one to the Dak and when no one could see us in the aircraft Speckle slit it open with his bayonet and made a long *shhhh* sound. It was packed with dollars, dollars and more dollars and then he said to me, "Do you really think Red and the others are going to keep quiet, Porra?" That was my nickname, Vergottini is Italian but because my father had a fish-and-chip shop in Bellville . . .

'I said no. And he said if I wanted to get out of the thing I had to keep my head because things were going to happen and then we went out to fetch more cartons and I saw him giving Bushy a sign, covertly, with one hand and when we reached the Landy he shot one American and when he fell, he shot the other.'

'Mr Vergottini . . .'

'Peter. Or Miller. Just give me a chance. If I could get something to drink?'

'Of course. I'll send for coffee.'

'Coffee would be good.'

'Sugar? Milk?'

'Two sugars and milk, please.'

'Just a moment.'

'Would you like to get up? Stretch your legs?'

'I'm fine, thank you.'

'Coffee is coming.'

'Thank you.'

'Wouldn't you like to take a break?'

'I want to finish.'

'We understand.'

'I wonder.'

'I'll remember Brits's face in that moment until the day I die. The disbelief. The fright. The surprise. It was all there, I think they were the first dead bodies, the first people he had seen with bullet wounds. There was nausea as well, which we all get the first time. But the disbelief was the greatest. He looked at Speckle, at the Americans, at Speckle again, his mouth open, his eyes big and round, his hands trying to stop something but Speckle had already turned to the others.

'"Now I want to know who's going to talk," he said. "Bushy and I know where we stand. And I think I know where Porra and Rupert stand," and Bushy turned and aimed his rifle at Gerry and Clinton and Red and Koos. "The others must think very clearly," Speckle said and then he walked to the plane and climbed in and we heard another shot. It was the pilot, he shot the pilot.

'Some day someone must explain to me how the psychology of the thing worked. I know we were tired. We had barely slept in four days, we were finished. I doubt whether any of us could think any longer, we were simply a bundle of raw nerves. The Parabats haunted us, not only what had happened but what lay ahead. For me it was pitch dark, I knew it wasn't something you simply erased from your life, from your head, but hell . . .

'Bester Brits got his voice back. "What are you doing, what are you doing?" he asked Speckle when he climbed out of the Dak and Speckle thrust his Star pistol into his face and said "Where are we?" Brits shook like a leaf and tried to bat the gun away and Speckle hit him with the butt and he fell and Speckle held him down with his foot and asked again where we were. I think Bester knew he was going to die there, he had seen it in Speckle. "Botswana" he said. Speckle removed his foot and Bester tried to get up, got to his knees and then Speckle asked 'Where in Botswana?'

'"North, just west of Chobe," and then Speckle thrust the barrel into his mouth and he fired and turned round and asked me "Porra, are you with me?"

'What could I say, Jesus, what could I say . . .'

'Gently does it, Mr . . . Miller.'

'I'll see where the coffee is.'

'Please let me finish.'

'You don't have to.'

'I must.'

'Very well.'

'What could I say? There are only two choices, you die quickly or you die slowly and I wasn't prepared to die quickly. I wake up next to my wife and then I'm there again and I have to choose again and every time I choose to die there, but that night, that morning, I chose the other way. I said, "I'm with you, Speckle" and then he asked Rupert and Rupert's mouth contorted and he looked at Brits and he looked at Speckle and he said, "I'm with you, Speckle" and Gerry de Beer started crying like a child and Red Verster was the only man that night, he jerked up his R1 and then Bushy shot him and Speckle fired as well, shot Gerry and Red and Clinton Manley and Koos van Rensburg, shot them like dogs. And then it was quiet and I saw Rupert de Jager's body jolting with shock and Speckle said, "I know how you feel, Rupert, but I'm not throwing away my entire fucking life for an accident which was no one's fault in a war where it's kaffir against kaffir in a country that feels fuck-all for me. Not me. If you want to cry, you can cry but I want to know if you're still with me."

'He shook his head. "I'm with you Speckle."

'And then he made us carry the dollars and diamonds back to the Landy and we drove away. We left them just like that and drove away, just as it had begun to get light in the east.'

Q: How did you get back into the Republic?

A: We exchanged the Landy and a bag of diamonds with LPs for a ten-ton truck and civvie clothing and we drove during the night on back roads, Speckle making all the decisions, with that load of money and stones, for two weeks, buying petrol and food in small villages that didn't even appear on a map. We crossed the border somewhere north of Ellisras, simply flattening the fence, and drove to Johannesburg, Speckle said we would share everything there.

Q: Did you?

A: Yes.

Q: How much?

A: Each got about twenty million dollars and a few bags of diamonds.

Q: Twenty million.

A: Just about.

Q: Jesus.

Q: And then?

A: We talked. Talked a lot. About how we could change the dollars and the diamonds into rands. No one knew. Speckle went to Hillbrow, a few days after another guy and him got some of the dollars changed and then he said we must decide, he and Bushy were going to stay together, what about us? I wanted to go to Durban, I just wanted to get away, Rupert said he was going to the Cape. Speckle rented a box number in Hillbrow and said he had paid the rental for a year, here's the address, we must stay in contact. I bought a car, loaded my dollars and my diamonds into it and went to Durban. The diamonds were the easiest, even if I was stupid to start with. But you learn. There was a guy at a pawnshop I showed one to after I'd hung around there a few times, he said he'd take everything I could get. I was careful. I was scared but after the first deal nothing happened. And the money was good. I rented a flat, met someone in a nightclub. Said I was on holiday . . .

Q: Did you see Venter and the others again?

A: Once a year I wrote to the address and gave my own box number in Durban and then Speckle wrote after months and said we must have a reunion and I flew to Johannesburg. He and Bushy both had new IDs, Rupert and I had nothing. He gave us names and telephone numbers, he said he'd buy the dollars from us at thirty cents per dollar. I said I'd bring mine, Rupert said he'd think about it. Then we parted company.

I brought some of the money and got my rands and went back and the following year we were together again, Speckle bragging about his new business. He and Bushy were hanging around mercenaries but they weren't organized and he wanted to start an agency to sell their services and he had just the name for it.

Q: Orion?

A: Orion Solutions. He thought it was very funny.

Q: And then?

A: After the third year I didn't go back. I found a new name on the black market. I became bad. Too much money. Too much liquor. Pot. Cars, women. And seventeen dead bodies in my head. Until I woke up one morning and pissed blood and knew I didn't want to live like that. I couldn't change anything that had happened but I didn't want to go on living like that. So I packed my stuff and sold the flat and drove to Pretoria and looked for work. I started working for Iscor, in the stores. Became foreman. And then I met Elaine.

Q: Your wife.

A: Yes.

Q: You saw Venter or Schlebusch last year, you said?

A: Yes.

Q: Where?

A: At my home.

Q: How did they find you?

A: Speckle said it was his business to know where we were. He said he didn't gamble with his future.

Q: What did he want?

A: Money. He was big, all those muscles. He said he'd done body-building, said it was the only way to ensure respect without shooting people.

Q: His money was finished?

A: He said the world had changed. No one wanted to make war any more. No one had money for war any longer. He said they had lost everything. And Rupert and I were cosy, that was his word, cosy, we had women, we had children, the time had come to share again, we only had one another.

Q: Did you give him money?

A: I buried the dollars I still had in 1985, on a smallholding I'd bought for the children to keep their horses.

Q: Did your wife never ask where the money came from?

A: I told her I'd inherited.

Q: And you fetched the money?

A: It had rotted. Speckle was furious, he said I should've buried it in plastic bags. I thought he was going to shoot me. Then he told me to draw money. I told him it was invested, there was only a hundred thousand in cash and he told me to draw it.

Q: Did you?

A: Yes.

Q: And then they left?

A: Yes. With a final threat. I knew I'd see them again. But then I saw Rupert's photo in the newspaper and then I knew.

Q: And then you came to the Cape?

A: What else could I do? The thing just wouldn't go away. But I knew that, from the time beside the plane, I knew. This thing would never go away.

59

Hope Beneke came in the evening. 'He must rest,' the nurse said protectively.

'She's been waiting for a week,' his mother said.

'She's the last one today.'

'I promise.'

As if he had no say in the matter.

They both went out and then she came in. 'Van Heerden,' she said, her gaze taking in the drip, the now dormant monitors, the bandages and the deep, dark circles round his eyes as a worried frown clouded her face.

He looked at her and something registered: a glimpse, a shadow. Something had changed there, in the way she held her shoulders, the way she carried her head and her neck, in the fine adjustments of facial nerves and eyes. A certain acceptance.

She had lost her innocence, he thought. She had seen the evil.

'How can I ever thank you?'

'In the locker, bottom shelf,' he said, his voice not yet fully recovered from the oxygen tube. He didn't want her to thank him because he didn't know how to react.

She hesitated for a moment, surprised, then bent down and opened the metal door of the locker.

'The document.'

She took it out.

'You have the right to know,' he said. 'You and Tiny. But then it must be destroyed. That's my agreement with Joubert.'

She glanced at the first pages and nodded.

'You musn't thank me.'

Her face registered a series of emotions. She started to say something, then swallowed the words.

'Are you . . . are you OK?'

She sat down next to the bed. 'I've started therapy.'

'That's good,' he said.

She looked away and then back at him. 'There are things I want to say.'

'I know.'

'But it can wait.'

He said nothing.

'Kemp sends his regards. He says we needn't have worried about you. Weeds don't just wither.'

'Kemp,' he said. 'Always first in line with sympathy.'

She smiled vaguely.

'You must rest,' she said.

'That's what they all tell me.'

The morning of his discharge from the hospital, while he was dressing and packing, he received a parcel, an old six-bottle wine carton covered in brown paper and broad strips of tape. He was alone when he opened it. On top, in a white envelope, there was a message in painfully neat handwriting on a thin page of notepaper.

I got a rand per dollar because the notes are so old. The diamonds did somewhat better. This is your half.

Just the 'O' for Orlando at the bottom.

Inside the carton, filling it and tightly packed, were masses of R200 notes.

He closed the carton again.

Blood money.

His house was clean and shiny. His curtains had been replaced with light material, white and yellow and pale green which let the sun through. There were flowers on the table.

His mother.

He had to wash in the washbasin, a shower would wet the bandages. He dressed and walked slowly down to the garage, the keys to the van in his hand. He had to rest for a moment at the door. Light-headed.

He drove.

At the military hospital he had to wait while the male nurse went into Bester Brits's room alone, then came out again. 'He said you can come in but you won't be able to stay long. He's still very weak. And he can't speak. We'll have to reconstruct his vocal chords. He can communicate with a notebook and a pen but it's very demanding work. So please, not long.'

He nodded. The nurse held the door open as he walked in.

Bester Brits looked like death. Pale, thin, his head in a brace, drip in the arm.

'Brits,' he said.

The eyes followed him.

'I've read Vergottini's statement. I think I understand. As much as I can understand.'

Brits's eyes blinked.

'I don't know how you got out of Botswana alive but I can guess. Someone arrived in time, someone . . .'

He saw the officer drawing a notebook towards him and writing. He waited. Brits turned the notebook so that he could read.

CIA team. In chopper. Twenty minutes.

'The CIA had back-up?'

Bester blinked his eyes once.

'And when you recovered your career was over, the money and the diamonds gone, the CIA mad as snakes and the Boers looking like fools.'

Eyes blinking. Angry.

'And then you hunted them?'

He wrote in the notebook.

Part-time.

'The authorities would've preferred to forget about it?'

Blink. *Yes.*

'Jeeze,' he said in wonderment. Twenty-three years' worth of hate and frustration. 'I saw the media cuttings of the past two weeks. They still don't know what's going on. Know only parts of it.'

He wrote. *And it'll stay that way. Pressure from the US.*

Van Heerden shook his head. 'They can't. What about Speckle Venter? He has to stand trial.'

Brits's face contorting, a grimace?

Never.

'They can't let him walk.'

You'll see.

They looked at one another. Suddenly he had nothing more to say.

'I just wanted to tell you that I think I understand.'

Thank you.

And then he wanted out.

To the city. Roeland Street. To the computer people. Asked for Russell Marshall, the man who had doctored the photo of Schlebusch.

'Hey, man, you're a hero,' Marshall said when he saw who it was.

'You believe the media. That's not cool,' said van Heerden.

'Have you brought more photos?'

'No. I want to buy a computer. And I don't know where to start.'

'Avril,' Marshall said to the receptionist, 'hold the calls. We're going shopping.'

He unpacked the computer and the printer, plugged it in according to Marshall's instructions, waited for it to boot, and clicked the mouse on the icon with 'Word' below it.

The white sheet of virtual paper lay clean and open on the screen. He looked at the keyboard. The same layout as the typewriter at the University of South Africa. He got up, put on a CD. *Die Heitere Mozart.* Light. Music for laughter.

He typed a paragraph. Deleted it. Tried again. Deleted it. And again.

He swore. Deleted it. Got up.

Perhaps Beethoven would help. Fourth Piano Concerto. He made coffee, took the telephone off the hook, sat down.

Where did one start?

At the beginning.

My mother was an artist. My father was a miner.

60

Willem Nagel died in the hospital and I went back to my house in my bloody clothes.

She wasn't there. I drove to his house and she opened the door and saw the blood and my face and knew. I put my hands out to her. She pushed me away. 'No, Zet, no, Zet, no.' The same despair in her voice as I had in my soul. The same hysteria, the same torment.

She went into the house. She didn't just cry, the sounds were far more heart-rending than that. I followed her. She closed a door and locked it.

'Nonnie,' I said.

'No!'

I stood in front of that door. I don't know for how long. The sounds eventually subsided, much later.

'Nonnie.'

'No!'

I turned and walked out.

I was never given the opportunity to confess.

I didn't go to her that evening to take possession of her. I went to confess, to tell her that I had eventually been weighed as a man, as a human being, and found myself despicable. After so many years of hunting Evil, I had discovered an infinity of evil in myself. And I deserved it because I had seen myself as above it all.

But I cannot deny that I yearned for her forgiveness. I didn't go to her to tell her that I didn't deserve her. I sank far lower than that. I went to seek absolution.

After that it was a combination of self-pity and the extrapolation of my personal discovery – that the rot is hidden in every one of us – that drove me.

Despite my mother's best efforts. She came to the Cape, bought the smallholding at Morning Star and remodelled and rebuilt and I moved in there, something like a tenant farmer, while she tried to keep me from the abyss with love and sympathy and compassion.

This is who I am.

61

He stood in front of Kara-An's desk in the NasPers Building with the manuscript in his hands. The view over Table Bay was seductive. She sat there with a small smile, as if she had known that he would come.

'The agreement was that I would write the story of my life,' he said.

'I can't wait.'

'You don't understand,' he said. 'I never said I would give it to you.'

The smile turned sour. 'What do you mean?'

'Think about it,' he said.

He went down in the lift with a bunch of models. They twittered like sparrows and their soft, sweet perfume filled the space like an Eastern offering of incense. He walked out and crossed the Heerengracht to where the van was parked in Adderley Street.

Against a lamp-post he saw a poster for *Die Burger*.

MERCENARY
COMMITS
SUICIDE
IN CELL

He hesitated briefly at the door of the vehicle, key in one hand, manuscript in the other, and then walked on. Hope Beneke's office wasn't far away.

He was making a seafood mixture for the pancakes – prawns and mussels and calamari and garlic, the aroma rising with the steam, *The Magic Flute* over the loudspeakers, when she opened the door and walked in without knocking. He turned. She was wearing a black skirt, a white blouse and high-heeled shoes. The outfit of a professional woman. Her legs, in stockings, were gorgeous.

She put the manuscript down on the coffee table.

'I don't want to talk about it,' he said.

'Perhaps you're right,' she said. 'Perhaps there's some wickedness in each of us that lies dormant until the moment of truth. But in that warehouse you were willing to die to save my life. What does that tell you?'

He stirred the seafood mixture.

'Would you like to eat?' he asked.

About the Author

Deon Meyer lives in Durbanville in South Africa with his wife and four children. Other than his family, Deon's big passions are motorcycling, music, reading, cooking and rugby. In January 2008 he retired from his day job as a consultant on brand strategy for BMW Motorrad, and is now a full time author.

Deon Meyer's books have attracted worldwide critical acclaim and a growing international fanbase. Originally written in Afrikaans, they have now been translated into twenty-five languages.

Find out more about Deon Meyer and his books:
Visit his website at www.deonmeyer.com
Follow him on Twitter at @MeyerDeon

Also by Deon Meyer
and published by Hodder & Stoughton

Dead Before Dying
Dead at Daybreak
Heart of the Hunter
Devil's Peak
Blood Safari
Thirteen Hours
Trackers

Turn the page now to read the opening chapters of Deon Meyer's riveting new thriller

TRACKERS

I

31 July 2009. Friday.

Ismail Mohammed runs down the steep slope of Heiliger Lane. The coat-tails of his white jalabiya robe with its trendy open mandarin collar flick up high with every stride. His arms wave wildly, in mortal fear, and for balance. The crocheted kufi falls off his head onto the cobbles at the crossroad, as he fixes his eyes on the relative safety of the city below.

Behind him the door of the one-storey building next to the Bo-Kaap's Schotschekloof mosque bursts open for the second time. Six men, also in traditional Islamic garb, rush out onto the street all looking immediately, instinctively downhill. One has a pistol in his hand. Hurriedly, he takes aim at the figure of Ismail Mohammed, already sixty metres away, and fires off two wild shots, before the last, older man knocks his arm up, bellowing: 'No! Go. Catch him.'

The three younger men set off after Ismail. The grizzled heads stand watching, eyes anxious at the lead they have to make up.

'You should have let him shoot, Sheikh,' says one.

'No, Shaheed. He was eavesdropping.'

'Exactly. And then he ran. That says enough.'

'It doesn't tell us who he's working for.'

'Him? Ismail? You surely don't think . . .'

'You never can tell.'

'No. He's too . . . clumsy. For the locals maybe. NIA.'

'I hope you are right.' The Sheikh watches the pursuers sprinting across the Chiappini Street crossing, weighing up the implications. A siren sounds up from below in Buitengracht.

'Come,' he says calmly. 'Everything has changed.'

He walks ahead, quickly, to the Volvo.

From the belly of the city another siren begins to wail.

She knew the significance of the footsteps, five o' clock on a Friday afternoon, so hurried and purposeful. She felt the paralysis of prescience, the burden. With great effort she raised up her defences against it.

Barend came in, a whirlwind of shampoo and too much deodorant. She didn't look at him, knowing he would be freshly turned out for the evening, his hair a new, dubious experiment. He sat down at the breakfast counter. 'So, how are you, Ma? What's cooking?' So jovial.

'Dinner,' said Milla, resigned.

'Oh. I'm not eating here.'

She knew that. Christo probably wouldn't either.

'Ma, you're not going to use your car tonight, are you.' In the tone of voice he had perfected, that astonishing blend of pre-emptive hurt and barely disguised blame.

'Where do you want to go?'

'To the city. Jacques is coming. He's got his licence.'

'Where in the city?'

'We haven't decided yet.'

'Barend, I have to know.' As gently as possible.

'*Ja*, Ma, I'll let you know later.' The first hint of annoyance breaking through.

'What time will you be home?'

'Ma, I'm eighteen. Pa was in the army when he was this old.'

'The army had rules.'

He sighed, irritated. 'OK, OK. So . . . we'll leave at twelve.'

'That's what you said last week. You only got in after two. You're in Matric, the final exams . . .'

'*Jissis*, Ma, why do you always go on about it? You don't want me to have any fun.'

'I want you to have fun. But within certain limits.'

He gave a derisory laugh, the one that meant he was a fool to put up with this. She forced herself not to react.

'I told you. We will leave at twelve.'

'Please don't drink.'

'Why do you worry about that?'

She wanted to say, I worry about the half-bottle of brandy I found in your cupboard, clumsily hidden behind your underpants, along with the pack of Marlboro's. 'It's my job to worry. You're my child.'

Silence, as if he accepted that. Relief washed over her. That was all he wanted. They had got this far without a skirmish. Then she heard the tap-tap of his jerking leg against the counter, saw how he lifted the lid off the sugar bowl and rolled it between his fingers. She knew he wasn't finished. He wanted money too.

'Ma, I can't let Jacques and them pay for me.'

He was so clever with his choice of words, with the sequence of favours asked, with his strategy and onslaught of accusation and blame. He spun his web with adult skill, she thought. He set his snares, and she stepped into them so easily in her eternal urge to avoid conflict. The humiliation could be heard in her voice. 'Is your pocket money finished?'

'Do you want me to be a parasite?'

The *you* and the aggression were the trigger, she saw the familiar battlefield ahead. Just give him the money, give him the purse and say take it. Everything. Just what he wanted.

She took a deep breath. 'I want you to manage on your pocket money. Eight hundred rand a month is . . .'

'Do you know how much Jacques gets?'

'It doesn't matter, Barend. If you want more you should . . .'

'Do you want me to lose all my friends? You don't want me to be fucking happy.' The swearword shook her, along with the clatter of the sugar bowl lid that he threw against the cupboard.

'Barend,' she said, shocked. He had exploded before, thrown his hands in the air, stormed out. He had used *Jesus* and *God*, he had mumbled the unmentionable, cowardly and just out of hearing. But not this time. Now his whole torso leaned over the counter, now his face was filled with disgust for her. 'You make me sick,' he said.

She cringed, experiencing the attack physically, so that she had to reach for support, stretch out her hand to the cupboard. She did not want to cry, but the tears came anyway, there in front of the stove with a wooden spoon in her hand and the odour of hot olive oil in her nose. She repeated her son's name, softly and soothingly.

With venom, with disgust, with the intent to cause bodily harm, with his father's voice and inflection and abuse of power, Barend slumped back on the stool and said, 'Jesus, you are pathetic. No wonder your husband fucks around.'

* * *

The member of the oversight committee, glass in hand, beckoned to Janina Mentz. She stood still and waited for him to navigate a path to her. 'Madam Director,' he greeted her. Then he leaned over conspiratorially, his mouth close to her ear: 'Did you hear?'

They were in the middle of a banqueting hall, surrounded by four hundred people. She shook her head, expecting the usual, the latest minor scandal of the week.

'The Minister is considering an amalgamation.'

'Which Minister?'

'*Your* Minister.'

'An amalgamation?'

'A superstructure. You, the National Intelligence Agency, the Secret Service, everyone. A consolidation, a union. Complete integration.'

She looked at him, at his full-moon face, shiny with the glow of alcohol, looking for signs of humour. She found none.

'Come on,' she said. How sober was he?

'That's the rumour. The word on the street.'

'How many glasses have you had?' Light-hearted.

'Janina, I am deadly serious.'

She knew he was informed, had always been reliable. She hid her concern out of habit. 'And does the rumour say when?'

'The announcement will come. Three, four weeks. But that's not the big news.'

'Oh.'

'The President wants Mo. As chief.'

She frowned at him.

'Mo Shaik,' he said.

She laughed, short and sceptical.

'Word on the street,' he said solemnly.

She smiled, wanted to ask about his source, but her cellphone rang inside her small black handbag. 'Excuse me,' she said, unclipping the handbag and taking out her phone. It was the Advocate, she saw.

'Tau?' she answered.

'Ismail Mohammed is in from the cold.'

Milla lay on her side in the dark, knees tucked up to her chest. Beyond weeping she made reluctant, painful discoveries. It seemed as though the grey glass, the tinted window between her and reality, was shattered, so that she saw her existence brilliantly exposed, and she could not look away.

When she could no longer stand it, she took refuge in questions, in retracing. How had she come to this? How had she lost consciousness, sunk so deep? When? How had this lie, this fantasy life, overtaken her? Every answer brought greater fear of the inevitable, the absolute knowledge of what she must do. And for that she did not have the courage. Not even the words. She, who had always had words, in her head, in her diary, for everything.

She lay like that until Christo came home, at half past twelve that night. He didn't try to be quiet. His unsteady footsteps were muffled on the carpet, he switched on the bathroom light, then came back and sat down heavily on the bed.

She lay motionless, with her back to him, her eyes closed, listening to him pulling off his shoes, tossing them aside, getting up to go to the bathroom, urinating, farting.

Shower, please. Wash your sins away.

Running water in the basin. Then the light went off, he came to bed, climbed in. Grunted, tired, content.

Just before he pulled the blankets over himself, she smelled him. The alcohol. Cigarette smoke, sweat. And the other, more primitive smell.

That's when she found the courage.

2

1 August 2009. Saturday.

Transcription: *Debriefing of Ismail Mohammed by A.J.M. Williams. Safe House, Gardens, Cape Town*

Date and Time: *1 August 2009, 17.52*

M: I want to enter the program, Williams. Like in now.

W: I understand, Ismail, but . . .

M: No 'buts'. Those fuckers wanted to shoot me. They won't stop at trying.

W: Relax, Ismail. Once we've debriefed you . . .

M: How long is that going to take?

W: The sooner you calm down and talk to me, the sooner it will be done.

M: And then you'll put me in witness protection?

W: You know we look after our people. Let's start at the beginning, Ismail. How did it happen?

M: I heard them talking . . .

W: No, how did they find out you were working for us?

M: I don't know.

W: You must have some sort of idea.

M: I . . . Maybe they followed me . . .

W: To the drop?

M: Maybe. I was careful. With everything. For the drop I did three switch backs, got on other trains twice, but . . .

W: But what?

M: No, I . . . you know . . . After the drop . . . I thought . . . I dunno . . . Maybe I saw someone. But afterwards . . .

W: One of them?

M: Could be. Maybe.

W: Why did they suspect you?

M: What do you mean?

W: Let's suppose they followed you. They must have had a reason. You must have done something. Asked too many questions? Wrong place at the wrong time?

M: It's your fault. If I could have reported via the cellphone, I would have been there still.

W: Cellphones are dangerous, Ismail, you know that.

M: They can't tap every phone in the Cape.

W: No, Ismail, only those that matter. What have the cellphones to do with this?

M: Every time I had to report, I had to leave. For the drop.

W: What happened after the drop?

M: My last drop was Monday, Tuesday, the shit started, there was a discreet silence between them. At first I thought it was some other tension. Maybe over the shipment. Then yesterday I saw, no, it was only when I was around that they got like that. Subtle, you know, very subtle, they tried to hide it, but it was there. Then I began to worry, I thought, better keep my ears open, something's wrong. And then this morning, Suleiman sat in council and said I must wait in the kitchen with Rayan . . .

W: Suleiman Dolly. The 'Sheikh'.

M: Yes.

W: And Rayan . . . ?

M: Baboo Rayan. A dogsbody, a driver. Just like me. We worked together. Anyway, Rayan never said a word to me, which is really strange. And then they called Rayan in too, for the very first time, I mean, he's a dogsbody like me, we don't get called in. So I thought, let me listen at the door, because this means trouble. So I went down the passage and stood there and heard the Sheikh . . . Suleiman . . . when he said, 'We can't take any risks, the stakes are too high.'

W: The stakes are too high.

M: That's right. Then the Sheikh said to Rayan: 'Tell the council how Ismail disappears'.

W: Go on.

M: There's no going on. That's when they caught me.

W: How?

M: The Imam caught me at the door. He was supposed to be inside. They were all supposed to be inside.

W: So you ran.

M: I ran, yes, and the fuckers shot at me, I'm telling you, these people are ruthless. Intense.

W: OK. Let's go back to Monday. At the drop you talked about 'lots of sudden activity' . . .

M: The last two weeks, yes. Something's brewing.

W: Why do you say that?

M: The Committee used to meet once a week, for months. Now suddenly, it's three, four times. What does that tell you?

W: But you don't know why.

M: Must be the shipment.

W: Tell me again about the phone call. Suleiman and Macki.

M: Last Friday. Macki phoned the Sheikh. The Sheikh stood up and went into the passage so that I couldn't hear everything.

W: How did you know it was Macki?

M: Because the Sheikh said, 'Hello, Sayyid'.

W: Sayyid Khalid bin Alawi Macki?

M: That's him. The Sheikh asked Macki as he was walking away, 'Any news on the shipment?' And then he said, 'September', like he was confirming it.

W: Is that all?

M: That's all I heard of their conversation. Then the Sheikh came back and told the others, 'Bad news'.

W: Bad news. Do you know what that means?

M: How would I know? It could be because the shipment is small. Or the timing is wrong. It could be anything.

W: And then?

M: Then they left, the Sheikh and the two Supreme Committee members. They went off to the basement. Then you must know, it's top secret.

W: Would you say the shipment is coming in September? Is that the conclusion you came to?

M: Best guess.

W: Is that a 'yes'?

M: That is what I think.

W: And the shipment. Have you any idea what it is?

M: You know, if it is Macki, it's diamonds.

W: What does the Committee want with diamonds, Ismail?

M: Only the Supreme Committee knows that.

W: And no one else talked about it?

M: Of course they talked about it, on the lower levels. But that is dicey intel, you know that.

W: Where there's smoke . . . What did the lower levels say?

M: They said it was weapons. For local action.

W: What do you mean?

M: That was the rumour. They wanted to bring in weapons. For an attack, here. For the first time. But I don't believe that.

W: A Muslim attack? In South Africa?

M: *Ja*. Here. Cape Town. The fairest Cape.

DEON MEYER ON THE NEW SOUTH AFRICA

My South Africa

If books are windows on the world,[1] crime fiction mostly provides a view of the underbelly and back alleys of cities and countries. This is my only genuine regret writing as an author in this genre.

Because the real South Africa, the one that I love so passionately, is very different from the narrow and dim view my books probably allow. It is also quite unlike the one you see in those pessimistic fifteen second television news reports in the UK, Europe or Australia.

So let me try and set the record straight.

My country is breathtakingly beautiful – from the lush, subtropical east coast of Kwazulu-Natal, to the serene semi-desert stretching along the Atlantic in the west (which blooms in indescribable colour and splendour in Spring). In between, there's the magnificence of the Lowveld, the Bushveld, the Highveld, the towering Drakensberg mountains, the aching vastness of the Karoo and the dense silence of the Knysna forests . . .

Diversity is everywhere. In the climate (mostly perfect sunshine and balmy weather, but we have extremes too, summer highs of more than 50°C in Upington, and winter lows of -15°C in Sutherland – both in the same Northern Cape province), and in the cities (Durban is an intoxicating fusion of Zulu, Indian and British colonial cultures, Cape Town is a heady mix of Malay, Dutch-Afrikaans and Xhosa, Johannesburg is . . . well, modern African-cosmopolitan, utterly unique, and always exciting).

The biodiversity of South Africa is truly astonishing. "With a land surface area of 1.2 million square kilometres representing just 1% of the earth's total land surface, South Africa boasts six biospheres, and contains almost 10% of the world's total known bird, fish and plant species, and over 6% of the world's mammal and reptile species."[2]

Of course we are also world-famous for our huge collection of wildlife regions and game parks – both public and private – encompassing every possible landscape from deserts to forests, mountains to coast, teeming with wildlife species, including Africa's Big Five: Leopard, Lion, Buffalo, Elephant and Rhinoceros.[3]

But most of all, the diversity is in the people who constitute the Rainbow Nation. Our black ethnic groups include the Zulu, Xhosa, Basotho, Bapedi, Venda, Tswana, Tsonga, Swazi and Ndebele. The so-called 'coloured' (no, it's not a derogatory term over here) population is mainly concentrated in the Western Cape region, and come from a combination of ethnic backgrounds including Malay, White, Khoi, San, and Griqua. White South Africans are descendants of Dutch, German, French Huguenots, English and other European and Jewish settlers. And our Indian population came to South Africa as indentured labourers to work in the sugar plantations in the British colony of Natal in the late 19th and early 20th centuries.

The population of more than fifty million people is made up of African (40.2 million, or 79.5%), White (4.6 million, or 9.0%), Coloured (4.5 million, or 9.0%), and Indian/Asian (1.3 million, or 2.5%).

And, having travelled most of the world, I can confidently say, you won't find friendlier, more hospitable and accommodating people anywhere, irrespective of their race, culture, language or creed.

We have nine provinces (Eastern Cape, Gauteng, KwaZulu-Natal, Mpumalanga, Northern Cape, Limpopo, North West, Free State, and Western Cape) and eleven official languages: Afrikaans (13%), English (8%), isiNdebele (1.6%), isiXhosa (18%), isiZulu (24%), Sesotho sa Leboa (9%), Sesotho (8%), Setswana (8%), siSwati (3%), Tshivenda (2%), and Xitsonga (4%).[4]

Throw all of this together in a democracy only eighteen years old (a tempestuous teenager, if ever there was one), and you get an effervescent, energetic, dynamic, and often a little chaotic, melting pot – of cultures, people, views, politics, opinions, and circumstance. After the tragedy and oppression of Apartheid, we are still very much coming to terms with – and are sometimes a little overwhelmed by – all the facets of the freedom-diamond. Which means that we argue incessantly, shout, point fingers, blame, accuse, denounce, complain, and criticize, mostly loudly and publicly, like all enthusiastic democrats should.

But when our beloved Bafana-Bafana (the national football team), Springboks (our twice World Cup-winning rugby team) or Proteas (the cricket guys) walk onto the field, we stand united, shoulder to shoulder. And mostly, in our day-to-day-lives, we get along rather well. We increasingly study and work and live and love and socialise together, in great harmony.

Of course, we have our problems.

Poverty is the major one. "There is a consensus amongst most economic and political analysts that approximately 40% of South Africans are living in poverty – with the poorest 15% in a desperate struggle to survive."

However, we are making steady progress. The percentage of the South African population with access to clean drinking water has increased from 62% in 1994, to 93% in 2011. Access to electricity has increased from 34% in 1994, to 84% in 2011.[5]

In 2010, 13.5 million South Africans benefited from access to social grants, 8.5 million of whom were children, 3.5 million pensioners and 1.5 million people with disabilities. In 1994, only 2.5 million people had access to social grants, the majority of whom were pensioners. And since 1994, 435 houses have been built *every day* for the poor.[6]

And you might have heard about our other challenge – South Africa has a bit of a reputation when it comes to crime. I am most definitely going out on a limb here, but having studied the statistics, and looked at the (often unfair) comparisons over the past five years, I honestly believe we don't quite deserve it.

". . . in relation to the overall risk of victimisation, South

Africans are not much more likely to become victims of crime than people in other parts of the world," Anthony Altbeker recently wrote in a carefully considered and exhaustively researched contribution to the marvellous *Opinion Pieces by South African Thought Leaders*.[7]

To put the matter into further perspective: In the two years leading up to the FIFA World Cup held in South Africa in 2010, almost every British, French and German journalist who interviewed me, asked the same question, more or less: "How big a slaughter is it going to be for fans attending the games?" Some were downright accusatory: "How dare you host this magnificent event in such a hazardous country?" A British tabloid even predicted a 'machete race war' waiting for visitors.[8]

And how many soccer fans died during the tournament?

None.[9] Furthermore, the attendees who were affected by crime-related incidents represented a very meagre 0.009% of the fans. That is far, far less than, for instance, the crime rate in Wales. When World Cup tourists were asked if they would consider visiting South Africa again, 96% said 'yes'.

As a matter of fact, if you are a tourist from the Northern Hemisphere visiting my beautiful country, your chances of becoming a victim of violent crime is less than 0.67%.[10] (Compare this to the fact that "the 2011 British Behaviour Abroad Report published by the UK's Foreign and Commonwealth Office (FCO) noted that the death rate (including murder and natural causes) of Britons in Thailand was forty-one per 100,000 tourists and for those visiting Germany was twenty-four. Tourists from the UK are far safer visiting South Africa"[11] – with just 14.6 per 100,000.[12])

South Africa's murder rate dropped by 6.5% in 2010-2011, attempted murder by 12.2%, robbery with aggravating circumstances was down by 12%, and house robberies by 10%.[13] Our police services are slowly but surely turning the tide.

We struggle with inadequate service delivery, our politicians don't always live up to our expectations, and our unemployment rate is too high.

But our economy is robust, and easily out-performs first-world countries like Greece (no surprise there), Italy, and Spain. South African Tax Revenue has increased from R100 billion in 1994 to R640 billion in 2010. Our debt to GDP ratio is 32% (USA 100%, Japan 200%, UK 90%). (The World Bank recommends a ratio of 60%.) And we are ranked first out of 142 countries in respect of regulation of security exchanges by the World Economic Forum Global Competitiveness Report 2011/12.[14]

According to the Open Budget Index, South Africa has the most transparent budget in the world. We are the only African country that is a member of the G20. In the Economist Intelligence Unit's Survey of Democratic Freedom, South Africa ranks 31st out of 184 countries. And according to the Global Competitiveness Report 2010/11, South Africa has the 34th most efficient government out of the 139 countries ranked.[15]

The number of tourists visiting South Africa has grown from 3.9 million in 1994 to 11.3 million in 2010. South Africa is ranked among the top five countries in the world in respect of tourism growth (growing at three times the global average).[16]

I could go on. South Africa's learner-to-teacher ratio improved from 1:50 in 1994 to 1:31 in 2010. According to the Global Competitiveness Report 2011/12, South Africa is ranked 13th out of 142 countries for its quality of management schools. 61% of South African primary school children and 30% of high school children receive free meals as part of the school feeding scheme.[17]

But none of these facts and figures, as inspiring as they are, will reveal the real reason why I am so unwaveringly optimistic about my country's future.

It is one of the major reasons for the peaceful transition miracle of 1994, it is something woven into the texture of everyday South African life, hidden from the fleeting eyes of foreign journalists on a flying visit, mostly talking only to important folks: The goodwill of ordinary people.

Every day, in cities, towns, and tiny villages, small acts of kindness happen between human beings. Individuals who extend a helping hand across racial, cultural, political and linguistic divides, who extend friendship and kindness and empathy. I have been witnessing this for more than forty years, and I absolutely believe it is this goodwill that will carry us through, no matter how challenging the future may be.

Deon Meyer
January 2012

1 "Books are the carriers of civilization. Without books, history is silent, literature dumb, science crippled, thought and speculation at a standstill. They are engines of change, windows on the world, lighthouses erected in the sea of time." - Barbara W. Tuchman, American popular historian and author, 1912-1989.
2 http://www.bcb.uwc.ac.za/envfacts/facts/biosa.htm
3 http://www.sa-venues.com/game_lodges_nationwide_south_afr.htm
4 http://www.safrica.info/about/facts.htm (percentages rounded off)
5 http://www.sagoodnews.co.za/fast_facts_and_quick_stats/index.html
6 *Ibid.*
7 Penguin, 2011. p. 47.
8 http://www.dailystar.co.uk/posts/view/129402/WORLD-CUP-MACHETE-THREAT/
9 http://www.truecrimexpo.co.za/
10 http://www.info.gov.za/issues/crime/crime_aprsept_ppt.pdf
11 http://www.issafrica.org/iss_today.php?ID=1394
12 *Ibid.*
13 http://www.sagoodnews.co.za/crime/crime_statistics_show_drop_in_murder_rate.html
14 http://www.sagoodnews.co.za/fast_facts_and_quick_stats/index.html
15 *Ibid.*
16 *Ibid.*
17 *Ibid.*